I0846836

# all this

# TIME

BLOSSOM PEAK SERIES

Copyright © 2025 by Harlow James

All rights reserved.

No part of this publication may be reproduced, distributed, or transmitted in any form or by any means, including photocopying, recording, or other electronic or mechanical methods, without the prior written permission of the publisher, except as permitted by U.S. copyright law. For permission requests, contact Harlow James at harlowjamesauthor@gmail.com

The story, all names, characters, and incidents portrayed in this production are fictitious. No identification with actual persons (living or deceased), places, buildings, and products is intended or should be inferred.

Book Cover by Abigail Davies

Edited by Jenny Ayers (Swift Red Pen)

Proof Read by Emma Cook

ISBN: 9798991541930

# Contents

*To all of the women who have ever had a crush on your brother's best friend...*

*This is the story where it all works out.*

*But if it did, I hope your man is like Fletcher Adams.*

*When two people are destined to be together, don't worry. Just wait.*


*The love that you seek will come to you in the right time, the right place, and with the right person, that was meant to love you the way you always wanted.*


**Mustafa Alam**

# Prologue

**Fletcher**

***When the Shit Hits the Fan***

"You motherfucker!"

I slam my father to the ground before landing a punch to his face. Rationality leaves my brain, red clouds my vision, and my fists keep landing on his face as all the rage from my childhood up until now leaves my body.

"Don't you ever talk about her like that!" I roar.

Henley yanks me back before I can get another punch in. "You're not fucking thinking straight, Fletch!"

"I'm done," I snap, tossing my hands in the air, even though every part of me wants to get more hits in—as many as he's delivered to me over the years.

"Get out of here." Henley pushes me toward my truck. "Go! Before it gets worse."

I reach for Laney's hand and help her into my truck before I round the hood and hop inside myself. Gravel kicks up as I peel out of the parking lot.

My heart is racing as I drive away from the chaos. The truck is silent, the only sound the whir of the tires beneath us.

"Fletcher... You shouldn't have done that."

"What was I supposed to do? Stand by and let him talk about you like that?"

"No, but—"

"He fucking deserved it, Laney. Punching him is the least I could do after everything that man has put me through."

"I don't blame you. But the cameras... People were—"

"I know." I slam my palm against the steering wheel. "Fuck!"

The crazy thing is, I would do it all over again—every single fucking thing that has led me to this point. Because if there's one thing coming back to Blossom Peak has taught me, it's that true feelings don't fade, even after all this time.

# Chapter 1

**Laney**

*Three Weeks Earlier*

*Dildos, Orgasms, and Lucifer*

"God, I wish I could visit you next weekend." My eyes drift to the rearview mirror as I change lanes, inching closer to Blossom Beauty, the full-service salon I opened six years ago.

"I know. You're gonna miss out on all the new products Adeline is bringing. I think this passion party is going to be my biggest one yet," Hazel, one of my closest friends, says through my car's Bluetooth as I continue my drive to work.

Hazel Sheppard and I met years ago when I needed some professional photos done for my salon, and I stumbled upon her photography page online, instantly enamored with her work. Even though Blossom Peak is seven hours away from her hometown of Carrington

Cove on the North Carolina coast, she ventured out here, completed the job, and we hit it off, becoming instant friends.

She regularly hosts passion parties for all the women in her town, and I've made it a point to attend as many as I can, extending my visit for a few days just to break up the monotony of my life and spend time with her.

Laughing, I flip on my blinker as I stop at a red light. "Does Gage know what he's getting himself into?"

"Well, we're already married, so it's not like he can do too much about it."

"Touché."

"Honestly, I think he might be more excited about the party than I am. The man has no problem bringing toys into the bedroom."

"You know that I'm genuinely thrilled that you're so happy, but part of me really hates you right now."

Hazel laughs. "Why?"

"Because you found the perfect man," I say, pulling into the parking lot behind the salon and shutting off my car.

"Oh, Gage is not perfect by any means. But he's definitely perfect for me." Her words hit me right in the center of my chest. "And one day, you're going to find the man that is perfect for you too, Laney."

"I'm not so sure about that anymore," I groan, dropping my head against the headrest of my seat. "I mean, my last relationship was over a year ago, I haven't attempted another one since, and my date the other night was more focused on my potential connection to you-know-who than me."

Even twelve years later, being associated with Fletcher Adams is still messing with my love life.

"First of all, fuck any man that would rather talk about football than get to know you, okay? And second, you dodged a bullet with

Spencer as far as I'm concerned. I mean, he couldn't even make you come!"

A knock on my window makes me jump. "Jesus Christ!" My hand flies to my chest as I look over to find Glenn, one of my employees, waving at me as he bites the straw of his iced coffee.

"What happened?" Hazel asks as I will my heart rate to calm down.

"Glenn is trying to give me a heart attack this morning."

"Oh, Glenny-poo. How is that beautiful man?"

I roll down the window so Glenn can hear her. "Hazel says hello."

"Hazel! Girl, when are you gonna come visit so I can meet that fine-ass man of yours?"

Hazel laughs. "I don't know, Glenn. Maybe never if you aren't going to be able to keep your hands to yourself."

Glenn holds up his free hand like he's making a solemn oath, even though she can't see him. "I swear I won't touch. Looking only."

I roll my eyes. "Don't believe him, Hazel. Glenn is notorious for making straight men question their sexuality."

Glenn pops his shoulder. "It's a gift. I won't apologize for that."

"But he never went after Spencer, did he?" Hazel asks.

Glenn dry heaves. "Ew. No thank you."

"Oh, come on... Spencer wasn't *that* bad." I say, trying to make myself feel better, even though I know he was a safe choice, not the right one, and definitely didn't make me desperate for him.

Glenn chuckles. "Laney, I'm beginning to think you need your eyes checked. You were way out of his league, first of all. And if he couldn't make you come, that should have been your first clue to run far, far away."

I close my eyes and blow out a breath. "You heard that, huh?"

"Your volume is up loud enough for the entire town of Blossom Peak to hear, sweetie." Glenn clutches his iced coffee to his chest.

"Now, I'm going to head inside and get things ready for the day." He pushes his head through the window. "Hazel, it was good to hear your voice, honey. Come visit us soon."

"Will do, Glenn!" Hazel calls.

I watch Glenn unlock the back door to the salon as I roll the window back up. "Note to self, turn the volume down when I pull into the parking lot."

Hazel lets out a laugh. "Glenn is right though, Laney. You are way too good for Spencer."

Staring down at my hands in my lap, I groan. "I know. But I can't help but feel like I played a part in the downfall of our relationship too."

"How so?"

Staring out the front windshield, I press my lips together as I consider how to explain. "Well, I mean, he cheated on me. I obviously wasn't giving him what he needed physically..."

"Oh, hell no. You are not about to take responsibility for his infidelity. That's all on him, regardless of how he felt about your sex life."

"I wasn't initiating, though," I counter. "That was one of his biggest arguments as to why we drifted apart."

"Laney, if he'd actually been good in bed, you would've wanted it more."

"That's true..."

"And a mature man would have had a conversation with you about it instead of sticking his dick in another woman. Joke's on her, though, because you know he didn't make her come either."

I snort. "That is also true."

"Well, if you really want to escape and ditch the wedding festivities, you know where to find me. Just look for the house full of silicone penises."

"Don't tempt me. I was already questioning why I even agreed to be Tori's maid of honor, but now that I know you-know-who is Elliot's best man, the list of injuries I could fake is getting longer each day."

"Maybe I can call you and say there's an emergency here, like how girlfriends do for each other when they're on a really bad date so you don't have to see *him*. What should be our code word?"

"How about pathetic? Because that's how I'm beginning to feel." My hand covers my eyes. "I don't even have a date for the wedding."

"I think that's for the better, actually. Then you can flirt with whoever you want."

"You act like I don't already know all the single men who will be there."

Hazel hums. "Good point. I, uh...will be praying for you then?"

I huff out a laugh. "Gee, thanks."

"Hey, if I remember correctly, you were basking in my emotional turmoil last year when I was basically bribed to marry Gage. I guess the tables have turned, huh?"

"You know what? I'm beginning to question our friendship."

"No you aren't," she says as I glance at the time and note I have to end this call soon to get ready for my first client. "You're going to keep your chin held high, pretend Fletcher doesn't affect you, and in three weeks, he'll be gone and everything will go back to normal."

"When you told those lies to yourself about Gage and your six-month marriage, did they work?"

"No."

"Exactly."

"But Gage and I realized we were meant to be, Laney. So...maybe you and Fletcher—"

"Please don't finish that sentence," I cut her off, shaking off memories as I do. "We had our chance, and he made his choice. I just wish seeing him didn't bring all those emotions back up again."

"I get that. Your first love shapes you… But, whatever happens, just know I'm here if you need to vent or process."

"Thank you. I really appreciate it."

"Always, girl. Good luck!"

"Thanks, I'm gonna need it."

After ending our call and making my way into the salon, I finish some paperwork from the night before and prepare the color and tools for my first client.

Two hours later, her hair is transformed and she leaves with a smile on her face just as Glenn comes up beside me, leaning close to my ear.

"Girl, you just worked magic on her. She was looking a little like a troll when she walked in, and now she looks like a movie star."

I roll my eyes, not at all surprised by his flair for exaggeration. "Being a new mom is rough, Glenn. The world doesn't revolve around you anymore, and a lot of women neglect themselves when they have a baby. She just needed to be reminded of the gorgeous woman she still is, despite her life now revolving around keeping another human alive."

A dull ache fills my chest.

*God, am I ever going to get the chance to be in the same position? A new mom, exhausted from taking care of my newborn baby, but overwhelmed with gratitude for the role?*

I just turned thirty, and I am not even close to making that a reality. I want a love like my parents had. I want a partner that looks at me as if I'm the center of his universe. And I want a family someday.

But then the fear of letting someone in again makes my chest tighten.

Heartache is difficult to recover from, and I'm not sure I'd survive it a second time.

Shaking off my plaguing thoughts before they burrow too deep, I head back to my station to clean and sanitize before my next client. Glenn's close behind. "And that is why I will never have children," Glenn declares as he shudders. "The smell of formula alone is enough to make me gag."

"You never know. You might meet the right man one day and want to start a family with him. Don't completely close the door on that opportunity."

Glenn rolls his eyes. "The chances of me finding a gay man in this town are about as likely as winning the lottery, Laney." He snaps his fingers as he heads back to his station. "But maybe a hot tourist will come in one day and prove me wrong."

As he walks away, I can't help but agree. Blossom Peak isn't exactly a dating hotspot. Especially if you aren't looking for a small-town high school legend turned hometown has-been with a hero complex.

"What's he going on about this time?" Yvonne, my lead massage therapist, asks as she joins me where I'm sweeping.

"Oh, nothing we haven't heard before. Ranting about how he'll never find a man."

"Ah... Speaking of men, how did your date with the guy from Asheville go the other night?"

I cringe. "Not great."

Yvonne plants her hands on her hips. "What was wrong with this one?"

"As soon as I told him where I'm from, he asked me if I know you-know-who." Rolling my eyes, I continue. "Like that's the only thing Blossom Peak is known for."

Claudia walks by us on her way to her nail station. "Are we talking about Lucifer?"

As my employees gossip about me right in front of me, I glance out the floor-to-ceiling windows of the salon. From here, I have a great view of The Village, a hub of shops and restaurants in the heart of town lined with sidewalks, iron street lamps, and plenty of trees to provide shade in the warmer months.

Named for the cherry blossom trees that bloom each spring and the peaks surrounding the valley our town sits in just north of Asheville, Blossom Peak boasts some of the best ski slopes in the area and the landscape is full of color throughout the year.

However, as demonstrated by my lackluster date, Blossom Peak is also known for producing one of the most talented wide receivers the NFL has ever seen—a fact I try to forget. Hence why his name is not to be uttered in my salon. It was one boundary I could put in place to help keep me sane.

As I continue to sweep, I admire the décor of my salon—olive green chairs at each station gleaming in the sunlight coming through the tall front windows, white walls that make the space bright and open, black-framed mirrors hung in front of each stylist's station, and smooth gray floors pulling it all together.

Past the stations on both sides of the room are three separate spaces—one for our nail technicians, one for our massage services, and one for facials and skin care.

I'm proud of what I've created, and even if I'm struggling in my personal life, at least I'm killing it in my professional life.

"She's ignoring us again," Yvonne says, pulling me back to the present.

I don't bother lifting my eyes to her. "I'm not ignoring you. I'm just choosing to remove myself from this conversation."

Yvonne tsks. "Nope. Not until you tell me why every time a man brings up Flet—"

I hold my hand up to stop her. "Say the name and you have to put a dollar in the jar."

She bats my hand away. "Oh, don't get your panties in a wad."

I sigh and pick up the broom again. "My date didn't want to know anything about *me*. He just wanted to know if I'd ever met you-know-who and if I knew when he might be in town again so he could casually drop by to try to run into him."

Yvonne shrugs. "It's not every day that a small town like ours produces a bona fide celebrity, Laney."

I know Yvonne is right, but it doesn't mean I have to talk about Fletcher as if I still know him. Once upon a time I did, but that changed quickly and drastically after that night twelve years ago.

Fletcher went on to get drafted to the NFL, fulfilling his dream of playing football professionally and leaving our hometown behind just like he intended. And thanks to his demanding schedule, I've only crossed paths with him a handful of times over the years.

There are other reasons he doesn't visit home often, though. Reasons only I and a few others know about.

Unfortunately, in a matter of hours, I'll be forced to come face-to-face with the man that not only broke my heart but showed me his true colors in a way that made me question if he was ever really honest with me.

Elliot Thorne, one-fourth of my older brother Rhonan's best friend group, is getting married in just a few weeks, which means the entire crew will be here, including the man who's still ruining my dating life, even after all this time.

And because he's the best man and I'm the maid of honor, I'll have to pretend like he doesn't still affect me while performing countless wedding party duties.

Some therapists might say I have suppressed rage and anger I should deal with when it comes to him. That maybe telling him how he made me feel back then would help me move on.

But that would mean admitting how naïve I was to believe we felt the same about one another, and my pride just isn't letting me go there—at least not yet.

"Laney? You still in there?" Yvonne reaches over and raps her knuckles on my forehead.

I swat her hand away. "Good gracious. Yes, I'm still here."

"You didn't answer my question."

"Which is?"

"Did you tell your date that Fletcher is actually coming to town tomorrow?"

I shake my head and resume sweeping. "No, and you owe me a dollar." She just sticks her tongue out at me.

Claudia comes out from her nail room, joining the two of us. "Well, he already booked a manicure with me, so..."

I stop mid-sweep and glare at her. "You're joking, right?"

"Nope." She pops the p before continuing to smack her gum.

"I guess now's the time to tell you that he booked a massage with me too," Yvonne says as she rubs her palms together. "God, I can't wait to rub that man down with oil."

"You're both fired." I turn my back to them and take the dustpan over to the trash can.

"Oh, please. We all know you need us, honey. And Fletcher booking appointments here is a good thing. It means more business, which means more money. You know, that stuff that keeps this place running?"

"The salon does just fine without him." I put the broom and dustpan away just as the door opens and Elliot's fiancé, Tori, comes walking in.

"Tori!" I paste on a smile, grateful for the distraction. "What are you doing here?"

"Laney!" she chirps, barely connecting her fingertips with my shoulder as we attempt to emulate a hug. "I just stopped in to make sure that we reserved spa time for the day before the wedding."

My brows draw together. "Um, yeah...we did that last month."

She sighs and smacks her palm to her forehead. "God, that's right. I'm sorry. I'm just really overwhelmed with this whole thing. That's why I'm so glad that I have you to keep everything straight for me."

I grind my teeth together as I smile, fighting to hide my annoyance. "Well, that's what maid of honors are for, right?"

Yvonne calls out to me as she heads back to her space. "This isn't over, Laney!"

"Yes, it is!" I yell over my shoulder before turning back to Tori. "What's going on?"

I lead her over to the waiting area where we take a seat in two of the olive green chairs.

Tori sighs as she stares off to the side. "My boss isn't being very flexible about the wedding, and it's stressing me out. Looks like I'm going to be stuck in Nashville most of the time leading up to the wedding."

I blink slowly. "Okay..."

"It just means I'm going to have to lean on you even more than I already have." She says it like an apology, but her smile doesn't exactly seem sorry.

Aggravation builds at my temples, but I breathe it away.

The truth is, I remember Tori from high school, but only vaguely since she was a couple of years ahead of me with my brother and his friends. We never really crossed paths after that, and since Elliot proposed after only six months of dating, there wasn't much of a chance to get to know her better.

So, when she asked me to be her maid of honor, shock is too soft of a word to describe what I felt. But Tori doesn't have many girlfriends, and Elliot said it would mean a lot to him if I did this, so here I am, planning this woman's wedding because she's too busy to do it, apparently.

I nod like I'm totally fine with this development. "I mean, I'm happy to help however I can..."

She immediately brightens. "Gah! I knew you were the right person for the job." Her phone chimes in her purse. She pulls it out, skims the screen, and begins typing, not even bothering to meet my eyes as she continues. "Elliot and I have been putting together a list of things that you and Fletcher can handle for us leading up to the wedding, which will allow me to focus on work."

The reminder of having to collaborate with Fletcher makes my jaw clench even tighter, but I shove it down. "Okay."

She launches herself from the chair, still staring down at her phone. "Excellent. I'll talk to you soon," she says, leaving the salon without a backward glance.

Yvonne comes up behind me. "Tell me why you agreed to be her maid of honor again?"

"Because saying no felt...rude."

"*You*? Worried about being rude? That's new..."

I swat at her playfully. "Oh, shut up."

As I head to the break room, Yvonne follows behind. "I'm being serious. The Laney I know would have shut that down *real* quick."

I sigh, pushing open the door. "Well, that Laney has been thrown off-kilter this week, so how about you cut her some slack?"

"Okay, but only if she stops referring to herself in the third person."

I chuckle. "Deal."

"God, I can't wait to see how long it takes for you to crumble under Fletcher's blue eyes. Either that, or how quickly you slip a laxative in his coffee."

"Laxatives aren't a bad idea... Thanks for the suggestion. But as for the crumbling? Yeah, not gonna happen."

The lie feels dirty leaving my lips because I know from personal experience how those blue eyes of his can suck you in—and how damaging they can be to your heart when they're full of lies. I'm sure fame hasn't changed him for the better.

But it has been almost three years since I've seen him, and I've moved on. Maybe I'll find that Fletcher doesn't have the same effect on me anymore. Maybe being older and wiser will help me realize that the boy who broke my heart at eighteen is just a part of my past, and I really shouldn't compare every man that's come after that to him.

One thing is for sure, though: for the next few weeks I'm going to have to put my aversion of Fletcher Adams aside as a sacrifice for Elliot's happiness. Because after everything Rhonan's friends did for me after my world was flipped upside down, it's the least I can do.

# Chapter 2

**Laney**

*Control, Wine, and Responsibilities*

"Honey, I'm home!" Dilynne calls as she walks into my house right after six, just as I'm popping the cork on the bottle of wine I've been dreaming about since Yvonne brought up Blossom Peak's impending visitor earlier.

"Nothing like the smell of rubber and grease to let me know you're here." I hold out a glass of wine to her as she kicks off her boots and heads toward the kitchen.

Dilynne Clark and I have been best friends since middle school when she and her brother Henley, one of Rhonan's other best friends, got placed in a foster home in Blossom Peak. She was sassy and spirited, unapologetically confident, and she sat down in front of me in math class one day, asked me what my name was, and the rest was history.

A few years ago, we moved into two brand new houses built right next door to each other. Even though I love my best friend dearly, living with her would be a disaster. But living close? Perfect. We trade off dinner and wine nights a few times a week, keeping each other sane in this small town.

Part of me dreads the day that either one of us finds a man because we won't have these nights as frequently. Though, after the past few years of our combined dating history, or lack thereof, I'm beginning to think that won't be a problem.

"You know you love it. Hell, the smell doesn't even faze me anymore."

"Perks of owning an automotive shop."

"Exactly. And I know you feel the same way about hair dye."

"I do." We clink glasses and then both take a sip. "How was your day?"

"Oh, same as always. Oil changes, tire rotations, broken air conditioners. Though, there was a bit of excitement when a girl's car broke down in the intersection right in front of the garage. She was able to coast into the parking lot before the thing finally took a shit."

"Oh God, poor thing. That's awful."

"I know. Her brother had to come get her so she wouldn't be late picking her kids up from school. I think she might be new in town, but I didn't really get a chance to ask. It took me a while to diagnose her disaster on wheels."

"And?"

"Her transmission is toast. It'd cost more to fix it than the car's even worth."

I take another drink from my wine. "That's a bad day."

"Yeah, pretty much." Dilynne brushes away the wisps of her jet-black hair that have fallen from the red bandana she always wears while she's at work but hasn't bothered to remove yet.

One thing about my best friend that I admire the most is that she's never afraid to be herself. Dilynne has always been a bit of a "black cat," standing out from the crowd instead of trying to fit in. She likes what she likes, dresses the way she wants, and has a love for everything vintage, especially classic cars and anything from the 1950s.

When she told me she wanted to open her own automotive shop and specialize in custom restorations, it didn't even surprise me. Blossom Peak didn't have a reputable repair shop anyway, so it made sense, especially with the number of tourists we see year to year. But now, she's been contacted by people from all over the state thanks to the internet and social media, and she goes to car shows every month to show off her restorations. She's the definition of a badass, and sometimes I wish I could channel her don't-give-a-fuck attitude.

"What about you? How was your day?"

"Well, Tori came into the salon, wanting to make sure she reserved spa time for the day before the wedding, even though she already had. She seems a bit overwhelmed with the whole thing."

Dilynne rolls her eyes. "Then she shouldn't have agreed to getting married so quickly."

"She and Elliot are in love," I counter.

"No, Elliot is mesmerized by her fake boobs and *amazing* personality," she quips.

"She's not *that* bad." I don't even sound convincing to myself.

"I know you don't remember her well from high school, but I do, and Tori is *the* definition of a mean girl."

"People can change..."

Dilynne scoffs. "Oh, okay. So there's hope for Fletcher?"

I harden my gaze. We stare at each other before Dilynne finally breaks eye contact. "Fine, and the only reason I'm agreeing is because you're my best friend and I know how the whole thing with him has affected you. But do you honestly think this thing between Tori and Elliot is going to last? They only dated for *six* months."

"It doesn't matter what I think. This is what they want, and our job as their friends is to support them."

"I am *not* friends with Tori, and I merely tolerate Elliot." She takes another sip of her wine.

I practically snort. "Yes, I'm very aware of how you feel about Elliot. Anyway, apparently she's too stressed with work, so she and Elliot have made a list of things for me and you-know-who to do before the wedding."

"God, she's annoying. I mean, she's not even the one who wanted the traditional wedding, right? That was all Elliot?"

"More Elliot's family, but yeah. I think the timeline is what's making it overwhelming. She seems excited about it, though, and I assured her everything would be okay, but that's when she brought up..."

Dilynne shakes her hands in the air. "Lucifer himself?"

I groan. "I'm seriously considering just staying drunk the entire time he's here."

Her eyes widen like I've just suggested setting myself on fire. "Uh, that's a terrible idea. Alcohol is a truth serum, Laney. One glass too many and you might tell him every thought that's crossed your mind over the past twelve years. You'll end up sobbing in his lap or punching him in the nuts."

Dilynne has always been my sounding board when it comes to Fletcher, but he hasn't been a topic of conversation between us in a very long time.

I bury my head in my hands, propping them up on the kitchen counter. "God, how am I going to survive this, Dilynne? Being near him makes my body and mind do weird shit. It's like he has a forcefield surrounding him, and when I get too close, I get sucked back into his orbit. It's happened every time I've seen him since *that* night."

"This isn't an alien romance book, Laney. He doesn't have magical powers."

"I'm not so sure about that. And you know what I found out today?"

"What?"

"He booked a manicure *and* a massage at the salon this week."

Dilynne's head rears back as she takes a seat on one of the stools at the kitchen counter.

"What the hell?"

"Exactly. I wonder if he even knows I own the place."

Dilynne tilts her head and arches a brow. "Laney. Babe. You really think in the past six years the guys haven't told him you opened a business? One of those guys is *your brother*."

I grimace. "Okay, so if he does know, what the hell is he up to? Trying to get close enough to me that I might be tempted to pluck his toenails off, one by one?"

Dilynne shudders. "The fact that you came up with that so fast tells me you've put a lot of thought into that."

"I have." I stand up from the counter again and take my glass back in my hands. "I never should have agreed to be Tori's maid of honor."

"I tried telling you that, but you insisted that it was the right thing to do," she sing-songs, mockingly.

"Yeah, well, if things were going well in my personal life, I don't think I'd feel this off-kilter. I just hate that he still has this effect on me after all these years, and yet again, I'm single with no prospects of moving on with someone better. There has to be someone else who can make me feel the way he did."

"As your best friend, I'm going to tell you something you may not like, but I think you need to hear it."

I swallow roughly, preparing for the truth she's about to deliver—because if there's one thing Dilynne's good at, it's telling it like it is. "Okay…"

She leans forward in her seat, locking her eyes on mine. "*You're* the one giving him this power over you. You've spent so much time and energy hating him for what he did… And you're the only one who can decide when to let it go."

Emotion clogs my throat—because just hearing that reminder from Dilynne reminds me of all of the ways I've had to pick myself up and keep going, even when life felt hopeless and unfair.

I stare at her, knowing she's right. But it doesn't change how I feel.

Fletcher Adams broke my heart and it's never been the same since.

"How do I do that?" I whisper.

"You just channel your inner Elsa." She shrugs like it's so simple. "Besides, I think you romanticized a lot of your relationship with him because of your age." I can't deny that the thought has crossed my mind as well. I was a teenager when I became obsessed with him. I bet if I was dating someone else right now, I wouldn't even care that he's in town.

*Sure…keep telling yourself that, Laney.*

"And if that doesn't work, you tell him the truth. You finally tell him how he made you feel that night, and then maybe you can start to move on."

"Ugh, that sounds exhausting."

She takes a sip of her wine. "No matter what you decide, you know I'm here for you."

"I don't know what I would do without you." I reach for her hand, covering it with mine.

"You've been here through all the shit life has handed me."

"Right back at you, Laney. And that will never change." She smirks over the rim of her glass. "Although, I have to admit, I can't wait to see what happens between you two leading up to this wedding. My Costco order of popcorn is already on its way."

***

"Hey, you made it!" Rhonan pulls me into a hug as soon as I enter the tasting room of Hart Winery, kissing the top of my head.

"Did you think I wouldn't? That would make me a shitty maid of honor."

He grins as he hands me a glass of sparkling wine, one of the signature wines that made my parents' winery famous. Leaning in close, he whispers, "I wouldn't blame you if you did, though."

"Be nice," I fire back. "We're trying to be supportive friends, remember?"

"If I were being truly supportive, I'd tell him he's rushing into this too fast."

I raise a brow. "I'm pretty sure you proposed to Sarah less than a year after you started dating."

My brother tenses up at the mention of his late wife. "True, but Sarah fit into our family and friends seamlessly, like she was always meant to be there. Tori is...different," he says, even though I'm sure he had another word in mind.

"Well, maybe if you didn't scowl at her every time she came around, she would be more relaxed around you."

His brows draw together even further. "I don't scowl."

I snort. "Yeah. Okay." I'm pretty sure there's a picture of my older brother under the definition of the word *grumpy*, but in his defense, when life robs you of your wife, leaving you to raise your daughter alone, grumpiness is understandable.

"I miss her," he says as his eyes find Ellis, my niece, across the room.

"Me too. She was the type of person that lit up a room when she walked in—just like Mom."

Bringing up our mother makes my heart twist in my chest too.

Being here never fails to remind me of my mother's dream, my parents' hard work, and the legacy they built that is now a staple in Blossom Peak, drawing even more tourists to our town.

The walls of the main building on the vineyard are all made of taupe stone mixed with brick to give the space a rustic feel, transporting visitors to Italy, and the entire back wall of the tasting room we're standing in is lined with old oak barrels from floor to ceiling, embossed with the Hart Winery logo. Ivy vines climb the outside of the winery, and inside there are live plants scattered throughout. The smell of grapes and oak fills the room, and each time I step in here, memories slam into me from my childhood, running around while my mother and father worked until I was old enough to learn about winemaking and taste the fruits of their labor myself.

But after our mother died unexpectedly, and Rhonan joined the Marines, I felt the responsibility to make sure my dad knew he wasn't alone as he fought to keep the winery running. Those were some trying years. Sacrifices had to be made, including what *my* future was going to look like, but I would gladly make the same choices now that I did back then.

"Hi, sweetheart." My father comes up behind me wearing the signature burgundy polo that all our staff wear, interrupting our conversation. His lips meet my temple. "I feel like it's been ages since I've seen you."

"It's been three days, Dad."

His grin spreads. "That's too long."

"Well, I have a business to run and a wedding to help plan, so…" My eyes drift over to Tori standing in the corner of the room, typing on her phone, confirming Rhonan's observation that she doesn't quite fit in. I get that her work as a talent manager's assistant is demanding, but she could at least try to include herself in conversations.

"Yes, well, let Anabelle know if you need anything," my father says, referring to the wedding planner for the winery.

"I will. Thanks, Dad."

"And maybe come over for dinner one night so I can get some Laney time."

I wrap my arms around his waist, resting my head on his shoulder. "That sounds perfect."

My father releases me just as Elliot comes striding up to me and my brother, his smile blinding.

"Laney!" Elliot pulls me into a side hug as he presses a kiss to the top of my head. "Tori told me she stopped by the salon yesterday and you calmed her down by offering to help with the wedding prep. Thank you."

With his arm around my shoulders, he leads me deeper into the room as I spot Henley and one of the employees talking to my right, Dilynne flirting with Thomas, the employee behind the bar, and Ellis and her nanny, Joanne, at a table playing Candy Land. A few more customers are sprinkled throughout the room, enjoying their tasting flights on this Friday evening.

My smile feels forced. "It was nothing. She seemed overwhelmed."

Elliot gestures for me to take a seat with him at the bar made from old oak barrels. "She is, but I think it's more because she has to travel between here and Nashville a lot these next few weeks for work when all the wedding details have to be finalized. At least she's getting time off for our honeymoon in Aruba." He grins suggestively behind the rim of his glass.

"I'm happy to help."

"I know you are." He leans closer to me. "I know I've said this before, but it really means a lot that you agreed to be her maid of honor. Tori doesn't have many girlfriends."

"And don't you think that's a problem?" Dilynne interjects, leaning against the back of my stool.

Elliot glares at her. "The problem I have is that *you're* inserting yourself into my business."

Dilynne shakes her head. "You know, I thought lawyers were supposed to be smart. I guess I was wrong." Shrugging, she leaves us just as quickly as she appeared.

Elliot turns to me. "Your friend needs to get over whatever happened between Tori and her in high school. She's about to be my wife and..."

I almost explain why those memories are especially difficult to let go. Adolescence is a critical time in your life, and it shapes us in ways we will never entirely understand.

I take a sip from my glass, deciding to change the subject instead. "You sure you need the big, fancy wedding?"

His brows draw together. "What are you asking?"

"I mean, didn't she suggest eloping?"

"Yeah, but I think she just didn't want to add anything on to our already crazy schedules." He takes a drink from his own glass. "The truth is, my parents would never forgive me if I did that. Mom is already infatuated with her future daughter-in-law, and my dad is relieved that I'm actually getting married. As my legal career takes off, and he considers retirement, he's been worried that all I've been focused on is my job and taking on too many cases. But if he'd never sent me to the conference in Nashville, I never would have reconnected with Tori though, so..." He shrugs. "She deserves a big wedding, Laney. And hell, after everything my family has been through, we all deserve a day full of happiness and celebration."

"What are you two talking about?" Tori asks as she approaches, kissing Elliot's cheek and situating herself on his lap.

"You, babe." His hand grips her thigh possessively, and for one split second, I'm jealous. I've never had a man touch me like that, owning me in a way that speaks to his need to be near me and make sure everyone in the room knows I'm his. "And how amazing the wedding's going to be."

Tori sighs. "Part of me is just ready for it to be over though, you know?"

"Me too." He rubs his nose against her cheek. "And then we can just focus on starting our lives here in Blossom Peak."

Tori nods, a satisfied smile on her lips. "Yeah."

"So, you've made a decision about that?" The last time Tori and I spoke about it, she hadn't landed on a final choice.

"We did," Elliot answers. "With the law firm based here, and my parents wanting to be close by when we have kids, it just made sense to find a place in Blossom Peak."

Tori nods. "I managed to get my boss to agree to let me work here remotely after the wedding, which I think is why he wants me there as long as he can have me. We even talked about me starting my own talent agency down the road. Of course, that will probably be after we have kids, but that's our plan."

"Sounds great," I say, but confusion clouds my mind. The last time I spoke with Elliot about his future, he said he never wanted kids. People are allowed to change their minds, though, and maybe being in love changed his.

Speaking of children, Ellis squeals as she races across the room to me. "Auntie Laney!"

"Well, it's about time you came over and said hello." I place my glass on the bar and reach down to lift Ellis into my lap, the pink tulle skirt on her dress fanning out around her. Rhonan marches over as well, wiping something off his daughter's cheek.

"I was playing Candy Land and I was winning, so I couldn't stop." She narrows her eyes at me. "I don't like to lose."

"Did you win, then?"

Joanne comes up next to us, wrapping her sweater around her waist. "She did. I think she should be a professional Candy Land player when she grows up."

Ellis's eyes widen as she looks over at her father. "Can I?"

I chuckle while my brother debates how to answer that question. Luckily, Dilynne jumps in. "Sure you can. You can be anything you want to be, Ellis. With the way the internet changes every day, who the hell knows what kind of jobs there will be in fourteen years?"

"But essential jobs like lawyers, doctors, and teachers will always be secure," Elliot interjects, his infamous smirk on his lips.

Dilynne glares at him over her shoulder. "Bor-ing," she says, drawing out the word.

Tori clears her throat. "I'm sorry, but don't you work on cars for a living?" Spite laces her words. "That sounds pretty boring to me."

Dilynne turns, slow and deliberate, smile razor-sharp. "Why don't you refrain from speaking on things you don't understand before you hurt the few brain cells you have left?"

The women stare each other down, years of tension crackling between them.

If Tori weren't perched on Elliot's lap like a trophy, I'm pretty sure she'd have already thrown a wine glass at my best friend's head. And judging what Dilynne does for a living is the best possible way Tori could get under her skin.

Elliot straightens his tie as he directs his gaze back to Ellis, replying to my niece before Dilynne speaks her mind. "Just because Dilynne thinks those jobs are boring doesn't mean they aren't good choices."

"I don't want a boring job," Ellis says. "I want something fun! Like a princess!"

"Being a princess would *definitely* be fun," I reply, bopping her on the nose.

Elliot, ever the realist, can't help himself. "Being a princess isn't a job."

"Ha!" Dilynne chimes in. "Tell the Princess of Wales that and see what she says."

"All right, you two," my brother interjects, knowing that Dilynne and Elliot are just getting started in their natural repertoire, and if someone doesn't stop them, they'll go on all night. "Let's quit while we're ahead."

"Sorry, but I'm not going to let this stick-in-the-mud rain on your daughter's dreams," Dilynne says as she juts her thumb in Elliot's direction.

Elliot huffs out a laugh, still holding Tori on his lap as her eyes bounce back and forth between the two of them. "Stick in the mud, huh? Maybe you should look in the mirror and see if you can locate the stick that's shoved up your—"

"Is this the right place? I'm looking for some people I used to know!" A voice cuts through the tasting room like a record scratch, and I don't even have to look to know who just arrived. Nonetheless, my eyes travel from his feet to his eyes in a slow perusal that wakes up every nerve ending on my body, particularly the ones between my legs.

Fletcher Adams smiles from ear to ear wearing a Carolina Thunder T-shirt as he walks deeper into the room—his stride long, his spine straight, and his cocky grin that should be classified as a weapon on full display. Greeting my brother, Henley, and Elliot first, he makes his way around the room while I finish the wine left in my glass and avoid staring at him any further, gathering the confidence I need to face him.

And as my heart hammers so wildly that I think I might pass out, I accept that he's here, that nothing could have prepared me for how my body still reacts to him after all this time, and that the next three weeks might just be the longest of my life.

# Chapter 3

**Fletcher**

*Memories and Strippers*

"Is this the right place? I'm looking for some people I used to know!" With my arms outstretched, I pull the attention of the entire room toward me as I project my voice over the noise.

I can't deny that walking into the tasting room at Hart Winery feels like coming home, as cliché as it sounds. But it's not just the fact that Blossom Peak is the only place I've ever really considered home, no matter how many shitty memories this place holds. It's the people in this room, the people that kept me going through all those moments when I truly wanted to give up—*one* person especially.

"Adams, you look like shit," Elliot says as he walks up to me and pulls me in for a hug and a slap on the back.

"Right back at you, Thorne. Good thing you're getting married before your looks disappear completely."

"Looks like it'll be too late for you, then," Elliot fires back as he takes a drink from his glass.

"Yeah, no marriage for me, thanks."

"The small-town celebrity returns," Henley declares as he steps up to me, reaching out to shake my hand.

"I had to return to my roots, you know, just so my head doesn't get too big."

Henley huffs out a laugh. "Good to know you're still humble in there." He points to my chest.

"He doesn't need to be humble with the yards he's been putting up the past two seasons," Elliot adds. "Seriously, dude, you are fucking killing it."

I slap him on the shoulder, sighing heavily. "Thanks, man. I feel fucking good, better than I have in my entire career. But until I get that championship ring, it's not enough."

When you make it to the NFL, there's always one goal in mind: make it to the Super Bowl and win. And I have several reasons why I won't quit until I do.

Elliot pulls a vaguely familiar blonde closer to him, locking his fingers with hers. "You remember Tori from high school, right?"

"Yeah," I answer not too convincingly, holding my hand out to shake hers. "Nice to see you."

Her eyes slowly dip down my body and when they return to my gaze, she licks her lips. "Nice to see you too."

*Okay...*

Rhonan clears his throat behind me, pulling my attention just in time. I spin around and pull him into a hug.

"Glad you could find some time in your celebrity life for us little people back home," he says dryly.

When he releases me, I adjust my backwards hat. "Ah, come on. It hasn't been that long..."

Rhonan arches a brow. "The last time you came home was Ellis's second birthday party, and she's about to be five in a few months."

Guilt slams into me. Not because I didn't realize how long it's been since I visited Blossom Peak, but because my friends think my life is too busy for them. Meanwhile, they've all come to Charlotte to attend games and spend time with me in the offseason whenever they could.

But coming back here means facing all the bullshit that plagues me when I come into town, things not even my best friends know the full extent of.

One person does, though.

My eyes scour the room and find her instantly, like always.

*Laney.* She's across the room, sitting with that perfectly blank face that somehow still radiates annoyance, glaring like she hopes I spontaneously combust.

I see some things haven't changed, including her ability to make my balls shrivel up with one angry look. She didn't always look at me like that, though. There was a time when looking into her eyes felt like the safest place in the world.

But one fucking night back in college burned our friendship to the ground. I know I fucked up that night, but Laney and I have never discussed the details, and honestly, I wonder if revisiting it might fix things—or just blow up whatever's still left.

Luckily, my boys remained a constant for me as I gave all my focus to making it to the NFL, but the three of them have also been busy building their own lives and futures.

Rhonan spent six years in the Marines, but he came back to Blossom Peak to be a sheriff after he met Sarah. They fell fast and started a life together. Then came Ellis—but due to complications during delivery, Sarah didn't make it. Now Rhonan's living the single dad life and raising one of my favorite humans on the planet. And he's damn good at it, but I can still see the pain behind his eyes no matter how hard he tries to hide it.

Henley has always been the daredevil of the group. He waited for Dilynne to graduate from high school and then took off to travel for a few years, seeking his next thrill. However, when he broke several bones during a street luge course, Dilynne begged him to stop, so he returned to Blossom Peak and now runs Sky's The Limit, the town's ski resort and adventure park.

And then there's Elliot, the overachiever. After attending Florida State, he went to Duke for law school to be closer to home and came back to work at his family's law firm. The Thornes are generational lawyers and their name is well-known throughout the state of North Carolina, but they also have some skeletons hidden in their closets. Elliot travels to Charlotte a lot to work on corporate cases, but he chose to live here to be close to his parents, and now he's getting married, which of course, is why I'm here.

"Fuck, it's good to see you, man." Elliot shoves Rhonan and Henley aside to get to me, wrapping me in another hug, this time lifting me from the ground and shaking me up and down a few times before setting me back on my feet.

I fix my shirt as I regain my footing, studying my friend who seems way more cheerful than he typically is. "Jesus, have you been working out?"

Elliot bats his eyelashes at me. "You trying to flatter me already?"

"I mean, as your best man, that's part of my job, right? Motivational speeches and encouragement?"

"Not sure I'll need them." Elliot pulls Tori into his side and kisses the top of her head. "What's the saying? When you know, you know?"

I nod, though I'm still wrapping my head around the fact that this is really happening.

When Elliot called and told me he reconnected with Tori and had never felt this strongly for a woman before, I was more than happy for him. The guy's been a workaholic since he graduated from law school, and even before that, his nose was always stuck in a book. He never failed to find time to flirt with women, but marriage was never a goal of his. So, I was shocked when he called to say he was engaged after just six months of dating. Having never been in a serious relationship before, I know I have no room to judge. But anyone would agree that timeline was fast.

Tori rolls her eyes as she giggles. "This guy was adamant about a big wedding too. I said we should elope."

"I mean, I'm always down for a trip to Vegas."

"But if you go to Vegas, then I can't go!" A tiny voice behind the group of grown men and Tori breaks through our conversation as Ellis pushes her way toward me.

I crouch down to intercept her as she runs into my arms. "Ellis, my girl!" Inhaling deeply, I take a moment to savor seeing this little ray of sunshine again in person instead of through a cell phone, kissing the top of her head through her brown hair as dark as her father's. "How are you, princess?"

"I'm not a princess yet, Uncle Fletcher." She leans back in my arms as I stand to full height again. "But in the wedding, I get to wear a princess dress."

I reach down and toy with the tulle on the dress she's wearing right now. "Then what do you call this thing?"

"A dress, duh." She rolls her eyes.

"Looks like a princess dress to me."

She wriggles in my arms, so I set her down on the floor. "No, this dress is just for twirling." Holding her hands above her head, she proceeds to turn in a circle but loses her balance and falls to the floor.

"Careful, Ellis." Laney pushes her way into our circle, helping her niece stand up again.

Her voice slides across my skin like a memory I can't shake—sharp, warm, and still too goddamn powerful.

Her long brown hair with soft blonde highlights covers her face as she bends down, but when she stands upright again and our eyes meet, a flurry of emotions slam into me all at once.

*Laney.*

*My Laney.* Even more beautiful than the last time I saw her.

*Fuck. These three weeks are going to be torture.*

"I'm okay, Auntie," Ellis says, pushing Laney away before attempting to twirl again and nailing it this time.

We all clap in celebration.

"Finally came over to say hello?" I say, directing my attention to my best friend's little sister.

Laney arches a brow at me. "I was just letting your fan club fawn over you first."

I huff out a laugh, grateful to see that her sass hasn't diminished. "Nice to see you too, Laney."

Rhonan walks back toward the bar in the tasting room, the rest of us guys following. "Thomas, can you get Fletcher a drink?"

"Just water, Tom," I call out quickly—the last thing I need right now is alcohol.

"Come on, we're celebrating. And it's the offseason, right?" Rhonan pouts amusingly.

"I know, but I just don't feel like drinking tonight, man."

"Save it for the bachelor party then," Elliot says.

Rhonan turns to me, the corner of his mouth turned up. "You're in charge of that, by the way."

I rub the back of my neck, feeling more out of my element and overwhelmed the longer I stand in this room and reality sinks in. "I figured, but..."

Rhonan hands me my glass of water as Elliot slaps me on the back. "Don't worry. Tomorrow, Tori and I are gonna sit down with you and Laney and tell you exactly what we need your help with and what we want as far as wedding stuff goes."

Wincing, I ask, "You sure you don't just want to go to Vegas? I mean, there are strippers there."

"What's a stripper?"

The question comes from about three feet down, where Ellis is tugging on my shirt and looking up at me like I'm some kind of life encyclopedia.

I peer down at her, not sure how to safely answer this question. "Uh, a stripper is a...a dancer," I answer proudly, pleased with my quick response.

Her eyes light up. "Then I want to be a stripper when I grow up!" she shouts, catching everyone's attention in the room as she proceeds to twirl around again.

Rhonan glares at me. "Thank you for that."

I put my hands up as I lower my voice and lean toward him. "What was I supposed to say? I mean, technically I told the truth."

Rhonan shakes his head and pinches the bridge of his nose. "I can't wait until I get phone calls from preschool about this."

Patting his shoulder, I say, "I'm sorry. I'll make it up to you while I'm here, all right? Maybe with some babysitting..."

"So you can teach her more about strippers?" He shakes his head. "Nah, I think I'm good."

My eyes dart over to Laney—my partner for the next three weeks apparently—who's standing across the room, laughing at something Dilynne says while Joanne watches Ellis spin in circles.

As if she can sense my staring, Laney looks up and our eyes lock.

Only for a second—but it lands like a punch. And then she looks away, her expression tightening like I'm a bad taste in her mouth.

This woman's irritation toward me hasn't diminished at all in the nearly three years since we've seen each other. The handful of times I came home since the night everything fell apart were Laney-free. She was always conveniently unavailable, busy or out of town. And while I have a pretty good idea as to why she might wish I would fall off the face of the planet, part of me wonders if there's anything I can do to make things right.

Because being near her again has my body reacting to her as if I'm seventeen all over again.

I miss the way things used to be between us—the way I felt like I could tell her anything and she wouldn't judge me, the way I *did* tell her things that no one else knew.

I miss our fucking friendship.

I miss the way she used to smile when she saw me instead of these icy glares that she's downright perfected.

I miss the girl that became the one person I could trust above all others, even more than her own brother and my best fucking friends.

I miss the girl that I grew to want, but knew I could never have.

# Chapter 4

**Laney**

*Age Fifteen*

*Spaghetti and Ice With Friends*

"Come on, Bobcats!" I shout, cupping my gloved hands around my mouth, trying to shield the part of my face still exposed to the elements. Even my warmest jacket and beanie aren't doing much tonight.

Winter has descended upon Blossom Peak a little earlier than usual, which means everyone gathered at the high school tonight to cheer on the varsity football team is freezing their asses off, myself included.

I watch the field, trying to keep my eyes locked on my brother, who plays tight end. But my eyes keep drifting to the boy in the wide receiver position, even though I know they shouldn't.

It's getting harder and harder to conceal my crush on Fletcher Adams, but I'm still trying everything in my power to keep it to myself—and Dilynne, of course.     .

The ball is snapped, and Fletcher makes a run for the end zone. As he turns, the football spirals through the air before landing perfectly in his outstretched arms. Fletcher turns to find a defenseman lunging for him, but he blasts to the right to dodge him before gliding across the goal line for a touchdown.

"Yes," I scream, along with the rest of the home-team crowd.

Dilynne laughs next to me, bumping my shoulder. "Your boy is on fire tonight!"

I roll my eyes at her but don't say anything.

"If the boys keep playing like this, they're going to the playoffs," my father says from beside me, pulling me into his side and rubbing my arm through my jacket. My mother claps wildly beside him in celebration.

The Blossom Peak High School football team hasn't had many shots at the state championship. When you have a small population, it's hard to build a solid program from year-to-year. But the new coach has rebuilt the program and created a team that has been smashing the competition all season long.

I guess that's what can happen when the coach is a former NFL star himself.

Our team punts the ball with only a few minutes left on the clock, and even though Castle High School tries their best, they aren't able to put more points on the board, sealing the win for Blossom Peak.

After the teams shake hands, people start trickling onto the field, and my parents and I join the crowd to congratulate my brother and his friends.

My father finds Dilynne's brother, Henley, first and claps a hand on his shoulder. "Great game, son."

"Thanks, Mr. Hart." Henley plays center, which makes sense given his size.

"You coming over for a late dinner to celebrate?"

"Nah. I promised Dilynne I'd take her to Ruthie's."

Dilynne chimes in next to me. "I'm in the mood for pie." She rubs her stomach before turning to me. "Talk to you tomorrow?"

"Yup. See ya."

She waves before following Henley toward the field house.

Elliot sees us from where he's standing with his family, waving in acknowledgment. He always has something going on with his parents, so I know he won't be joining us either. Which only leaves...

"Did you see Fletcher's catch?" Rhonan asks as he runs up to us with Fletcher trailing behind him.

"Yes, honey. We saw." My mother intercepts my brother in a hug, pressing a kiss to his sweaty cheek.

"Hell of a play, Fletcher," my father says, reaching out to shake Fletcher's hand.

My pulse picks up at the smile that lights up his face. "Thanks, Mr. Hart."

"You're having an impressive season."

"I'm trying," Fletcher says sheepishly, and for a moment I'm wondering where the cocky boy I've grown to know is hiding.

Coach Adams walks up to us, extending a hand to my father. "George, Elizabeth. Good to see you both."

My father reaches out to shake his hand. "Likewise, Luke. Your boy looked great tonight."

Coach Adams glances over at Fletcher. "He could have done more."

Fletcher's jaw ticks as he looks away from his father.

My mother's eyebrows draw together. "Well, I was impressed," she replies as Fletcher offers her a tight-lipped smile. "Will you two be joining us for dinner?"

"I can't. I need to review game footage and get ready for next week's game," Coach Adams says.

"I'll be there," Fletcher says enthusiastically, which makes butterflies take flight in my stomach again. They started fluttering a few months ago, anytime Fletcher's around.

"Perfect," Mom says. "Well, you boys get cleaned up and we'll meet you out by the car."

"See you at home later, son," Luke says to Fletcher before heading back to the sideline to finish clearing out.

Fletcher doesn't even acknowledge him. "Are you making spaghetti, Mrs. Hart?"

My mother winks at him. "Just for you, Fletcher."

He rubs his stomach, which causes his jersey to move up, offering a glimpse at his abs underneath. "A woman after my own heart."

Dad gives him a mock glare. "You'd better watch it, son. That's my wife you're flirting with."

Rhonan rolls his eyes as I giggle. "Oh, Dad. Get real."

Fletcher holds his hands in the air. "I mean no harm. Promise."

My dad grins and then grabs my mother's hand. "Come on, honey. Let's go wait in the car where it's warm." Then he turns to me and grabs my hand as well. "I know you're cold too, Laney."

With one more glance at Fletcher and my brother, I take my father's hand and let him lead me to warmth. But the truth is, I haven't been cold since Fletcher walked up. Apparently, my crush affects not just my mind, but also my body.

And I'm afraid that it's only getting worse with each encounter.

***

"This is the best spaghetti, Mrs. Hart," Fletcher groans and mumbles around his mouthful of food. "I don't know what you put in this, but I could eat it every day."

My mother laughs. "It's a pretty standard recipe, Fletcher. Although, I guess I do add one special ingredient." She looks over at me and winks. "Love."

I roll my eyes. "Jesus, Mom. That was cheesy."

My father pipes up. "It's true, though. Something about home-cooked food just tastes better, and your mother is one hell of a cook." My father blows a kiss across the table toward my mom, and I groan, rolling my eyes. But honestly, I admire what they have. They are still head-over-heels for each other, they genuinely respect and admire one another, and even when they argue, they never forget they're on the same team. It makes me hopeful that I can find that kind of love one day because they've shown me that it's possible—plus, it makes those novels I've been reading more realistic.

Fletcher points his fork toward me and my entire body becomes alert. "He's right, Laney. Trust me. You're lucky you have a mom who can cook like this."

Rhonan chimes in. "You don't hear me complaining," he says as he shoves a forkful of pasta into his mouth.

Once we all finish eating, I help my mother clean up the kitchen.

Our house is on the back of the property, tucked into the base of one of the mountains behind the vineyard, offering expansive views of the grape vines and mountains surrounding our small town. The house itself is made of beautiful red brickwork, with massive picturesque windows and ivy vines cascading up the sides, matching the aesthetic of the winery's main building. The inside, though, reflects my mother's touch—vaulted ceilings with broad oak beams, soft brown and green décor, and deep colored wood throughout.

Once I finish helping my mom, my dad drives Fletcher home, and I make my way to my room to hang out and read until I go to sleep. I've been really into YA romance novels lately, and the one I'm reading now is about a girl who's in love with her brother's best friend—go figure.

It's just after eleven when I hear scratching at my window.

I bolt upright, my heart pounding violently in my chest. It's not uncommon for a tree branch to kiss my window when the wind whips outside, but it's a still night.

*Oh God, someone is breaking in. I'm going to be murdered in my own room and I haven't even kissed a boy yet.*

When my window shakes and begins to rise, I jump from my bed and prepare to bolt from my room when the voice behind me stops me in my tracks. "Laney?"

Twisting around, I find Fletcher staring at me as his body is halfway in and halfway out of my bedroom window. "Fletcher? Wh—what the hell are you doing? I thought someone was coming to murder me."

He huffs out a laugh as he steps all the way into my room and shuts the window behind him. "No murdering on my mind, I swear."

Keeping my back to my door as I try to process what's happening here, I eye him warily. He looks massive to me, even though my bedroom isn't especially small. "Didn't my father drive you home a while ago?"

He brushes a hand through his hair. "He did."

"So, what are you doing back here?"

His eyes dart around my room, taking it all in, and I suddenly realize he's never been in here before.

Fletcher and his father moved to Blossom Peak when he was a freshman, so I was only twelve at the time. Any time Rhonan had his friends over, I was told to stay away—annoying younger sister rules and all that.

It wasn't until I started going to Blossom Peak High last year that I actually started interacting with Henley, Elliot, and Fletcher more—mostly so people knew not to mess with me since I'm Rhonan Hart's little sister, but also because it's a small school and they can't avoid me as easily.

"Your room doesn't look like I imagined," he says, pulling me back to the present and the reality that he's here, in my room, just the two of us, just like I wished he would be more times than I can count.

"What do you mean?"

He takes a step further into the space and heads toward my dresser, examining the postcards I've wedged between the mirror and its frame. "What are these?"

"Those are postcards, Fletcher."

He flashes me a deadpan look. "You don't say?"

I take a deep breath and blow it out before moving into the same space that he's occupying, making sure to prepare myself for the proximity.

"These were actually written by my grandfather." I take one down and flip it to the back. "He was a soldier in World War II and wrote them to my grandmother while he was overseas. He'd write her letters too, but sometimes a postcard was quicker. Before she died, she gave them to me."

He takes the postcard from my hand and begins reading. "My dearest Jane, the world is a mess, but what I know is that our love can stand the test of it. I will return to you, my love, as soon as I can. Please wait for me. I look forward to our future together." He hands the card back to me. "Wow. People actually felt that way?"

My brows draw together in confusion. "Um, yes. Believe it or not, there is such a thing as true love."

He shrugs as he moves to my bookshelf. "I wouldn't know."

I frown. "What do you mean?"

"I mean, when your parents are divorced, it makes you skeptical about the idea of love."

I knew his parents weren't together, but I didn't know much more than that because Fletcher doesn't talk about his mom, and I've been too nervous to ask. "I'm sorry."

He glances at me over his shoulder. "Me too."

"Where *is* your mom?"

"No clue. She took off and never looked back, leaving me with my dad." He scoffs. "Lucky me."

As Fletcher walks closer to me, I notice something in the dim light that I didn't before. "Oh my God. Fletcher…" I reach up to touch his face, but he turns away from me.

"It's nothing."

"That doesn't look like nothing."

"It's from the game," he says, reaching up to touch the side of his face that is swollen and red, on the brink of turning purple.

"But it wasn't there during dinner…"

"Some hits take longer to show." The reply is automatic, as if rehearsed.

Swallowing down the lump in my throat, I make a decision in that moment. "I'll be right back."

"Laney!" he whisper-shouts, but I don't stop as I quietly exit my room and make my way toward the kitchen. My parents are in bed, and Rhonan is probably passed out, but there's no way I'm not going to do something about the lump on the side of Fletcher's head.

I fill a plastic bag with ice, grab a clean dish towel to wrap it in, and head back to my room, finding Fletcher back at my dresser reading the other postcards. When he hears the door click shut, his eyes follow me as I make my way over to him. "Come sit." I direct him to my bed, taking a seat as I wait for him to follow.

With a roll of his eyes, he reluctantly obeys and takes a seat right next to me, playing into many fantasies I've had about this boy in my room, but none of them involved him being hurt.

"I appreciate this, but—"

"Stop talking." I cut him off, pressing the ice to his face, watching him wince. "It's swollen."

"No shit." We sit there for a few moments, studying each other before he lets out a yawn. "Do you mind if I lie down if you insist on me keeping this ice on?"

I glance back at my pillows. "Uh, sure."

Fletcher crawls up my bed and lays his head on my pillow, sighing. He takes the ice and presses it back to his face. "You didn't have to do this, Laney."

"Well, you're the one who crawled into my room with a knot on the side of your head."

He closes his eyes. "I thought this was Rhonan's room."

Suddenly, my dull excitement about this turn of events evaporates. "Oh."

His eyes pop open and he stares at me. I'm sitting next to him, my feet still dangling off the edge of the bed. Unexpectedly, he reaches out and touches my glucose monitor attached to the back of my arm. "Is this new?"

I dip my eyes down to the white object attached to the back of my arm. "This one is, yeah."

He's never mentioned it before, and suddenly, I feel even more self-conscious about it. I'm not naïve about the looks I get at school when people see my glucose monitor, but the harsh reality is, without this monstrosity on my arm, I'd die. At least this one is a lot smaller than the other one I had.

"Is this a newer model or something?"

"Yeah. It's supposed to monitor my insulin more closely."

He shakes his head slowly. "I can't imagine dealing with that."

"Having type 1 diabetes?"

"Yeah. Having to watch what you eat all the time..." There's a compassion in his eyes that's unnerving, so I look away from him before I reply because talking to Fletcher about this right now is making me feel uncomfortable.

"I'm used to it now. I was diagnosed when I was eight."

"How did you know you had it?"

I huff out a laugh as I stare down at the floor. "We don't have to talk about this, Fletcher."

He places his hand on my forearm, drawing my gaze to him again. "I want to know, Laney."

My pulse picks up as I watch his blue eyes bounce back and forth between mine. "Okay..." I draw in a breath. "Well, according to what my mom has told me, I was hungry all the time and eating everything in sight, but I was losing weight. I was moody and irritable, and I started getting sick to my stomach and vomiting. They took me to the ER one night when I started slurring my words, the doctors ran a bunch of tests, and my blood sugar was off the charts."

"Jesus."

"From then on, I just remember going to lots of doctors' appointments, crying every time I had to be poked with a needle, and feeling like I was different than everyone else." I turn away from him. "I still do."

"I think you're a rock star."

I spin back to face him. "What?"

He props the pillow behind his head so he can sit up a bit more, a hint of a smile on his lips. "I mean, you're smart as hell, nice to everyone even though most kids at our school don't deserve it, you aren't afraid to tell it like it is, and you do it all while dealing with an autoimmune disease." The corner of his mouth lifts even higher. "You don't realize how incredible you are, Laney."

*Somebody pinch me, please. Fletcher Adams is complimenting me.*

"You're also true to who you are. You don't put on a show to try to fit in with people."

"I literally only have like two friends, Fletcher, and one of them is Dilynne."

He chuckles. "Well, we're friends, aren't we?"

I feel my smile start to build. "Yeah, I guess we are."

Fletcher lets out a yawn and closes his eyes, ending our moment, and I'm grateful—because my heart feels like it's about to launch itself from my chest.

"Do you mind if I just close my eyes for a minute before I leave?" he asks.

I stand from my bed, not sure how to answer. If my parents knew I had a boy in my bed right now, I'm pretty sure I'd be grounded until I turned thirty.

"Uh, shouldn't I get Rhonan? I mean, you can sleep in his room…"

He shakes his head, turning on his side and repositioning the ice pack against his temple. "No, don't bother him. I won't be here long."

I bite my thumbnail, growing more anxious by the second. "Fletch-er…"

"Thanks for the ice, Laney," he mumbles. "You're an angel."

After a few moments, his breathing grows heavy.

Looking around my room, I fight with myself over what to do. I should wake him up and tell him to leave, but I just can't find it in my heart to do it.

So I don't.

Instead, I slip into the bathroom to get ready for bed. When I return, Fletcher is still fast asleep in the same spot I left him.

After I pull back the covers that he's not on top of, I slip underneath and stare up at the ceiling, basking in how close I am to my crush. It takes me a while, but I finally drift off to sleep.

And when I wake up, Fletcher is gone.

But the memory of our time together is not.

It's very much alive and only feeding my endless crush on him.

# Chapter 5

**Fletcher**

***Present Day***

***Blackjack and Brews***

"Aw, Rhonan. You're gonna make me cry." With my hand pressed to my chest, I walk into George Hart's office in the back of the winery, finding the card table set up and ready for action.

Our obsession with blackjack developed after Rhonan's dad made us watch *21*, the movie where an MIT professor teaches a group of students to count cards then takes them to Vegas to hustle the casinos. None of us ever got *that* good at counting cards, but nonetheless, we fell in love with the game and try to play whenever we get together.

"Has playing football professionally made you that soft?" Elliot asks, shoving me as he strides past, draining his beer before heading to the mini fridge George keeps stocked. He pulls out four beers and places them around the green felt, waiting for us.

"Nothing about me is soft," I say, heading to my seat at the table. "I just can't remember the last time the four of us have played a game together."

Rhonan has a stupid grin on his face as he joins Henley, Elliot, and me at the table. "That's what I thought. What better way to welcome you home, Fletch?"

I settle back in my chair. I've only been back in Blossom Peak for about two hours and already I'm being slammed with feelings left and right—gratitude, longing, and a gnawing guilt for not being around more, especially for the people who never stopped showing up for me.

"You know I wouldn't miss Elliot getting married, dickhead." I take the beer Elliot got for me and return it to the fridge, taking a water back to the table instead.

Elliot studies me. "You're seriously not going to drink with us?"

"I told you. I just don't want to drink tonight."

"But this is a special occasion," he fires back. "I'm getting married and you're home for the first time in almost three years."

I twist off the cap and chug half of the bottle. "I'm just not much of a drinker anymore."

Elliot raises a brow while scratching the black scruff on his chin. "You? Fletcher Adams? If memory serves me correctly, you were somewhat of a beer pong champion back in college, right? Or did I dream that?"

"That was back when my body could recover from that shit with just a few hours of sleep. We're in our thirties now, gentlemen. Alcohol and professional football don't mix very well."

All of us have turned thirty-two in the past year, which means we are fully immersed in a new decade with new experiences, one of which is our bodies hurting in places they didn't before. I know part of my aches and pains have come from playing football for a living, which makes me apprehensive about how much longer I have in my career. But as long as I stay healthy and maintain my strength, I could go another three to five years, easily.

It'd be a lot longer than my father got to play, that's for sure.

Henley clears his throat, darting his eyes to me before he looks back over to Elliot. "The man doesn't want to drink. Let it go."

Elliot shrugs before bringing his beer bottle to his lips. "Whatever. More for me."

I give Henley a small nod in thanks before focusing on Rhonan, who's busy shuffling cards, getting ready to deal.

This isn't the time to tell my friends that I haven't had a drink since my first year in the NFL. Honestly, I'm not sure they'd believe me. But I have my reasons for my decision and reasons for not telling even my best friends.

Some things are better left in the past.

"All right. I can only play a few hands because Ellis will be up with the sun, so less talking and more blackjack."

"Isn't Joanne there?" I ask.

"Yes, but I have tomorrow off, so I'll be the one to get up with Ellis. Joanne is the single best thing that ever happened to us, and I'm not about to take her for granted."

I nod in understanding. "Fair enough."

"Besides, she's old enough to be my mom and scares me a little bit."

Elliot snorts behind his beer bottle. "Aren't you her boss?"

"Technically. But I can't survive without her, so we're a team."

Rhonan hired Joanne as a full-time nanny shortly after Ellis was born and his wife died. With the crazy hours he works as a sheriff, he needed someone who could be in his life day and night. We all remember how difficult that first year was for him, and he's correct—he wouldn't have survived without Joanne's help.

"That's how I feel about Tori," Elliot interjects, a dreamy smile on his face.

"Seriously, Fletcher. You should see this guy now." Henley juts his thumb toward Elliot, who's sitting on his right. "He shits rainbows most days. It's scary how much Tori has changed him."

Elliot shrugs but doesn't refute what Henley says. "Yeah... Before Tori and I reconnected, I probably wouldn't have settled down just to spite my mother."

Henley chuckles as he turns to me. "Momma Thorne was putting pressure on him to find a wife."

Elliot rolls his eyes. "I swear, if she tried to set me up one more time, I was going to sue her for emotional distress."

I laugh. "Damn, she must have upped her game since I've seen her last."

"She had, but luckily, that's not a problem anymore." Elliot slaps the table in front of him, knocking over the piles of chips. "I'm getting married, fuckers."

"Yes, we know," Henley says flatly. "Better you than me."

"You're not looking to settle down anytime soon, Clark?" Rhonan interjects.

Henley scoffs. "Ha, no. I'll stick to one-night-only deals, gentlemen. They get what they want, I get what I want, and everyone leaves satisfied. I don't believe one person for the rest of your life can make you *that* happy." Henley visibly shudders as he begins stacking back the fallen chips. "I think I'll just stick to my freedom, thank you very much."

Rhonan clears his throat as he tosses a look at Elliot and begins dealing the cards. "Elliot, it is a little surprising that you're willing to give up your single status so quickly, especially given how short of a time you've been with Tori..."

Elliot's smile falls as he locks eyes with Rhonan. "Don't start."

"Start what?" I ask, glancing around the table. Henley darts his gaze to the other side of the room as Rhonan turns his attention to me.

"I offered to do a background check on her—"

"And I said no," Elliot cuts in. "Look, I know her, okay? We went to high school with her, so she's not a complete stranger. And we want the same things—she understands my life and she has goals herself."

Henley clears his throat. "Can we not get into this tonight, boys? We're supposed to be having fun, and I'm supposed to be kicking all your asses in blackjack."

"Am I missing something?" I say as I pick up my cards and check to see if I got dealt anything worthwhile.

"I just..." Rhonan blows out a breath. "Never mind. I guess I should just be grateful he's not marrying Laney, huh?"

Elliot tips his beer toward him. "Exactly. But we all know that wouldn't happen anyway thanks to our pact, right boys?"

"Ah, the pact," Henley says wistfully, dredging up memories for me as I fiddle with my cards.

There's nothing like four fourteen-year-old boys making a pact to solidify their friendship. The rules were simple: one, always have each other's backs, two, don't let anything come between us, and three, sisters are off-limits.

As an only child, the third rule didn't affect me, but only one short year later, I realized I was stupid to ever agree to such a stipulation when Laney became more to me than *just* Rhonan's little sister.

"Good. Now that that's over, I'll take a card, please." Elliot taps the table where his cards total twelve, pulling me back to our game. Rhonan flips over a ten, causing him to bust. "Shit." He lifts his beer to his lips and drains the rest of it. We aren't playing for money tonight, which is probably for the best, given the tension in the room.

Rhonan turns to Henley next, who shows two tens, so he splits them. Henley hits on both, getting a twenty on one hand, and twenty-one on the other. All of us acknowledge his stellar hand.

When all's said and done, I easily win my round with my eleven and the ten that Rhonan deals, and then we play a few more hands before our time together comes to an end.

Outside, as Rhonan locks up the winery, he says, "All right, boys. This has been fun, but the sun, and therefore my kid, rises in about five hours. I'll see y'all later."

With a wave, he heads for his car and Elliot lets out a yawn. "Sorry boys, but my bed is calling too. Tori's probably waiting for me." He slaps me on the shoulder. "Don't forget about the meeting with us and Laney tomorrow."

I tap my temple. "Got it written down in here."

"See ya then. Don't forget to bring protection for your junk." Laughing, he heads to his car and takes off, leaving me and Henley alone.

"What does he mean by that?"

Henley scoffs. "He's probably wondering how you're going to survive this when Laney would probably Lorena Bobbitt you if she had the chance."

I take off my backwards ball cap and run a hand through my wavy brown hair, putting it right back in place. "Honestly, I've been trying to figure that out myself. If looks could kill, I'd already be a dead man."

Henley shoves his hands in his pockets. "Well, in my experience, when you've wronged a woman, it's almost impossible to get back on their good side."

"How many women have you wronged?"

Henley smirks. "A few."

"Well, Laney hasn't been the same toward me since her mom's funeral, so…"

"And you still don't know why she flipped a switch?"

"Not really."

Admitting my and Laney's past to Henley right now is only going to open a floodgate of more shit to deal with, especially since he wasn't there the night the line of our friendship was blurred.

But my goal for the next three weeks is simple: remind Laney of our friendship, get her to lighten up on the icy looks, and hopefully be on a more even playing field with her before I go back to Charlotte—all while trying to keep my contact with my father to a minimum and avoid letting my feelings for her rise back to the surface.

I think it's feasible. Either that, or I'm much more delusional than I thought.

"I wish you luck, then." He slaps me on the back. "You're going to need it. By the way, are you staying in one of the McNallys' rental cabins while you're here?"

The McNallys run a cabin rental business in Blossom Peak. Their son, Vince, was a buddy of ours in school and his parents have always been welcoming to me anytime I'm in town, so I did ask them to hold a place for me so I wasn't imposing on anyone or—heaven forbid—forced to stay with my dad. I never bought my own place in town because I never planned on returning for any real length of time.

"Yeah, I am."

"Okay. Well, if you get lonely and want to have pillow fights in our underwear and stay up late talking and painting our nails, you know where to find me." He waggles his eyebrows at me before heading toward his truck.

Laughing, I pull my keys from my pocket as I walk backward. "Thanks. I'll keep that in mind." After I hop into my own truck, I head for the cabin that will be my temporary home during this stay until I can race back to Charlotte—because when I told everyone I wanted to leave Blossom Peak and never come back here again, I meant it.

Guess not everything we think will happen comes true, huh?

***

"Fletcher Adams!" Justin Cook shouts my name as I enter Blossom Brews, the restaurant and brewery his family has owned for three generations. The place has been updated a few times over the years, but it's still got the same hometown welcome and the best onion rings I've ever had—and I've traveled all over this country.

"Justin, my man. How's it going?" I take a seat at the bar and reach out to shake his hand.

"Can't complain." He tosses a coaster onto the bar in front of me. "What can I get for you? I've got a new IPA people are raving about."

"How about a sweet tea with lemon?"

He laughs as he fills a glass with ice, then tops it off with tea from the pitcher behind the bar. "Watching your figure in the offseason?"

I pat my stomach. "You know it. Less for me to work off later."

"Smart." He slides the glass over to me. "You had one hell of a season this past year," he says. "It's a shame about the playoffs, though."

"The team just wasn't jiving," I say as I lift my drink to my mouth.

"He can blame it on the team all he wants, but the truth is, without a quarterback who can make the pass and a wide receiver who can find his mark, they didn't stand a chance." The voice behind me makes my hackles rise. His monstrous hand comes down on my shoulder. "Huh, son?"

I glare at him over my shoulder as he takes the seat next to me, the smell of beer wafting off him. I wonder how many he's already had.

"You know that more than anyone, right, *Dad*?" He doesn't hear the jab I intended, judging by the mile-wide grin on his lips.

He turns to Justin. "Yeah, I guess I might know a thing or two about the game."

Justin humors him. "Trust me. I feel like I'm standing in front of football royalty right now. Anything you two say I'll take as gospel."

My father slaps me on the back again. "I don't know about Fletcher here. He's still too green to know the game the way his father did, and I still don't see a ring on his finger."

My teeth grind together as I fight with myself not to say anything in return—because being the son of Luke Adams, one of the best quarterbacks to play the game in his time—comes with never-ending criticism and competition, among other things.

Justin nods toward me. "I don't know about that, sir. Fletcher is killing it. He's the top wide receiver in the league."

My dad takes a sip of his beer and then studies me. "Interesting. Last I checked he was number two."

I pick up my tea and start to chug, wishing it was alcohol and thankful that it's not at the same time—because then I'd be dealing with my issues the same way he does. When I'm done drinking the entire glass, I set it down and move to stand, fishing my wallet from my back pocket so I can pay and get as far away from this man as possible.

When I walked into Blossom Brews today, the goal was to just kill some time before I meet up with Elliot later about wedding shit. But after only a few minutes in my father's presence, I can think of a million other places I'd rather go.

"Thanks for the tea, Justin." I throw a twenty on the bar and move to leave, but my dad reaches out to grab my arm.

"Where are you going?"

"Oh you know, the usual. Going to study some game tape."

"Don't mock me," he growls just low enough that only the two of us can hear.

I glare at him over my shoulder as I shake my arm free from his grasp. "I wouldn't dream of it, *Dad*."

"Fletcher..." he draws out, and for a moment, he almost sounds sincere. But I know better. "Would it kill you to just be thankful for everything that I've taught you?"

And there it is. The classic Luke Adams cocktail—one part gaslighting, two parts self-congratulation, topped with a twist of emotional manipulation. According to him, my success on the road to the NFL had nothing to do with my hard work and everything to do with his athleticism, his knowledge of the game, and his tough love that ultimately made me a better player and man.

Jesus. What a load of shit.

"Nice to see you, Dad," I say instead of the countless rebuttals I've rehearsed over the years. I walk away, swallowing the bitterness he always leaves behind.

# Chapter 6

**Laney**

*Popcorn, Lies, and Thank-Yous*

"Did you get the popcorn machine to work, Dad?" Holding the stack of red and white striped cardboard buckets, I head across the grass in his direction. People are already starting to arrive, claiming spaces on the lawn and laying down blankets, trying to get the best spot to view the projector screen in the courtyard.

My father straightens from behind the old red steel popcorn cart, adjusting his pants and wiping the sweat from his brow. "I think so." A beat later, the sound of popping kernels fills the air, and his mouth spreads into a proud grin. "See? She's still got it."

I set the buckets on the table beside the cart. "But what happens when it doesn't work the next time?"

"Then I fix it again."

Titling my head, I make sure my tone is soft when I say, "You know we should think about buying a new one, Dad. Those things aren't meant to last forever."

His thick, gray eyebrows pull together. "I know, Laney. But as long as I can fix it, I'm gonna. There's no sense in buying something new for no reason."

My father's excuse sounds reasonable, but we both know the real reason why he doesn't want to replace this popcorn machine—it's the one my mother picked out when we started Hart Winery seasonal events.

It's the first weekend in June, which means it's the start of our summer event series, and as the seasons change, so do the experiences we offer. Normally, we host events during the week or Sunday afternoons, but since we didn't have a wedding on the calendar this Saturday night, my father decided to host an outdoor family movie night to fill the winery with people and take advantage of the warmer weather.

As the winery has expanded over the years, so has the property. We now have two main buildings—one has the tasting room and barrel room we use for private parties, while the other houses our farm-to-table restaurant and event spaces for wedding receptions, business conferences, and so much more.

Between those two buildings is our open and spacious courtyard, perfect for hosting events like tonight's. Trees, shrubs, and flowers are planted around the space, a playground is off to the left for kids to enjoy while parents relax with a glass of wine, and to the right are several cornhole sets, bocce ball courts, horseshoe pits, and fire pits for the cooler nights.

"Auntie Laney!" Ellis shrieks as she runs across the grass, her little feet carrying her as fast as they can, and leaps into my arms.

"Hey, Ellis." I tug on her shirt. "I like your pajamas."

She looks down at her shorts and matching shirt. "Princess Elsa is my favorite." Rhonan always brings Ellis to movie nights in her pajamas to make life easier when she inevitably passes out early.

"Oh really? I thought Moana was."

Rhonan whispers in my ear as he comes up behind me. "That was last week. You've gotta keep up, Auntie." He circles back to my niece. "And Elsa is a queen, honey. We talked about this."

"Ah, I see," I say, setting Ellis gently back on the ground. "Are you still excited to watch the movie, though? Papa chose Moana because you asked for it." My dad loves letting Ellis help pick the film for family movie nights. It's his way of including her in the legacy of our family business, and I know if Mom were still alive, she'd do the same.

"Yes, I still love Moana. But she's my second favorite now."

"Got it. Well, movie night means you get to stay up past your bedtime. Are you excited?"

Nodding, her brown hair sways as she dances in place. "Yes! I can't wait to eat popcorn and snuggle with Uncle Fletcher."

As if she summoned him, Fletcher appears out of nowhere, looking freshly showered in black shorts and a plain gray T-shirt. His signature backwards hat is missing, allowing him to push a hand through his thick curly brown hair, which looks in dire need of a cut.

Ellis can sing his praises all she wants, but I know the emotional turmoil this man is capable of inflicting.

"Wh—what are you doing here? I thought we were meeting at Elliot's later?" I ask while trying to keep my composure. My plan was to finish helping my dad set up, drive to Elliot's for our wedding talk, then head home and bury my feelings in a pint of ice cream later.

Ellis tugs on his hand, pulling his attention to her before he can answer. "Uncle Fletcher, where are your pajamas?"

"I don't wear pajamas to bed, sweetie."

Her nose scrunches up. "That's weird. Then what do you wear?"

His eyes lift to mine, as if he sensed me anticipating his answer as well.

When Fletcher slept in my bed all those years ago, he was always fully clothed, minus maybe a T-shirt depending on his injury.

But adult Fletcher?

Does he sleep in just shorts? Briefs? Nothing at all?

*You shouldn't even want to know the answer to that question, Laney.*

Smiling back down at my niece, he dodges her question, and I don't know who's more grateful for that, me or my brother. "Why don't you and your dad find us a spot to put our blanket? Then once I'm done talking to Auntie Laney, I'll be over to share your popcorn and the candy I brought."

Her eyes light up and then she's pulling Rhonan toward the grass. "Let's go, Daddy! We need to pick a spot."

Rhonan sighs as he follows his daughter, but not before saying over his shoulder, "Thanks for not telling my daughter that you sleep naked."

"Wouldn't want another stripper incident." Fletcher retorts.

Rhonan shakes his head and continues to walk away, leaving me and Fletcher alone. When his eyes find mine again, my pulse races even faster.

*He's just a guy, Laney. Just a guy you used to have a crush on when you were a teenager. He's not even that good-looking, so just calm the fuck down.*

Fletcher grins, and that dimple of his pops in his cheek.

*I'm screwed.*

"Excuse me? Are you Fletcher Adams?" a small voice asks.

A young girl a little older than Ellis approaches us before Fletcher can explain why he's here.

"I am," Fletcher answers, kneeling down to her level so they can see eye-to-eye. "What's your name?"

"Isabella."

"What a beautiful name. Do you watch football, Isabella?"

She shakes her head. "No, but my Daddy does."

A gentleman who can't be much older than Fletcher walks up behind her. "Sorry about that. My daughter swore she saw you, and she took off before I could stop her."

Fletcher stands, smiling. "Well, she was right." He extends his hand to the man. "Fletcher Adams. Nice to meet you."

The guy shakes Fletcher's hand with a grin. "Man, this is wild. I've watched you play for years. Big fan."

Fletcher's smile softens. "I appreciate that."

"Do you mind signing my hat?" the man asks, taking it off and handing it to Fletcher.

"Absolutely." Prepared for occasions such as this, Fletcher extracts a black marker from his pocket, uncaps it with his teeth, and scribbles his name across the bill. "There you go."

I'm so transfixed watching him interacting with his fans, that I am oblivious to the line of people that has formed behind the young girl and her dad.

Fletcher directs his gaze to mine. "Sorry about this."

"Why are you apologizing? This is what you wanted, right?" I ask without one ounce of sarcasm in my voice. I remember listening to Fletcher talk about how one day people were going to ask him for his autograph—and now I get to witness it.

While Fletcher takes pictures, talks, and signs autographs for his fans, I walk over to the refreshment table, needing something to do besides gape. I grab two water bottles and linger for a bit, pretending to organize popcorn buckets while mostly just watching him work the small crowd.

It takes nearly thirty minutes before the last fan finally walks away.

When he turns back toward me, I hand him a water.

"Thank you," he says, twisting the cap open and taking a long drink.

"Does that happen a lot?" I ask.

"Honestly, I'm surprised it hasn't happened before now. If I'm not keeping a low profile, it's pretty standard. I'm used to it by now."

"Comes with the territory, huh?"

It's in that moment that I realize just how much I don't know about the man standing in front of me, when once upon a time, I was the person who knew more about him than anyone else.

Maybe that's still true.

He takes a step closer to me. "Yes, and to answer your question from earlier, Rhonan texted me this afternoon, asking if I wanted to join him and Ellis for movie night. So I called Elliot to ask if we could reschedule, and he suggested we just meet here at the winery. Now I can spend time with Ellis *and* fulfill my duty as the best man."

"Oh." He spent thirty minutes talking to his fans instead of brushing them off *and* he didn't want to let down my niece, so he made other arrangements for our meeting?

*Knowing that makes it harder to hate him, doesn't it, Laney?*

His eyebrow lifts. "Oh?"

I plant a hand on my hip and shrug. "I mean, who knew you could consider other people's feelings?"

He huffs out a laugh. "Come on, Laney. You know I've always been a nice guy..."

I tilt my head. "That's weird...because I didn't think nice guys told lies?" The words slip out before I have a second to process them. But if he was truly worried about how I felt, he wouldn't have acted the way he did all those years ago.

Regret fills my chest, but there's no taking it back now.

Fletcher's head rears back. "What?"

My heart hammers in my chest as I turn my back to him. "Never mind."

He steps up behind me, his chest brushing my back. And for one split second, I forget how to breathe.

"Don't think for a second that I'm going to let that comment slide, Laney." His finger dances up my arm, lighting my skin on fire as breathing begins to feel almost impossible. "You can't avoid me this time. You can try to pretend we weren't friends once and that we are strangers now, but you and I both know that's a fucking lie. Like it or not, we'll be working together for the next three weeks, and it'd be great if you didn't make the wedding duties more difficult than it needs to be. Don't you agree?"

"What's going on here?"

I lift my eyes to find Dilynne standing next to the popcorn cart, her arms crossed over her chest, smirking at me with a knowing grin.

Fletcher steps away from me—*thank God*—and I brush my hair from my face, forcing a smile while desperately trying to cool down. "Just helping set up a few things for the movie night. Have you—have you seen my dad?"

"He was talking to Elliot and Tori in the tasting room, last I saw." Dilynne rolls her eyes. "Of course they'd be here tonight."

Fletcher studies Dilynne. "I'm beginning to think you're just as much of a fan of Tori's as you are of Elliot's."

Dilynne feigns shock, placing a hand to her chest while her mouth drops open. "Why, whatever gave you that idea?"

Fletcher laughs. "What's the deal, Dilynne? Did she do something to you?"

"Just stupid shit back in school—saying a classroom smelled like a grease monkey whenever I walked into it, calling me a lesbian behind my back because I loved working on cars instead of painting my nails and doing my makeup like her and her friends, and generally always acting like she was better than everyone else. But don't worry, I got back at her."

Fletcher winces. "Uh, what did you do?"

Dilynne leans over the table and lowers her voice. "I slipped a laxative into her smoothie during first period drama class. About twenty minutes later, she was shitting her brains out in the bathroom, *American Pie* style."

*God, I love her.*

"Wow. Remind me never to leave a drink unattended around you. Does Tori know it was you?" Fletcher asks.

Dilynne smiles proudly. "Nope, but I have video of her running into the bathroom with shit on her leg in case I need leverage one day."

"Noted." Fletcher looks over at me. "And you knew about this story when you agreed to be Tori's maid of honor?"

"I did, and I never would have said yes if Dilynne asked me not to. But I agreed for Elliot's sake, not Tori's. And if Elliot is so crazy about her, she must have changed a little bit."

"And this way I have someone on the inside to get intel," Dilynne adds, popping her shoulder.

Fletcher hooks his thumb over his shoulder. "Well, I'm gonna go greet the bride and groom." He turns to me before walking off. "You coming?"

"I... I'll be there in a minute."

Dilynne and I watch him walk off before she rounds the table and comes to stand by me. "Sooo... Did I interrupt something?"

"Absolutely not." My eyes scour the courtyard and the crowd that has doubled in size since I last looked.

"You sure? You looked flustered when I walked up." She nudges my shoulder playfully. "In fact, your cheeks are still red."

Sighing, I pinch the bridge of my nose. "I'm beginning to accept that I severely underestimated how much he still affects me."

"Your hard nipples agree."

"Oh my God." Stomping across the lawn, I head for the main building, ducking inside a hallway where I can take a moment to gather myself, but Dilynne is hot on my heels.

She places her hand on my shoulder as I lean against the wall, looking up at the ceiling. "Okay, the nipple thing was a bit far. I'll admit that. But what's going on? You seemed to handle last night okay. Why are you panicking now?"

I lower my chin and meet her eyes. "Because I could avoid him last night. There were other people to talk to, and Ellis is the perfect distraction."

Dilynne folds in her lips as she fights her laugh. "God, she had me rolling when she screamed she wanted to be a stripper."

I roll my eyes. "Yeah, just one more thing to thank Fletcher for."

"Okay, so you'll actually have to talk to him now while you guys handle the wedding shenanigans." She shrugs. "You already knew this, so what's the big deal?"

"The big deal is I have no idea how to act around him. Like, what am I supposed to say to him? We haven't had a conversation in *years*. And then he shows up tonight and asks Elliot to move our meeting here so he can watch the movie with Ellis?"

Dilynne tsks. "Damn. Well played, Adams." She lets out a heavy sigh. "Well, I say you just try to keep things casual, very PG. Only talk about the weather, your business, and the winery. But if he asks you about your dating life, tell him you bang a new guy every week."

"What? Why?"

"So he knows you're not sitting around still pining after him, or worse, full of cobwebs down there." She dips her eyes down to my crotch and then back to my face. "Now that I think about it, when's the last time you got any?"

I pinch the bridge of my nose. "God, I'm so glad that you're concerned about my sex life right now. Truly."

"I appreciate your sarcasm, and I think that's why we're such good friends. But my point is, if Spencer was the last guy to go down under"—she points to the juncture between my legs—"then we need to get you laid. All the pent-up sexual frustration is probably why Fletcher is having such an effect on you."

I can't deny that she may have a point. "Yeah, maybe."

She snaps her fingers. "Then that settles it. We go out next Friday and you don't come home until you've seen a dick *and* felt it in your vagina."

I stare at her, blinking slowly. "You'd think, given how long we've been friends, that nothing you say could shock me, yet here we are."

"It's a gift."

"When's the last time *you* had sex?"

Staring up at the ceiling, she thinks for a second before answering. "Last weekend."

"What? With who?"

"Jeremy."

"Asheville guy? You're still seeing him?"

Holding a finger up in the air, she replies, "Correction, we're not *seeing* each other. We have sex. There's a difference."

Jeremy is a guy Dilynne met at a car show last year. He's been her unofficial fuck buddy ever since. Part of me wonders why she doesn't want more with him, but I know my best friend better than that. Dilynne has never really been interested in relationships. She's had a hard enough time with men given the industry she's in, and most guys she's dated can't handle her outsmarting them when it comes to cars, or the fact that she's not the type of girl that will change who she is to make them happy.

Those are the qualities that I love most about her, but I know she struggles with that when it comes to relationships.

"Well, you know I have no experience with casual, and I'm kind of busy being a girl boss in my life right now."

She sighs. "Yes, but this is the time to try something new. You need to enjoy your single status while waiting for Mr. Right."

"Hey, I've been on a few dates recently."

"Yeah, literally two in the past three months and besides that, nothing. What's stopping you from going on more?"

"Uh…well…" I bite on my bottom lip. "I'm busy running my business, and you know… It's Blossom Peak. Not exactly a hotspot for eligible bachelors."

"Agreed, but that doesn't mean you need to continue to live in this monotony." Dilynne straightens her spine and tightens her ponytail. "So, I stand by my suggestion. We go out next Friday night, we find you a man to clean out the cobwebs downstairs, and hell, maybe you even invite him to the wedding as your date, just to give yourself a buffer for Fletcher."

I hate to admit it, but Dilynne might be onto something. "Ugh, fine."

She fist pumps the air. "Hell yes! Operation De-Cobweb is a go. And if all else fails, I'll kidnap Fletcher, tape his mouth shut, and let you say everything you've been holding in, so you can finally move on."

I arch a brow. "I swear, with the way your mind works, I'm fairly certain you could get away with murder."

She pops her hip out to the side. "Oh, I know I could. I didn't binge all those murder documentaries for nothing."

***

"Thanks for letting us use your office, George." Elliot holds the door to my father's office open, motioning for Tori, me, and Lucifer—I mean, Fletcher—to enter ahead of him.

The familiar room still smells strongly of oak like it did when I was a kid. The same family photos line the walls, and a few new ones have been added over the years. My father's desk sits in the far left corner, a beautiful picture window behind it that showcases the vineyards behind the building, and the conference table is off to the right where my father holds meetings for the staff when necessary.

Standing in the hallway, my father smiles as he shoves his hands into the pockets of his khaki slacks. "Of course. You kids can talk freely back here, and it's a hell of a lot quieter than anywhere else in the winery right now." Even as he speaks, the dull sound of the movie echoes through the walls. My father's eyes meet mine. "Lock it up when you're done, sweetheart?"

"Sure, Dad." He blows me a kiss before shutting the door. When I turn around, Elliot and Tori are sitting next to each other on one side of the conference table, and Fletcher is in a chair directly across from them.

Elliot waves me over. "Come on, Laney. Let's get this done so we can all go enjoy the rest of our evening."

"Thanks for being accommodating about this, by the way," I say as I head for the chair that's furthest away from Fletcher. "You know I always help my dad with these events."

Elliot nods. "No problem. After Fletcher called me, Tori and I agreed it just made more sense. Plus, it gives us another excuse to scope out the winery before the wedding."

"That's true." As I begin to take my seat, Fletcher's voice stops me.

"What are you doing?"

I blink. "Sitting down..."

Tori giggles. "Go sit next to Fletcher, Laney. We've got a few things to show you both." Her brows draw together. "Does he smell bad or something?"

Fletcher sniffs his armpit theatrically and flashes me his lethal grin. "I just showered before coming over here, so I'm fresh as a daisy."

Oh, I'm fully aware of how incredible this man smells after he was pressed up against my back earlier.

Sighing, I move to the chair to his left and sit, avoiding his gaze. "Okay, so let me have it. What is it that you need me to do?"

"Uh, I'm part of this too, remember?" Fletcher interjects.

Elliot darts his eyes between the two of us, laughing slightly before he shakes off our awkward interaction and starts talking. The truth is, my brother and his friends are in the dark about my history with Fletcher, and for good reason—because if they (my brother most importantly) ever found out, I don't think the four of them would still be friends.

"Okay. You two know we only have three weeks before the wedding, and Tori is going to be gone a lot for work."

"My boss just took on a new client, so we're building a social media campaign from scratch, and they need me," Tori states proudly as she flips her long blonde hair over her shoulder. "So that's why it's so important that we can count on the two of you to help."

"And I have two trials between now and the wedding that hopefully won't last long, so a lot of what we need you two to do will be running errands, putting favors together, making sure the details with the winery are finalized, and planning the bachelor and bachelorette party."

"Party? As in one?" Fletcher asks for clarification.

Elliot turns to his fiancée. "Yes. We want a joint one."

"Plus, I don't have many friends here, so if we had a separate bachelorette party, it'd just be you, me, and Dilynne," Tori adds through a laugh. "And I'm pretty sure she doesn't want that."

I offer her an understanding smile. "I think a joint party is a great idea. We could have it here at the winery too."

"Yeah! We thought it'd be more fun if we were all together. Go crazy—we're not opposed to having a little fun," Elliot adds.

Fletcher rubs his palms together. "I already have a few ideas."

"Which we can discuss later," I say through a placating smile without even looking in his direction.

Elliot grabs a list and slides it toward us before lifting a cardboard box from under the table. The box is full of organza bags, place cards, decorations, and several bags of what look like M&M's. I move the paper closer to me, but Fletcher reaches out and pulls it back toward him. I fight the urge to rip it from his hands.

"This is what we need you two to accomplish."

"Filling wedding favors, cake tasting, picking out a bridesmaid dress for me and a tux for Fletcher." I lift my eyes to Tori and then cast them over to Elliot. "I get the favors, but you honestly don't want to pick out your own cake, or what Fletcher and I wear?"

Tori shakes her head as she laughs. "I don't care about this stuff. If it were up to me, we wouldn't be having a traditional wedding at all."

Elliot chuckles. "And you know I'll eat anything, Laney. Just make sure we have a cake." He picks up Tori's hand and kisses the top of it. "Honestly, the details only matter to my parents. The only thing I care about is this woman walking down the aisle toward me on that day."

Tori swallows and leans forward, pressing her lips to Elliot's and then nuzzling their noses together. "You're too good to me."

"All right, you two. We get it. You're in love," Fletcher chimes in. "So what color tux are we talking?"

"Black," Tori answers. "Just simple and classic." Then she turns to me. "And for you, Laney, blush pink for the dress."

The moment she says it, I can feel my cheeks turn the same color. "Sounds good."

"What are your thoughts on Funfetti cake, though?" Fletcher asks.

I twist in my chair to face him for the first time since I sat down. "Are you serious?"

He shrugs before looking back at Elliot. "What? It is the best flavor of cake."

"We're not ordering the cake from Betty Crocker," I admonish. "And I highly doubt Bites & Bliss Bakery will do a Funfetti cake."

Elliot laughs. "Again, I don't fucking care what flavor the cake is. Funfetti is delicious, but maybe something a tad more sophisticated. The wedding is at the winery, after all."

I jut my thumb at Fletcher. "Apparently some of us still haven't grown up."

"And *apparently* some of us are snobs about cake."

I glare at him as he raises an eyebrow. Sighing, I turn back to the list while mentally finishing my argument with this insufferable man.

*Funfetti cake.* I mentally roll my eyes, too.

My parents started hosting weddings at the winery when I was very young, so for years I watched from afar as many a bride walked down the aisle to her groom waiting anxiously. My favorite part was watching his reaction when he saw her for the first time, which made me imagine what my future husband would look like when he saw me.

Let's just say that Ellis isn't the only little girl who was obsessed with dressing like a princess. I've envisioned my own wedding since I was just a few years older than her, down to every last detail, including the cake.

And, for a while, the groom waiting at the other end of the aisle was the man currently sitting to my right.

*Oh, to be young and naïve again.*

"So that's it?" I say, looking over the list again.

"Oh! The place cards," Tori says, standing from the table to dig in the box, pulling out a stack of place cards before sliding them across the table toward me. "Laney, you have beautiful handwriting, and you know everyone on the guest list." She gestures to the papers in front of me, causing me to flip to the next paper where I see the list of people who will be attending. "There should be enough, but try not to make too many mistakes. I don't have time to order more."

That makes me pause for a moment, but then Fletcher leans over my shoulder to see the list, and the second his cologne hits my nose, I'm transported back to my old bedroom, breathing in that same scent off my pillow long after he was gone.

"You invited my dad?" he asks, his voice strained. The concern in his voice makes my shoulders stiffen.

Elliot studies him, confused. "Yes. Why wouldn't we? You're in the wedding and he was my coach—*our coach*—for years."

The clench in Fletcher's jaw tells me all I need to know about how he feels about it. "Well, yeah. I mean, it makes sense." He rubs the back of his neck as his eyes find the floor.

"Is there something I should know about?" Elliot prods, but I interject before Fletcher feels like he has to.

"Nope. We've got this. I promise, the day will be perfect." Smiling over at Tori, I place my hand on top of hers.

She lets out a dramatic sigh. "I can't tell you how much easier this will be for me, knowing I don't have to worry about this stuff." When her phone chimes on the table, she lifts it and then stands from her chair. "Sorry, I need to take this. It's my boss."

Tori heads for the door as Elliot watches her. "He's always calling her. I told her she'd better put her phone on silent when we're on our honeymoon."

"I'm sure you'll both be able to disconnect once you get away."

Elliot pushes a hand through his hair. "Let's hope so—because my mother is already threatening to call and make sure we're working on a grandbaby on our trip."

"And that's my cue to leave," I say as I stand from my chair. "If that's all you needed to talk to me about, then I'm going to head home." As I gather the papers in front of me, and move to stand, Fletcher reaches out and puts his hand on my forearm.

"Leaving so soon? What about the movie?"

I pull my arm away and grab the bags and M&M's, placing them back in the box to carry out to my car. "I have work to do and plenty of errands to run tomorrow."

Elliot points to the door of the office. "I'm gonna go check on Tori. See you two out there?"

"Yup. Be there in a minute," Fletcher replies as he stands, the screech of his chair echoing in the room. "Well, before you leave, let me get your number."

"Why?"

He looks at me as if I'm certifiable, but there's a hint of a smile on his lips. "So we can communicate." He pulls his phone from his pocket and waves it in front of my face. "These are called cell phones, Laney. It's how people keep in touch in the modern age."

I give him a deadpan stare before I rattle off my number and he programs it into his phone. My phone starts to vibrate in my pocket a few seconds later.

"That was me. Now you have mine too." Fletcher shoves his phone back in his pocket.

"Awesome." I lift the box and turn for the door, but Fletcher stops me.

"Let me take that to your car for you." Without asking, he takes the box from my arms and opens the door to the office, allowing me to walk out first.

"That's really unnecessary." I pull the door shut and lock it before turning to face him.

"Doesn't matter. I'm here to serve. Now, lead me to your car, *angel*."

My entire body ignites with a live wire of intense emotion from hearing that nickname, and I'm afraid nothing could have prepared me for what that would feel like again.

Does Fletcher even realize he said it? Was it intentional, or just a slip of the tongue?

When we arrive at my car, I pop the trunk open and gesture for Fletcher to place the box inside. After shutting the trunk, I turn to face him once more. "Thank you, I guess."

He chuckles. "Wow. That sounded like it hurt to say."

"To be honest, it kind of did."

With that infamous smirk still on his lips, he says, "Man, it's good to see you, Laney."

His words make my heart pound harder because there was once a time when I felt that way about him too.

"I, uh…need to get going." I reach to open my car door, but Fletcher beats me to it, holding it open until I'm fully inside. "Thanks."

He leans forward, resting his forearms on the top of the door, smiling down at me. "Be careful, Laney. That was two thank-yous you just gave me."

"It's sad that you're counting."

He locks his eyes with me and says, "I'll always remember what you say to me." Tapping his temple, he continues, "Every. Single. Word." As my mouth drops open, he slams my car door shut and waves at me through the window. "Bye, Laney! Talk to you soon!"

I start my car as fast as I can, pulling out of the parking lot while my mind spins from his words.

He remembers everything I've ever said to him? Is he referring to *that* night? And if so, does that mean he still thinks about it too?

Or is this all a game to him? A test to see if he still has that kind of power over me. Spoiler alert: he does.

I don't even need to glance in the rearview mirror to clearly envision the smug grin on his lips as he stands there, watching me drive away, knowing how easily he just fucked with my head.

But at least this time he has to watch me leave. Because he didn't get that luxury last time—when I walked away for good, heart in pieces, because I was stupid enough to think he felt the same way I did.

Now, if only my heart would catch up to the decision my brain made all those years ago... These next three weeks would be much easier to get through.

# Chapter 7

**Laney**

***Massages, Manicures, and a Banana***

"Good morning!" Yvonne glides through the front door of the salon on Monday morning, looking much happier than usual.

"Well, apparently it is for *you*," I reply.

Chuckling, she walks past me to the break room to put away her things, so I follow her. "Oh, it is. My first client today has the body of a Greek god, and I can't wait to get my hands on him." She wiggles her fingers like she's already kneading divine biceps.

I lean against the doorframe, crossing my arms over my chest. "I thought massage therapists weren't supposed to ogle their clients."

She waves me off as she moves to the fridge and puts her lunch inside. "Oh, Laney. Anyone in the industry who says they don't appreciate what they're working with is a liar." She turns and faces me with a satisfied grin on her lips. "Besides, I think you might agree that with *this* client, ogling is unavoidable."

It takes a few seconds, but when it dawns on me, the smile falls from my face. "Oh God. It's..."

"Lucifer is coming today!" she exclaims, brushing past me toward her massage room.

I face-palm my forehead. "Jesus, I forgot."

"That's surprising. You usually check the schedule when you come in."

She's right. I *do* usually check the schedule when I open the salon for the day. But ever since Fletcher came back in town, everything has been thrown off and my thoughts have just been one tornado after another, leaving destruction and distraction in their wake.

Yesterday I spent most of the day at home, bingeing *Grey's Anatomy* just to check out for a while. And apparently, it worked—because Fletcher's appointments completely slipped my mind.

My mood turns instantly as I head back to my station, catching my reflection in the mirror, adjusting my black tunic and slacks, the same outfit all employees wear. The uniform helps us look polished, adding to the upscale vibe I wanted for my salon.

"Hey, boss." Claudia strides through the front door next, followed by Glenn.

"Today's the day, Laney! Lucifer is coming!" Glenn bounces with excitement. "Do you think I can talk Fletcher into letting me cut his hair while he's here?"

I point a finger at him. "Go put a dollar in the jar."

He throws his head back and laughs. "Gladly." And as he heads toward the break room, he repeats, "Fletcher, Fletcher, Fletcher!!!"

"That's four dollars now!" I call after him. Claudia is still standing next to me when I turn back to my mirror. "Yes?"

"This guy really gets to you, huh?"

Just her asking that question makes my shoulders fall. "Let's just say that growing up with him makes him way more normal—and annoying—to me than he is to the general population. I just think it's ridiculous how people fawn over him. I mean, he's a regular guy that gets sock lint stuck between his toes like the rest of us."

Claudia purses her lips. "That was an oddly specific example, but I get your point. Although, I think we can both agree he is way too good-looking for his own good."

"Oh, believe me, he knows it too."

Her smile is small but comforting. "Just breathe and remember this is all temporary."

"Thank you."

"And also, I hope you get laid this Friday. I think it will help you move past all the lust threatening to spill out of you."

My eyes bug out of my head as my heart starts to race. "Uh... What are you talking about?"

"Dilynne texted us last night and told us we're all going out Friday to get you laid. I agreed it was the perfect way to help you forget about your crush."

"I don't have a crush," I lie. "And who is 'us'?"

"Me, Glenn, Yvonne, and a few other people from the salon."

I close my eyes and take a deep breath, fighting with myself and the idea of marching across the street to my best friend's automotive shop to give her a piece of my mind right now. Sadly, I know it won't do any good. The damage has been done. "Joy."

Claudia laughs, rubbing my shoulder. "It will be great. But just so you know, if you want to hide out today, I wouldn't blame you. You know the rest of us can handle everything."

Her suggestion is tempting, but the last thing I'm going to do is hide like a coward. "Nope. This is *my* business. He's stepping into *my* territory. *He's* the one who should feel uncomfortable, not me."

"I make you feel uncomfortable, huh?"

*Of course he walks in at this moment.*

Clenching my jaw, I plaster on the fakest smile I can muster and turn to find Fletcher smirking at me, his hands stuffed in his pockets, and his hat on backwards in his signature way, covering up his hair that I already noticed is in desperate need of a cut, but refuse to tell Glenn.

"Good morning, Fletcher."

His eyebrows lift. "Wow. I get a 'good morning' from you today?" He reaches forward and places the back of his hand on my forehead. "Are you feeling okay?"

I gently push his hand away. "I'm fine, thank you. No need for touching."

His smirk grows. "Pretty sure you used to like it when I touched you."

Claudia's eyes widen because his words sound way more suggestive than they really are. "Oh my."

I spin to face her so fast I nearly fall over, pointing a finger at her while I regain my balance. "It's not what it sounds like."

"And what did it sound like?" Fletcher asks, pulling my attention back to him, my glare coming on strong.

"Now is not the time nor the place to have this discussion."

Claudia chimes in again, crossing her arms over her chest. "Oh, on the contrary, I think it's the perfect time. It would make her disdain toward you make a lot more sense, at least for me."

My jaw drops open. "Claudia! I thought you were on my side?"

"I am, but seeing you two together? Now I'm invested." She waves her finger between us. "This is the first time I've seen him in person," she says as she dips her eyes up and down his muscular body. "And now I understand why he gets you all riled up."

Fletcher starts to laugh while rubbing the back of his neck. "Okay, so Laney hates me *and* I get her all riled up... Good to know."

"Oh my gosh, he's here!" Glenn hops over to where we're standing, Yvonne trailing behind him. "Mr. Fletcher Adams, football god, can I just say I'm a huge fan?" He reaches out to shake Fletcher's hand, which Fletcher obliges.

"Oh yeah? Huge fan?" Yvonne asks behind me. "What position does he play?"

Glenn giggles. "Oh, you misunderstood, I'm a huge fan of the pants he wears." Glenn licks his lips before dipping his eyes up and down Fletcher's body, much like Claudia just did. "But I play catcher if you're looking for one."

I should feel bad for how blatantly my employees are harassing Fletcher, but I'm sure he's used to this reaction from people. In fact, I'd bet money that he uses it as an opportunity to sleep with many of his female fans to feed his ever-growing ego.

Fletcher casts his gaze toward me, looking for help, before landing back on Glenn and perfecting that polite smile I've seen him use with sportscasters and the public—not that I've been watching him. "Uh, thanks, man. Always grateful for the support."

I roll my eyes, growing more irritated with my employees—who are supposed to be my friends—by the minute. "Okay then. Yvonne, Claudia, Glenn," I say while pointing to each of them and then over to our guest of *dishonor*, "this is Lucif—I mean, Fletcher Adams. There, now everyone's met. Claudia, is he with you first or Yvonne?"

Yvonne rubs her palms together. "I get him first." It's her turn to eye-fuck him, but Fletcher looks to me for guidance.

I shrug and fold my arms over my chest. "Looks like it's your massage and then manicure, Fletch. Are you sure you thought this through?

The corner of his mouth rises ever so slightly as he reaches behind him and removes his shirt, knocking his hat to the floor in the process and shocking all of us.

"Good lord," Glenn pants before fanning his face.

"Lucifer has muscles," Claudia whispers as she tilts her head and stares at Fletcher's torso.

"Oh, I can't wait to rub you down," Yvonne adds as her smile grows.

I can't look away.

My eyes linger on every divot in his chest and abs, every line in his arms, the sprinkle of hair on his chest and just below his belly button, and that V of his hips, dipping just below the waistband of his shorts, leading to the motherland—a place I've visited a thousand times in my imagination.

As Uncle Jesse from *Full House* would say, *have mercy.*

Fletcher has filled out in the most delicious way—such a contrast to the boy who used to lie next to me and talk for hours. His muscles have muscles.

I didn't think men like this existed outside of Marvel movies.

"Laney," Fletcher says, pulling me back to the present as I realize I have no idea how long I've been staring.

I blink myself back to reality. "What?"

I hear giggling behind me, but my eyes stay locked on Fletcher's. "I said... I know *exactly* what I'm doing here." And with a wink, he follows Yvonne back to the massage room, leaving me standing there in a pile of my own drool.

Claudia clears her throat. "You might as well wave your white flag now, lie down, and spread your legs open because there is no way you're going to make it three weeks without sleeping with him."

Glenn hums. "Yup. I totally agree."

My jaw drops. "I can't believe you just said that to me." Pushing my hair from my face, I take a deep breath. "You know what, I think the Lucifer jar needs to extend to any innuendo involving him as well."

Glenn takes out a wad of dollar bills and hands them to me. "Then I'd like to pay in advance."

***

My cell phone chimes in my pocket. I pull it out and groan. My glucose monitor's app is notifying me that my blood sugar is low, so I need to eat something.

Sounds about right since the only thing I've had this morning was a protein bar, of which I only ate half because as soon as I realized Fletcher was coming in, I lost my appetite.

"You need to eat."

Spinning around, I come face-to-face with the man of my nightmares *and* fantasies, but at least he has a shirt on this time. "Um, I'm aware. Thank you."

Fletcher grins. "Wow. That's three thank-yous now." I roll my eyes. "But I hope you still take those alerts seriously..."

"I'm alive, aren't I?"

His brows draw together as he takes a step closer to me, pointing at my phone. "You have an app now, huh?"

His proximity is distracting, but I try to focus on the screen and not how good he smells. "Yeah, technology has come a long way in twelve years."

He looks to my arm where I used to wear my glucose monitor. "Where's the..."

"On my lower stomach now," I say quietly, tapping the bulge underneath my tunic that conceals it.

He hums thoughtfully, which only confuses me more.

"Okay, Lucifer. Claudia is all ready for you," Yvonne says as she approaches, interrupting this bizarre display of concern from Fletcher.

I'm thankful for the interruption because this exchange is just taking me back to so many conversations where I felt like he genuinely wanted to know about how I felt living with it, how my body didn't work normally, and how I wondered if it would turn guys off to know that my glucose monitor would be a permanent fixture in my life.

Fletcher smiles as he spins to face her. "Awesome. I just want to make sure Laney eats something."

I laugh, waving him off. "That's really not necessary."

His eyes meet mine again. "Where are your snacks?"

Yvonne clears her throat. "I'm sorry. Did I miss something?"

"Laney's blood sugar is low, so she needs to eat," Fletcher replies before I can speak for myself.

Yvonne smirks, crossing her arms over her chest. "I see. Well, boss, you heard the man. Let's make sure you eat something."

Rolling my eyes, I set my phone down at my station and then head to the break room to get myself a snack like the thirty-year-old woman that I am. I grab a banana, and when I turn around, I find Fletcher leaning against the doorframe, his arms crossed over his chest as he watches me. I begin to peel the banana slowly and then take a bite out of it a tad too aggressively. "There. You happy?" I mumble around my mouthful of fruit.

His punchable face spreads into a grin. "Very."

I chomp off another bite of the banana. "You know, I'm not the same teenager you knew as Rhonan's annoying little sister, Fletcher. I'm a grown woman, so I can manage my own blood sugar just fine without you hovering."

He drops his arms and crosses the room slowly, each of his strides eating up the space between us until he's just a few inches from me, holding my gaze so intensely that I pause my chewing.

His eyes—deep pools of blue with flecks of green and gold—still hold the same allure for me that they did back when I would stare at them for hours. His lips—still full and kissable—are moving but I don't hear a word they're saying.

Because being this close to him is only making me remember what it felt like to be close to him back then—back when we were friends and this display of concern would make me feel cared for instead of insulted.

And for one split second, I deliriously wonder if we could ever get back to that place.

"Laney?" Fletcher reaches up and cups the side of my face, pulling me right back to reality with one spark of electricity.

"Huh?"

"Fuck, you weren't even listening to me, were you?"

I blink and take a step back, but Fletcher just follows me, his hand still on my face. "I said, I know damn well that you're a grown woman." His eyes dip down to my lips and back up as his jaw tightens. "Believe me, I fucking noticed. But that's not going to stop me from making sure you're okay, especially when I'm around."

My voice drops to a whisper. "You—you haven't been around in a long time, Fletcher."

"But I'm here now." His eyes dip down to my lips again, lingering there.

"Oh, Lucifer?" Claudia singsongs as she walks into the break room, catching us in this compromising position.

Fletcher mumbles something under his breath, drops his hand from my face, and spins to face her. "Yeah?"

"I'm ready for you," she says, gaze flicking between us like she's trying to piece together what she just walked into.

He nods. "Great. I'll be right there."

Claudia's eyes meet mine, but I turn away quickly, trying to get a handle on my blood pressure.

*What the hell is going on?*

The way Fletcher was looking at me just now, I could have sworn he was thinking about kissing me. He touched me like he was legitimately concerned, like...old Fletcher. The one who used to sneak through my window and hold space for all the things I never told anyone else. For a second, it felt like we were still those people—the ones who hadn't ruined everything yet.

"Laney."

"Yeah?" I ask, looking over my shoulder at him.

"I made these appointments because I wanted to support your business," he says, putting another crack in the wall around my heart.

"Why?"

"Because you've built something incredible here, and I'm proud of your success and wanted to see it firsthand." I stand there in shock, trying to process what he's telling me. He shoves his hands in his pocket, his boyish grin returning. "I just wanted to support my friend."

God, I've never hated that word more than I do right now.

"I've never had a manicure in my life, but when in Rome, right?"

I nearly gasp as I laugh. "Pretty sure the Romans weren't getting their cuticles buffed."

The corner of his mouth lifts higher. "Yeah, well, when in Blossom Peak." He turns around and walks out of the break room, leaving me reeling and feeling way more unsteady than I care to admit.

***

"How are your online reviews?" Fletcher asks as he hands me his credit card.

I tap it on the machine and hand it back to him. "Pretty solid. They've been helping bring in tourists."

"I'm not surprised." He shoves his wallet back in his pocket and readjusts his backwards baseball cap. "I mean, Yvonne's hands are so magical, I think she unknotted something in my soul. And Claudia may have turned me into a manicure kind of guy." He fans his hands in front of him, admiring his nails.

Fighting to contain my laughter, I hand him his receipt. "Well, feel free to brag to the entire internet that Blossom Beauty has changed your life."

"Don't worry. I will." He rocks back on his heels. "We should probably work out some sort of schedule, right?"

"Schedule?"

"Yeah, I mean, for the wedding stuff. I'm free tonight if you want to get started."

The ball of anxiety that's been hanging out in my chest starts to bounce around again, but I know he's right. If we don't figure out a schedule, things are going to get done at the last minute and that's going to stress me out even more.

"Look, you don't have to pretend to be interested in this stuff. I can handle it all and just say that you helped..."

He scowls. "Fuck no. Elliot is one of my best friends, and he picked *me* to be his best man. Granted, it was luck of the draw..."

"What do you mean?"

"The boys and I agreed that each of us would get to do it once in the event we ever got married. Elliot chose my name first, so this is my only shot to be a best man, and I don't take that lightly. Besides, he wanted us to work together, and you know this would go a lot smoother if you'd just let me help."

"I don't need your help..."

"Well, too fucking bad, Laney. You're getting it." He taps the reception counter between us. "I'm only here for the wedding and a few days after, so I'm going to make each day count." His face relaxes and then his voice softens too. "Besides, it's been a long time since we've spent time together, just the two of us."

I huff out a laugh as I mutter, "Yeah, well, that's been intentional."

"Care to explain why?" he fires back.

I don't answer him because now is not the time nor the place to get into our history, and I can't deny that his little speech was endearing. He truly cares about this, so I need to put aside my own issues and commit to what I signed on for. "You know what, fine. Come over to my place tomorrow since tonight I have plans, and we can work on the favors if you're insistent on helping."

He licks his lips, but there's still a pinch in his forehead. "I'll be there."

"Good."

"Great."

We stand there awkwardly until Glenn comes racing up to us. "Mr. Adams!"

Fletcher's face changes drastically from analytical to grateful. "Just Fletcher, please."

Glenn sighs. "I like Mr. Adams. It's more authoritative, and I'm all about following authority." He winks and I close my eyes, warding off the secondhand embarrassment. "Anyhow, can you sign this please?" He holds out a Carolina Thunder calendar, one that I recognize because I *may* have flipped through the pages when I was at the general store a few weeks ago, just inspecting the layout, of course. It wasn't because I wanted to see the picture of Fletcher in his uniform, which didn't do much to hide the bulge in his pants.

"Sure, Glenn. I'd be happy to." He takes the calendar and sharpie from Glenn and flips to the month of April, signing across the page under his picture. "There you go, man."

"Gah. Thank you!"

"Why on earth do you have that calendar? You don't even watch football," I say.

Glenn laughs. "Oh girl, the pictures alone are enough spank bank material for me. Plus, when I heard that Lucifer was coming, I had to get something for him to sign."

"Hey, Glenn?" Fletcher asks.

"Yes, Mr. Adams?"

He looks directly at me while he speaks. "Why do y'all call me Lucifer?"

"No reason," I interject, but Glenn literally hip checks me out of the way and leans over the counter, staring straight at Fletcher.

He flicks his eyes over to me and then back to Fletcher. "We aren't allowed to say your name in the salon because Laney thinks bad things will happen. If we do, we have to put a dollar in the jar."

I grind my teeth together as Fletcher grins in my direction. "Is that so?"

"Glenn, you're fired," I say.

Glenn waves me off. "Honey, if I had a dollar for the number of times you've fired me, I could retire early." He winks at Fletcher. "Thanks again, Mr. Adams."

Fletcher waits for him to leave before turning to me, crossing his arms over his chest. "So, I'll be at your place at six tomorrow with food, and then you're going to tell me why you hate me so much."

Shaking my head, I say, "You can come over at seven, food isn't necessary, and we won't be talking about anything except wedding stuff." Walking backwards, he grins before reaching for the door. "Laney, it appears you've forgotten how persuasive I can be. See you at seven."

With that, he's gone.

Standing frozen in place, adrenaline races through me, thinking about being alone with him tomorrow in my house with no one else as a buffer and very little space I can put between us.

Yup. It's official. This man will be the death of me.

# Chapter 8

**Fletcher**

### *Ropes Course, Reality, and Rage*

*God, how could I have forgotten how stubborn Laney Hart is?*

"You okay back there?" Henley calls out to me as he increases the distance between us on the ropes course, leaving me further behind while I continue to mentally revisit my time at Laney's salon yesterday.

She's pissed. Like, deeply, soul-level pissed. I knew there was tension, but I didn't realize she'd been nursing a full stadium's worth of resentment for years. Clearly, I've got work to do.

"I'm trying not to injure myself so I don't have to explain to my coach why I can't play the game I'm paid to!" Holding onto the ropes even tighter, I traverse the boards beneath my feet, keeping a slow pace so I don't fall, even though I'm strapped into a harness and connected to the cable above me.

Henley laughs. "We can't have that now, can we?"

"Not until I get my Super Bowl ring." As I cross the last few boards and land on the platform, I release the breath I was holding. "Jesus, what a workout."

Henley adjusts his helmet. "This is the beginner's course, Fletch."

"You're kidding me."

He holds his stomach while he laughs. "Nope. Sorry to deflate your ego."

"Well, consider me humbled."

I decided to pay a visit to Henley at Sky's the Limit ski resort and adventure park since I don't have much else to do while waiting for seven o'clock to get here. Business was slow today, so Henley convinced me to tackle the ropes course while we caught up.

I would have been fine just sitting at a table and talking, but Henley's not the type to sit still. When he told us he was going to take over the resort from the previous owners a few years ago, it didn't surprise any of us. Honestly, this job was right up Henley's alley, given his daredevil tendencies.

On the other hand, the only adrenaline *I* like to chase is that which occurs with my feet planted firmly on the ground.

During the winter when the snow sticks, this place draws skiers, snowboarders, and families with young kids to enjoy the winter activities, scenery, and Santa's Village that the resort transforms into in December. But during the summer, the slopes shut down and the adventure side of the property opens with ziplining, rock climbing, hiking, biking, and apparently near-death rope challenges.

Hence why I'm sweating my balls off while my fear of heights keeps me from moving too fast so I don't fall to my death.

Henley leads me through the rest of the course, and when I'm back on earth, I take a seat at the bar in the lodge while Henley orders us some lunch and checks on his employees from behind the bar.

He slides me a water and leans in front of me. "Well, it looks like all of your body parts are still intact, so I take it that Laney hasn't tried to jeopardize your football career yet with any physical harm?"

"Nope, you're doing a better job at that than she is, making me do that course."

"Oh, stop whining or I'll make you do the mountain bike trail next."

"Hard pass." Sighing, I lean back in my chair. "I knew having to spend time with Laney for Elliot's wedding was going to be interesting, but I severely underestimated how much she wants to avoid me."

"The Fletcher Adams charm isn't working on her, huh?"

"Nope. The nicer I am to her, the more riled up she seems to get." Chuckling, I spin my glass on the bar in front of me while remembering how flustered she was when I ripped my shirt off in front of her yesterday, or how painful it was for her to thank me for carrying a box to her car Saturday night. Yeah, so maybe that wasn't me being nice, exactly.

In fact, watching her struggle with how to handle me is starting to become its own source of entertainment. The way she glares, how her lips purse like she's trying to hold back a whole monologue.

But the only thing those annoyed expressions do is remind me that once upon a time, I couldn't think of anything but what those lips would feel like against mine.

Yeah, it's official—my feelings for Laney Hart haven't diminished over the years, even though I've shoved them down and ignored them with alarming success... Until now. Being near her again is bringing everything back to the surface, reminding me of the girl I fell for in the first place and how those feelings never went away. I've just been avoiding them because it was easy to do with space and time between us.

But Laney's not the same girl I knew. And, against my better judgment and my loyalty to Rhonan, I want to know how the brave and fascinating girl who captivated me back in high school has become the version of herself she is now, with thicker walls than Fort Knox.

"Riling her up probably isn't the best plan," Henley says while he fills up his own glass of water just as his phone rings in his pocket. When he fishes it out and glances at the screen, he rolls his eyes and declines the call.

"Not someone you wanted to hear from, huh?"

"It's this girl, Meghan, that I hooked up with last year. She's been calling me for a few months now, but I was clear it was a one-time thing. Apparently, she can't take the hint."

"You aren't even interested in a couple dates?" I ask, already knowing the answer since Henley is not the relationship type. I always assumed I wasn't either... But things can change.

"You know that's not my style. One night only works just fine for me," he says.

"Normally, I wouldn't even keep a girl's number, but now I'm glad I did so I know to avoid her. Anyway, back to you pissing off Laney."

Chuckling, I say, "I'm not doing anything horrible to her, but apparently it doesn't take much to get on her bad side. Yesterday I went to her salon because I booked a few appointments there to support her business, you know? And I thought that would help, but then I found out she calls me Lucifer and makes her employees put a dollar in a jar every time they say my name."

Henley throws his head back in laughter. "Oh, fuck. That's priceless."

"I can't deny that it is pretty funny, but fuck, Henley... How the hell am I supposed to come back from that?"

"Why don't you ask her what the problem is?"

"I'm gonna try tonight. We're meeting at her house at seven to start working on wedding shit, and I'm determined to wear her down."

Henley crosses his arms over his chest. "Does it really matter if she has a problem with you, Fletch? I mean, you're only here for the wedding, and then you're headed back to your life in Charlotte and the NFL. Sure, Laney is Rhonan's sister, but..."

"What about my sister?"

Rhonan's voice cuts through the room like a warning shot. He steps up to the bar next to me wearing his sheriff's uniform with his hand placed firmly on the gun holster at his hip, but his eyes are locked on mine, full of curiosity.

"I was, uh, just telling Henley that Laney and I are starting to work on Elliot's wedding stuff tonight." Henley and I share a look as I silently ask him to drop the previous subject.

Rhonan taps the bar in front of him. "Can I get a burger and fries to go, please? And the biggest Coke you've got?" he asks Henley before he turns back to me. "Good luck with my sister. I think we both know that Laney can be a bit of a control freak, but her organizational skills and inability to say no to people is what got her in this mess to begin with."

Henley scoffs as he stands at the computer, plugging in Rhonan's order. "Dilynne doesn't understand it either, but Laney has a bigger heart than any of us, I guess."

Little do they both know that I have firsthand experience with Laney's generosity and compassion, which makes my predicament even more complicated.

"I was worried about her being involved with the wedding planning, but she's handling it better than I thought she would," Rhonan adds as he pulls his phone from his pocket and checks it.

"What do you mean?"

My friends share a look before Rhonan answers me. "Laney was engaged a couple of years ago to that guy Spencer she was dating."

My pulse instantly skyrockets. "What?"

Henley clears his throat before adding, "And the fucker cheated on her."

*How the hell did I not know about this?*

Rhonan mentioned she was dating someone a while ago, and I knew that it didn't work out, but I never knew they were engaged or that he was unfaithful to her.

*Fuck.*

Rage fills my veins, the type of anger I can only recall feeling a handful of times in my life—because the thought of any man hurting Laney like that makes me want to rip this guy apart with my bare hands.

"Are you fucking serious?"

Rhonan scoffs. "Yeah. She seemed to bounce back pretty quickly, but I don't know..." He shrugs as Henley hands him a plastic bag with his food and a to-go cup. "She just hasn't been the same since. And when Tori asked her to be her maid of honor, I thought for sure she'd say no, but part of me thinks she might just be trying to prove she's all right to everyone, you know?"

I can't stop clenching my fists as I sit there and process this revelation. No wonder Laney doesn't seem the same, and given our history, she's probably keeping me at arm's length because the last time we were on good terms was before she told me...

"Fletcher?" Rhonan's voice pulls me from my thoughts.

"Yeah?"

"Keep an eye on her for me, will you?" he asks, his question genuine, but the protective instinct it lights within me is already there. "Let me know if you feel like she's struggling or needs to bow out."

"Of course."

"Tori will survive if Laney can't handle everything."

Henley chuckles. "But who will fill in for her? My sister?"

Rhonan shakes his head, a smile on his face. "Fuck, that would be a disaster. But I won't lie, I'd pay to watch it."

I think back to the story Dilynne told me at the winery, knowing if she had the chance, her revenge on Tori the second time would be even worse than the laxatives.

"I think Laney will be fine, but I'll definitely try to take on as much responsibility as I can."

"Thanks. I know I can trust you to look after her."

Henley grunts. "What about me? You don't trust me?"

Rhonan points a finger at him. "Your method for helping women get over their exes is getting them *under* you."

Henley grins. "What can I say? I'm dedicated to the cause." He laughs before adding, "But Laney is your sister. Even I know she's off-limits."

"True, but I feel like Fletcher is less of a threat than you are."

Henley bounces his eyebrows up and down while he looks at me. "You hear that? Rhonan thinks I'm better looking than you."

"Do you want a trophy or something?" I say, grinding my teeth together at the thought of Henley touching Laney at all.

I respect Henley's carefree attitude toward sex. He's honest with the women he hooks up with, never pretends it's more than it is. If that works for them, no harm, no foul.

But Laney isn't just any woman.

She's my Laney—*my angel*.

And the irony is, as Rhonan says his goodbyes and heads out to his cruiser, he has no idea that Henley isn't the one he should be worried about making a move on her.

# Chapter 9

**Fletcher**

*Age Seventeen*

*Angels, Future Plans, and Admissions*

"Fletcher?"

Laney twists around in her desk chair just as I finish climbing through her window. I wince as I slide all the way through. "Hey, Laney."

Her expression instantly morphs into concern. "What's wrong?"

I hold my ribs as I walk up to her, forcing a smile. "It's nothing."

Yanking my arm away from my body, she lifts my shirt and gasps. "Holy shit! That doesn't look like nothing."

I glance down at the spot that was only red when I snuck out of my house and see that it is now turning purple. "It looks worse than it really is. It happened during football practice. Comes with the territory." Another lie, but at this point, they're beginning to sound like the truth even to me.

Laney's frustration is visible. "Sit down. I'll be right back." Before I can argue, she quietly exits her room, leaving me alone.

My eyes scour her space, taking in this light blue and lavender room that has become the only place I feel like I can really breathe. The first night I ended up here was by accident. I honestly thought it was Rhonan's window I was crawling through.

As soon as I realized my mistake, I should have left. But being able to talk to Laney without anyone else around—most of all her brother—was too tempting to resist.

Laney Hart is intriguing, intelligent, a tad feisty yet kind, and her green eyes shine when the sunlight hits them—a detail I shouldn't know but now can't seem to forget.

I remember when I first met her—she was twelve and I was fourteen. Back then, I just saw her as Rhonan's annoying little sister, even though I couldn't deny that when she came around, she made me laugh and I loved that she didn't let Rhonan boss her around. But then when she came to Blossom Peak High as a freshman, something changed.

It was a slow change. I no longer minded if she came around when Rhonan and I hung out. I made sure to wave when I saw her at school, and when she smiled back, something funny started happening in my chest.

But now, in my senior year, I can finally admit what's been happening to me.

I'm developing a crush on my best friend's little sister.

This past summer, she changed—not just physically, but in her confidence as well.

I definitely noticed the physical part, though.

Her hips got wider, her boobs got bigger, and her hair got longer—the type of long hair that flows down her back in soft curls that look so classy and feminine.

Yeah...Laney Hart was suddenly a girl I couldn't ignore anymore, even though thinking of her this way went completely against the pact my friends and I made our freshman year—always have each other's backs, don't let anyone come between us, and sisters are off-limits.

That last rule made sense three years ago, but now? I fucking hate it.

Laney returns to her room with a bag of ice and a towel. "You know the drill, Fletcher. Shirt off."

Her bossiness makes me smile. "Yes, ma'am." Carefully, I peel my shirt off, tugging my left arm out of the sleeve slowly since that's the side I'm banged up on.

Laney winces again when she takes in my purple and red bruising. "You said this happened during football?"

I hiss as she presses the ice to my skin, enjoying the burn even though I know the next few days are going to suck. "Yeah."

"Huh."

"What?"

Her eyes lift to mine. "This looks pretty fresh, Fletcher. Practice ended hours ago, right?"

My throat grows tight. "Well, it wasn't hurting then."

She looks away, but I can't tell if she believes me or not. I need her to, though, because telling her the truth would mean admitting out loud to someone else what it's like being an only child to a man who resents you for the one thing he used to love.

"Maybe you should lie down."

I motion to her mattress. "Trying to get me in bed already?"

Her cheeks turn pink, which I'm not going to lie, makes me proud. "Just lay down, Fletcher."

"Yes, boss."

"First ma'am, then boss? Which is it?" She waits for me to lie flat on my back before placing the bag of ice back on my ribs.

I reach out and gently place my hand around her wrist. "How about, angel?"

Our eyes lock as her brows rise. "Angel?"

"Yeah. I mean, you are kind of saving me right now, right?"

"Saving you from what?" she whispers as we stare at each other. But I don't know what to say that won't give away too much.

We both grow quiet before I finally break the silence and cut through the tension. "Have you thought about college yet?"

"Wow. Okay, that was out of left field."

"Sorry." I point across the room to her desk. "I saw your brochure."

"Oh." Laney blows out a breath before tucking her hair behind her ears. "I mean, I'm just exploring all my options. I don't want to go far unless I get a scholarship. Then I'll go wherever is the cheapest."

"Smart plan."

She nods slowly. "But I'm having a hard time thinking about being that far away from my parents. That's the part that's getting to me the most—the idea of leaving them."

"Well, I can't wait to get out of my dad's house," I say a little too quickly.

Her eyes flick to mine. "Really?"

Trying to recover from my mistake, I quickly add, "Yeah. I mean, college is supposed to be the best four years of your life, right?"

She shrugs. "I guess. My parents always tell Rhonan and me that life doesn't really get great until your late twenties and early thirties."

"Why do they say that?"

Laney clears her throat before continuing, lifting the ice to check on my bruise before placing it back down. "My mom says that you go through a lot of growing pains between high school and the age of twenty-five—learning about what you want for your life, who your true friends are, and who *you* are as a person. Once you get past that, that's when life gets good because you're more secure, more driven, and more content. I guess that's what I'm looking forward to—that part of my life."

I smile. "That makes a lot of sense. And what is it that you want to do with your life?"

She smiles and tilts her head, looking at me curiously. "You sure are full of questions tonight."

"I'm just making conversation."

"Why?" she asks, her brows drawn together.

"Because we're friends, right?"

She swallows. "Yeah. Friends."

I hate the way that word tastes in my mouth, but I hate the way it sounds coming out of hers even more. Because the last thing I want as of late is to be just *friends* with Laney Hart.

"So, tell me," I say, keeping my voice light. "What's the life plan?"

Her eyes dip down to the floor. "If I tell you, you might think it's stupid."

"I would never."

"Sure, you say that now."

I squeeze her wrist that I'm still holding. "I promise, Laney. No judgment. I mean, hell, you know what my dream is."

"To make it to the NFL," she replies without hesitation.

"Exactly. And to most people, that dream sounds crazy."

"I know you'll make it, though, Fletcher. You're so good, and you work incredibly hard."

I scoff, looking away. "Yeah, well... Not everyone agrees."

"Like who?"

I shake my head, putting the focus back on her. "Never mind. Now tell me what your dream is."

She stays quiet for a while, but just when I think she's going to let that stubbornness of hers win, she surprises me when she says, "I really want to be an author."

"Really? That's fucking cool. Why would I think that's stupid?"

"Because the chances of actually becoming a published author are pretty slim."

"Slimmer than making it to the NFL?"

She chuckles. "Well, I guess not."

"What do you want to write?" I'm still lying on the bed staring up at her as she stands next to me on the floor, but this view just gets better and better the longer I stay here. The soft light coming from her desk lamp makes the shadows on her face more pronounced, highlighting the curve of her lips, the fan of her eyelashes, and the slope of her neck.

*I wonder what she would do if I kissed her there...*

"I'm not sure yet. I like to read YA novels, but I'm not sure that I'd want to write one."

Her voice pulls me from my thoughts. "What's YA?"

"Young adult."

"Oh. So, the characters are teenagers?"

She chuckles. "Most of the time, but it's really the age bracket that the stories are meant for. The books are targeted for readers twelve to eighteen but still include adult themes but from a young character's perspective."

"Give me an example."

She glances over at her bookshelf for a minute, and then turns back to me, her expression a little hesitant. "Okay. Well, there's one book

I read where the girl has a crush on the popular football player at her high school, but she's convinced that he doesn't even know who she is. Then out of the blue, he asks her out and she's thrust into this world that she's unfamiliar with and has to learn how to navigate dealing with the popular kids and her feelings for this guy. She's not sure if she can trust him, though, because he's different with her than he is with his friends." She shrugs. "That's just one example."

"You don't think you could write something like that?"

She shrugs. "I mean, maybe. But my high school experience is very tame so far compared to some of those stories."

"You *are* a little bit of a goody two-shoes, aren't you?" I tease her.

"Um, you're in my room after curfew lying shirtless in my bed. That seems a little rebellious, if I do say so myself."

*Fuck. This girl is something else.*

Shaking my head, I laugh lightly. "I guess you're right."

Laney lets out a yawn. "It's getting late." We both glance at her alarm clock on her nightstand.

*Shit. How is it past eleven already?*

"Is it okay if I stay a little while longer?" I ask a little too desperately.

She bites her bottom lip. "I guess. But you need to get under the covers this time because you were so heavy I couldn't move them last time," she says, pointing a finger at me, and then she heads for her dresser to gather some pajamas. "I'm going to get changed. I'll be right back."

"All right." Watching her leave, I wait until the door is shut before carefully standing from the bed and walking over to her mirror above her dresser, seeing those familiar postcards that her grandfather wrote to her grandmother before examining the bruise on my side.

The fucker got me good this time, but at least I can hide this one.

It's going to hurt like hell at practice tomorrow, but I just have to make sure he doesn't see that I'm in pain. That will only make him happier.

Shaking my head, I grind my teeth together on my way back to Laney's bed, kicking off my shoes before lying under the covers and putting the ice back on my ribs. I just hope to God nothing's broken.

Laney enters the room again a few minutes later in green flannel pajama pants and an oversized T-shirt.

*Fuck, she looks cute.*

"You better scoot over and make some room, Adams."

"You got it, angel."

She shakes her head, but there's a smile on her lips. "Not sure I'm a fan of that nickname."

When she climbs into the bed and slides under the covers with me, I don't leave too much space between us. She radiates this quiet warmth—not just in her body, but her soul. Being alone with Laney after a long time is like feeling sunshine on your skin after a week of cloudy days.

But then as soon as my dad comes around, the storm returns and I become accustomed to the darkness, forgetting how bright the sun can shine.

It's part of the reason I came back to her again after my dad and I got into a fight, much like I did the last time and the time before that.

"Do you want to live in Blossom Peak for the rest of your life, Laney?" I ask, watching her as she gazes at the ceiling.

She considers my question, turning on her side and sliding her hands under her head as she faces me. And fuck, those green eyes of hers captivate me when we're this close.

"I do. This is home. My parents are here, the winery is here, and honestly, I could write from anywhere." She sighs. "I've always had this vision of living in a house up on one of the mountains that encircles the town, you know?"

"I think so," I say, trying to picture it.

"The house would have these giant picturesque windows, kind of like the ones we have in our living room, but I could set up a desk right in front of them and write, staring out at the town full of cherry blossoms in spring, admiring the snow-covered peaks when winter comes, and watching the gorgeous sunsets that come late in the summer."

As she describes the image, I can see her there too. "Sounds like you've put a lot of thought into it."

"A little," she says with a shrug. "But I'm also a realist."

"What do you mean?"

"Well, I'm going to get my degree in English so I can teach while I work on my novel. Or... I've always wanted to own a beauty salon."

"Those are two very different things," I reply, which makes her laugh.

"I know. I feel like a little kid when you ask them what they want to be when they grow up, and they tell you an astronaut, the president, or a ballerina." She waves her hand in the air. "I'm all over the place."

"That's not a bad thing. It's good to have other interests. Sometimes I wish there was something else I wanted more than making it to the NFL."

"You don't have a backup plan? Something that would keep you in Blossom Peak at any point?"

"Nope. I want to start somewhere fresh, even if it isn't playing football for a living. But if I do make it to the NFL, I'll have to live in the city of whatever team drafts me."

"True."

"But if not? Well, I'm not sure where I'll end up. I haven't lived here all my life like some people in this town, so I don't think it will be as difficult to leave."

"Yeah, this is the kind of place that's hard to leave when it's all you've known."

"Rhonan wants to leave, though," I counter, remembering for a moment that my friendship with him is the reason I met her in the first place... And also why I shouldn't be lying in her bed.

Laney shrugs again. "For school, yes, but he hasn't said that he wouldn't move back when he's done."

"Yeah, I haven't really talked to him about it. Maybe I'll ask him the next time I see him."

Laney grows quiet. "Does—does Rhonan know that you've been sneaking into my room?"

"No," I answer honestly.

"Are you going to tell him?" she asks, her eyes locked on mine.

"Probably not."

"Oh. Okay."

I reach out and stroke my hand up and down her arm, loving how soft her skin is, admiring her freckles and the way her pulse is thrumming when I reach her wrist. "I don't think it's any of his business."

"But weren't you looking for his room that first time?"

My heart pounds harder as I look at her, our eyes locked. "I was, but I found yours instead."

Her eyes dip down to my mouth and then back up. "You did."

"And I'm glad." I tuck her hair behind her ear, hearing her breath hitch. "You're my angel, remember. You saved me."

I watch her tongue dart out to lick her lips, and I struggle not to reach out and pull those lips to mine.

"And what am I saving you from, Fletcher?" she whispers, throwing a bucket of ice water on our heated moment.

I take my hand back and avert my eyes from hers. But she grips my jaw and forces me to look at her again. "How did you really get that bruise on your ribs? Because I know damn well it wasn't football, and you thinking that I'm that stupid just pisses me off."

"I know you're not stupid."

"Then talk to me."

I clench my jaw, but she keeps my chin in her hand while she takes my hand and places it over the center of her chest where I can feel her heart hammering as hard as mine. "Fletcher, it's *me*. You know me. I promise, I won't tell anyone, but I need you to be honest with me."

I swallow the lump in my throat. "You already know the answer, Laney."

"I think I do, but I need to hear you say it."

"Fine." Fury and shame race through me as I close my eyes and say, "No, I didn't get hurt playing football, but it's a good thing I can blame my injuries on that because, otherwise, I'd have to admit to people that my dad fucking hits me." My eyes pop open as I add, "There. Are you happy?"

Her eyes fill with tears as she reaches out and pulls me into her, our chests now pressing together, my head resting on her shoulder. "No, I'm not fucking happy, Fletcher. I'm so sorry..."

I push her away gently and avert my gaze from hers. "Don't feel fucking sorry for me, Laney."

*Fuck, I need to get out of here.*

This is exactly what I didn't want. I don't want her pity or anyone else's because it's *my* fault. I'm the one who mouths off. I'm the one who says shit that makes him angry. I'm the one who has a love for the same game that he lost, but I refuse to quit because football is the only thing that makes me fucking happy.

Dad never hit my mom, but she got sick of the drinking and left him. But she left me too. And now, when Luke Adams gets pissed—and it's usually about football—he takes it out on me.

I whip off the blankets and start to get up, but Laney pulls me back down to the bed and shocks me when she pins my arms at my sides and straddles me.

*Oh fucking hell.*

"Laney..."

"No, Fletcher. You aren't going anywhere."

I close my eyes and beg my dick to calm down. Otherwise, this conversation is going to take a turn that I'm afraid might freak her out more than the information I just shared.

"Okay. I won't leave. But can you please lie back down?"

She slides off me and I quickly pull the covers back over me to conceal my boner.

"Fletcher..."

"You can't tell anyone, Laney," I say, cutting her off as we lie facing each other again.

"I won't. I promise." She bites her bottom lip. "But can I ask you something?"

I mentally prepare myself for the inquisition. "Sure."

"When did it start?"

Memories assault me like raindrops hitting a windshield during a storm, fast and at random. But pinpointing the first time it happened is easy.

"The first time, I was twelve. It was after a peewee football game... He told me I didn't execute a play correctly, and I told him he was wrong. He smacked me, and I was so shocked that it probably took me five minutes before I realized what happened."

Laney pulls in her bottom lip between her teeth. "Jesus."

"It didn't happen for a while after that, so I thought it was maybe just a fluke, you know? But then freshman year when we moved here because he got the coaching job, I started to put two and two together."

"What do you mean?"

"We moved because he got fired from his last coaching job. I guess when you show up to coach kids smelling like alcohol, people get concerned."

"Oh my God."

"Yeah, so now he saves his drinking for after work, and when he's had a lot, he comes looking for me to pick a fight with. Most of the time, I don't say anything back. Sometimes he'll just walk away when he doesn't get a rise out of me. But tonight, I said something back to him, so I got hit."

A tear slides down her cheek. "Fletcher..."

I brush her tear away with my thumb, hating that she's shedding any for me, but also feeling lighter—like letting her in eased a weight I've been carrying alone for too long. "I'm tough, Laney. I can handle him. But I sure as fuck know that I'm never getting married or having kids. I don't ever want to end up like him."

"You are *not* like him, Fletcher."

"Maybe not now, but look at how him not being able to come to terms with losing a fucking game has affected my family." I shake my head. "I could never do that to someone. What if I do end up like him one day?"

Her hand curls around the side of my face. "You won't. That's not who you are."

"I hope you're right." Sighing, I continue, "I love coming here so I can escape for a while. I didn't know that I'd end up being taken care of by you, but I'm grateful."

Her green eyes lock onto mine. "You come here anytime it happens, okay? Or before you think it will get to that point. I don't care. I don't care if my parents find out, but I can't stand the thought of you getting hit. You..." She sucks in a shaky breath. "You don't deserve that, Fletcher. You're a *good* person."

"I don't know about that—"

"I do," she says, cutting me off. "You're smart, funny, kind to everyone, and loyal."

"Not so sure about loyal..."

"Why do you say that?"

*Because if your brother found out, he might murder me.*

*Because your parents trust me—and they wouldn't if they knew how I feel.*

"Because I break rules," I say instead, opting for a vague answer.

"Well, some rules are stupid."

I laugh and can't deny that being near her is making it just a slightly bit easier to breathe.

"Yeah, they are."

She grows quiet for a moment. "So, the first time you came here...the hit on your head?"

"I ducked before he could hit me completely, so it was just a graze."

"And the time after that?"

I point to my forearm, where he had wrapped his hand so tightly around my wrist, I thought he might break it. "Him too."

"And last week?"

"The bruise on my back? He shoved me into the door and I hit the knob."

She gently rests her hand on the ice pack that I put back on my ribs. "But this?"

"This was his fist."

Her eyes become glossy again, her voice a whisper. "You don't deserve this."

"Maybe I do," I whisper back.

"In what world does anyone deserve to be hit?"

When she says it like that, something in me shifts, like she pulled back a curtain and revealed a window I didn't know was there.

I know that I try to take the blame when he gets physical, but no matter how mad he gets, it doesn't excuse his behavior.

"Next time I'm going to hit him back."

She sits up. "What?"

"I'm about to be eighteen, Laney," I say, which reminds me that in a few months, me being alone with her in her room has bigger implications if her parents or Rhonan finds out.

"So..."

"Well, then I can press charges against him if he hits me. It's not child abuse then. It's assault."

"What if you move out instead?" she suggests as she lies back down.

"And where would I go?"

"Here," she replies like the answer is so simple.

"Ha. Yeah, I don't think your parents would want me here if *you* asked them. That would be suspicious."

"Then we have Rhonan ask."

"Rhonan can't know about this," I say quickly. "And neither can your parents."

"Why?"

"You promised you wouldn't say anything, Laney."

"I won't. I just... I want to help."

I reach out and cup her face. "You *are* helping. You help me more than you'll ever know." A yawn escapes my mouth, so I take this as the perfect time to let this conversation die down.

I know Laney won't let this go, but she has to. I really hope I didn't fuck up by telling her the truth. My gut tells me that I didn't, but when emotions get involved, people can do things they wouldn't normally.

"Let's get some sleep."

"Fine. But this conversation isn't over, Fletcher."

Chuckling, I reply, "Oh, I'm aware." Despite the pain that it causes me, I lean over and press a kiss to her forehead, even though I really want to go for her lips. "Thank you, angel...for everything."

"You're welcome, Fletcher."

"Can I hold you?" I whisper as she stares at me, her eyes bouncing back and forth between mine rapidly.

"Okay."

She turns, pressing her back against me, and I slide my arm around her waist. She places her hand over mine, and we fall asleep like that, holding each other.

And when I sneak out before the sun comes up, I try not to think too hard about how it might have been the best night's sleep I've ever had.

# Chapter 10

**Laney**

***Present Day***

***Onions, Lemons, and Crumbling Walls***

I light the lemon-scented candle...and immediately blow it out.

*Candlelight would send the wrong message, wouldn't it?*

This isn't a date. Hell, this little meeting wouldn't even be happening if it were up to me, but Fletcher stressed that his role in Elliot's wedding is important to him, so I'm trying to be level-headed as I wait for him to arrive. I remind myself that I am in control over what happens tonight.

After Fletcher's visit to the salon yesterday, a part of me felt guilty and slightly embarrassed that my employees revealed my nickname for him.

I can't deny that hearing it from someone else made it seem so much more childish than when I instituted the rule years ago. But in my defense, I was just trying to protect my mental peace in the business that I built, wanting *some* sort of control over how present he was in my life.

He never truly left my thoughts completely, though.

But then yesterday, he hovered over me while I ate after my glucose monitor went off, acting all protective when he has no right to, and suggested that he intends to wear me down and make me tell him why I hate him during our meeting tonight.

The truth is, I don't hate him. Believe me, I think my feelings toward him would be so much easier to manage if that were true.

I just hate the way he makes me *feel*.

And no matter how hard I've tried to convince myself over the years that I've moved past the things that happened between us, the past few days have proven otherwise.

Having him back in town and no longer at a distance that I can control is only fueling this loop in my life of me feeling like I'm living in the past, unable to move on from him and all of the other instances that have shaped me into the woman I am today because Fletcher is like a tether, holding me there.

At thirty, I thought I'd be in a much different place than I am, and letting go of that disappointment feels like trying to swim in quicksand—virtually impossible.

I light the candle again and keep it lit this time. The scent does help calm me, and my house smells like onions from the dip I made earlier.

*Jesus, I even made dip and put out chips after I told him not to bring food.*

The whiplash happening between my head, heart, and vagina right now makes me feel like I'm on one of those state fair rides that basically throws you in a blender as you spin around in the air while you hope not to die.

That's what having Fletcher back in town and in my space is doing to me, and the sad part is, I didn't even feel this unsettled after my breakup with Spencer.

The knock on the door signals that my time to freak out is over. Bracing myself for the impact of seeing him, I take a deep breath as I open the front door.

*Fuck. I can't do this.*

Fletcher is freshly showered, his head void of the hat that he's worn since he got back in town, and his body is covered in a simple black shirt and khaki shorts, his feet in black sneakers.

He looks effortlessly handsome, which makes me even less confident in my ability to keep a level head tonight.

He looks like the boy who captured my heart at fifteen and never gave it back.

"Laney."

"Fletcher."

Shutting the door behind him, I watch him as he walks further inside, looking around the space.

"Wow. So this is your house..."

"It is."

He chuckles as he walks around, taking in my wall art and pictures.

My house isn't big, however, I wanted this space to feel like my parents' house—warm and cozy, yet also my own.

Everything is in shades of gray and cornflower blue. I have several plants around the living room for that pop of green, and the furniture is dark walnut. Two shelves flank the television on a far wall that hold my books and various pictures, and the only light in the living room comes from two floor lamps flanking the couch.

Fletcher walks up to the shelves, picking up a frame and staring at it. "This is a great picture of them."

I don't even have to look to know which one he's referring to. "I know. That was my—"

"Sixteenth birthday," he finishes for me, looking up to find me staring at him. "I remember."

My heart feels like it's in my throat. Shaking off the moment, I head toward the kitchen. "Are you thirsty?"

"Sure. Water would be great."

"That's all I have besides wine."

"No wine for me, thanks."

I momentarily debate having some myself, just to take the edge off. But losing my composure around Fletcher is the last thing I need right now.

Taking two glasses of water over to the dining room table, I signal for Fletcher to follow me. He takes his glass and downs half of it. "Thanks."

"Of course. I also made some dip." I point to the chips and dip on the table.

Fletcher smirks. "I thought you said no food."

"I'm a snacker. But if you don't want any, that's fine. More to get stuck to my thighs."

His eyes dip down to my legs. "Your thighs look perfect to me." I don't bother responding because what the hell am I supposed to say to that?

*Is Fletcher flirting with me?*

He takes a chip, scoops it into the caramelized onion dip, and pops it in his mouth. "Holy shit."

"Yeah." I take a taste for myself. "I saw this recipe online and I've made it three times in the last two weeks."

"Is this why it smells like onions and lemons in here?" he asks as he pops another dip-filled chip in his mouth.

"The onions are from the dip. The lemons are from the candle." I point to where the candle rests on the kitchen counter.

His lips lift in that signature grin, his dimple appearing just slightly as he arches a brow. "Are you trying to seduce me, angel?"

*Angel.*

There's that nickname again.

I choose to ignore it, even though my heart is hammering from hearing it. Unfortunately, it always reacts that way at hearing that term of endearment. "In your dreams, Fletcher."

"If you only knew," he mumbles before taking a seat at the table and assessing the supplies I gathered. "Uh, why do we need tape?" he asks, picking up the plastic holder and examining it.

"I don't know. I wasn't sure what we were going to need. I figured we could complete the favors tonight since that's easy enough," I say as I reach for the organza bags, placing them on the table beside me. Next, I grab the bags of monogrammed M&M's and toss them on the surface as well. But when I turn back to Fletcher, an unattractive snort leaves my lips. "What on earth?"

"What?" he asks, his voice more nasally than before. He's taped the tip of his nose to his forehead, lifting his nose entirely so I can practically see up into his brain.

"Fletcher, you're ridiculous," I say through a laugh.

"I'm just making good use of the supplies you took the time to provide."

Shaking my head, I take the organza bags out and start separating them. "That was not what I had in mind. But apparently your listening skills haven't improved over the years, so now I know to be clearer."

He rips the tape off of his face, balling it up and tossing it into the cardboard box. "At least I got you to smile, which is a far cry from the snarl you've had on your face since I got here."

I gasp. "I don't snarl."

"You do at me, angel."

I drop my eyes back down to the table. "Please don't call me that."

"Why not? That was always my nickname for you."

"Yeah, but that was a long time ago, Fletcher."

He scoots closer to me in his chair, grabbing one of the bags of M&M's and tearing off the corner with his teeth. I hate the way I watch his forearms flex as he does. "Believe me, I'm very much aware of how things have changed since then."

"Exactly. I'm not the same girl I was back then, and you aren't the same guy, so I think we should just leave the past behind us."

"Doesn't mean that we can't still be friends..." he says, trailing off. "But I think in order for that to happen, I can't be Lucifer anymore."

Laughter bubbles out of me. "Oh God." Face-palming my forehead, I take in a deep breath. "I'm sorry you had to hear about that."

He pulls my hand from my face as I turn toward him. "Honestly, I thought it was creative, though a little scary."

"Yeah, well, sometimes people don't handle their emotions in a healthy way."

"And what kind of emotions were you trying to handle, Laney?"

"It doesn't matter," I reply as I reach for another bag, avoiding his eyes even though I can feel him watching me.

"It does to me," he counters before reaching for my forearm and pulling my hand into his.

"Please just drop it, Fletcher," I whisper, hating how I can already feel my throat growing tight with emotion.

He releases my hand and throws his hands up in the air dramatically. "Fine. I guess I just have to put the tape back on my face so you'll keep talking to me."

He reaches for the roll of scotch tape, but I grab it before he can. "Oh no you don't. You're not going to waste any more of my tape."

"Oh, it's just tape."

"But if you use it all, the next time I need tape I won't have any, and then I'll remember that you're the reason it's all gone, and it's just going to put me in a bad mood."

His head falls back as he laughs. "Okay then. Point made. No more scary faces with the tape."

"Good." I push the bags and M&M's toward him. "Let's get to work on the favors then, shall we? This shouldn't take very long."

"How many people are coming to this wedding anyway?" Fletcher asks, grabbing a handful of bags.

"You saw the guest list."

"Just briefly. You snatched the paper away from me, remember?"

I roll my eyes, but don't argue with him. "About a hundred. A lot of people are from town, people we've known for years. But there are several guests coming from out of town that know Elliot's parents through the court system."

Fletcher nods in understanding. "Naturally."

"Tori's parents live in Florida now, and they're coming, but she doesn't have a lot of other family. A few of her coworkers from Nashville are attending, but other than that it's mostly people that Elliot knows."

Fletcher's brows draw together. "If she has work friends, why didn't she ask one of them to be her maid of honor?"

"She said they're not that type of friend, whatever the hell that means."

"Well, it doesn't surprise me that you agreed to do this for her. That's who you are."

I glance over at him. "And who is that exactly?"

"Someone who steps up for people when they need them."

My cheeks grow hot as I look away from him, but my heart twists in my chest. "Everyone needs a friend sometimes."

"Exactly," he says, reaching for my hand again. "And you can talk to me if this gets to be too much for you, okay?"

Confusion floods my mind. "Why would this be too much for me?"

"Because of what happened with your ex."

I feel the blood drain from my face before my dread turns to anger. "What about my ex?"

Fletcher leans back in his chair, releasing my hand and blowing out a breath, hesitant to answer me. "Your brother and Henley told me what happened...with the engagement."

Grinding my teeth together, I stand from my chair and walk into the kitchen. "Of course they did."

"Look, don't be upset..."

"Don't tell me what I'm allowed to feel," I fire back as he stands from his chair, the sincerity in his gaze being replaced with determination as he walks toward me.

"I'm not telling you what you're allowed to feel, Laney. But if this wedding shit gets to be too much for you, given how your engagement ended—"

"I'm fine," I say, cutting him off.

Fletcher huffs out a laugh. "Yeah, that's what they said you'd say."

"Because it's the truth!"

And I'm not lying. The sad part is that what happened with Fletcher devastated me ten times more than what happened between me and Spencer.

"Then why are you yelling?"

"I'm not yelling!"

"You're definitely raising your voice."

"Because this isn't any of your business and they had no right to tell you!"

He tilts his head at me. "Well, they did. And you know what? I'm glad they did."

"Why?"

"So I can tell you this..."

His feet carry him across the kitchen until he's so close that I have no choice but to back up until my ass hits the counter behind me. His body closes me in as he lifts one hand to rest on the cabinets above me, and his other hand comes up to cup my jaw.

I'm frozen as my heart beats a mile a minute, his scent infiltrating my nose and transporting me back to the last time I was in this position with him, our mouths so close that all it would take is one of us throwing caution to the wind and moving forward just an inch so that our lips touch.

Fletcher lowers his voice, but his words still hit every nerve ending in my body. "Any man that puts a ring on your finger but doesn't honor that commitment is a fucking coward, and he sure as hell doesn't deserve you." My breath grows shallow as his eyes dance across my face. "Any man foolish enough to cheat on you deserves to have every one of his limbs ripped from his body." He pulls my bottom lip down with his thumb as I hold my breath. "And any man that can't appreciate the incredible, selfless, intelligent, tenacious, and fucking gorgeous woman that you are will be kicking himself when the next guy comes along and treats you like you're the best fucking thing that ever happened to him—because *that's* what you deserve, Laney Maddison Hart."

*Oh. My. God.*

My voice is shaky when I finally speak. "You—you shouldn't have said any of that, Fletcher…"

"Well I did, so what are you going to do about it?" Our eyes bounce back and forth between each other, but I don't have a response. All I can think about right now is how close he is, how amazing he smells, and how badly I want to taste his lips. "Your ex was a fucking idiot, and if I ever run into him, he's gonna know how badly he fucked up by not choosing you."

"Are you—" But I don't get a chance to finish because he keeps talking.

"But the part that kills me is, I think I understand why you're so guarded now."

"I'm not—"

"Yes, you fucking are. But I want you to remember…" His words trail off as one of his fingers slowly glides down my neck. "You don't have to be that way with me."

Little does he know that my walls are even more important when I'm around him. But after that little speech, they're already starting to crumble.

"Thank you," I say because anything else doesn't feel right. I could snap at him again, tell him to back away, and stop talking to me as if he still knows me, but that wouldn't reflect how I really feel—*seen*.

Fletcher truly sees me for who I am and all I have to offer someone.

The corner of his mouth lifts as he toys with my bottom lip again before dropping his arms and taking a step back from me. "That's four thank-yous, by the way."

Rolling my eyes, I move around him and head back to the table, fixing my hair and straightening my clothes on the way. "And you just ruined the moment."

"As long as I made my point, that's all I care about."

*Oh your point was very clear.*

But did he say those things just to be nice, to not make me feel bad? Or were they genuine?

I'm not sure which option is worse.

"Let's just get this done." Sighing, I pull the opening apart on one of the organza bags, desperate to move past what just happened in the kitchen. But while tipping the bag of M&M's into the bag with my other hand, I end up spilling them all over the table. "Shit."

"Why don't I hold the bags open and then you pour? That way it goes faster."

"Sure."

"See? This is why there's two of us." He grins at me and then moves his seat even closer to me than he already was.

I can feel my nipples tighten beneath my bra and curse my body's reaction to him. Clearing my throat, I opt to change the subject. "Anyway, how does it feel being back in Blossom Peak? Have you seen your dad?" As soon as the words leave my lips, I regret them.

I can see Fletcher's entire body tighten from the corner of my eye. "I have. I ran into him at Blossom Brews actually."

"Really? How—how was it?"

"Same shit, different day," he answers bluntly, continuing to fill the bags as I open up each new one. "But he didn't exactly know I was coming to town, so I caught him off guard, which pissed him off."

"Are you going to be all right with him coming to the wedding?"

He grunts. "Yeah, I'll be fine, Laney. I'll tell you this though, it sure was nice to see *your* dad the other night."

My lips instantly curl into a smile at the mention of my father. Fletcher empties one of the bags of M&M's and then reaches for a new one, tearing off the corner with his teeth again.

*God, why is that so hot?*

"Yeah, he's doing well, and he sure does love those movie nights we do at the winery."

"I can tell, although he spent most of the time at the popcorn cart, making sure it was working."

Sighing, I open up another bag and watch him fill it up before pulling the strings together and tying them. "I keep telling him we need to buy a new one, but he doesn't want to replace it yet."

"Why not?"

"Because that's the one my mom bought," I answer.

Fletcher nods in understanding. "I see."

"Anyway, other than that, the events have been doing well, and I help out with them as much as I can."

"You're always fucking helping people, Laney," he says, pulling my attention back to him. "Your dad, Rhonan, Elliot..."

"Yeah, so..."

"Let me ask you something."

"Okay..."

"When's the last time you let someone help *you*?" Just as the words leave Fletcher's mouth, his hand covers mine, gently removing the organza bag from my fingers.

"Fletcher..." My throat grows tight because I'm startled by his observation.

Luckily, my glucose monitor app goes off before either of us can say anything else.

But it's not just my phone that goes off. Fletcher's also chimes from inside his pocket. He takes it out and looks at his screen. "Your blood sugar is too high. You need insulin."

"Uh, how do you know that?" He flashes the screen to me where I see an account he's made on the same app that I use. "What the...how did you…" I launch myself up from the table. "What in the actual hell, Fletcher?"

He stands up just as fast. "Can you please just give yourself insulin, Laney, so you don't start getting loopy on me?"

"When the heck did you add yourself to my app?"

"While I was at your salon yesterday. You left your phone on your station when you went to grab a banana."

I cross my arms over my chest. "Wow. So you just took it upon yourself to…" I can't even finish the sentence because my thoughts are spinning. "You—you have no right to—"

He presses a finger to my lips, silencing me. "I know I don't. You're right about that. But while I'm here, while we're spending time together, I need to know that you're taking care of yourself. Call it an old habit, but…"

I'm speechless, truly and utterly speechless. How the hell does he think that what he did was okay?

But more importantly, why is it making me want to cry?

Why does it make me feel seen and cared for?

And why do I like that so much?

"You know I can just delete you from my account, right?"

"I do. But I'll just sign up again."

Shaking my head at him, I reply, "I've never wanted to punch you more than I do right now."

"Maybe you should do it just to see if it makes you feel better. Or, how about telling me why you started calling me Lucifer so I can fix it?"

"It's not something that can be fixed," I answer honestly.

"Let me be the judge of that."

We stand there, in a silent standoff, waiting to see who will make a move first. But then the app chimes at me again.

Before he can say something else, I spin away from him and walk to the bathroom to administer the insulin through my pump in private. When I look at myself in the mirror, I almost don't recognize the girl staring back at me.

My eyes are wild, my face flushed from anger, but my lips? I reach up and touch them—because feeling Fletcher's finger on them earlier and again just now has them tingling in desperation for more of his touch.

Sighing, I take a few deep breaths, trying to get my blood pressure under control before I walk back out to face him. When I exit the bathroom, I find Fletcher pacing the living room, running his hand through his hair.

But I don't say a word. I take my seat again at the table and hold out an organza bag toward him. "Let's just finish this."

Clearing his throat, he nods and then takes his seat back at the table, holding the bag open as I begin to fill it up with the candy. We sit in silence as we go through the motions, filling one bag after another. I can feel his eyes on me the entire time, but I don't look at him once.

I'm too angry, too anxious, and there's something else that I'm feeling—hope.

It's that hope that him acting completely out of line is a sign that he still cares about me, even though I shouldn't hope for that.

But why else would he do such a thing? Is it just friendly? Or does he have another reason?

When we fill the last bag, I begin to place them in the cardboard box.

"Sure you don't want to tackle something else while I'm here?" Fletcher asks from beside me.

"I think this was enough for tonight."

"Then what's on the agenda for tomorrow?"

"Why do we need to do anything tomorrow?"

"Uh, because tomorrow's Wednesday, and in case you forgot, we have a party next Saturday we need to plan. Not to mention, if we're going to order a cake, we need to do that as soon as possible."

I glance over at him and sigh. "Yeah, I guess you're right."

"Damn, hearing that from you just made my day."

I narrow my eyes at him. "Don't get used to it." Lifting the box of favors, I take them back to my spare room and place them inside so they're safe and out of the way. But when I turn to leave, Fletcher is standing right in the doorway. "Excuse me," I say, motioning for him to move.

But he just stands there, staring at me, a crooked smile on his lips. "I'm going to get you to admit we're still friends before this wedding is over, Laney."

"Ha. Friends is a strong term, Fletcher. Let's just agree to be civil while we handle this wedding crap, and then we can both go back to our separate lives." I move to walk by him, but he shifts to block me inside. "Come on, Fletcher."

He lifts his hand and moves to tuck my hair behind my ear, his soft touch sending shockwaves across my skin. "*You* come on, Laney. There was a time where we talked about everything, where you were the person I looked forward to seeing the most—a time when you were my *friend*."

"Well, a lot has changed since then."

His thumb caresses my jaw as his fingers trail down my neck. I can hear my heart racing in my ears. "Oh, I'm aware. But how we used to be? That's something that I'll never regret."

Any words I had ready to say back to him die on my tongue. Instead, I wait for him to move aside and then walk past him and head straight for the front door, eager for him to leave. The push and pull between us tonight was far more intense than I anticipated, and what I need right now is space to process it all.

"I guess I'll be going then." Fletcher appears from the hallway to find me at the door, my hand on the knob.

"Yeah. It's time."

When there's only a fraction of space between us, he shoves his hands in his pockets. "So, what time should we meet at the bakery tomorrow?"

"My first client is at eleven, so I can meet before that. How's ten?"

"Sounds good."

When I open the door, he stares at me for a few moments before walking through. And even though I want to hang on to my icy demeanor, I can't let him leave without saying one last thing.

"Fletcher?"

He turns to face me as he's halfway down the driveway. "Yeah?"

"Thank you," I state softly.

The corner of his mouth lifts. "For helping? I thought that was the point."

I shake my head. "Not just that." With a deep inhale, I say, "Thank you for supporting my salon yesterday."

His face softens as his lips spread wider. "My pleasure, Laney. You should be proud of what you've created."

"I am."

"And now my thank-yous are up to five."

I roll my eyes at him. "You're ridiculous."

He laughs. "Have a good night, Laney."

"You too, Fletcher."

And then he hops in his truck and drives away, leaving me standing there, feeling the ice around my heart I've grown so used to beginning to melt away.

# Chapter 11

**Fletcher**

***Cake is Better Than Orgasms***

Walking into Bites & Bliss Bakery is like getting smacked in the face with a cloud of sugar. I swear you can gain ten pounds just inhaling the air in here.

In fact, this place reminds me a lot of a bakery in Carrington Cove, this small town on the coast. My tattoo artist, Gage Kingston, lives there now and he's friends with the owner of Smells Like Sugar, their local bakery that makes some of the best damn blueberry muffins I've ever had.

When I look outside to see if Laney has arrived yet, I'm met with disappointment, even though I know I'm early. But the last thing I wanted was to be late today and give Laney a reason to harden up around me again.

Last night was a fucking test of my restraint if there ever was one. I used to think that those nights I would lie in her bed, talking to her for hours and holding her while we fell asleep were the worst kind of torture.

But now, as a full-grown man having to be this close to her again? To have to act like we don't have a history, to look directly into her eyes and hear her laugh for the first time in years?

Yeah, I can safely say I didn't know what torture was back then.

And I won't lie. Not seeing her much since I left Blossom Peak has made it easier to bury all those feelings, so I can't fault her for doing the same.

If there's one thing that's become apparent since I've been back, though, it's this: when you've been harboring feelings for your best friend's little sister for over twelve years, it's easier to pretend she doesn't exist than have to face the fact that she actually does.

Yet, in less than a week, I've recalled every detail about the girl who captivated me as a teenager, and discovering who she is as an adult is only making me more interested.

I glance around the bakery while waiting for Laney to show up, taking in the changes since my last visit as people flood inside to place their orders for the day. Display cases are filled with muffins, scones, and donuts, and several examples of custom cakes sit on a shelf behind the counter. The walls are painted purple with swirls of white drawn throughout. In fact, this whole store is covered in purple now, indicative of a complete remodel, which must have happened between now and the last time I was here.

"Oh my God! You're Fletcher Adams!" A young boy to my right gains my attention as I join the line. All I've had this morning was a protein shake after my workout, so I need something else in my stomach before we taste cake.

Smiling, I lift my hat up a bit so I can see him better. I knew it was only a matter of time before I was recognized by someone again, and the kids are my favorite fans to meet.

"I am. What's your name?"

"Collin," he replies, practically vibrating with excitement.

I hold my hand out to shake his. "It's nice to meet you, Collin."

"You're my favorite player. Whenever I play football at school, I always pretend I'm you."

My smile grows. "Thank you. I'm honored."

"Can I get your autograph?" he asks with tears in his eyes.

I remember being so emotional over meeting the players I looked up to when I was a kid. Of course, I met most of them in a stadium or on a practice field as I followed my dad around during his career. Still, I know what those moments meant to me, so when kids come up to me, I give them every ounce of attention I can.

"Of course."

The boy's mom comes up behind him. "Sorry, we weren't prepared for this. I don't have anything for you to sign."

I look around the bakery and find a stack of napkins on the condiment station to my left. Taking a few, I find the marker in my pocket that I keep on me for moments like this, uncap it with my teeth, and begin scribbling my name on a few napkins as a line starts to form behind Collin and his mom.

"Well, well. Look at what the cat dragged in..."

My head lifts to find Carolina, the owner of the bakery and one of my favorite people in Blossom Peak, smirking at me with her hands on her hips.

"Good to see you, Carolina."

"You're holding up the line, Fletcher," she teases me as I hand the napkin to Collin and his mom motions for us to pose for a picture.

"If you want to pour me a cup of coffee and put a breakfast croissant sandwich aside for me, I would really appreciate it."

Her laughter rings out. "Sure thing, Mr. Famous."

Multiple families wait their turn for a few minutes with me, and even more show up as customers start texting their friends about my location. I smile and chat with kids and their families for a good thirty minutes before the crowd seems to start dwindling.

And for just a second, I remember that this is one of my favorite parts of the job—being a role model, someone that young kids can look up to and realize that hard work can truly pay off.

These are the moments that help me forget all the shitty ones I had to endure to get here.

Once the line dies down and the last person leaves, Carolina locks the door behind the last customer, leaving the two of us alone. She hands me my coffee and sandwich, which I proceed to inhale in just a few bites.

"You didn't have to do that," I tell her as I finally make my way to the cash register to pay, even though the silence is welcoming.

She waves me off when I try to hand her my credit card. "Your money is no good here."

I scowl at her. "Come on, Carolina. Let me pay."

"Nope. You just doubled my profit from yesterday with the crowd you brought in, so we'll call it even." I stick my tongue out at her as I place a hundred dollar bill in the tip jar just to spite her. She laughs. "So, what brings you to town, Fletcher? If memory serves me correctly, it's been years..."

"Almost three, but who's counting?" She arches a brow at me, waiting for me to explain. "I'm here for Elliot's wedding, actually."

"Ah, that's right. The boys must be happy to see you."

Carolina has owned this bakery since Henley, Elliot, Rhonan, and I were in high school. We used to ride our bikes down here every Sunday morning to get donuts before going to the park to toss the football around. She's followed my career from the beginning, and I always appreciate seeing her when I visit.

"They are."

"How long are you in town for?"

"About three weeks. Training camp starts shortly after the wedding, so I'll be heading back to Charlotte." The sound of someone trying to open the door pulls my attention behind me, only to find Laney angrily yanking on the handle. I try not to laugh as I say, "Uh, Laney's here."

"Perfect." Carolina moves toward the door, unlocking it so Laney can step inside. The sunlight hits her face when she turns to face me, highlighting her green eyes and glossy lips.

*Fuck, she's so damn gorgeous.*

"Good morning, Laney," Carolina says as she moves back to the counter.

"You lock the door now?" Laney pushes her hair from her face before meeting my eyes.

"It was my fault. A little kid asked me for an autograph and picture, and then a crowd started forming."

Laney shakes her head at me, but there's a hint of a smile on her lips. "Always causing trouble wherever you go, huh?"

I lean close to her. "You have no idea how much trouble I can cause, angel."

Her throat bobs as she swallows roughly, her eyes darting down to my lips for only a second, but I catch it before she moves away from me and heads closer to Carolina. "Okay then. Are we ready to taste some cake and get this over with?"

"You act like eating cake this early in the morning is a hardship."

Carolina laughs. "For some people, it is, but to answer your question, Laney... Yes, I'm ready for you. I planned on leaving the door locked while you're here though, just to give you some privacy."

"You don't have to do that, Carolina. I'm used to the attention," I interject, shoving my hands into my pockets. "And I don't want to cost you customers."

"Nonsense. It gives me a break too." She motions for us to take a seat at one of the tables. "I'll be right there with everything."

Laney heads for the table, but I pull her chair out for her before she can sit down. "Thank you," she says as she sits.

"And that's number six."

"God, you're infuriating," she mumbles, checking her phone before placing it in her purse and hanging it on the back of her chair.

"Infuriating but hot, right?"

Her eyes meet mine, but dart away after only one second. "I'm not even going to comment on that."

Before I can give her shit about her lack of response, Carolina comes out from the back of the bakery with a notebook in hand. "Okay, let's get started." She flips the paper over on her notebook, scribbling something at the top of the blank page. "So, y'all are here to pick out your wedding cake, right?"

"Oh, no. The cake's not for us," Laney corrects her immediately.

Carolina winks at me, and that's when I realize what she's doing. "What? You're kidding. When you called to schedule a cake tasting for you and Fletcher, I thought you two had finally figured out that you belong together?"

Laney's eyes bug out so much that I have to twist my face away from her to cover up my smile. "You thought Fletcher and I..."

"Oh, heck yes. You two might have thought you concealed your crush on each other well, but I've been around a heck of a lot longer than you kids. Trust me, I know love when I see it."

Laney clears her throat, but her cheeks are pink now and she's practically squirming in her seat. "Well, uh...sorry to burst your bubble, but the cake is for Elliot and his fiancée. We're the maid of honor and best man, and they asked us to do this for them since they're both extremely busy."

Crossing my arms over my chest, I lean back in my chair. "Had to make sure to clear that up, didn't you?"

The glare I get from her could slice right through my nipples. "Well, it's the truth."

Carolina looks at me. "Oh dear. I just assumed, but clearly I've misread the situation."

"What?" Laney asks.

She waves her pen back and forth between us. "I'm sensing some tension here."

Laney huffs. "There's no tension."

"Oh, there's plenty of tension," I say just as quickly, knowing it's the sexual tension building between us that has my fucking stomach twisted up.

When I crowded her against the counter in her kitchen last night and told her what I thought about her ex, it was all I could do not to kiss her and show her how a real man would treat her. And her darkened eyes, hard nipples, and shaky breath all indicated that she probably would have let me.

Carolina pops her brows as she begins scribbling a few things on a piece of paper in front of her. "Okay then. Let's just get down to business. How many people will there be?"

"One hundred." Laney looks over to me and then back to Carolina.

"Three tiers should do it, then," Carolina replies. "Do you want them all the same flavor, or different?"

I stare up at Carolina from my chair. "You can make them different flavors?"

"Oh yes. And we can add filling, different frostings…the list goes on and on."

I look over at Laney. "We might be here a while."

She blinks at me. "No, we won't. I have a client at eleven, remember?"

Carolina smiles as she continues to write, clearly finding our interactions amusing. "Okay, well…let me go get the cake samples then so you can start to make some decisions."

"Thank you, Carolina," Laney says, watching her walk away before turning back to me. "I need you to take this seriously because I can't be here for too long. I have a business to run, remember?"

"I'm well aware."

"Then act like a grown-up, please."

I lean closer to her, getting my mouth as close to her ear as I can. "Trust me, Laney. I'm all grown up now, in more ways than one. Would you like a demonstration?"

Her breath is shaky as I lean back, smirking at her just as Carolina comes back to our table.

"Okay, here we go."

Laney clears her throat as Carolina sets the tray down and I pull out my phone.

"Fletcher, now is not the time to be on your phone," Laney chastises.

I hold up the screen so she can see that I'm checking her glucose level through her app. "Just making sure you can handle the cake right now, angel."

Laney's eyes grow wide. "Oh."

I glance up to see Carolina grinning like a Cheshire cat. "Is she good to go?"

"Yup. Perfect." Holding my hand out, I say, "Please give us the spiel."

Carolina clears her throat emphatically. "Perfect. Now, the flavors are labeled, and here are the scoring cards to help you decide. I'm going to leave you two to sort this out. Just ring the bell when you're ready with your choices and then we can talk other details like colors, ribbons or flowers, etcetera."

"Sounds good, Carolina. Thank you." I smile as she leaves and then immediately scour the tray for a Funfetti flavor. "Oh, hell yes." I lift one of the squares and pop it into my mouth, moaning as the cake melts on my tongue. "Automatic winner for me."

Laney sighs. "See? You are a child." I finish chewing as she reaches for the other square of the Funfetti, but I beat her to it. "Hey!"

"Open up, angel."

"Can you *please* stop calling me that?"

"If you open up."

She crosses her arms over her chest. "I'm not letting you feed me."

"Then you won't get to sample this one and when I tell Carolina to make the whole thing out of Funfetti, I'm going to tell everyone it was your idea."

Her glare gets deeper each time she flashes it at me, and it only makes my dick harder.

She sighs, licks her lips, and then opens her mouth just enough that I can slide the piece of cake inside, but I make sure to graze her lips with my thumb before pulling my hand away.

*What the fuck are you doing, Fletcher? You're definitely sending mixed signals, and not just to Laney, but also your own fucking dick.*

Every time I touch her, I know I'm playing with fire. But the more I do, the more I don't fucking care.

She reaches up to dust off a few crumbs from her lip, rubbing the spot I just grazed as she chews. "It's...not bad."

"Don't lie. It's perfect. Moist and sweet, but not overly so. Classic."

"You seem to have a lot of opinions about this flavor."

I tilt my head, studying her. "You seriously don't know why that cake is my favorite, do you?"

She doesn't glance in my direction as she marks her scoresheet. "Nope, and I don't really care either."

I reach for her hand and pull her toward me, our faces inches apart. Laney's eyes widen and her lips part slightly, just far enough that I can smell the sweetness of her breath.

"That's funny," I say. "Because I don't think I'll ever forget the cupcakes that a certain someone made for my eighteenth birthday and brought to school."

Our eyes remain locked when she says, "Interesting how you remember that, but you've forgotten other things, Fletcher."

"Like what?"

Laney's eyes dip down to my mouth as she licks her lips. But then she shakes herself out of the moment and glares back down at her paper. "Just forget it."

I huff out a laugh. "And you think I'm the one acting like a child."

Her mouth drops open before she scowls, familiar tension building between us.

*Fuck, if we weren't in a public place, I'd kiss that fucking snarl right off of her goddamn lips.*

I'm getting really sick of this whiplash—one moment where she's standoffish, and the next where her edges are soft. But I also know that if I push this woman too hard, too fast, she's never going to talk to me about how the hell we ended up in this tug-of-war where no one's winning.

Exhaling, I push away from her and grab both squares of the chocolate cake, popping one in my mouth, savoring the flavor before vocalizing my opinion. "The chocolate is solid."

I hold the other in front of her lips again, and even though she rolls her eyes, surprisingly, she opens up and lets me feed her once more. Her lips graze the tips of my fingers this time as I pull away. Our eyes remain locked as she chews.

"I agree. Not too rich, and something most people would enjoy." She marks her grade on the scoresheet before leaning over the table and choosing the red velvet next, popping one piece in her mouth. "Oh, sweet baby Jesus," she moans, and fuck—my dick twitches from the sound.

"That good, huh?" I manage to grate out.

"So good," she mumbles as she continues to chew. "God, that's almost better than an orgasm."

"Ha. I doubt that."

She closes her eyes as she finishes chewing. "Well, when you haven't had one in three years from something other than your vibrator or hand, it's hard to be sure." But then her eyes pop open, wide and shocked as she slowly slides them in my direction.

The damage has already been done, though.

"Wait a minute..."

She covers her face with her hands. "Oh my God..."

"Three years?"

Groaning, she shakes her head. "I cannot believe I just said that out loud."

I tear her hands from her face and wait for her eyes to open. "Laney..."

"You know what? Let's just forget I ever said that." She fakes a smile before attempting to reach for another flavor of cake, but I stop her.

"Oh, hell no. That's not something I can just forget."

"Fletcher…" Her bottom lip trembles. "Please… I didn't mean it… I was…"

Part of me wants to keep pushing her for more information, but I've already done the math in my head. Laney and her ex broke up a year ago, and if she just said it's been three years of her own self-satisfying, that means not only did that dipshit cheat on her, but he sure as fuck wasn't keeping her satisfied to begin with.

I *really* want to chop off all his fingers one by one now. But the more troubling thought? The overwhelming urge to throw Laney down on this table and fuck her with my tongue until she can't breathe and forgets her own name.

Yeah, this little piece of knowledge isn't helping my dick calm down at all.

"Fine." Leaning back in my chair, I cross my arms over my chest and open my mouth.

"What are you doing?" she asks cautiously.

"Waiting for my sample."

"You want me to feed you?"

"I think it's only fair. You got a turn, now I get one."

Eyeing me curiously, she reaches for the other piece of red velvet and slowly brings it to my lips. I open my mouth and watch her cautiously place the cake inside, but before she can pull away, I grab her wrist, holding it in place as I close my lips around her fingers and swirl my tongue gently around them, keeping my eyes locked on hers as I do.

She gasps but doesn't move as I toy with her thumb and index finger, torturing her with my tongue and teasing her before releasing them from my mouth with a pop.

Her green eyes grow darker, her pupils bold and large, and then she stares at my mouth for so long, I almost fucking grab her by the back of the head and smash my mouth to hers right here in this fucking bakery.

*Making Laney Hart come has just become the number one thought in my mind, and that's a big fucking problem.*

"So, have we made some decisions?" Carolina surprises us both, making Laney jump in her seat as I move to discreetly adjust my cock.

Laney nods, directing her attention to Carolina. "Um, yes. We'll go with the small tier in red velvet, the middle tier in chocolate, and the bottom tier in Funfetti." Her eyes bounce over to me for one split second, and hope blossoms in my chest while I mentally war with the lines I crossed in the past fifteen minutes.

But I don't regret any of it for a fucking second.

Laney and Carolina discuss the other details like flowers and colors, we help her clean up the mess, and then Carolina asks for a deposit for the cake. I slide my credit card across the counter before Laney can blink. "I'll pay for the whole thing."

"You don't have to do that, Fletcher," Laney argues. "Elliot said...."

"I don't give a shit what Elliot said. I'm paying for the cake. End of story."

Laney sighs as Carolina hands me the receipt to sign. "Well, that's very nice of you."

"It's the least I can do. I have all of this money and no one to spoil. Might as well spoil my friends."

Carolina arches a brow. "Are you looking for someone to spoil? Because last I recall, Fletcher Adams had no interest in love."

I turn toward Laney and wait until she looks my way. "I guess I'm just waiting for the right person."

Laney clears her throat as Carolina looks between the two of us. "You know, she might just be closer than you think. And when you find her, I expect you to come back so I can make your wedding cake as well," she says cheerily. "Have a good day, you two. I'll have the cake ready to be delivered in two weeks."

"Thank you," Laney says as I hold the door open for her and we step out of the bakery. She checks the time on her phone as we reach the sidewalk. "Shit, I need to get to the salon."

"Did you drive?"

She shakes her head. "No, I just walked over from the salon since I went in early this morning to take care of some paperwork."

"Then let me drive you."

"It's not that far of a walk, Fletcher."

"It's five to eleven, Laney. You don't want to be late for your client." She bites her lip, clearly weighing her options. "Don't overthink it," I add. "It's just a ride."

She exhales. "Fine."

I take her by the hand and lead her to my truck, not wasting another second or giving Laney the chance to argue with me again. Holding her hand makes my body stay in the hyperaware state I was in while feeding her cake.

Opening the door for her, I help her inside.

"Thank you."

"Wow. We're up to eight thank-yous, ladies and gentlemen." She shakes her head at me before I close her door, round the front of the truck, and drive her the short distance through The Village to her salon.

When I get out of the truck as she does, she asks, "What are you doing?"

"Walking you inside."

"That's unnecessary."

I meet her at the front of my truck, right in front of the entrance to the salon. Glancing inside, I see her employees begin to gather at the front reception desk.

Great, now we have an audience.

Smiling, I shove my hands in my pockets. "It's completely necessary. This way, I know you made it inside safely."

"Fletcher, I appreciate the ride, but you can't do this."

"What?"

"Be all sweet. Support my business. Drive me to work." She lowers her voice. "Feed me cake."

I take a step closer to her so she's forced to crane her head back to meet my eyes. "Why not?"

"Because...you're...confusing me," she admits on a whisper, but finally giving me a glimpse of just how much I affect her.

If only she knew how much she affects me too.

I reach up and tuck her hair behind her ear as her eyes grow heavy from my touch. "How so?"

"You know how."

I shake my head. "Nope. I'm an idiot—been hit one too many times in the head. I need you to spell it out for me."

Laney's eyes flick between mine and then drop down to my lips for the hundredth time since I arrived back in town. And for a moment, I'm taken back to that night—the night she told me she had feelings for me, but I was too stupid to do anything about it. And when I wanted to, it was too late.

Laney blinks herself out of her trance, stepping away from me and averting her eyes from mine. Blowing out a breath, she hoists her purse up higher on her shoulder and then reaches for the door handle to Blossom Beauty. "See you later, Fletcher."

"Yes you will, Laney."

She flashes me a tight-lipped smile and then disappears inside.

But I know what I saw.

The fire that started burning when we were teenagers is still there.

The question is: is now the time to do something about it?

Or am I still going to let all of my excuses prevent me from going after the one thing in my life that I've always wanted, but never thought I could have?

***

"Fletcher?" Elliot comes out from the back of the Thorne Family Law Group office after I showed up unannounced and asked the receptionist if he was around.

Standing from the chair I've been waiting in, I reach out to shake his hand. "Hey, man."

He reciprocates, greeting me in a more professional way than jumping into my arms as we've been known to do in the past. "What's up? You need a lawyer? I have to tell you, I'm getting married in a couple of weeks, so now's not a good time." Pushing his shirt sleeves up his tattooed forearms, he crosses them over his chest, an amused grin on his face.

"No legal services necessary. I was in the neighborhood and just thought I'd stop by. Laney and I ordered the cake this morning, FYI."

"Nice. Don't tell me the flavors, though. I want to be surprised."

"Deal."

"Well, I'm in the middle of some paperwork, but if you want to come back to my office to chat, I can multitask."

I shove my hands in my pockets. "Sure. Sounds good."

After dropping Laney off, I drove around a bit and took in the town I've always thought of as home. There have been some changes since I was here last—new buildings, repaved roads, expanded intersections—but most things have stayed the same.

Even driving past Blossom Peak High School felt like traveling back in time. The field that held some of the best memories of my life is the same as I remember it—although, I'm sure my father has enjoyed having new players to torture with drills.

Elliot leads me into his office, a more than ample space filled with floor-to-ceiling bookshelves and the biggest mahogany desk I've ever seen. The walls are filled with his framed degrees and accolades he's earned throughout the years, and one of the walls is almost entirely taken up by a window that looks out toward the mountains that surround the town. "You want something to drink?"

"Water would be great."

He points to the mini fridge in the corner next to a couch as he takes his seat. "Help yourself."

After grabbing a bottle of water and drinking down half of it, I take a seat in one of the cushioned chairs opposite his desk. "So, how's business?"

Elliot can't hide his smile. "Really fucking good, man. The practice is thriving, our win rate is nearly perfect, and I'm getting married. Life is fucking great right now and I feel like I'm living the dream."

A small twinge of jealousy hits the center of my chest. "I'm happy for you, man."

"Thanks, Fletch. I know I said this to you on the phone when I called, but it really fucking means a lot that you're here for the wedding."

"I wouldn't have missed it, Elliot."

"I guess it was lucky that it happens to be the offseason too, huh?"

I nod. "That definitely helps. I've still got about a month before training camp."

"You ready to get back on the field?" he asks as he begins glancing between two spreadsheets and scribbling down some numbers.

"Always. I feel kinda antsy between seasons."

"So, what do you plan on doing between the wedding and then?"

"Probably just go back to Charlotte and train."

"You could always hang around here for a while longer," he suggests, glancing up with a knowing grin.

"I mean, I could..."

"You're always in a hurry to leave when you come to visit... I mean, at least the handful of times I've seen your face in the past few years."

*Yeah, and there's a fucking reason for that.*

"Well, my life is in Charlotte now."

"Yeah, but Henley, Rhonan, and I are here," he counters. "It's fucking weird not having *you* here too, man."

"You act like my job *just* took me away from here, Elliot. I've been in the NFL for ten years now."

"Yeah, but you've also missed a lot."

*Don't I fucking know it.* Sometimes it feels like my life here in Blossom Peak was a movie I watched as a teenager but never got to see the end of. "I can't be in two places at once."

Elliot sighs. "Fuck, I know. I'm not trying to lay on a guilt trip, I just..." He blows out a breath as he drops his pen to his desk and leans back in his chair, reaching up to make sure that his black hair is still styled in place. "I guess with the wedding coming up, it's just making me sentimental. You guys are the brothers I never had, you know?"

"Take that up with your parents," I joke.

Elliot laughs. "You're right, and fuck. They're so over the moon about the wedding. Since the moment I introduced Tori to them, my mom acts like she's her biological child and I'm chopped liver. Dad just wants to make sure I have a son to carry on the family name." He rolls his eyes at that.

"I thought you didn't want kids," I say, curious what changed his mind.

"I didn't, but when Tori and I talked about it, it didn't sound so fucking scary anymore. Like, with her, I think I want to take on that challenge. Plus, my parents are dying to be grandparents, so having them close by means they'll be here to help when we need a break, you know?"

Hearing Elliot talk about him wanting a family just reminds me that the man I share DNA with is the one who made me never want to have a family of my own.

Yet here's my friend, sitting right in front of me, saying words I thought I'd never hear him say.

Did he really have a change of heart, and is Tori the reason for it?

Can the right person suddenly make everything click into place?

Or does growing up truly mean that the life we were avoiding was just our fear of the unknown?

My phone starts ringing in my pocket. I pull it out and see my dad's name—talk about speaking of the devil himself. I immediately send it to voicemail. "Sorry," I say, sliding it back in my shorts.

"You can take that if you need to."

"Nope. I can call them back." *Yeah, that's not going to happen either.*

Elliot grins. "Was it a lady friend?"

"No."

He leans forward in his chair. "Come on, you can be honest with me. You've got to have a roster of women on standby, right?"

*Actually, I haven't had sex in almost two years,* I think to myself. But Elliot certainly doesn't need to know that.

But after cake tasting with Laney earlier *and* her little secret she spilled, sex is certainly on my mind.

I reach down to discreetly adjust my dick in my shorts, yet again. "There is no woman, and there hasn't been one in a long time. But if I recall correctly, *you're* the one who used to have a roster."

"I'm not going to apologize for enjoying myself and showing women a good time. But that was my life before Tori. Now I'm a changed man."

I blow out a breath as I contemplate my next words, but there's no time like the present. "Dude, I have to say this as your best man, okay? And the only reason I'm bringing it up is because I want to hear it from you."

He rolls his eyes and crosses his arms over his chest. "All right. Give it to me."

"You sure you're not rushing into this?"

His smile falls and his eyes narrow. "Did you talk to Henley and Rhonan?"

"No. This is all me." I tap the desk right in front of me. "I just want to make sure you're thinking this through."

"I get it. It's not like me to be the impulsive one, right?"

"Well, yeah, that's part of it. Ever since I've known you, you've been analytical about shit."

"Exactly, and for once, I was listening to my heart instead of my head, Fletcher. Does it make this sound crazy? Probably. But it also feels right. And not that it's any of your business, but Tori was the one that brought up marriage, not me."

"Really?"

"Yeah." His lips spread into a boyish grin. "We were lying in bed one night after fucking so hard I nearly blacked out..."

"Didn't need to know that," I mutter, but he ignores me and continues.

"And she turned to me and told me that I'm exactly the type of man she wants to marry—smart, responsible, good looking," he says, bouncing his brows. "And when I looked at her and really listened to what she said she wanted, I just decided right then and there to be that man."

"Okay...so she wanted this too?"

"We both do, Fletch. I know she wasn't the nicest girl in our class back in high school, all right? And she's even admitted that to me, how she wishes she could go back in time and act differently. Hell, she even told me about things she did and said to Dilynne, which makes more sense why she's been a pill ever since Tori's been around." He rolls his eyes. "But Tori isn't the same person she was back then. Hell, none of us are, right? She's fucking gorgeous, hardworking, and wants the same things I do. Why should I question it? When you feel that strongly for someone, you have to react. If you don't, that's how you live with regrets, right?"

His words strike a chord once again. If only he knew how true that statement is for me, how often I think back to not giving in to what I've felt for Laney since I was seventeen, and how different my life might be if I had.

"You're right."

He points at me. "I know. So, yeah... It's fast, and you, Henley, and Rhonan might not understand it. But one day you'll find a woman who will make you want to be impulsive for the first time in *your* life, and if you don't act on it, I'm going to be pissed at you."

"Is that so?"

"Yup. And I'm going to remind you of this conversation when you come to me on the fence about listening to your goddamn heart."

"So no matter the cost, no matter what issue may arise... You're saying that if I find the woman that makes me want that life—marriage, kids, the white picket fence—to go after her?"

He nods. "That's exactly what I'm saying."

*So, you're saying that I should go after Laney?*

Am I using this as a bit of a loophole? Maybe. But at the same time, hearing one of my best friends talk about taking control of his life and not waiting, despite the risks, has my brain spinning.

There are a million reasons why I shouldn't push things with Laney. Hell, reason number one being her hot-and-cold demeanor that still hasn't chilled out. But if there's one thing I've learned over the past twenty-four hours, it's that I still have an effect on her, so maybe this time in Blossom Peak is the perfect opportunity to explore it.

Am I fucking crazy? Probably.

Do I care? Not even a little.

"Fletch?" Elliot's voice pulls me from my thought spiral.

"Yeah?"

He glances at his phone that's chiming at him. "I have a call in ten minutes that I completely forgot about."

Pushing myself up from my chair, I readjust my hat. "No worries, man. I'll let you get back to work."

"We'll talk more soon, yeah?" He wakes up his computer by jostling the mouse. "Maybe you can come over one night and I'll order some pizza. It's just me right now while Tori is out of town for work."

"Aw, are you lonely, Elliot?"

He flips me off. "Do you want free pizza or not?"

"I don't know." I pat my stomach. "Not sure my waistband can afford it."

"Fuck off," he says through a laugh. "Just text me later."

"Will do." I leave Elliot's office and head back out to my truck, reeling over my friend's epiphany about his life, and wondering if coming here for his wedding is helping me find my own.

# Chapter 12

**Laney**

### *Rods, Feelings, and a Charming Bull*

"Hey, Steven. Where's Dilynne?"

Steven, one of the mechanics at Clark Customs & Auto Repair, rubs his hand on a rag as he jerks his chin toward the back of the shop. "She's head-down in an engine, just the way she likes it." He sticks his tongue in his cheek, fighting back his grin.

"God, Steven. Do you kiss your mother with that mouth?"

He points a finger at me. "My mom thinks I'm a saint, and that's exactly the way we're going to keep it, you got it?"

Placing my hands on my hips, I tilt my head at him. "I don't know. Maybe it's time I let her know how filthy her son really is."

"Snitches get stitches, Laney." He shrugs. "Don't forget that."

Laughing, I round the counter and pull him in for a hug. "It's good to see you."

"You too. What brings you in?"

I step back and push my hair from my face. "Girl stuff. I kinda need to talk to my best friend, and it can't wait."

Steven picks up a pen from the counter and starts scribbling something on the paper in front of him. "You know how she gets when she's close to finishing a project. I'm pretty sure she slept here last night."

"That's what I figured when there weren't any lights on at her house." After trying to call her three times with no answer, I peeked through the blinds in the window of my house that faces hers, and found hers pitch black. Hence why I'm here on my lunch hour to get the advice I'm in desperate need of.

"Excuse me?" A voice behind me makes me jump. When I turn and find a customer who just walked in, I slide out of the way so Steven can assist her.

He morphs from a dirty-minded jokester into the professional that he is right before my eyes. "Welcome to Clark Customs & Auto Repair. How can I help you?"

A short, blonde woman in a pink sundress walks up closer to the counter, clutching her purse at her side. "I was interested in getting my brakes checked. They're squeaking something awful and I don't want to drive home after my trip if something is wrong."

"We can definitely take a look. Most of the time, the noise is just dirt that's gotten in between the brake pads, but if not, we'll assess for any other issues."

She covers her chest with her palm, sighing in relief. "Thank you. I swear, one of my worst fears is getting in a car accident because of something that was totally preventable, you know?"

"I agree." Steven pulls out an invoice from under the counter. "Let me just get your information."

But before the woman replies, she turns to face me and her eyes widen. "Oh my goodness. You work at the salon, don't you?"

"I do."

"Can I just say that the facial I had there the other day was the best I've ever had?"

Smiling, I reply, "Happy to hear that. Are you just visiting Blossom Peak?"

"I am." She begins to fiddle with her necklace, catching my eye, especially as recognition dawns on me.

"Oh my gosh. Your necklace," I say, reaching out to touch it but stopping myself. "My—my mom used to have one just like it."

The lady pulls it out in front of her to peek down at it. "I love pink diamonds."

"She did too." Goosebumps spread down my arms as my eyes stay fixated on the woman's jewelry. "She—she died twelve years ago."

The woman frowns and reaches out to stroke my arm. "I'm so sorry for your loss."

"Thank you." I keep staring at the woman as I fight back tears, finding myself apologizing quickly. "Sorry. I'm—I'm just having a moment."

"Take all the time you need. Grief can hit you when you least expect it."

I nod, but don't say anything else as I regain my composure.

Steven clears his throat, gaining the woman's attention. "If you have your driver's license, that would help me create a customer profile for you."

"Oh, absolutely." The woman digs through her purse for her wallet but glances over at me again. "Are you going to be okay?"

"Yeah. I'm good. Thanks for being so..." The word I'm looking for dies on my tongue.

Luckily, the woman squeezes my hand, giving me the emotional support that I need in that moment. "Anytime."

Shaking off the sensitive moment, I walk past Steven, down the hall of the office space, and into the garage, looking between the bays to find my best friend.

"Steven, I need that tie rod over here, please!" Dilynne calls out as I make my way toward her, and Steven appears out of nowhere, hot on my heels.

"I thought you were helping that lady. That was quick," I say as I glance back at the front office and find it empty.

"I got her info, but I knew Dilynne was waiting on me, so I told her I'd be right back." He glances over at me, grinning. "Isn't this car sick?"

"What car is it?"

"A 1968 Cadillac Coupe de Ville, 62 series. Dilynne's gonna show it off next month and make all the men in the room walk around with hard-ons for the rest of the day."

Dilynne slides out from under the classic car she's working on, spinning on her rolling board to face us. Steven and I both stare down at her. "You know, you're lucky I'm a cool boss because that kind of talk wouldn't fly everywhere." She holds out her hand, waiting for Steven to hand her the rod he was speaking of, I assume. Dilynne may be my best friend, and I may have listened to her drone on and on about cars over the years, but I still have no clue what the hell any of this is. "And you're lucky I know your wife."

"My hot as fuck wife," he corrects her. "Don't forget that part."

"Of course. How could I forget?"

"How is Chelsea doing by the way?" I ask him as I run my hand along the body of the car Dilynne is working on.

"Getting hotter by the day."

Dilynne kicks his shoe as she takes the rod and sets it on top of her stomach. Luckily, she wears Carhartt coveralls anytime she's working in the garage, so the grease tends to only end up on those, and not everywhere else. "Now, if you'll excuse us, Laney and I have some important business to discuss."

"Business about wieners and smut?"

"Always," I tease him.

"Hell yeah!" Steven fist pumps the air as he heads back to the office.

I point my thumb in the direction he just went. "Does he ever not say something that's laced with innuendo?"

"Nope," Dilynne answers frankly before brushing her forearm against her forehead. Her red bandana slides back a bit, but she pulls it back into place to keep her hair out of her face while she works. "So, what's up?" She rolls the board back under the fender well of the car, but I know she's listening. You'd be amazed at how many conversations we've had like this.

Sighing, I say, "It's Fletcher."

"Yeah, I assumed as much. Fill me in. What's happened since Saturday?"

I've only given Dilynne bits and pieces of what the past few days have been like.

"So, you know how he scheduled appointments at the salon?"

"Yeah..."

"Well, he found out that I call him Lucifer and keep a swear jar for anyone who says his name."

Dilynne snorts. "Let me guess, Glenn let it slip?"

"Yes, and speaking of my employees, why didn't you tell me that you invited them out with us on Friday?"

She slides toward me just far enough that I can see her face, pointing a wrench up at me. "Because I knew you'd back out if I did. And this way, I have peer pressure to keep you from canceling."

I glare at her. "I really hate you sometimes."

"No you don't. Now, continue. How was he while he was at the salon?"

"He was…fine." *Fine* is putting it lightly. Everyone fell in love with him, he tipped the entire staff very generously, even those that didn't assist him, and the image of him ripping off his shirt in front of me has been burned into my brain for all eternity. Not to mention, Glenn pinned his signed April calendar page up next to his station so he can brag about it to all his clients.

"Nope." She waves a finger at me from under the car. "That's what you said when I texted you. Now spill."

Sighing, I cross my arms around my waist and give my best friend the Cliff Notes version, but only the things that irritated me. "Well, he took his shirt off in front of everyone, admitted that he only made the appointments because he was trying to support my business, and then programmed his contact information into my glucose monitoring app so he gets alerts now when my sugar is out of whack."

Dilynne slowly rolls out from under the car and sits up on the board, blinking a few times. "Holy shit."

"Right? And then when he came to my house the next night to fill favors, I was trying to be cool, pretend like things between us were normal because it actually really did mean a lot that he came into the salon. But then I found out that my brother and Henley told him about Spencer—the whole story."

Dilynne rolls her eyes. "I swear, those boys gossip worse than teenage girls."

"Seriously… And Fletcher insisted that if I felt like being Tori's maid of honor was too much, to let him know. So I assured him that I'm fine, and he doesn't need to worry about me."

She arches a brow. "And what was his response to that?"

"Umm..." I can feel my cheeks grow hot from the memory of Fletcher pressing me up against the kitchen counter and the words he said in that deep timbre of his voice. "He basically told me that Spencer was an idiot, and he'd like to rip his limbs from his body."

Dilynne's eyes bug out as she stands, looking me in the eyes. "Holy shit. Laney..."

I throw my hands in the air. "I know!"

"He really said that?"

"Yes, but what the hell am I supposed to do with that information? I mean, shit, Dilynne..." I begin to pace. "What he said, how close he was to me, the way he toyed with my bottom lip..."

Dilynne visibly shudders. "Damn, that's hot."

I freeze and lower my voice. "It was one of the hottest moments of my life."

She studies me for a moment, tapping her wrench on her palm. "What happened after that?"

"We finished filling the favors, and then he went home."

"Huh." Dilynne sits back down on the board and starts to roll back under the car, but I put my foot on the board, stopping her.

"Huh? That's all you have to say?"

"What more do you want from me?"

"I don't know. Tell me what to do! What does this mean?!"

"Laney, only you can answer that."

"But—"

She sits up, resting her arms between her legs, peering up at me. "Look, you could have asked him, or hell, even kissed him, but you didn't." She shrugs.

"Well, I mean... Why would I?"

"I think the more important question you need to ask yourself is, why *wouldn't* you?"

I blink. "What?"

I'm used to blunt honesty from her, but I never imagined this being her advice.

"Why didn't you give in to the moment?"

"Because... Because I don't want to cause any issues for Elliot, Tori, and their big day," I say, but Dilynne's eyes narrow.

"Nope. Try again."

"That's the reason—"

"No, it's not." She gives me a full once-over. "You're scared. I don't know why I didn't see it sooner. We've known each other most of our lives, and I can tell when you're letting fear run things."

"I am not *scared.*"

"Yes, you are, and now you definitely have a reason to be."

"What's that supposed to mean?"

"A man—not just any man, but your brother's best friend, the guy you had the most insane crush on—would *not* go to those lengths and do those things, or say those things, if he did not have feelings for you."

I suddenly feel dizzy. Bracing myself on a toolbox behind me, I say, "You really think so?"

Dilynne shrugs. "Yeah, I do. But, I wasn't there. You were. So, you're the only one that truly knows what happened between you two, but I will say this." She points her wrench up at me again. "You've spent almost twelve years wondering if the man felt the same way about you because you never got that validation back then. I hate to say it, babe...but I think you got it from him the other night."

"I—I don't know."

She straightens her spine. "I'm gonna ask you something and don't be mad at me."

"I hate when you lead with that."

"I'm just forewarning you. But Laney...do you think there's even a chance that maybe what you saw that night twelve years ago wasn't what you thought it was?"

The image of Fletcher in that final moment that sealed the deal for me flashes in my mind. "I know what I saw. And I know what he said—or didn't say."

"Then why would he be putting forth all this effort to get on your good side?"

"Because he's Rhonan's best friend. Because he cares about Elliot and is taking this best man duty seriously. Or maybe he doesn't remember that night because he'd been drinking. Or maybe he thinks he can get laid while he's here on his little mini-vacation and then go back to his life as a playboy wide receiver in the NFL."

"You know what's weird, though?" She taps her chin in thought.

"What?"

"He's never actually been confirmed to be dating anyone."

"Yeah, because he probably just has one-night stands and licks cake off of their fingers too."

Dilynne clears her throat while arching a brow at me. "Is that...from personal experience or...?" Her eyes widen. "Oh my God. Did he do that when you two went cake tasting yesterday?"

I close my eyes and nod. "Yes. He was flirtatious, hand-fed me samples of cake, and sucked on my fingers to the point that I thought I was going to have an orgasm right there in the bakery." I cover my face when I remember what that led to. "Then I made the mistake of admitting out loud how I haven't had an orgasm from something other than my hand or a vibrator in three years..."

Dilynne stares at me, barely blinking. "You are so fucked, so the only thing left to do is fuck him and get it out of your system."

"That's your advice?"

"What?" She throws her hands to the side. "You know I'm not the relationship type. Sex without feelings is my love language, Laney."

"God, I wish I could do that."

She shrugs. "You can. You just live out the fantasy of being with him, enjoy these next couple of weeks hopefully full of mind-blowing orgasms, and then move on knowing you'll no longer wonder what if."

"I just really wish I didn't feel anything for him at this point. It would make this a lot easier."

"Again, I think you've built this whole thing up in your head, so maybe it's just time to face it and find out the truth."

"I think I'd rather get a root canal."

Dilynne laughs before looking back at the car. "To each their own, but don't forget we're going out Friday night, if for nothing else than to get your mind off of this whole thing."

I fake a cough. "I don't know. I think I feel a cold coming on."

She glares at me. "Don't even think about it. You're going."

"Ugh." I stomp my feet and then turn to exit the shop. "You know, you're not my mom. You can't make me go."

"Oh, yes, I can. Remember that I know how to do wicked things with a pair of pliers." She shakes her finger at me. "Don't say I didn't warn you."

***

"Who are these people?" Lifting my drink to my mouth, I suck on the straw between my lips. The strawberry and lime margarita is going down smoothly with only a hint of a burn from the tequila.

Dilynne wraps her arm around my shoulders. "Who the hell cares? The point is, there are a ton of men in here, so you have your pick of which one gets to help you burn off some sexual aggression."

"You make it sound like I'm about to mount someone in the middle of the bar and hump his leg."

Dilynne pops her brows. "Dry humping is severely underrated."

"I'm gonna need more alcohol," I mumble around my straw as I suck down the bottom half of my drink.

It's Friday night and, as planned, I'm out with Dilynne, my coworkers, and a few of our friends from around town. When Dilynne suggested this little excursion, I just imagined it would be just the two of us. Unfortunately, all of my friends are now involved in Operation: Laney Gets Her Groove Back.

The Charming Bull, a bar located about thirty minutes outside of town, is bustling with more people than I've ever seen. Although, I can't tell you the last time I was out at a bar, so this could just be a normal Friday-night crowd.

"Maybe to take the edge off, you should ride the mechanical bull?" Dilynne gestures to the roped-off area where a girl is gyrating her hips against the bull beneath her, one hand thrown up in the air, her hair cascading wildly around her, exuding sexuality that I don't think I've ever possessed.

"You want me to get off on a fake animal?"

"The stimulation is great if you press down hard enough."

Shaking my head at my best friend, I signal to the bartender for a refill.

Ginny, our friend who manages the grocery store in Blossom Peak, comes sauntering up to us. "All right, I scoured the room and landed on two groups of potential men for you." Brushing her red hair from her face, she discreetly points to the far-right corner. "That group looks like all blue-collar men—dirty hands, worn jeans, and steel-toed boots." She licks her lips. "Those would be my first pick."

Dilynne nods in agreement. "Two of them are wearing cowboy hats too, so that's a plus."

"Dear God," I mutter, sucking down my second drink at record speed.

Ginny motions to the other side of the bar. "Now, over here we have the business type—button-down shirts, pressed slacks, leather loafers. I saw quite a few ankles over there, and a smattering of chest hair peeking out from the collars of their shirts, so also very good potential."

"God, I love chest hair. It's so under appreciated," Dilynne adds. "A man with hair on his chest makes me feel a bit more like a cavewoman, and what we're doing is more animalistic than not."

Ginny motions to clink her glass against Dilynne's. "I'll toast to that."

Glenn comes up to us now, a pout on his lips. "Straight, straight, straight," he whines. "This bar is full of straight men. What does a gay man have to do around here to find someone to bang?"

"Go to a gay bar," Dilynne replies dryly.

"Then next time, that's where we're going. The operation that night will be to get *Glenn* laid."

"You know, we could do that right now, if you want?" I interject as the anxiety rises in my chest. I thought the alcohol would help me relax, but all it's doing is feeding this uneasy feeling in my gut that I don't want to be here.

Sure, there are some very attractive men in this bar, men that romance novels are written about, looks-wise. But none of them are making me want to put myself out there. None of them are familiar.

None of them are Fletcher.

*Yup. It's official. I think my head, heart, and vagina are broken.*

Dilynne tsks. "Nice try, Laney. Tonight is about you. Now, which corner do you want to shimmy on over to first?"

"I'm not shimmying anywhere."

"Girl, you've got to shake your ass a bit in that skirt. I'm telling you, as soon as you walk by that table of bona fide cowboys and they see the way your ass looks, they'll start fighting over which one of them gets to take you home."

"Knowing my luck, I'm gonna trip as I walk by and fall flat on my face."

Ginny perks up. "Even better! Then they get to rescue you, and that's always a great way to make a man hard."

"You two have issues."

"No, we are concerned for you and your vagina," Ginny clarifies.

"I appreciate it, but my vagina is just fine."

Glenn dry heaves. "Can we stop with all of the vagina talk, ladies? Please?"

"If you're hanging out with the girls, you know vaginas are a topic of discussion, Glenn. Don't act offended," Dilynne says as Yvonne and Claudia approach us.

"How many drinks have you had, Laney?" Yvonne asks as she tips her beer bottle to her lips.

I hold up my half-empty glass. "This is my second."

"Good. Let's dance then." Yanking on my free hand, she pulls me to the dance floor in the center of the bar. High-top tables are situated all around the hardwood floor full of people swaying their hips, and on the next level up are pool tables, dart boards, and neon signs all over the walls.

"Don't You Worry Child" pulses through the bar as we move into the crowd. Yvonne pulls me to the middle of the dance floor, only releasing me to put her hands in the air as she shakes her ass to the beat of the song.

Knowing there's no way she'll let me sneak away, I give in and let the music overtake me. I sip on my drink, feeling my body get warm as the tequila does its job, and after a few minutes, the tightness in my chest starts to loosen up.

Maybe Dilynne was right. Maybe I just needed a night out to take the edge off. That doesn't mean that I have to go home with anyone, and honestly, I've already decided that I'm not. But, being out instead of alone on my couch watching reruns of Friends is exactly what I needed to shake things up.

I'm so busy dancing that I fail to notice a man approaching me from behind.

"Hey, darlin'," he says in my ear before stepping in front of me. "Name's Easton."

"Laney," I say while staring up at him, his face etched from stone and his dark hair covered by a cowboy hat.

*I bet this man knows how to ride that mechanical bull.*

"Mind if I join you?" he says as his feet start moving to the beat of the next song.

"Uh, sure."

He moves closer to me, planting his hands gently on my hips. My eyes land on his chest, admiring how broad it is. The flannel he's wearing is almost bursting at the seams as his arms move. When I look back up to his face, I lock eyes with his.

"How come I haven't seen you around here?" he asks, his voice deep and gravelly.

"Oh, uh... I don't go out very often."

"Shame." He grins and I admire the dark stubble dusting his cheeks and his green eyes that are framed by dark, thick lashes.

God, he really is handsome.

Maybe Dilynne and Ginny are onto something. Suddenly, I have sparked an interest in cowboys, which is a far cry from football players, am I right?

"Easton!" One of his friends calls out to him from the side of the dance floor, gaining our attention.

"What?"

"Come here!"

As my eyes volley back and forth, I realize that Easton and his friends are the group of men that Ginny was scouting earlier, as indicated by their similar attire and cowboy hats.

"I'm busy!" he calls back before looking down at me again. "Sorry about them, sugar."

"It's okay. You can go over there if you need to."

His grip on my hip tightens, pulling me closer. "I'd rather stay right here."

"I think you should go over there," a deep voice says from behind me, making my entire body tense up.

"Do you?" Easton challenges as he looks directly over my shoulder. I don't have to turn around to know who he's talking to.

"I do." His words are clipped, but I hear the warning in his tone.

Easton dips his eyes down to me. "Do you want me to go?"

"Easton!" His friend calls again from the side of the dance floor. Easton's eyes bounce back and forth between mine, waiting for my answer.

Shrugging my shoulders but fighting off my irritation, I say, "Maybe it's for the best."

He sighs, releasing me from his grip and glaring at the man behind me before stomping over to his friend.

I watch him leave and don't bother looking behind me before moving in the opposite direction, but I'm pulled back by warm hands before meeting another broad chest, this time at my back.

"Laney..." Fletcher murmurs in my ear as we stand still, bodies dancing all around us.

I look up at him over my shoulder. "What are you doing here? Are you stalking me?"

"I swear, it was purely coincidence," he replies, his breath ghosting across the sensitive skin at my neck.

"Well, next time, you should just pretend you never saw me, okay?"

His grip on my waist tightens, and the way his touch feels compared to Easton's is like night and day.

Easton was polite, not too aggressive, and genuinely interested in me, or so it seemed.

But the way Fletcher is holding on to me right now is filled with possessiveness, and I can't deny that it makes me want to obey anything he tells me to do, even though as soon as I get the courage to open up to the possibility of someone new, he appears out of thin air.

*Seems to be my luck, doesn't it?*

"You act like that's easy to do," he says as his body starts swaying behind mine, his hand commanding my body to follow suit.

My breath hitches as his fingers find the sliver of skin between my denim skirt and white tank top. "It should be. You've done it before."

"I planned on turning away, had every intention, but then that guy came over here and started dancing with you, and I just..."

"You what?" I ask breathlessly, borderline embarrassed at the extent this man is affecting my breathing.

"The thought of him touching you..." His growl is low, but I don't miss it. "It made me want to put my football cleat to his chest and dig it in as far as it would go."

"What is it with you and these murderous tendencies?"

"Well, that's how you make me feel. In fact, I haven't stopped feeling this way since the cake tasting, when you admitted..."

"I told you to forget about what I said."

He pushes his very hard body closer to mine—and when I feel just how hard every part of him is, wetness builds between my legs.

Glad to know there are no cobwebs down there, but the fact that it's Fletcher making me aware of that is an even bigger problem to manage.

"There's no forgetting something like that, angel."

The nickname rolls off his tongue so effortlessly that it makes me forget where we are.

"In fact, seeing that guy touch you made me realize that any man you are with is going to leave you disappointed."

"And how do you know that?"

He inhales deeply before muttering against the shell of my ear, "Because none of them are me."

# Chapter 13

**Fletcher**

*Jealousy and an Orgasm*

Every nerve ending in my body is on high alert, but that's what being near Laney does to me, what she's always done to me.

When Henley suggested we go out tonight to blow off some steam, I never imagined we would run into Laney and her friends. I spotted Dilynne first, actually. And since I know those two rarely go anywhere without the other, it only took a few more minutes to find the woman that's made the past few days difficult to get through.

"What makes you think you're the better option?" she asks, her voice a purr above the music playing around us.

"Because making you come is all I've thought about since you uttered those words," I admit. She twists her head so our eyes connect, but she doesn't say anything. I trail my fingers from her wrist to her forearm, moving them across her shoulder before teasing her neck. "If you were mine, Laney, every man in this place would know it."

"Fletcher..." she mewls as she pushes her ass back into me. And I know she has to be able to feel how fucking hard I am right now, but I honestly don't give a shit.

Holding her, touching her like this—it's years of repressed need flowing out of me all at once.

"If you were mine, I'd make sure that every orgasm was better than the last."

Her free arm moves behind my neck, allowing me to drag my nose up the column of her throat while we continue to sway to the music.

"And if you were mine, I'd need to watch you come so badly that I'd find a place in this bar where we could be alone, just so I could watch you fall apart from my touch." Her entire body shudders and my dick twitches.

Neither of us speak for so long, I wonder if she's even aware that we're still dancing, and the people around us are starting to stare.

I wore my hat tonight in an attempt to avoid attention, but all it takes is one fan to spot me, and then there's no dodging the chaos.

Just when I'm about to pull us off the dance floor, Laney says something that makes me freeze where I stand. "Show me," she says, weaving her fingers through mine where they're wrapped around her hips.

"What?"

She turns her face toward me again, and her eyes are filled with a desire I don't think I've ever seen from her before. "Show me, Fletcher. Show me what it's like to be touched like that."

A match is lit within me, but I stand there for a moment, making sure I'm hearing her correctly. "Laney, I—"

"Either prove it to me, or walk away," she says, cutting me off, her eyes darkened and penetrating mine with a command I can't deny.

And in that moment, I know there's no turning back.

Laney Hart just gave me permission to make her come, and that's exactly what I intend to do.

"Fuck it." Grabbing her empty drink from her hand, I weave our fingers together and pull her behind me, off the dance floor and away from prying eyes. Keeping my head down to cover my face as much as possible with the bill of my hat, I move toward the back corner of the bar where I know there's a hallway we can duck into for a few moments.

Laney's grip on me tightens as I lead her through the crowd, her desperation confirmed in her touch. As soon as the hallway is within reach, I walk up to the bouncer guarding the entrance.

"This area is closed," he says, crossing his arms over his chest and widening his stance.

I pull my wallet from my back pocket, hold out a wad of cash in front of his face, and arch a brow at him. "Is it, though?"

He takes the cash from my hand and unclips the rope, allowing us to pass by him. "Take your time."

"Thank you."

"Fletcher," Laney says behind me. "Fletcher?"

Once I reach the end of the hallway where barely any light remains, I spin Laney so her back is to my chest and plant her hands above her on the wall. Her breathing quickens, but I stand there, holding her hands to the wall while pressing my body against hers.

"You know we shouldn't be doing this," I mutter against her ear.

"I know, but I'm getting really tired of being told what I shouldn't do."

"Me too, baby." My grip on her wrists tightens as I thrust my erection against her back, letting her feel how fucking hard I am. "Now, you're going to listen to everything I say to you, do you understand?" She nods, but I need to hear her. "Use your words, angel."

"Yes."

"And you're sure that you want this?"

"Yes," she answers again, her chest heaving as she struggles to take in air.

Moving her hands closer together so I can hold them with only one of mine, I drag my nose up the side of her neck. Her hair is pulled up in a ponytail, she's wearing a white tank top that shows a sliver of her tan stomach, and the little denim skirt she has on is making me even harder while I imagine just what's underneath it.

"Fuck, Laney." I nip at her skin. "You have no idea how many times I've thought about this."

"Then make it real. Make me come, Fletcher," she whispers while pushing her ass into my crotch.

With my free hand on the button of her skirt, I pop it open, pull down the zipper slowly, and then tease the top of her underwear with my finger before pulling it away from exactly where she wants me.

"Ugh…"

"Patience, baby."

"*Three years*, Fletcher. Remember?"

"I told you, it's all I've been able to think about." I bring my hand to her chest, dragging my thumb across her pebbled nipples, loving how she lets out soft little whimpers with each pass. My gaze is locked on the rise and fall of her chest and the part in her lips as her eyelashes flutter closed. Moving my hand back down, I skim my fingertips across her stomach, loving how her skin breaks out in goosebumps, before slowly dipping my index finger beneath the fabric of her underwear again, just far enough that I can feel her slit and discover how fucking soaked she is. "Jesus, Laney…"

"Don't stop. Please."

I dip my finger lower, parting her to find her clit swollen and needy. Softly, I move the tip of my finger around her bundle of nerves, slowly and with just enough pressure to build her up, but definitely not as much as she needs.

Her hand starts slipping on the wall. "Oh God..."

I lift it and put it back in place with the other one, holding them together tighter in my hand this time while my finger slides down further to find her entrance, teasing her by just inserting the tip.

"Hands stay on the wall," I command.

"But..."

I move my lips right next to her ear. "Hands on the wall or I stop, Laney. You decide."

She closes her eyes, groans in frustration, and then leans her head back on my shoulder, sighing as I move my finger just a few inches deeper inside of her. "Fine."

"Attagirl." Pulling my finger back up to her clit, I use two fingers this time to circle the bud, moving her arousal around as her hips start to move along with the motion. "So needy, aren't you?"

"Yes..."

"How's the pressure?"

"Perfect," she sighs.

Sliding my fingers back down to her entrance, I push both inside of her now, slowly and as best I can due to the confines of the denim fabric of her skirt and her underwear. But I'm determined to make this woman break for me, and nothing is going to stop me at this point.

"I need my other hand, Laney. Are you gonna keep yours on the wall like I told you?"

"Uh huh."

"Good girl."

Removing my hand from her pussy and releasing her wrists, I slip my hand under her thigh and lift her left leg up, pushing her body forward slightly and her skirt up over her ass so that I can access all of her now. "Keep your hands on the wall."

"Fletcher, I..."

"You're gonna come for me like this, Laney. You're going to ride my fingers and show me how needy your pussy is for this release, how fucking much you want me to finger fuck you and make you come. Understood?"

"Yes." Her head falls back on my shoulder again as I keep her open to me. I move her underwear to the side and slide my fingers back inside her wet cunt, loving how wet she is as I move my fingers in and out of her.

She moans. "Oh God..."

"Your pussy is dripping on my fingers, angel. I can't wait to lick my fucking fingers clean and taste you." Her moans get louder, but the music in the bar drowns them out. Her walls grow tighter and her breathing shallower as one of my hands continues to fuck her, and the other is rubbing her clit, making sure that her buildup is slow and deliberate. But when I feel her clench around me, I know she's almost there. "You're getting close, aren't you?"

"Yes!" she cries.

Applying a bit more pressure so I can get her to break, I listen for her cues so I know when she's about to detonate.

Laney's nails dig into the wall, sliding down as her hips rock forward against my hand, but I keep her leg up, her pussy open for me as I curl my fingers deep inside of her, thrusting and stretching her open while applying pressure where she needs it.

"Oh fuck!"

"Come for me, Laney." My fingers keep moving rapidly over her clit. "Let me see you fall apart."

"Fletcher...I..." But her words die on the tremor that rips through her body, her moans echoing in the hall around us. She rides my hand, taking every last ounce of pleasure as I continue to rub her clit and slide my fingers in and out of her, her arousal dripping all the way down my wrist to my elbow.

*Fucking perfect.*

When her body finally goes slack, I catch her in my arms as her hands leave the wall and she leans back against me. Slowly, I drop her leg down, situate her skirt back in place, lifting the zipper and re-buttoning it before planting a kiss right at the juncture where her neck meets her shoulder.

Before she turns around, I line my lips up to her ear. "That's how it feels to be touched by a real man, angel. And if you find that you need more, I'm more than willing to give it to you."

Taking a step back, I adjust my cock in my jeans, knowing that the pain I'll feel while waiting to release my own tension at home is worth it just from getting to experience Laney Hart climaxing on my fingers.

I can only hope that next time, it'll be on my tongue or my cock.

*There shouldn't be a next time, Fletcher.*

*Oh, but there will be.*

I lift my hand to my mouth and lick it clean. "Fucking delicious, just like I knew you'd be."

"I—I need to get back to my friends," she says, her voice shaky.

"Probably a good idea."

"Uh huh." She straightens her spine, turns and walks down the hallway, back the way we entered, never meeting my eyes before she leaves.

Reaching up to readjust my hat, I wait a few minutes before exiting the hallway myself.

My eyes scour the space, looking for Laney even though I know that I shouldn't. But before I can spot her, Henley makes his way over to me. "Dude…where the fuck did you go? I was giving the bartender our order, and when I turned around, you were gone."

"I—I thought I saw someone I knew, so I went to check."

Henley eyes me curiously as he tips his beer bottle to his lips. "Okay…"

"You wanna get out of here?" I turn to meet his gaze.

"We just got here."

"Yeah, but it's loud and I got bombarded in the restroom when I went in to take a piss. I'm really not in the mood to be rushed by fans." The lie feels dirty coming from my lips because I never take my fans and my job for granted, but I need to get out of here before I find Laney and fuck her up against that wall this time.

Not gonna lie—part of me is curious if she'd let me.

Fuck, I'm unraveling the longer I stand here, and the last thing I need to do is tell Henley what the hell just happened. Before I talk to anyone about the waves of emotions and lust rolling through me, I need to talk to Laney about what this means.

"Fine." Henley drains the rest of his beer. "It *is* loud as fuck in here, but that's the only reason I'm leaving. A redhead was eyeing me earlier and I had every intention of taking her home tonight."

"Sorry to be a cock block."

"I'll survive." Henley follows me closely as we make our way toward the exit. "Funny how we used to enjoy this shit a few years ago, huh?"

"Well, we *are* in our thirties. Now, a good time is music low enough I can talk over, going to bed at a reasonable hour, and not waking up with a hangover the next day."

Henley eyes me from the side. "You sound like Chandler from that episode of *Friends* when the boys realize they're too old to party anymore."

When the cool air hits us as we walk through the front door of the bar, I chuckle. "Hate to break it to you, man, but I relate to that episode more and more every day."

"This is just sad. Are you gonna be in bed by ten the night of the bachelor party then?" he asks as we head out to my truck. We had to park far away since this place is packed.

"Depends on how the night goes."

I pull my phone from my pocket as we continue walking, bringing up my text thread with Laney.

**Me:** *How are you getting home?*

She responds almost instantly.

**Laney:** *Claudia. She isn't drinking.*

**Me:** *Good. Be safe.*

**Laney:** **rolling eye emoji**

**Me:** *And Laney?*

**Laney:** *What?*

**Me:** *I certainly hope that orgasm was better than the cake.*

Laughing, I listen to Henley drone on about me being an old man now before we hop inside my truck. But I barely pay attention to anything else he says because as I drive us both back to Blossom Peak, the only thing on my mind is what it felt like touching, listening to, and seeing Laney come apart in my arms.

And as I grip the wheel, her scent still lingering on my fingers, one thing becomes crystal clear.

That was not a one-time thing.

Not even close.

# Chapter 14

**Laney**

***Benefits and Training Wheels***

"You're alive." Hazel's groggy voice says through the phone.

"I am, but are you?" Tucking my leg underneath me, I take a seat on my couch, holding my coffee cup in my hand.

"Just waking up," she says before she bursts into a fit of giggles.

Sounds of rustling come through, and then a male voice replies. "She's lying to you, Laney. I just fucked her hard into the mattress and she's still recovering."

The reminder of what Fletcher and I did on Friday night hits me hard, followed by the thought I've had a thousand times since... *What if we'd kept going?*

Hazel returns to the line with a groan. "Sorry. Gage doesn't have a problem with sharing every detail of our lives, apparently."

"It's okay... But can I ask you something?"

"Always."

"How does it feel to be God's favorite?"

She laughs. "Really fucking good. But enough about me, how's everything going? It's been a week since we spoke last and I figured I would have heard from you by now, especially if you needed bail money for the attempted murder of Fletcher Adams."

Now it's my turn to laugh. "No bail money necessary, thankfully."

"So he's not driving you insane?"

"Oh, he is, but not in the way you'd think."

"And what way is that?"

I take a deep breath before admitting the truth. "Well...he sort of made me come Friday night. At a bar."

There's a loud clatter on her end, followed by Hazel's voice in full panic. "Oh my God! Sorry, I dropped the phone from shock. What? He made you come? How? Mouth or fingers? Dick?"

Closing my eyes, I visualize that moment again. "Fingers, but that's not the point."

"Let me guess...you're freaking out?"

"Uh, naturally. I mean, the last thing I expected during all this wedding chaos was Fletcher and I crossing that line. I was more worried about not accidentally-on-purpose shoving him into oncoming traffic."

"Well, how was it?"

I pause for dramatic effect. "I've never come that hard in my life," I admit on a whisper.

Thinking back on how his touch made me feel makes my entire body shiver.

Hazel chuckles. "Nice. But back up. How did we get to the orgasm that rocked your world?" I spend the next several minutes catching Hazel up on everything that has transpired since Fletcher arrived—his appointments at the salon, him hacking into my glucose monitoring app, his feelings about Spencer, and the flirting that kept building until eventually we snapped at the bar.

Hazel lets out a long whistle. "Well, girl. I'd say you have a problem on your hands, but honestly? I don't think this is a bad thing."

"You're joking, right?"

"No, I'm not. Clearly there's still something between you two and after sampling his talents, I say you enjoy them while he's there."

I shake my head, even though she can't see me. "It feels messy, Hazel, like I'm just going to end up hurt again."

"Not if you both go into the arrangement knowing that it's temporary. I mean, you deserve to have some mind-blowing orgasms for a few weeks, Laney. It doesn't mean you have to marry the guy."

"Says the woman who married a man first and then got her orgasms."

"What's your point?"

"My point is, when you and Gage agreed to get married, you were both on the same page about no feelings too, and then look what happened." Sighing, I fiddle with the hem of my shirt. "The thing with Spencer was humiliating, and I don't think I could handle if things blow up with Fletcher too. If you hadn't realized, I sort of have some trust issues now."

Hazel hums. "All right. I understand where you're coming from, but let me ask you this... Do you want him to touch you again?"

I haven't thought about anything else since I walked away from him that night, eager to find my friends so they wouldn't start asking questions. Yvonne did, of course, because she was on the dance floor with Fletcher and me, but I told her I went to the bathroom, and she didn't press me further.

And the texts Fletcher has been sending me aren't helping me push it from my mind either. I haven't even responded because I don't know what to say.

"Well…"

"The fact that you're hesitating tells me all I need to know. You want more, so why aren't you taking advantage of the opportunity?" Before I can think of how to respond, she speaks again. "When's the last time you did something for you, Laney? When's the last time you put your needs before anyone else's? And when's the last time you were with a man who could actually make you come?"

"Okay, I see your point."

"Good, because if you didn't, I was contemplating driving over to Blossom Peak to convince you myself."

"You should anyway because it's been way too long since we've seen each other."

Hazel sighs. "I know. Gage and I will look at our calendars and pick out some dates for a trip, okay? I promise."

"Thank you," I say softly because, even though I still feel uneasy about the brazenness I exhibited the other night, Hazel's encouragement to do what I want for once instead of overthinking everything—which I'm an expert at doing—is the push I needed to allow myself to want this.

"I'm always here. Good luck and happy humping!"

Laughing, we end the call and then I pick up my coffee again, taking a sip while I swirl this idea around in my brain. Hazel is right. Fletcher will be gone right after the wedding, and then life will go back to normal. This could just be one of those spontaneous things I'll look back on fondly when I'm older and reminiscing about my life.

Sex without feelings. If other women can do it, I should be able to, right?

Just because I haven't doesn't mean I'm not *capable* of it.

And yes, there may be some feelings simmering under the surface where Fletcher is concerned, but maybe I need to focus more on *what* I'll be receiving instead of *who's* delivering.

Dilynne made a valid point as well—I've always wondered what being with Fletcher would be like, and after the taste of it I got Friday night, I'm definitely interested in more.

Orgasms. No feelings. That's what I need, what I deserve.

I just hope that Fletcher can agree to that too.

***

"I'm gonna let go now," Rhonan says as he walks alongside Ellis, who's teetering on her bike without training wheels. They've been at this for days, and she's still having trouble with her balance.

"No, Daddy!" she cries, legs pedaling furiously beneath her.

"You've got this, Ellis. Just keep pedaling."

"No, Daddy...please." Her voice pitches into panic.

"Ellis..."

She drops her feet to the ground, bringing them both to a halt. The bike wobbles beneath her and Rhonan reaches out, easing her off the seat as the bike clatters to the asphalt beside them. Crossing her arms over her chest, she shoots my brother a glare that I might have some firsthand knowledge of—because at this moment, my niece looks alarmingly like me.

"I hate this bike!" she announces with all the conviction of a four-year-old betrayed by the laws of gravity.

"But it has Elsa on it," my brother counters.

Ellis steps over the bike and stomps off. "I don't care. I want my training wheels back!"

From his perch in the garage, my father stifles his laughter behind his hand. As Ellis walks past him and into the house, he arches a brow at my brother. "You've pissed her off good this time."

It's Sunday night and the four of us are having dinner together at Rhonan's house. We try to get together at least once a week, but sometimes our schedules don't allow for it. Tonight, Rhonan hoped having us here would encourage Ellis to give riding her bike without training wheels another try.

Rhonan pushes a hand through his hair as he walks back up the driveway. "She's the one who wanted the training wheels off. Some kid at preschool was making fun of her, so she insisted I remove them. Now *I'm* the asshole."

"She's just struggling with her balance," I interject. "She's still little, Rhonan. Give her time."

He shrugs. "Yeah... Joanne said she'd give it a try with her when she comes back tomorrow."

"I wish her luck," my father says.

My brother snaps his fingers, turning to me. "That reminds me, do you mind looking after Ellis Friday night? Joanne's niece is in a play in Charlotte, so she asked for the night off. She'll be back Saturday for the bachelor and bachelorette party, though."

*Shit. I forgot all about the party Fletcher and I have yet to plan.*

*Well, someone has been keeping you rather distracted lately, Laney.*

I mentally think over my schedule, wondering when I'm going to fit planning a party in there. But I've made lemonade out of lemons before, so I'm not too stressed about it. "Yeah, that should be fine."

"Thanks. It'll be a sleepover since I'm working the night shift."

"Not a problem. We'll have a movie night."

My father clears his throat. "You haven't forgotten about yoga at the winery on Tuesday, have you?"

"No, Dad. I'll be there."

He cranes his neck from side to side. "Good, because there's no way I can do that stuff. I'll end up with a broken hip."

Laughter bubbles out of me. "You act like you're eighty."

"Some days I feel like it, Laney. But nonetheless, fifty-seven is still a risky age."

"I heard yoga-related injuries are on the rise too," Rhonan interjects sarcastically.

"Then how about you put on some spandex and join the fun?" my father chides.

Rhonan tsks as he shakes his head. "No can do. Sheriff duty calls."

My father glares at him. "How convenient."

"Oh stop, you two. You know if Mom were here, she'd make you both participate, video tape it, and then keep it for blackmail if need be."

My father's mouth spreads into a wistful smile. "Sounds about right." But as his smile fades, melancholy rests between us, reminding us of her absence even though we're all aware of it every minute of every day.

Even after all these years, grief still sneaks up on us when we least expect it. It's not sharp like it used to be, but it's always under the surface, flaring up in moments like this.

"Daddy?" Ellis comes back into the garage, still wearing her bike helmet.

"Yes, sweet pea?"

"Can I have cavities?"

My father and I share a look.

"Cavities?" I ask.

Rhonan sighs. "I made the mistake of telling her that candy gives her cavities, so now that's what she calls it." He clears his throat while walking up to his daughter. "Only two pieces."

"But I want five."

"Well, then you need to get back on the Elsa bike and try riding again."

"Bribery? Really?" I mutter out of the side of my mouth.

My father shoves his hands in his pockets while shrugging. "Until you've had kids, you can't judge, Laney. You and your brother would do some crazy things for sugar."

The dull ache that rests in my chest from the reminder that I'm nowhere near close to being a mom finds its way right to the center.

Fooling around with Fletcher might feel good in the moment, but it's not going to get me closer to the life that I want. Am I stupid for wasting time on him when I could be investing time in a man that I can actually see a future with?

I still haven't responded to his texts. Maybe I'm entirely too naïve to think that enjoying a physical relationship is going to help solve this lull I've found myself settling into.

Ellis tips her head back and groans. "Fine."

My brother turns to me, a pleased smile on his face. "See?" he mouths to me.

As I watch him attempt to get his daughter to ride her bike again without falling, I mentally go back through my schedule for the week.

Late client on Monday. Yoga at the winery on Tuesday. Wednesday is open because that's usually when Dilynne and I have dinner together. Late night at the salon again on Thursday. Babysitting Ellis for Rhonan on Friday. Bachelor party on Saturday for Elliot and Tori.

And that's when it hits me.

My whole life revolves around other people—what they need and how I can be of service to them.

Hazel is right.

I deserve a few orgasms, *especially* from a man who's eager to give them to me. And two weeks is not going to make or break my future. I just hope I can keep my feelings out of it.

# Chapter 15

**Fletcher**

### *A Bet, Yoga, and Drowning*

"Thank you so much. We hope to see you again soon!" Yvonne waves to the customer leaving as I walk through the front door to Blossom Beauty. Our eyes meet and her lips curl up into a knowing grin. "Well, if it isn't Lucifer himself. Are you here for another massage?" She wiggles her fingers in the air.

Chuckling, I reply, "As much as I'm tempted, I'm actually here to see your boss."

"Oooh. The plot thickens." Her eyebrows bounce up and down before motioning for me to follow her. "This way."

As we walk through the salon, several customers begin whispering. But right now, my only focus is getting to Laney and un-fucking this entire situation.

After two days of reaching out to her with no response, I knew the only way I would get her to talk to me would be to force her to.

And what better place to do it than her salon, where she can't escape without inviting questions, or where she's least likely to make a scene.

Yvonne knocks on the door to Laney's office at the end of the hall. "Boss?"

"I'm on the phone!" she calls back.

Yvonne turns to me. "There was a mistake with one of our orders and she's been on the phone all morning. Do you wanna wait?"

"Yup. I'm not going anywhere." Folding my arms, I lean against the wall.

Yvonne chuckles. "Good man." Leaning up against the door herself, she says, "You have a visitor. When you're done, they're out here waiting for you."

"Not sure how long I'll be," Laney calls back.

I lean in toward the door this time. "Don't worry. I've got *all* day."

Laney grows quiet on the other side.

"Fletcher?" she finally asks.

"Nope. It's Lucifer."

Yvonne snorts. "You two are perfect for each other." She slaps my shoulder and walks off, leaving me there to wait.

I'm not entirely sure what Yvonne knows about Friday night, but until I verify from Laney, I'm not going to assume anything.

Surprisingly, Laney doesn't keep me waiting long. After only ten minutes, the knob to her office turns and she appears, peering up at me with wide eyes through a crack in the door. "Um, hey."

"We need to talk."

The gap in the door gets smaller. "I'm kind of working, Fletcher."

"The salon is running just fine." I put my hand on the door, prepared to press it open with force. "Now, you can either let me inside on your own, or I'm going to push my way inside. But either way, I'm coming inside and we're talking. You decide how you want this to go."

She folds her lips between her teeth and slowly opens the door to let me through. "Good girl," I mutter before walking inside and waiting for her to shut the door behind me.

"Fletcher," she starts, but I cut her off, pressing my finger to her lips as I back her up against the door. Our bodies are pressed together, allowing me to feel every curve of her, curves that are even more tempting than they were when we were younger, and a body I got up close and intimate with the other night.

But wanting Laney is so much more beyond the physical. She's the only woman I've ever felt like I could be myself around, the only person that makes me want to bare my fucking soul, the only person who knows every part of me—the good and the ugly.

She's the one who got away, but she's not getting away from me this time—not when I know with each interaction how strong our connection still is. How, even though it's been twelve years, being around her makes me feel just as safe and secure as I did back then.

Now I just need to convince her to give us a chance, but I know I can't push that yet. Laney scares easily.

But Friday she let me touch her in a way I've never done before, so perhaps that's what I need to explore more first.

Laney's chest rises and falls with her rapid breaths and her pupils are dilated, making her otherwise bright green eyes appear darker. My cock grows painfully hard in just the few seconds we've been touching, and I don't even bother to hide it.

"It's my turn to talk, Laney Hart," I say, removing my hand from her lips. Her eyes grow wider before they drop to my mouth for a split second. "Friday night, you came all over my hand in a dark corner of a bar, and then you ran off."

She arches a brow at me. "Is that a problem?"

Technically, no. But I don't like the way we left things.

"Nope. No problem at all, except that you've been avoiding me the past two days." I drag my finger along her exposed collarbone, like I'm drawing a map across her skin.

Laney visibly swallows. "Well, I'm fine."

Narrowing my eyes at her, I feel her pulse fire rapidly under the skin along her neck. "I think you're lying. Tell me the truth."

"There's nothing you need to know," she fires back as she straightens her spine, her eyes fixated on my mouth.

"Really?" My eyes drop to her lips and the animalistic part of me I've been holding back comes out to play. "Well, how about we bet on it?"

Her gaze lifts to mine. "What?" she asks, her voice full of surprise.

"I bet I can make you come with my name on your lips in less than three minutes. And when I do, you're going to answer any question I ask."

*Jesus, Fletcher. Do you honestly think that was the correct thing to say at this moment?*

But instead of smacking me like I expect, she steels her gaze. "Is that so?"

"I wouldn't put it out there if I didn't know I could."

"And if you don't?"

"Then I'll back off. I won't push you to talk to me."

Some might call me crazy or insane, but I know what I feel between us. And if I can use this as a way to prove it to Laney so she can stop fucking denying it, then that's what I'm going to do.

Her jaw moves back and forth as she contemplates my challenge, but then she says something that shocks me and makes me snap at the same time. "Fine. Then prove it."

Smashing my lips to hers, I block out the rational part of my brain that's telling me I'm handling this situation all wrong and instead focus on letting out twelve years of pent-up need for this woman, consequences be damned.

If Laney truly didn't want me, she wouldn't have challenged me, she wouldn't have given me permission to make her come, and she sure as hell wouldn't be kissing me back the way that she is right now—passionately, obsessively, and full of fucking need.

*Well, that makes two of us, Laney Hart.*

I lift her by her hips and pin her to the door as her legs wrap around my waist. We claw at each other as I assault her mouth, controlling her tongue with my own. Her nails scrape through my hair like she can't get close enough. I spin us around, stalking toward her desk, shoving papers aside as I set her down and reach for the clasp on her slacks. She helps me strip them off, breathing fast.

"Now's the time to tell me if you don't want this, Laney," I grate out as our eyes lock. My hand moves straight toward her pussy, feeling the heat between her legs, finding her underwear soaked already. "But even if you did, I wouldn't believe you."

"Just shut up and make me come, Fletcher," she snaps, spreading her legs.

*Fuck me.*

I drop to my knees in front of her.

"You have no idea what you've just asked for," I say as I grip the sides of her thong and rip it in half. The gasp she lets out spurs me on as I lean forward and drag my tongue all the way through her soaking wet slit. "Are you going to set a timer, or shall I?"

She closes her eyes and drops her head back with a moan but doesn't respond. So, I reach into my pocket, take out my phone and set a timer for three minutes, setting it on the desk next to her before parting her pussy and sucking her clit between my teeth.

"Oh fuck," she groans as she buries one of her hands in my hair, the other braced behind her for support.

Time starts ticking, but I'm not even thinking about the constraint because tasting Laney's pussy is like taking a drink of water after trekking through the goddamn Sahara Desert—it's fueling me, replenishing something inside of me, reminding me why this woman caught my attention all those years ago and never left my mind, despite the distance between us.

"You're so fucking wet, Laney. You like the idea of me on my knees for you, don't you?"

"Yes," she says through a sigh.

"Do you realize how long I've wanted this?" Her head pops up and her eyes connect with mine. "While you've been hating me, all I've thought about is how to get you to see that I would gladly get on my knees for you to prove I'm not the asshole you think I am."

She blinks a few times. "Fletcher..."

I slide two of my fingers into my mouth to wet them, and then slowly push them inside her, curling them toward me as she gasps.

"Don't worry. I'm gonna make you come first, angel. But then we're going to fucking talk and you're going to realize that the last thing I could ever do is hate you back." Before she can say anything, I drop my mouth back down to her pussy and continue to build her up with my fingers and my tongue. "Fucking hell, you're drenched."

Her body bucks under my mouth. "Don't stop," she pants, hands trembling in my hair.

I peer up and see her head thrown back again, her eyes shut, her mouth agape, taking in short breaths as I bring out every drop of ecstasy that I can from her body. Her pussy tightens around my fingers as I flick her clit with my tongue and that's when I know she's close.

"Come on my fucking face, Laney. Give me every drop."

"Oh God." Her head pops up again as she watches me swirl my tongue in circles and flick her clit over and over until she screams, her orgasm slamming into her as her pussy tightens around my fingers. I quickly reach up and place my free hand over her mouth, quieting her because I'm sure the entire salon heard her just now. And when the last tremor rushes through her, I release her clit with a pop, extract my fingers from her pussy, and lick them clean as I stand up.

We just stay there, staring at each other until the chime of the timer on my phone goes off. Smirking, I reach over and turn it off. "Now, why have you been ignoring me?"

Laney closes her eyes and shakes her head. "We shouldn't have done that."

"I believe it was your idea."

She glares at me as she hops down from her desk and pulls her pants back up. "No, you brought it up, I just ..."

I close the distance between us again and cup her face. "You wanted me to make you come. You can admit it."

"Fine, I did. And I've been ignoring you because...Well? I enjoyed Friday night way too much, and I wasn't sure how to feel about that."

Irritation builds at my temples again, reminding me of the point I was going to make. "You know, you could have just responded to my messages to let me know that instead of leaving me on 'read.' I wasn't sure if I should send out a search party for you or assume it would be another three years before we spoke again."

"If you saw that I read your messages, then you knew I was fine."

"True, but why couldn't you just send something back?" I hate how desperate my voice sounds right now, but as I stand here and stare down into those hypnotizing eyes, my hand moves to her jaw before I stroke the skin right behind her ear. "Like thank you?" I drag my finger down the front of her throat now, loving how her breathing grows shallow each time I move my touch along her skin. "I'm still keeping count of those, you know."

"Not sure why."

"Because each one reminds me that you don't entirely hate me."

She sighs. "I don't hate you, Fletcher…"

I lean forward and press my lips to hers softly. As I retract, an idea comes to me. "Let me ask you something…"

"Okay…"

My voice comes out sounding like gravel, indicating the restraint I'm demonstrating right now. "Did you enjoy me touching you?"

"Yes," she admits on a whisper.

"Do you want me to do it again?"

Her tongue darts out to lick her lips. "I wouldn't be opposed to it."

"Then that's all we need to agree on right now."

When her eyes lift and lock on mine, something flashes in them that I instantly recognize—fear of rejection. And how do I know that? Because I am fairly certain that my eyes look the same.

But we don't need to have all the answers right now. I don't need to know everything that's going to happen next. Focusing on the fact that Laney wants me is enough fuel to keep me pushing forward while I figure out how the hell to make this woman a permanent fixture in my life.

"So, we agree this is just physical?" she asks timidly as her eyes darken.

"If that's what you want."

"Yeah, I mean…some decent sex would be nice for a change."

I thrust my hips against her pelvis, letting her feel how fucking hard I am. With my hand back on her jaw, I dip my head down so my lips are just an inch from hers. "Let me be clear about something, Laney Hart. Sex between us would be much more than *nice*. It would be carnal, sensual, and downright dirty. In fact, I'm pretty sure that fucking you would be a goddamn religious experience."

"Fletcher..."

Before I do exactly what I'm thinking, I change the subject. "Now, we have a bachelor party to plan, remember?"

Brows drawn together, she clears her throat, but her voice still cracks when she answers. "Um, yes. I'm aware..."

"Well, we should probably meet up tonight then."

Laney's eyes dart around the room, clearly thrown off by my change in topic. "I, uh...have a client at seven. I'll be home late."

"Tomorrow?"

She shakes her head. "I can't do tomorrow night either. We have yoga at the winery."

My jaw tightens as I fight off my irritation, but I know if push comes to shove, I can call some people in Charlotte, wave my credit card around, and get what we need in a few days' time. "Fine. Wednesday?"

Laney licks her lips. "Yeah, that will work. I'll have to postpone my dinner with Dilynne, but she'll understand."

"Okay." The corner of my mouth tips up as I chuckle, but I pull her flush against me, my hands gripping her hips possessively. "One more thing, though." Dipping my mouth to her ear, I wait a few seconds to speak, just listening to her breathing. "Laney, there's something you need to understand about what you just agreed to." I push my hand under her shirt against her back, letting the warmth of her skin soothe me while also making her shiver in response. "I might have agreed to make you come again, but I'm the one who gets to decide *when* and *where* that happens."

A groan leaves her lips as I drag her earlobe between my teeth, and then I release her and head for the door again. "Talk to you soon, angel."

Without a backwards glance, I exit the office and head for the front door.

"Leaving so soon?" Yvonne calls out to me as I walk past the receptionist's desk.

"My work here is done."

She snickers behind me. "You work fast."

Glancing over my shoulder, I say, "Nope. I just know that some things are worth waiting for." With a tip of my hat, I walk onto the sidewalk outside, even more determined to give this opportunity all I've got.

Laney might think she just wants sex, but I want much more than that. I want all of her.

And I'm not going to give up this fight until she wants that too.

***

"I can't believe you talked me into this," Henley mutters beside me.

I lean closer to him and lower my voice as we walk to the front entrance of Hart Winery. "What's the matter, Mr. Adventurous? You scared of a little yoga?"

"Yes, I am. What if I stretch the wrong way and tear my ball sack open?"

"I'm fairly certain that won't happen."

"How do you know?"

"Because we aren't going to be doing the fucking splits, Henley."

Footsteps sound behind us, and when I turn around, I find Elliot just a few feet behind us. "I'm not late, am I?"

"Nope."

Elliot takes in my gym clothes and Henley's athletic attire before staring down at his three-piece suit. "Why are you guys dressed like that? I thought we were gonna have some drinks and hang out?"

Henley shoots a look over at me. "You didn't tell him why we're at the winery tonight?"

Wrapping my arm around his shoulder, I continue to move us through the courtyard and that's when I see the realization on Elliot's face. "Oh fuck."

"We're still gonna have some drinks. We're just going to do yoga first."

Elliot glares at me. "I could kill you right now."

"Well, if you do that, then you won't have a best man."

Henley raises his hand in the air like a fucking kindergartener. "I volunteer as tribute."

"Not sure you're using that right, Henley," I say as I guide us to a spot on the grass near the front, but off to the side. I find three mats next to each other and drop my water bottle on one of them.

"I can't do yoga in a fucking suit, Fletcher." Elliot loosens the tie around his neck.

"Just do the best you can."

Henley groans. "First, you cock block me the other night, and now this?" He takes a step closer to me and lowers his voice. "If this interferes with my sex life too, we're going to have some words."

"Honestly, boys...this might help your sex life. Yoga increases your blood flow and flexibility."

"You sound like you're speaking from experience," Elliot replies, crossing his arms over his chest.

The truth is, I've done yoga throughout the course of my football career, but not consistently. Yoga fucking hurts. The first time I tried it, I thought I was having a heart attack because I couldn't breathe after just fifteen minutes.

So, the only reason I'm here tonight volunteering for this torture is to support Laney, and the winery, of course. Putting any significant length of time and space between us right now is the last thing I want to do. Plus, seeing Laney in spandex is icing on the cake.

"I'm not a professional by any means, but I promise, it's not that bad." *Lies, Fletcher. All lies.* Slapping both of my friends on the shoulder, I say, "I'm going to use the bathroom before it starts. Don't lose our spots."

Henley grumbles. "No promises."

As I cross the courtyard, more people filter in. But the one person I'm looking for is nowhere to be found.

"Fletcher?" George Hart turns a corner and almost runs into me.

"Hey, Mr. Hart."

He scoffs. "Please, call me George."

I shake my head. "Sorry, I can't do that. I've called you Mr. Hart since I was fourteen and the habit is ingrained."

Laughing, he shoves his hands in his khakis. "What are you doing here?"

I toss my thumb over my shoulder. "Yoga. I dragged Henley and Elliot along too. If Rhonan wasn't on shift, I'd have lied to get him here as well."

George chuckles. "I would have paid good money to see that. Seems you're still able to get the boys to go along with practically anything, huh?"

*Yeah, except for agreeing to lift a pact that we made when we were fourteen.*

Of course, I haven't exactly brought up the subject and won't until I know where Laney and I stand.

"I can be pretty persuasive," I reply, thinking about how giving Laney only one orgasm led to her wanting more. It wasn't the outcome I was looking for, but I'm taking advantage of the opportunity.

Hence why I'm here tonight—to remind her that there's more between us than just an intense physical connection. I mean, hell, I'm willing to endure fucking yoga for this woman. That has to count for something.

"Speaking of persuasion," I say, "there's something I wanted to speak to you about, sir."

"Me?"

"Yeah. It's actually related to the winery," I begin, knowing that part of my mission tonight involved a conversation with Laney's dad as well. But I don't get a chance to finish my thought because the woman I'm here to impress interrupts us.

"Dad? The sound system isn't working." Laney has her eyes on the clipboard in her hands as she walks toward us, oblivious that she's about to run into me.

So I decide to just let it happen.

"Oof!" Bouncing off my chest, she loses her balance and almost falls backward, but I catch her just in time, pulling her back into me.

*Smooth, I know.*

"Easy there, angel."

Staring up at me, it takes her a minute to register that I'm the one who caught her. But when she does, her eyes grow comically wide. "Fletcher? Wh—what are you doing here?"

"I'm here for yoga."

"What? Why?"

"Am I not allowed to do yoga?" I say, releasing her slowly to make sure she's not going to lose her footing again. Thankfully, she remains upright.

"He brought Henley and Elliot too," George adds, drawing Laney's gaze to him and then back to me.

"Really?"

I stick my hands in the pockets of my gym shorts. "I kind of didn't tell them what we were doing, so they're pretty pissed at me right now, but they'll get over it. I'll just let them beat me in a couple of hands of blackjack and all will be forgotten."

Her gaze moves between me and her father. "Okay. Well, I, uh…" Whether it's the yoga crowd or the fact that we discussed our... . arrangement yesterday, I can't tell. But she's flustered. And gorgeous.

George clears his throat. "I'm gonna go check on the sound system so we can get started, honey."

"Okay. Thanks, Dad," Laney says as she looks over at him and then back at me. "I guess I'll see you out there then?"

"Yup. Go easy on me, will ya?"

But she doesn't respond. As she walks away, my eyes trail her the entire time, fixated on her purple spandex-covered ass, of course.

George clears his throat again, alerting me to the fact that he hasn't left yet, which means he just watched our exchange. When our eyes meet, one of his brows lifts. "I see the way you look at my daughter hasn't changed at all."

I feel the blood drain from my face. "Sir?"

He takes a step closer to me. "I might be older now, Fletcher. But I'm not blind. Never was." Swallowing down the lump in my throat, I debate on how to respond. But then he winks and starts to walk off before I can speak.

Holy shit. Did Mr. Hart just admit that he knows and has known that I have feelings for his daughter?

And is that a good thing or a bad thing?

If I had his support, that might help Rhonan be more at ease with the idea too. But then again, was his statement more words of encouragement, or a warning to stay away from her?

"Mr. Hart?" I call after him before he gets too far.

"Yes, Fletcher?" he says when he turns around.

Hustling to catch up with him, I decide to follow through with my initial plan and test out the waters. "About that thing I wanted to talk to you about..."

***

"My elbow just popped. My fucking elbow!" Henley whisper-shouts at me from his mat where he fell into child's pose, or at least I think that's what he's supposed to be in. With a second glance, I confirm he's just in a contorted heap on his mat.

"If I rip the crotch on these slacks, you're paying for me to get them fixed," Elliot groans next as we transition into warrior pose. "Better yet, you're buying me a brand-new fucking suit, Adams."

"Shhhh!" the lady behind us hisses for the third time now.

I look over at Laney to find her eyes wide, telling us to shut up without actually saying the words.

"Motherfucker," I mumble through clenched teeth as my entire leg starts shaking.

Elliot growls. "Sweat just dripped down my ass crack, Fletcher. My fucking *ass crack*."

"And release," Laney says just as Elliot and I both crumble to our mats, joining Henley in a sweaty heap of tangled arms and legs. "Thank you everyone for joining us tonight. I hope you enjoyed yoga, and now let's celebrate with some wine!"

Murmurs of agreement filter through the crowd, and the lady behind us flashes us one more dirty look before heading for the main building.

With her water bottle in her hand, Laney walks up to us, but she's upside down since I'm still lying on the ground, fighting to catch my breath. "So, boys... What did you think?"

"I came up with three possible ways to get my revenge on Fletcher during that last pose, so it wasn't a total waste of time," Elliot replies.

Laney laughs. "Henley? You okay?"

"Why do people do that for fun?" he wheezes.

"Yoga has amazing benefits for the mind and body," Laney replies. "You don't have to do anything super crazy or strenuous to get a good workout."

"It's a good thing Tori is out of town for a few more days because there's no way I'd be able to fuck her after that," Elliot admits.

Laney rolls her eyes. "I think you'll survive, but I'll make sure to tell Tori that if you ever piss her off, yoga should be her go-to form of punishment."

Henley finally pushes himself up from his mat. "I need water, ibuprofen, and a shower."

Elliot rolls to his side and sits up too. "And a heating pad." When he stands, he glares at me one more time. "If you ever coerce me into doing that again, we aren't friends anymore. Understood?"

Staring up at him from my position on the ground, I reply, "You're the one who wanted me around more, remember? I mean, if I were in town more, we could do yoga every week."

Elliot taps his chin in thought. "I formally retract that request. You can take your yoga-loving ass back to Charlotte as soon as the wedding is over."

I bark out a laugh as Henley and Elliot walk away from the scene of their demise, leaving Laney and me alone.

"Were you trying to end two of your friendships tonight?" she asks, a smirk on her lips.

"They'll be fine."

Her smile falls and then she crouches down as I sit up, facing her now. "Why are you here, Fletcher?"

"Is it a problem that I am?"

"No, but..."

"Just trying to support you and the winery, Laney."

She glances around us for prying ears. "This wasn't part of our arrangement, though."

Irritated that she's irritated, I decide to push past my desire to argue with her and give her a piece of information that will appease her. Leaning closer to her, I say, "Well, men are visual creatures. Watching you bend your body in half for the past forty-five minutes was like me studying a playbook—now I know all of the different positions I can put you in to make you come."

Her cheeks are already red from the workout, but I don't miss the way they darken. "Oh."

"Yeah, oh." I push myself up from the ground and lift my shirt to wipe the sweat from my forehead. Laney's eyes drop to my abs as I do, locking onto my skin glistening with sweat. "Laney?"

She jumps, knowing she was just caught. "What?"

Chuckling to myself, I shake my head. "Nothing."

She sighs loudly. "I—I need to finish cleaning up and then I've got an early morning."

"All right. What time should I come over tomorrow night?"

"Oh, uh... Six should be good."

"Six it is." Taking a step closer to her, I lean down and line my lips up to her ear. "See you then, angel."

Letting out the breath she was holding, she takes a step back from me, blinking up at me slowly. "Good night, Fletcher."

I reach down to grab my water bottle, check my pocket for my keys, and start heading in the direction of the parking lot. I assume Henley left with Elliot, which is probably for the best since he might have tried to murder me while I drove us back to his place.

Feeling like I'm on cloud nine, I close my eyes and savor the feel of the breeze on my skin as the heat from today evaporates from the air. I made a point tonight by showing up here. It may have been subtle, but Laney needs subtle right now.

As I close in on my parking spot, the last person I expected to see locks eyes with me before I can pretend that I don't see him.

"Son."

"I'm busy, Dad." Increasing my pace, I head straight for the driver's side door to my truck, but I can hear his footsteps still behind me.

"Fletcher! Damn it, stop walking." The command of his voice instantly puts me on high alert. I know that tone. He's irritated, which can only mean one thing.

Spinning around to face him, I take in his sullen eyes and the pallor of his skin. "Let me guess. You need money?"

"I just need a few hundred to hold me over until payday."

Shaking my head, I contemplate what to do, but I also know that the quicker I decide, the faster I can get away from him.

I pull my wallet from my pocket, open it up, and take out all the cash I have on me. Tossing it at him, I watch it float to the ground. He doesn't bend down to get it at once though. He has more pride than that. "That's all I've got."

"Thank you."

Pointing a finger at him, I feel my jaw grow tighter. "Don't. Don't act like you're fucking grateful. You're just grateful that I keep feeding your habit."

He takes a step closer to me and lowers his voice. "One day, when you can't play anymore, you won't judge me like you do now. In fact, you'll probably join me..."

"I will *never* end up like you," I spit out.

"Never say never, son." He turns around and picks up the cash off the gravel, peering around us to make sure no one saw him, and then heads inside the entrance to the courtyard to get his fix before the winery closes. He must go home before he causes any problems. That must be the only logical explanation as to why they continue to serve him.

As I sit in my truck and stare out the front window, the two thorns of my life come at me from both sides—my unrelenting feelings for my best friend's little sister, and my alcoholic father.

Then the conversation with Elliot comes back to me, reminding me of how short life is. I'm tired of avoiding parts of mine because of my dad. I need to let shit go so I can move on.

I'm just not sure how I'm supposed to do that when every time I feel like I can breathe, he pulls me back underwater with him, leaving me fighting for air.

# Chapter 16

**Laney**

### *Party Planning and Asking for What I Need*

"When is the Wicked Witch of the West supposed to get here?"

Rolling my eyes, I check my phone on the table where we're seated in Blossom Brews. "She's only a few minutes late."

"Good to know she doesn't value your time. I mean, it's not like you're trying to run a business or anything." Dilynne purses her lips, clearly annoyed. "Maybe a house fell on top of her on her way here."

"You know, you don't have to stick around. I'm pretty sure *you're* the one who sat down on your own accord."

"Well, excuse me for wanting to check on my best friend when I saw her across the restaurant." Dilynne plants her hands on her hips. "If you hadn't canceled our dinner date tonight, then I wouldn't have even bothered to stop by. You'd have gotten a quick wave and then I'd be on my way."

"I'm sorry, but this is the only night I have free this week, and we've yet to make any concrete decisions regarding the party. It has to get done tonight."

"Yeah, you've been too busy letting Fletcher drag you into a dark hallway and have his way with you to plan a party, huh?" she whispers, and I'm very grateful she had the decency to do that.

After my phone call with Hazel on Sunday, I sauntered next door and filled in my best friend about what happened the night before while she was getting ready for her car show. And when I told her that I was considering propositioning Fletcher for a physical arrangement, she was more than supportive, even though I was still concerned about my lingering feelings.

Dilynne's advice was to focus on the physical feelings during the act and avoid kissing.

I'm still not sure I'm capable of that, but I'm damn sure going to try because I owe it to my vagina. She's been neglected for far too long.

"Oh, look who's here..." Dilynne turns toward the front door of the restaurant as Tori waltzes in, tossing her long blonde hair over her shoulder.

"Hi, Laney." Her voice is cheerful as she greets me. But when she turns to Dilynne, her smile falls, her eyes narrow, and one of her brows lifts. "Dilynne."

"Triple W," Dilynne fires back.

Tori's brows draw together. "What?"

"Dilynne was just leaving," I say as Tori's phone starts to ring.

She glances at the screen and sighs. "Ugh. Excuse me, I have to take this. Order me an iced tea, will you?" she asks. But as she walks away, she answers the phone, "Hey, baby."

Dilynne tilts her head to the side. "That was weird."

"What?"

"She seemed annoyed when she saw who was calling, but judging by how she answered, it was Elliot."

I process what she's saying. "Oh, uh…maybe she's talking to someone else?"

"Who else would she call 'baby' then?"

"A friend?" I say, growing more uneasy.

"One, I thought she didn't have any friends. And two, do you call your friends 'baby'?"

My shoulders fall as I suggest, "Maybe that's not what she said. Maybe we heard wrong."

Dilynne shakes her head, her brows still furrowed. "Nope. I'm pretty sure I heard her correctly."

As Tori approaches, I say quietly, "Look, I'm sure it's nothing. Now scram if you don't want to be around her anymore."

Dilynne glares at me. "I'm beginning to resent the fact that you agreed to this." She turns and walks right past Tori, the two of them glaring at each other in passing.

When Tori sees me again, though, her smile returns as she slides into the other side of the booth. "Sorry, work has just been insane."

"I bet you're looking forward to the honeymoon, huh?"

Tori nods. "You have no idea."

When the waiter stops by our table, we place our order and then get down to business. "Well, let me catch you up to speed on everything," I say, revisiting everything that Fletcher and I have taken care of so far. "Other than the favors and cake, I plan on getting my dress next week. There's a store in Charlotte that has a great selection and a tailor on-site if I need any adjustments. The flowers are confirmed for delivery on Saturday morning, the caterer has confirmed with the winery and will arrive an hour before the ceremony so the food is ready for the reception, and the photographer just needs you or Elliot to pay the remaining part of your deposit."

Tori sighs. "I really appreciate you, Laney. I hope you know that."

"Of course," I say, even though part of me is definitely ready for this obligation of mine to be over. I've already mentally prepared a speech to politely decline if someone else asks me to be their maid of honor. After this weekend, it's become abundantly clear that I haven't been putting myself first, and I'm determined to change that.

"Any last-minute requests for the party this Saturday?" I say, reaching for my water. "I know you and Elliot said you didn't care very much, but..."

Tori's eyes light up. "Oh, we should have an ice luge that you do shots out of! There was one at a frat party I went to in college, and it was a huge hit!"

*Where on earth am I going to order one of those?*

"I'll, uh, see what I can do."

"Perfect." Her phone rings again, but before she picks it up, I see the name flash across the screen. "Speaking of the groom," she says, rolling her eyes before answering, "Hey, baby."

*See? She called Elliot 'baby.' Dilynne must have misheard her earlier.*

"Oh, I'm at lunch with Laney. We're talking wedding details." A moment of silence while Elliot speaks on the other end of the call. "Elliot says hello."

"Hey," I reply back.

Tori laughs at something he said. "Well, I told her we should have an ice luge." She nods. "Elliot agrees it's a great idea."

I give her a thumbs up. "I've added it to the list."

After a few more minutes of sitting there, waiting for her to end the call, my phone chimes with a notification from my glucose app. Shit, I need to eat.

As if I summoned him, the waiter appears and delivers our food, but my phone chimes again, this time with a text.

**Fletcher:** *You'd better be reaching for food right now.*

**Me:** *Your supervision is unnecessary.*

**Fletcher:** *Think of it as taking care of you, not supervising.*

**Me:** *I told you, I can take care of myself.*

**Fletcher:** *If that were true, why did you agree to let me make you come again?*

His response makes a shiver run down my spine and my entire body grow hot. I glance up to see Tori still on the phone, so I continue to text.

**Me:** *I could retract my verbal consent, you know.*

**Fletcher:** *But that's not what you want.*

Damn him. He's right. In fact, all I've thought about today is his comment about knowing how flexible I am is giving him ideas for when he touches me again.

I snap a picture of my burger and fries instead.

**Me:** *There. Happy? This burger is about to be consumed.*

**Fletcher:** *Good girl. I can't wait to reward you later.*

Heat builds between my legs, but before I can respond, Tori ends her phone call.

"Elliot is working on his case right now, but he made us dinner reservations at this restaurant that I've been dying to try." She reaches for a fry on her plate and pops it into her mouth.

"How sweet."

She sighs. "He really is. He's always trying to make me happy, always asking what I need or want, always taking care of me in a way I didn't realize I wanted. I mean, a girl can't really ask for much more, can she?"

"No, she can't," I say. But even as the words leave my lips I can't help but wonder—will I ever find that too?

***

"You didn't have to do this, you know." Gesturing to the pizza boxes on my kitchen counter that are half empty now, I wipe my mouth with my napkin and then toss it onto my paper plate.

"What? Bring food?"

"Well, yeah."

"Do you not believe in dinner or something? Is that a new belief of yours you've developed since high school?" Fletcher grabs our plates and napkins, taking them to the trashcan. When he turns back around and leans against the kitchen counter facing my dining room table, he crosses his arms over his chest.

I mirror his position, leaning back in my chair. "Is only responding with sarcasm a thing that *you've* developed since high school?"

Fletcher's chest bounces as he silently laughs. "It was pizza, Laney. I was starving, and I can't think on an empty stomach. Sorry I was concerned about yours as well."

I roll my eyes, but inside my mind is at war.

When Fletcher arrived tonight, I had this fantasy of what would happen.

I would open the door, he'd take one look at me, and then pin me up against the wall, slamming his mouth to mine. He'd make me come on his hand again, and then on his tongue. And maybe, depending on how riled up I was, I'd let him take me to bed.

But that didn't happen. Not even close.

Instead, I opened the door to find Fletcher freshly showered, holding two pizza boxes, and a single serving of the red velvet cake from Bites & Bliss.

And he didn't bring just any pizza.

He brought my favorite: chicken alfredo with mushrooms and spinach, no onions.

Now I'm confused because two people in a friends-with-benefits situation shouldn't do things like that for each other, right?

"So, are you ready to plan this party?" he asks, bringing me back to the present.

"Um, yeah." Standing from my chair, I reach for my notepad on the counter, catching a whiff of his clean, freshly showered scent as I do. "Just so you know, Tori requested an ice luge at lunch today."

Fletcher huffs out a laugh. "Really?"

"Yeah. Apparently, they had one at a frat party she attended in college, and it was amazing," I say, attempting to impersonate her.

Fletcher shrugs. "I found them to be too fucking cold, honestly. My tongue got stuck to it."

"Well, I wouldn't know, but I told her that I would see what I can do."

Fletcher clears his throat. "Do you regret not going? To college, I mean."

His question makes my head snap to meet his eyes, and my heart starts pounding. The last thing I expected him to want to talk about was this. "Sometimes."

He nods. "Have you ever thought of going back?"

"I actually got my degree."

His eyes widen in surprise. "You did?"

Staring at the notepad, I start scribbling the title to the lists, one for him and one for me.

"Yeah, I did it online a few years ago."

"How come I never knew this? What is it in?"

"English," I reply. "I actually finished my last class on the ten-year anniversary of my mom's passing."

You can almost hear the silence resting between us. "She'd be so fucking proud of you, Laney."

When I lift my eyes to find Fletcher staring down at me, something passes between us, but I can't put a name to the feeling. "Thank you. I'd like to think so too."

"Just so you know, I'm still counting those thank-yous."

I roll my eyes and head back to my chair. "Let's get this done, shall we?"

He lets out a heavy breath and then makes his way over to the table, taking the seat next to mine. When our knees brush, I move away, but he pulls my knee back to his and rests his hand there.

My body temperature instantly rises.

Clearing my throat, I try to focus back on the reason we're here. "So, we have less than seventy-two hours until this party, and no concept of a plan. My dad said we can have it at the winery, which I think is better than the ski lodge. But we need a theme, food, decorations, games..."

Fletcher blows out a breath again. "Okay, let's do a Vegas theme..."

"Is that because you would have preferred to be there right now instead of here in Blossom Peak?"

The corner of his mouth lifts as his thumb rubs my kneecap, his eyes locked on mine. "Actually, I'm rather enjoying my time in Blossom Peak."

*Is he talking in general, or right at this moment, here with me?*

*It doesn't matter, Laney. Focus.*

"Oh. Okay, well Vegas would work," I continue, bypassing his comment while simultaneously trying to decipher it. "Elliot would love that."

Fletcher chuckles to himself before sitting up tall in his seat, his hand still on my leg. "That's what I'm thinking. We can have poker and blackjack tables, slot machines, and everything in black, gold, and red."

I drop my pen to my notepad. "Great ideas, but uh—how do you plan on getting all of this stuff by Saturday, Fletcher?"

His smirk grows. "You'd be surprised what you can get done when you know people and have a credit card with no limit, Laney."

I know his comment is meant to make me feel less stressed about the situation, but all it does is remind me of how different his life is now—how when he goes back to Charlotte after this wedding, that's the kind of reality he returns to.

*That's why you need to focus on the here and now, Laney. Stuff like that doesn't matter.*

I pick up my pen and finish my note. "Okay then. You're in charge of all of that, and I'll handle food and games."

"I told you, we can do poker—"

"We need something else too, not just cards." Tapping my chin with my pen, I think for a moment, but ultimately shake my head when the ideas don't come. "I'll think of something."

"Do you want me to get alcohol too?"

"Obviously we'll have wine, but I'm sure hard liquor and beer would be good to have too." I scribble the details of what we discussed and who is responsible for what in the two separate columns. "Anything else?"

"Does Rhonan still drink Pappy Van Winkle?" Fletcher asks, surprising me.

"Uh, I'm not sure. I haven't seen him drink bourbon in a long time. Although, after the other night, I'm sure he could use a glass."

"What happened the other night?"

I put my pen back down and lean back in my chair. "Sunday night we had dinner at his house with my dad, and he's trying to teach Ellis how to ride her bike without training wheels. Let's just say it's not going well."

Fletcher laughs. "I see. Well, I was thinking I could grab a bottle for us boys. I don't drink anymore, but…"

"Wait. You don't drink? Like ever?"

He shakes his head. "Nope. Haven't since I got drafted."

"But…why?"

The tilt of his head should alert me to the reason, but when his words follow, all they do is remind me of our history. "Come on, Laney. I'm sure you already know the answer to that question."

"You're not him, Fletcher."

"And I never will be." He stands from his chair, pushing a hand through his hair since he didn't wear his signature hat tonight. "I just didn't want to risk it." When he glances at the clock on the wall, he sighs. "It's getting late."

I didn't realize it's been almost two hours since he arrived, but that really shouldn't surprise me. Time always passed slowly when Fletcher and I talked years ago. Last week, I would have told you that being in his presence would have felt like being stuck in a time warp where everything slowed down, but honestly? Each time Fletcher and I have been together since he arrived in town has felt like it's slipped away in a blink of an eye.

Even our little rendezvous at the bar the other night and in my office on Monday wasn't long enough.

"Oh, yeah. It is." I take a picture of the list and send it to him. "There. Now you have a copy of what we agreed to."

"That wasn't necessary, but thank you." He moves for the front door, and as I watch him, I remember what he said yesterday.

The text messages. The flirting. Fletcher promised he'd touch me again, but it doesn't seem like that's going to happen anymore.

Disappointment builds in my chest—and even though I want to believe it's only because I've been thinking about him making me come again since it happened the last time in my office, the reality is that part of me doesn't want him to leave for other reasons—reasons I shouldn't be thinking about.

Before I can catch myself though, my libido takes the reins of my mind. "So that's it? You're just leaving?"

With his hand on the front door handle, he turns to look at me over his shoulder. "I mean, we have the details of the party decided. Is there something else we were supposed to do tonight?"

Our eyes lock, but after a few seconds, I break the stare. Shaking my head, I turn away from him. "Forget it."

Suddenly, he's at my side. His fingers wrap around my upper arm, his skin warm and his touch possessive, but not overly so. "Use your words, angel. You've got to tell me what you want. I'm not a damn mind reader."

Closing my eyes, I prepare to speak. "I—I thought you were going to make me..."

"Make you what?" His hot breath skates across the skin at my neck. "Come."

"You *thought*, or you *want*? Be clear, Laney."

*He's giving you the chance to speak up, Laney, just like you decided you were going to from now on.*

With much more conviction, I straighten my spine and say, "I—I want you to make me come, Fletcher. *Please*."

I can practically hear his smile. "Attagirl. Now let me take care of you, angel."

# Chapter 17

**Fletcher**

## *Job Offers and a Meatball Sub Full of Honesty*

I finish the last set of push-ups and then fall to the floor, waiting for the burn in my arms to subside. There's not much room to work out in this cabin, but I've been managing with the limited space.

Before I can fully recover, my phone rings on the coffee table next to me. It's Thursday morning, but as far as I can remember, I don't have anything going on. Last night at Laney's we finalized the details of the bachelor party, and then I pinned her up against her front door, stripped her shorts off, and made her come on my tongue again.

Fuck, I'm getting hard just from the memory.

Welcoming a distraction, I pick up my phone but hesitate when I don't recognize the number. The area code is from Blossom Peak though, so I answer more out of curiosity than anything.

"Hello?"

"Is this Fletcher?" A deep voice comes through the line, one that sounds familiar, but I can't place exactly.

"Who is this?"

"This is Principal Hastings," the man says. "But you probably remember me as Mr. Hastings, the history teacher."

I sit up from my spot on the floor. "No kidding. You're the principal now at the high school?"

When his laugh hits my ears, I'm brought back to the years I spent in his classroom, listening to the same sound as he cracked jokes, making history as entertaining as it could be. "I am. I'm surprised you didn't know that."

Pushing a hand through my sweat-soaked hair, I sigh. "It's hard to keep up with everything in Blossom Peak these days," I say, thinking back to Laney's revelation last night.

She finished her degree, just like she planned before her mom died, and I hate that I didn't know that—that I wasn't one of the people who got to cheer her on in that pursuit.

"I can imagine," Mr. Hastings says, pulling me back to the conversation. "I'm sure your life is exceptionally busy, but I heard you're in town. Is that correct?"

"I am."

"Well, I know this is short notice, but I was wondering if you'd have time to come down to the school and speak with me while you're here?"

I mentally debate what on earth he could want to talk about. "Anything I should be concerned about?"

"I'd rather talk more in person."

Glancing at the clock on the wall, I notice it's just after nine. "Today is the only day I would have time."

"Today would be perfect if that works for you. I'm at the school right now. Summer isn't really time off for the principal, you know?" He laughs.

"Can I meet you there in an hour?"

"Perfect. Just call when you arrive so I can let you in."

"Sounds good."

"Thanks, Fletcher. See ya soon."

After I shower and change my clothes, I stop by Bites & Bliss Bakery for a breakfast sandwich and coffee before making the drive over to the high school. Even though I drove by here last week, I haven't stepped foot on the campus since graduation.

As I lock up my truck and start walking toward the main building, the football field taunts me on my left. The smell of the freshly cut grass mixed with the humidity in the air brings back long practices during the same weather. The bleachers are empty, but I can still hear those hometown crowds cheering when I'd scored a touchdown. And the same scoreboard stands at the far end of the field, one that I looked up at so many times I lost count.

But that field holds some not-so-great memories as well, memories that I shove down with expert precision each time they try to crawl their way to the surface.

Mr. Hastings opens the front door to the main building as I approach.

"Fletcher Adams...Blossom Peak's own bona fide celebrity." I step through the door and wait for him to lock it behind me.

"I'm still a regular guy."

As I follow him down the same halls I once walked through as a student, eerie familiarity creeps up my limbs. When we arrive at the principal's office—the same one Principal Bell had back when I went to school here—we both take a seat in our respective chairs across from each other at his desk.

"So, how can I help you, Mr.—" I stop myself. "Principal Hastings."

He acknowledges my correction with a nod. "Well, I've been watching your career, as you can imagine."

"I appreciate the support. Thank you." Lacing my hands together, I rest them in my lap.

"Of course. So how much longer do you think you have left in the game?"

If I had a dollar for every time I've been asked this question recently, I could probably retire a year early.

The truth is, when it comes to the NFL, I'm getting toward the age where I'm practically considered ancient. Ten years in the league is a long time, but very long for a wide receiver, with an average career length of just under three years.

"Taking it season by season at this point, sir."

He nods. "Have you thought about what you might do when you're ready to hang up the cleats?"

"A little bit, but I'm just not done yet. Why? What's up?" My nerves are humming under my skin right now.

"Well, I was wondering if you've thought about coaching," he says, clearing his throat as he shifts in his seat.

"Oh. Well, uh..." I rub the back of my neck. "I honestly don't know." But then something dawns on me. "Wait. My dad is the coach. Are you saying..."

"Think of what a full circle moment it would be to have the two of you coaching together, or you even taking over for him one day. I mean, Blossom Peak having two back-to-back NFL stars as coaches would be pretty spectacular."

Nausea swirls in my gut over the idea of working alongside my dad. I mean, it was bad enough being his player and son. But trying to be his colleague? Expecting him to respect me as an equal? I think pigs would fly before that would happen.

"Look, I appreciate the offer, Principal Hastings, but..."

He holds his palm out toward me, cutting me off. "Just think about it, okay? There's been a few...complaints," he says with an arch of his brow, "about the coaching staff and I'm just trying to be proactive and look out for the program."

"Complaints?"

He nods but says nothing more.

Is he alluding to my father? Has he put his hands on another kid? If so, I'd beat the shit out of him myself, consequences be damned.

Luckily, his cell phone rings on his desk before I can spiral too far. "Uh, I'm sorry, Fletcher, but I need to take this."

"Yeah, no problem." Standing from my chair, I reach out to shake his hand. "Thanks for the offer."

"It would be an honor to have you. Keep me in the loop on your career decisions, will ya?"

"Sure thing."

But as I head back out to my truck and glance at the football field once more, this uncertainty builds in my chest.

I know I want Laney. That much has become clear to me since I returned.

But do I want Blossom Peak too?

Her life is here, and mine...isn't.

My job, my house, my other friends and teammates—they're all in Charlotte. But once my career is over, does that mean I'll leave Charlotte too?

Could I see a life back here with Laney?

But that would mean a life with my dad in it again too.

***

"At least some things haven't changed around here," I say as I lift my meatball sub to my mouth and take another bite. The Happy Belly Deli is a staple in Blossom Peak, and when Rhonan called to see if I wanted to grab lunch with him, he didn't even have to finish his thought when he mentioned sandwiches.

"Trust me, the locals would riot if Riley changed anything." Rhonan says, taking a sip from his drink.

"The seasonal menu is new though."

"Yeah, and he's had some winners on there too. But nothing beats the meatball sub."

Homemade meatballs and sauce, with thick slices of provolone cheese melted to bubbly perfection on toasted garlic, parmesan, and rosemary bread—this meatball sub would even make Joey from *Friends* weep with happiness.

"Agreed." I take another bite, savoring this meal because I'm not sure when I'll have it next, and I'm starving after signing autographs and taking pictures for a while after we first arrived.

For a moment, I debate bringing up the meeting with Principal Hastings, but decide against it. I don't want to cause rumors or false hope when I don't even know how I feel about his offer just yet. "So, how's bike riding with no training wheels going?"

Rhonan flashes me a deadpan gaze mid-chew. "I didn't realize there were multiple versions of hell until I became a parent."

My chest shakes with laughter. "Aw, come on. It can't be that bad."

"All I know is that my daughter's stubbornness will either be her greatest strength, or her doom. I thought maybe since it was her idea, she'd be more proactive about it, but she won't even touch her bike after this past Sunday when Laney and my dad were over."

"Laney was the one that told me about the whole ordeal."

Rhonan shrugs. "I figured. Speaking of my sister, how is she handling everything?"

*Oh, she's thriving. Your sister seems to be very fond of the orgasms I've been giving her.*

"It doesn't seem to be fazing her at all," I reply instead, knowing he's referring to the wedding planning. "And by the way, she wasn't too pleased with you and Henley telling me about Spencer."

"She can be mad all she wants, but someone has to look out for her."

"I agree. She seems to always be doing things for other people, but not herself."

"She takes after my mom in that regard." Rhonan lets out a sigh, dropping his eyes to the table. "Fuck."

"What's up?"

He shakes his head, clearly debating what to say as he glances to either side of us and then lowers his voice. "I don't mean to be a downer, but sometimes I just feel like Laney and I are so fucked up from losing our mom that our lives will never be normal."

My brow furrows. "That's a strong statement..."

Sighing, he picks up his drink. "You know how when we were kids, and every cut or scrape left a scar? Visible proof that something hurt."

"Yeah..."

"Well, those scars were on the outside as physical reminders of pain we felt. But the older I get, the more I feel like I'm collecting scars on the inside, Fletcher." He pauses, pushing his tray aside. "I lost my mom at twenty, so I ran off and joined the Marines to avoid it. Well, then I lost my fellow marines in combat. But when I came home after meeting Sarah, I thought she was my gift for all the loss I'd experienced in such a short time. Yet lo and behold, I fucking lost her too." He shakes his head. "If it weren't for Ellis, I'm not sure where I'd be right now."

"Fuck, Rhonan."

He blows out a breath. "Sorry to unload on you, but I guess Elliot's wedding is just bringing shit up for me."

"You know you can always be real with me."

He nods. "Yeah. Just be glad your life's been easy for the most part."

Defensiveness rushes through me. Tilting my head to the side, I say, "You think my life has been easy?"

"You know what I mean..."

"No, I don't. Please elaborate."

A heavy sigh leaves his lips. "Look, I just meant you haven't loved and lost like I have." He waves a hand up and down in my direction. "You've never even had a serious relationship, right?"

He's correct, but that's only because the one person I ever wanted that with never got a chance to hear that from me.

"And you like it that way—unattached and easygoing. So hopefully, you never do have to feel what it's like to lose someone you love."

Little does he know that I already have—his sister.

I huff out a laugh as I ball up my napkin and toss it on my tray. "Not that it's any of your business, but I've gone through shit that you don't even fucking know about, Rhonan."

"Like what?"

"It doesn't matter since, apparently, I'm shallow and you're the only one with real problems, right?"

"Fletcher..."

"No, this is good. I'm so glad that I know what you think of me now," I grate out.

"Fletcher, come on. I'm sorry," he says, making me pause before I stand up and walk out. My blood is pumping furiously and my jaw fucking hurts from how hard I'm grinding my teeth together.

Maybe I should tell him how I feel about his sister right now. Maybe I should tell him that she's the one who helped me when my dad threw his fists at my body. That without her, I might not even fucking be alive right now.

Rhonan continues. "I didn't mean it like that, man. Honestly, I fucking envy you."

That was the last thing I expected him to say. "You do?"

"Yeah. You made your dreams come true, you get to play a game that you love for a living, you don't have to worry about anyone else's happiness, and you don't have ghosts haunting you at every turn."

"People don't have to be dead to haunt you," I say without thinking.

He tilts his head. "What do you mean?"

Shaking off my comment because this is the last place I want to get into the details of my life that Rhonan doesn't know, I push my tray to the side as well. "Nothing, but I get what you're saying, man. Our lives are different, but did it ever occur to you that I might be jealous of what *you* have?"

He looks stunned. "Really?"

"Yeah. I mean, I know I'm the one that wanted this job and the fame that goes with it, but sometimes I wonder what it would be like to go out in public and not be recognized, to live in a quiet town and have a schedule that revolves around my family, not dodging paparazzi and fake people.."

"Well, shit." He sits back in his chair, soaking in my revelation. "Is this a new development?"

"Let's just say you're not the only one who is being affected by Elliot's wedding." Standing from my chair, I toss a couple of twenties on the table. "Looks like even after eighteen years of friendship, I can still surprise you."

Rhonan stands as well. "I think the only thing you could say to me that would really surprise me is that you'd be the next one of us to get married."

"Really? Even over Henley?"

Rhonan laughs. "I'd bet on Henley getting someone knocked up before you or Elliot with the way that guy fucks every woman within a 20-mile radius."

I lift my shoulders as I shove them in my pockets. "You're not wrong about that."

"But I don't see him getting married. Not with what his childhood was like."

What he forgets is that Henley and I both lived through shit as kids. Elliot had his share too. Trauma doesn't wait for adulthood—scars are formed no matter what age you are.

"Never say never, Rhonan."

We leave the deli and head back out to our cars. "Yeah, I guess I shouldn't assume what the future holds, right?"

"Yeah, because life can take you by surprise."

I might be speaking from my own experience, but it couldn't be truer than what I've gone through in the past week and a half.

I came back to Blossom Peak as one man, but I'm hoping to leave as another.

And after today, I'm starting to realize—my biggest challenge won't be changing my own future. It'll be convincing the people I love that this change is a good thing, not a threat to the friendship we've spent years building.

# Chapter 18

**Laney**

### *A Run-In and a Haircut*

"You got it, Laney," Justin says as he finishes scribbling down my order for the party.

"Do you think that will be enough?"

"I mean, you *are* feeding Henley, Rhonan, Elliot, and Fletcher, plus more. But you've ordered enough food for a small army, so I think you'll be all right," he teases.

"Okay." I sigh in relief and hand him my credit card. Blossom Brews only has a few customers right now because they just opened.

It's Thursday morning and I left the salon to come over here and place the order for the food for the bachelor and bachelorette party on Saturday.

"Do you ever eat at home?"

Dilynne's voice makes me jump. My hand flies to the center of my chest as she takes a seat at the stool next to where I'm standing at the bar. "Jesus Christ! You scared the shit out of me."

Laughing, she pulls her phone from her pocket, checks it briefly, and then slides it back into place. "Well, I hope you have an extra pair of pants on you, then."

Rolling my eyes, I inhale deeply, trying to get my heart rate back under control. "To answer your question, yes, I eat at home. I'm here to order the food for Saturday."

Dilynne nods in understanding. "Nice. The boys will like that."

"That's what Fletcher and I thought."

"Speaking of Lucifer, how are things going there? Any more magical spells from the talented man?" she asks, using her euphemism for orgasm that she thought was clever, so I humored her.

"Oh, um…" I can feel my cheeks turning pink. "Yes, there have been a few."

"And are you enjoying yourself?"

Tucking my hair behind my ear, I say, "Immensely."

Dilynne slaps me on the back a little too forcefully. "I'm proud of you. How does it feel taking what you need and not worrying about the implications?"

I wish I could say that I've been able to do that, but the truth of the matter is that last night when Fletcher was at my house, I felt way too many feelings. His gesture of bringing me my favorite pizza and that cake from the bakery, his comment about me finishing my degree, and then him admitting that he hasn't touched alcohol since he was drafted brought up way too many emotions.

The orgasms he gave me before he left helped remind me of what we agreed to, but I think I was naïve to think that I would be able to shut off everything that man makes me feel.

"Well, I definitely don't feel as tense."

Dilynne laughs. "Yeah, that's what a few orgasms will do for you. So, you guys have everything ready for the party? Not gonna lie, I'm dreading it a little bit."

"Why?" She gives me a flat look because I should already know the answer. Choosing to redirect, I say, "Anyway...I'm in charge of food and games. We're doing a Vegas theme with blackjack and poker tables, but I feel like that's more for the guys. The women need something too, you know?"

Dilynne taps her chin in thought before her whole face lights up. "Oh my God. I have a brilliant idea!"

"Really? What?"

Rubbing her palms together, she shakes her head at me. "Nope, I want this one to be a surprise."

"Dear God. That means it's probably going to make me question our friendship, doesn't it?"

She nods slowly. "Yup, but I guarantee the girls will get a kick out of it."

I press the heel of my hand to my forehead. "I don't know whether to just let this happen or fight it."

"Even if you fight me, you know you won't win."

"This is true." The sound of my glucose monitoring app interrupts our conversation. My blood sugar is low, so I need to eat something. But within a matter of seconds, my phone dings with a text.

**Fletcher:** *You'd better be reaching for food as I type this.*

Rolling my eyes, I pick up my phone to text him back.

"Who're you talking to?" Dilynne asks.

"It's Fletcher. Remember how I said he added himself to my account to get notified about my blood sugar?"

Dilynne chuckles. "Jesus. You sure Fletcher agreed to just orgasms?"

I ignore her insinuation and text him back.

**Me:** *I have a muffin waiting for me in the car.*

**Fletcher:** *I wish I was eating your muffin right now.*

"Oh my God."

"What?" Dilynne turns her head to read my text, her lips scrunching up as she does. "Aw, come on, Adams. You can do better than that."

I turn my back to her to type my response.

**Me:** *Dilynne says you can do better than that.*

**Fletcher:** *So Dilynne knows about us?*

**Me:** *She does. She was asking about what happened at the bar, so I told her. She is my best friend, you know...*

**Fletcher:** *It's fine. But I have a request for you...*

**Me:** *Okay.*

**Fletcher:** *Next time I see you, you'd better not be wearing any underwear. That way I can taste you even faster.*

Dilynne smacks the counter beside me. "Hot damn! Now that was much better, Adams." She slow claps. "Much better."

"You were still reading my texts?" I say, pulling my phone against my chest while my body hums from Fletcher's words.

"Girl, I could have stripped down until I was butt-ass naked and you probably wouldn't have noticed with how engrossed you were in your phone just now."

I roll my eyes just as Justin comes back over with my receipt, sliding it across the bar for me to sign. I do so, then slide it back to him, grateful for the distraction from Fletcher's words and my best friend's over exaggeration.

"Here's your order, Dilynne." He places a paper bag on the counter in front of her.

"Thanks."

"And you were giving me shit about not eating at home," I mutter to her out of the corner of my mouth. She sticks her tongue out at me.

Justin moves my copy of the order receipt to me. "Okay, everything is set for Saturday. Delivery will be at seven, as requested."

"You're the best, Justin. Thanks again for doing this on such short notice."

"My pleasure. Anything for you," he says, smiling. "Our dads were great friends, and I know he'd want me to make sure that we keep that tradition." Justin's dad passed away a few years ago, so he knows what it feels like to lose a parent, something we've bonded over since then.

I reach across the bar and place my hand on top of his. "I think our dads would too." He walks off just as Dilynne hums beside me. "What?"

She stands from her seat, grabbing the handles on her bag of food. "Perhaps when this thing with Fletcher is over, you could give Justin a call."

"Come again?"

Bopping me on the nose, she avoids answering me. "I've got to get back to the garage. Call me later if you need me."

I watch her leave and before I can do the same, a familiar voice calls to me from my back. "Laney?"

Spinning my head in that direction, my body instantly goes on high alert when I see who it is.

"Mr. Adams," I say, my stomach turning. I haven't seen Fletcher's dad in ages, mostly by design. Just being near him reminds me of what he did to Fletcher, and that memory alone makes me sick.

"Long time no see."

"Yes, it has been a while," I say as the smell of alcohol on his breath hits me.

"I take it you've seen my son since he arrived in town?"

"I have," I reply, silently wondering why he would bring Fletcher up. Did he see us together? Does he know that I know about their past?

"Funny how he couldn't even be bothered to tell his old man he was coming home, huh?"

"Well, it's only for the wedding," I say, hoping to remain as neutral as possible.

He nods. "Oh yes, Elliot's wedding. Glad to be invited," he says, the disdain in his voice dissipating. "Can't deny I'm surprised by how quickly the whole thing transpired, but..." Shrugging, he doesn't finish his thought.

"They're in love. When people feel that way, sometimes they don't want to wait to get married."

Luke scoffs. "Well, if my son knows what's good for him, he'll avoid the mess of marriage."

My pulse spikes. "Why do you say that?"

"Well, after what happened with me and his mom, and how dedicated he is to football, he'd be smart never to let a woman get in the way."

Fear builds in my chest, even though it shouldn't. Fletcher's future isn't my concern, but I can't deny that Luke strikes a chord because I've heard his son say himself that he's not interested in that kind of life.

But listening to Fletcher's dad right now—the snark in his voice, the resentment and animosity—it makes me wonder if he'll ever be able to let go of the past. Can any of us, really?

*Are you wondering about Luke, Fletcher, or yourself?*

Choking down my emotions, I take a step back from him and prepare to leave. "It was good to see you, Mr. Adams."

He reaches for the beer Justin just poured him, lifting it to his lips before saying, "You too, Laney. See you next week at the wedding."

As I leave the restaurant and return to the salon, a heaviness comes over me. I shouldn't be so affected by the words Luke spat, but I can't deny that they did make me stew on the situation I'm in with his son for the thousandth time.

*Just focus on you, Laney. That's what you're trying to do now, right? You don't have to help everyone.*

But what if there are some people you can't help but want to be there for, even if you know you're only going to get hurt in the end?

***

It's just after seven when my last client leaves and I lock the salon door behind her. All my employees left hours ago, but now that my workday is over, I can get a few business things done without any distractions or people in the way. So, color me surprised when I get a text from Fletcher while sitting at my desk in my office.

**Fletcher:** *Laney, open up.*

**Me:** *I'm not at home.*

**Fletcher:** *I know. I'm at the salon.*

Confused, I head to the front door and see Fletcher standing there, craning his neck back and forth as if it's bothering him.

"What are you doing here, Fletcher?" I ask curiously, cracking the door just enough to talk through it.

"Can I come in?"

"Um, we're closed."

"Come on. It's me, Laney."

I momentarily contemplate standing firm in my need to put a bit of distance between us, but when I take in his appearance, I decide against it.

Fletcher looks agitated and almost defeated. He has bags under his eyes, and his hair is a mess, probably from running his hands through it.

Sighing, I relent to that part of me that will always hold a soft spot for him. "Fine, but I'm working."

"Alone?" he asks as he steps through the door and I lock it again behind him. The blinds are closed, so the salon is much darker than it usually is, emphasizing the shadows on his face.

"Yes. I had a late client, and now I'm just trying to take care of some paperwork."

"Need any help?"

I arch a brow at him. "Are you bored or something?"

"Kinda," he says through a laugh, but then his smile transforms into a frown. "Honestly, I just needed to get out of my cabin."

"Okay, well, feel free to hang out, I guess..."

"Thanks."

Fletcher moves further into the salon, scouring the shelves of products that are stationed in the waiting area. "So, how was your day?" he asks before I can head back to my office.

I spin to face him, less eager to return to my work than I was before. "It was good. Long, but I did get the food ordered for the party." Momentarily, I debate telling him about my run-in with his father, but I decide against it, given his mood. "I also commissioned Dilynne to help us with games. Not so sure that was a good idea."

Fletcher nods as he continues to look through the shelves. "Nice. I made some calls for the decorations and such. Everything is set to be delivered to the winery Saturday morning."

"Great."

"I had lunch with your brother today too."

My shoulders instantly tense up. "Okay..."

Fletcher turns his head so our eyes meet. "Don't worry, I didn't say anything about us, obviously."

"I didn't think you would. That would be asking for him to pull his gun on you."

Fletcher laughs. "I honestly don't think he would have believed me even if I did tell him."

"Why's that?"

Fletcher pushes a hand through his hair. "It's not important."

I can tell he wanted to say something else, but he caught himself. He closes the distance between us before shoving his hands in his pockets, looking almost nervously at me, but his smirk appears before he talks. "Do you have plans tomorrow night?"

I'm momentarily stunned. Is he asking because he wants to hang out? Or is it about our arrangement?

"Um, I do actually." Tucking my hair behind my ear, I continue, "I'm watching Ellis for Rhonan. Joanne needed the night off."

Disappointment registers on his face as his smirk turns into a frown. "Oh. Okay, no biggie." His heavy sigh rests in the space between us as he walks over to my station and takes a seat in the chair, spreading his legs out wide, reminding me of how massive of a man he is. His muscular legs are on display under the hem of his khaki shorts, his arms full of sinew rest on the arms of the chair, and his massive hands clasp together as he hunches forward, bracing his forearms on his knees and holding his head in his hands.

It's been a long time since I've seen him like this—so up in his head, defeated and irritated. And that's when it dawns on me. "What did he do this time?"

His head pops up and his eyes connect with mine, but he's silent for a few moments. Finally, he exhales and drops his head down again. "How did you know?"

I move closer to him so I can look at him in the mirror in front of my chair. "There's only one person that makes you act like this. So, what happened, Fletcher?"

He leans back in the chair, meeting my gaze in the mirror. "I got a call from the high school principal today. He offered me a coaching job when I retire, and he was curious if I'd decided when that might be."

My brows lift. "Wow that's...wait..."

Fletcher huffs out a laugh. "Yeah, that means replacing my dad. Apparently, they've had some complaints from parents, but Principal Hastings didn't elaborate on what they were."

"Do you think..." I can't finish the thought because I don't want to assume the worst.

"I don't think my father is stupid enough to put his hands on another kid, but maybe he's been out of it during practice or games," he says, alluding to his substance problem. "He knows better than to drink on the job since that's how he lost his last one, but the other night..."

Without thinking, I place my hand on his shoulder. "What happened?"

Fletcher blows out a breath. "You know what? Never mind. I shouldn't be bothering you with this shit." He moves to stand, but I push him back down as best as I can. Our size difference is significant, but Fletcher humors me.

"You can talk to me, Fletcher."

"But I shouldn't. You don't need another thing or person to worry about. You have enough on your plate. And it goes against our arrangement, right?"

I move around the chair so that I can face him, crossing my arms over my chest. "Then why did you come here? Why not talk to Rhonan about it?"

His blue eyes lock on mine, and suddenly I'm transported back to when we were teenagers all over again, waiting on bated breath for what he'll say next.

"Because you were the only person I wanted to see." His answer is candid, honest, and my heart thumps in a way it shouldn't as we stare at each other. Silence rests between us as he pushes a hand through his hair again, pulling on the strands this time so they stand up as best as they can, given how thick his tresses are. Glancing up as if he can see the top of his head, he groans. "God, I need a fucking haircut."

Popping my shoulder, I say, "I wasn't going to say anything, but now that you brought it up..."

The corner of his mouth lifts. "Good thing I have a friend who knows how to cut hair, huh?"

"We're not friends, Fletcher, remember?"

"Keep telling yourself that."

I roll my eyes, but there's a smile on my lips. "Seems like you're the one that's in denial." I start to move, but Fletcher reaches out and grabs my wrist.

"Laney..."

Our eyes meet. "Yeah?"

I wait for what he'll say next as my skin breaks out in goosebumps. The truth is, I can't deny how being around him again has made me feel, especially after our interactions over the past few days. And seeing him like this now pulls on those same heartstrings I thought I had severed.

I'm still going to try to deny it, though.

His voice has a broken rasp to it when he speaks again. "Could you cut my hair, please?"

"Now?"

"I mean, why not? It won't take long, right?" He smirks up at me. "I'll even give you a big tip."

I raise both brows. "Is that code for something sexual?"

He laughs. "I mean, if you want it to be."

I take my arm back and reach for my scissors. "Boys never truly grow up, do they?" Our eyes meet in the mirror in front of us as I lay out my clippers, scissors, and straight razor on my rolling table, reaching for an apron to wrap around his neck.

Ten minutes ago, I was intent on finishing up my paperwork and getting home to relax before another long day tomorrow.

But suddenly, a burst of energy flows through me, part nerves from the idea of cutting Fletcher's hair—something I've never done, but can't deny having thought about.

"In some ways, no," he says, answering my question. "In others though, we change so much that it scares the ever-living shit out of us."

I button the apron and smooth it out over his chest and shoulders. "What do you mean?"

He grabs my hand from over his shoulder, stroking the top of it with his thumb before pulling me back around to face him head-on. "Like when we realize how foolish we've been. How one decision can change the entire direction of our lives, but we have to be brave enough to try to fix it."

The lump in my throat grows. "Oh."

He reaches out and toys with the necklace lying against my collar-bone. "This was your mom's, wasn't it?" Fletcher's fingers pass over the pink diamond stone in the necklace I put on the other day after seeing the woman at Dilynne's garage with the same one my mother had. I usually only wear this necklace on special occasions, but a part of me felt like I needed her with me recently, especially after that day, and I have a feeling I know why.

"You—you remember that?"

"I remember a lot of things, Laney." His head tilts to the side as he runs the chain between his fingers. "She loved pink diamonds."

"She did." Our eyes remain locked before I shake myself out of the moment, take a step back, and plug in the clippers. "So, how short are you wanting?"

His hand passes through his hair again. "Whatever you think would look good for the wedding."

"It's your hair, Fletcher."

"And you're the expert. I trust you."

Opting for a shorter look on the sides and slightly longer length on top, I get to work, concentrating a little too hard but hard enough that I can convince Fletcher that I can't talk and work at the same time. But then he drops a verbal bomb.

"I've been giving my dad money for the past few years now."

My stomach drops and the clippers go still in my hand as I lift my gaze to the mirror. "Why?"

"I wish I could tell you, but I ask myself the same thing every time, Laney."

My hands drop to my sides. "But after everything he did to you..."

His head spins in my direction. "You think I don't know that it's fucked up? That I give money to the man that used to hit me and bruise my body?"

"I'm not judging you, Fletcher," I say softly. "I just... What about his job?"

His brow arches. "I'll let you guess where his paychecks go."

"Alcohol," I answer instantly.

He snaps his fingers. "Bingo."

It's like pieces of the puzzle are all starting to fall into place. While I've been happy that Fletcher hasn't been around, I failed to consider that he's been avoiding his own past by not coming back to Blossom Peak nearly as often as he could.

"He's why you rarely come home, huh?"

God, my heart hurts just looking at him right now. He's that same boy I wanted to protect more than anything, yet he's a grown man and still fighting a battle with the demons of his past.

"You're the only person who knows, Laney."

"Even after all this time?"

His chin dips in a curt nod. "Yes. That's why I didn't go to talk to Rhonan, or Elliot, or Henley. And I'd like for it to stay that way, please."

I turn the clippers on to get back to work. "Of course."

Both of us go silent for a while as I buzz the sides of his hair. When I turn the clippers off, his voice makes me jump. "You know, there's something I've been wondering for a while now."

I look up to find him staring at me. "Be careful. Thinking too hard might hurt you."

He moves to pinch my ribs, and I barely dodge him. "Easy on the sass, woman."

"Never." Smirking, I move his head back in place and continue cutting his hair.

"I was wondering... Why did you open this salon?"

Shrugging, I reply, "Does it matter?"

"It matters to me. I remember you telling me that you wanted to be an author or teacher back in the day. I know you mentioned the salon too, but what made you land on that?"

"Everything," I admit on a whisper. Fletcher keeps his eyes on me until I start talking again. "Honestly, it was Dilynne. She always teased me for being a girly girl while she was a classic tomboy. After my mom died and I decided not to go to Florida State, she and I were talking about what we were going to do with our lives. She'd always mentioned owning her own auto shop and jokingly suggested that I could own a beauty salon right next door. Our businesses would be complete opposites like us, but we could support each other too, like offering manicures while customers get oil changes—stuff like that. A few Smirnoff Ices later, I had a business name, a plan, and something new to work toward, so I focused on that and made shit happen. It took longer than I wanted because I had to help my dad with the winery, but I'm proud of it."

"Well, this place is incredible. You can tell that you've created something special here."

"Thank you."

"Did you ever start writing your book, though?"

"No. It felt silly to bother with that after everything. I needed to be realistic, find a way to support myself with a stable income, so I got busy and I just kind of forgot about it."

"Well, I didn't."

Our eyes meet in the mirror again, talking to one another without saying anything.

*You could still do it*, he says.

*What's the point*, I reply.

*It was your dream*, he fires back.

*Not all dreams are meant to come true.*

I focus my attention back on his hair, finishing the edges with the clippers, then begin to trim the top and put product through it.

Fletcher lets out a moan as I weave my fingers through his hair. "Fuck, that feels good."

"I'm just tousling it."

He closes his eyes. "It might feel like nothing special, but there's just something about having your hands move through my hair that's doing something to me." He visibly shudders. "Fuck, you gotta stop that."

I laugh. "Why?"

"You want the honest answer?"

"Yeah."

He pulls me around to the front of the chair and onto his lap, making me gasp as I instantly feel the reason. Looking me dead in the eye while holding my hand, he says, "Because you're making me fucking hard, Laney."

*Jesus, take the wheel.*

"You didn't need to tell me that," I whisper, even though I feel like a hypocrite because heat is pooling between my legs as we speak.

He presses his nose against my cheek. "Fuck, you're making me want things I shouldn't."

My response comes out breathless. "You should get help with that."

"You're right. I should." When his face moves to the right, our lips brush ever so gently, but then he cups the back of my head and pulls me to his lips, deepening the kiss.

*You're not supposed to be kissing him, Laney. Remember?*

But I don't pull away. I let Fletcher tease my mouth with his own, swirling our tongues together as shivers race through my body. When we part, Fletcher rests his forehead on my shoulder.

"Being back here, with you…" I can hear my heartbeat in my ears as I wait for him to continue. "Thank you for letting me vent tonight," he finishes as my heart breaks from the sound of pain in his voice. "I should be past this shit, right? I shouldn't let him affect me anymore."

"I'm beginning to realize that *shouldn't* is a dangerous word."

# Chapter 19

**Laney**

### *Frozen, a New Bike, and a Plea*

"Auntie! You gotta hurry. Elsa is about to sing!" Ellis calls for me from the living room as I finish dumping popcorn into the bowl. Our sleepover ritual is about to begin, and of course my niece chose *Frozen* for the movie tonight.

Being an aunt is one of my favorite parts of my life. Even though helping my brother has added another level of responsibility to my plate, it's never felt like a burden. Watching Ellis grow up and become her own person is incredible, and I only hope that I get to do that one day with my own children.

"I'm coming, Ellis," I call, tossing the empty popcorn bag in the trash just as the doorbell rings. I glance at the clock, wondering who on earth could be here at six on a Friday. Dilynne is working late at the garage tonight on a project for a high-profile client, and besides her, I can't think of anyone else who would stop by unannounced.

Grabbing the bowl of popcorn, I head for the door. But when I pull it open, I freeze. Fletcher stands there with a Cheshire grin on his lips, holding a grocery bag.

"Fletcher? Wh—what are you doing here?"

"You said you were watching Ellis, and I figured you could use some help."

I tilt my head. "I've watched her by myself numerous times, thank you, so what's the real reason?" I take a step toward him and lower my voice. "If you were looking to get lucky, tonight is not the night."

He leans toward me. "I love that you think so highly of me. But just know, Laney, that if I was expecting to get lucky tonight, I would have told you I was on my way and for you to be naked when I got here."

"Uncle Fletcher!" Ellis shouts as she runs up behind me, launching herself at him. Luckily, he recovers from his shock in time to catch her, settling her on his hip. "Why should auntie be naked? It's not bath time."

"Ellie, girl. I heard you were having a sleepover and I got jealous." He glances over at me, winking. "Do you think I could join you?" he asks, avoiding her earlier question, thank God.

"Yes!" Ellis turns to me. "Can Uncle Fletcher sleepover too?"

Fletcher clears his throat. "I can't stay the night, but I do want to hang out with you girls, if that's okay?"

"Can he, auntie? Please?"

Leave it to Fletcher Adams to recruit my niece to guilt-trip me. "I guess."

"Yay!" Ellis yells before wiggling out of Fletcher's arms the second "Let It Go" starts playing from the television. "Come on! We have to sing!"

Fletcher steps inside, eyeing me curiously before joining Ellis in the living room and belting out the few lyrics that he knows to the song at a godawful, tone-deaf pitch. Stifling my laughter, I watch the two of them put on a performance, complete with hand gestures and everything. Fletcher winks at me at one point, cracking through the shell around my heart even further.

God, he's so good with her. He would make such a great dad.

My hand covers the center of my chest as I imagine Fletcher with kids, but then I remember him saying once upon a time that he never wanted them.

*That's why there's no point in entertaining that idea with him, Laney. That's why you two agreed on just orgasms.*

As that thought slams into me, the song ends and Ellis dramatically bows in front of us. Fletcher and I give her a round of applause.

"Ellis, I think you sing that better than Elsa does," Fletcher tells her.

She reaches for the bowl of popcorn and then walks back over to her spot on the floor. "I know. I'm a pro-tessional."

"I think you mean professional, sweetie," I say.

"That's what I said," she replies while shoving popcorn into her mouth.

Fletcher and I share a laugh before he walks back over to where I'm standing, shoving his hands in his pockets. "Sorry for surprising you, but I was worried if I asked to come over that you'd tell me no."

"I probably would have, but it was sweet of you to want to hang out with us."

He cups the side of my face, the warmth of his touch heating up my body. "I brought stuff for ice cream sundaes, and a gift for Ellis in my truck."

"Wait, what kind of gift?"

"It's a strider bike. It doesn't have pedals, so she uses her feet to move it. A few of my teammates swear by them for their kids. They learn the balance first, and then there's no need for training wheels later."

My mouth falls open slightly. "You—you bought her a bike?"

He takes a step closer to me, leaning his head down so his mouth lines up with my ear. "When are you gonna learn that I listen to everything you say, Laney?" He presses his lips to the spot behind my ear. "Especially when it involves people that I care about too."

My eyes close as his words wash over me. "This seems way beyond our arrangement."

When I open my eyes, his are narrowed at me. "Do you honestly think the only reason I would want to be here is to get you naked?"

"Uh, well..."

Leaning in again, he whispers in my ear, "I mean... Have I been thinking all day about all the ways I wanted to make you come tonight, to thank you for being there for me last night? Absolutely." My skin grows hot. "But do I want to be near you in any way I can, even if that doesn't include sex? Hell yes."

"Fletcher," I moan as his lips touch my neck ever so softly.

"I've thought about you all day," he whispers right before Ellis's voice cuts through our moment.

"Uncle Fletcher, why are you sniffing auntie?"

Fletcher's head pops up as I twist away from my niece, hiding my laughter. "Well, Ellis... Your auntie smells *really* good." He leans over and whispers, "Tastes amazing too."

Ellis drops the bowl beside her and runs up to Fletcher, holding her arm above her head, offering him her armpit. "I smell good too. Wanna see?"

Fletcher leans down to sniff her armpit. "You're right. You smell delicious," he says before pretending to eat her and tickle her all over. Ellis dissolves into a fit of laughter before Fletcher secures her on his hip again. "I have a present for you, but it's outside. Would you like to see it?"

Her eyes light up. "I love presents!"

"I know you do. You've got to get your shoes on first, though."

Ellis rushes to grab her shoes as Fletcher turns back to me. "Don't overthink it, Laney."

"I'm not," I say a little too defensively—because I hate that he can read me that easily.

Inside, my mind is spinning, fighting furiously to push down those pesky feelings I've been trying to avoid. But when he goes and does stuff like this, it's virtually impossible.

Fletcher sneaks outside to grab the bike from his truck while Ellis puts on her slip-on sneakers.

"I'm ready!" Ellis shouts, running to the front door and flinging it open to find Fletcher standing proudly by a bike with a giant pink bow on it. Her smile falls instantly and then she turns to walk back inside, shoulders slumping. "I don't want it."

Fletcher catches her by the shoulders and hoists her up in his arms before she gets too far. Walking back outside, he holds her as he explains the bike to her. "This isn't a normal bike, Ellis. It's special. It doesn't have pedals."

The quirk in her brow tells me she's still not convinced.

"I think you should at least try it, Ellis. Uncle Fletcher has friends who have them and the kids didn't even need training wheels on their bikes."

She eyes me skeptically. "I like my training wheels."

"What if I showed you how it works first?" He suggests, setting her down on the ground next to him.

"Uh, I don't think you'll fit on that," I say.

He gives me a look, then pulls out his phone. "You think?" He plays a video of kids riding the bike so Ellis understands how it works. By the end of the video, she walks over to the bike and tosses her leg over the seat to straddle it. "Okay, I wanna try."

"Let me go get your helmet." I race inside to get the spare helmet I keep here. When I return and clip it under her chin, Fletcher takes her to the driveway and helps her get started.

Effortlessly, she pushes herself forward with her feet, wobbling a bit but catching her balance instantly as she glides down the driveway and back up, her smile building as she rolls along the cement. "I'm doing it!"

"You are, sweetie!" I take my phone from my pocket and start recording her so I can send a video to Rhonan later. Ellis is laughing as she rolls along. "You're doing such a good job!"

"I like this bike!" she calls out to us. "Thank you, Uncle Fletcher!"

"My pleasure, Ellis." Crossing his arms over his chest, he stands there, watching her with a smile on his face.

I run after her, helping her stop when she gets going too fast. Once she gets that part under control, she's off. "Can I ride in the street?"

"Yeah. Let's do it!"

Fletcher runs after her, monitoring her distance along the residential street. Luckily, there's not much traffic on my road.

I'm so in awe watching her, eager to show my brother how much this bike is helping her, that I nearly miss Fletcher walking up behind me, pressing his chest against my back. "She's killing it."

"She is. This is amazing, Fletcher." Twisting my head so I can see him, I say, "Thank you."

He tips my chin up with his finger. "I'd do anything for you girls."

Once the sun has almost completely set and daylight is about to run out, we finally convince Ellis to come inside to finish the movie.

Fletcher takes Ellis back into the living room, setting her on the couch. She grabs the bowl of popcorn and offers it to him as he sits next to her, and they proceed to share the snack and watch the movie together.

Meanwhile, I'm still standing in the kitchen, watching this scene unfold in front of me with awe.

I know Fletcher isn't a complete stranger to my niece, but I haven't witnessed their relationship firsthand because I always avoided my brother's house when Fletcher visited. However, as I stand here, listening to them talk to one another, watching the way Ellis smiles at him or how hard she laughs when he makes a joke—it's showing me this entirely different side to the man that has been frozen in my memories for twelve years.

Fletcher Adams isn't the same boy I cared about all those years ago—he's grown up, and so have I. I've spent so long assuming I knew who he is that I've neglected to understand who he is now. And that version of him is even more dangerous to my heart.

"Auntie?" Ellis's voice pulls me from my thoughts.

"Yes, sweetie?"

She pats the space on the couch next to her. "Come watch the movie with us."

Nodding, I walk over and join them. Ellis offers me popcorn, but I decline. I'm staring blankly at the TV, trying to recall what part of the movie we're at, when I feel a hand at my neck. Slowly, I turn to the side to find Fletcher staring at the television, his eyes not pointed in my direction—but his arm is outstretched on the back of the couch, just long enough to reach my neck and tease the sensitive skin there.

His fingers trail along my collarbone, up the column of my neck to right under my ear before they make their way back down. He repeats the motion over and over again, making my skin pebble, heating me up from the inside out.

"I'm done," Ellis says, handing me the popcorn bowl before leaning in closer to Fletcher. I glance at the clock and notice it's almost her bedtime.

"You need to brush your teeth, Ellis," I say as she snuggles in closer to Fletcher.

"I don't want to miss the movie," she whines as if she hasn't seen it a million times.

"One night of not brushing her teeth won't kill her," Fletcher mutters out of the side of his mouth.

Rolling my eyes, I settle into my spot and let the argument die.

Fletcher's voice cuts through the silence. "Thanks for letting me crash your sleepover."

"You're welcome. Although I'm sure you're used to much wilder Friday nights."

He turns to face me. "How so?"

Shrugging, I say, "You know... Clubs, half-naked women dying for the chance to spend the night with you..."

"Actually, that sounds like hell." His eyes fall to Ellis as her eyes start to grow heavy. "This is much more my style."

"That's not what your father said," I mutter, catching myself right as the words leave my lips.

"What about my dad?"

*God, why did I say that?*

"I, uh, ran into your dad yesterday," I say. "He was at Blossom Brews when I ordered food for the party."

"Why didn't you tell me this last night at the salon?"

"You were already upset, and I didn't want to make it worse." Dropping my eyes to my lap, I continue, "I'm sorry. I shouldn't have even brought it up."

"But you did." He clears his throat. "So, what did he say to you?"

I look back up at him. "He was asking me if I'd seen you since you got back in town and mentioned the wedding and how he felt that Elliot was rushing into it. When I told him that some people don't want to wait when they find the right person, he said that he hopes you won't make the same mistake, that you'd be a fool to ever get married...to let a woman get in the way of the game."

Fletcher's brows draw together as his eyes move back and forth between mine. "Why are you bringing this up, Laney?"

"Like I said, it was my mistake. I shouldn't have said anything, but when you implied you enjoy Friday nights like this—" I gesture to Ellis and myself, "I just thought..."

He tilts his head to the side. "Is there something you want to ask me?"

I shrug and look back at the television. "Never mind." Fletcher continues to stare at me, but I don't look in his direction.

*God, Laney. Why did you even say anything?*

A few moments later, the movie ends, and I look down to find Ellis fast asleep. "I'm gonna take her to her room," I say, but Fletcher beats me to it.

"I've got her." He lifts her into his lap and then stands from the couch, carrying her in his arms down the hallway to the spare room I direct him to. I have a bed and toys just for her when she spends time here with me. He lays her down gently in the middle of the bed. "Does she sleep in here all night?"

"Inevitably, she'll end up in my bed with me, but I always start her in here."

We stand there, staring at her small size in comparison to the bed before I glance over at Fletcher and he does the same to me. Our eyes meet and that familiar electricity starts to flow between us.

"Where is your room?" he whispers.

"Across the hall."

"Can I see it?"

My mind tells me it's a bad idea, but my heart and libido have me leading Fletcher across the hall into my bedroom. When I spin around to face him, his eyes are on me. But then they dart behind me to where my dresser is before he walks in that direction.

He pulls one of the postcards from the mirror and studies it. "You still have these?" he asks, looking at the postcard from my grandfather that I've had on my mirror since high school.

"Did you think I'd get rid of them?"

He shakes his head. "No. It's just bringing back memories..." He trails off, not finishing his thought.

I watch him, waiting for him to continue speaking, but he remains silent. "Fletcher?"

He blinks and his trance is broken. Placing the postcard back in its place, he backs up from my dresser and then turns to face me. Reaching for my hand, he leads me out of my room, back to the living room and around the corner into the kitchen.

"My father chose football over everything in his life, Laney," he says, confusing me at first until I realize he's giving me insight to what his dad said earlier. "He chose the game over my mom and me. It's all he ever cared about."

"I know."

"But I'm. Not. Him." He punctuates every word.

"I know that, too."

"I sure as fuck hope so."

I reach up and run my hand down the side of his face, trailing my finger along his jaw, making this fire between us burn even hotter. "I do, Fletcher. I know you could never be your father."

"Why didn't you still come to Florida State, Laney?" His question is full of pain, curiosity, and longing.

"Fletcher…"

"No." He reaches for my hand on his face, putting his over mine. "I need to know."

"Why?"

Inhaling deeply, he says, "Because for the past twelve years, I've relived that night over and over again. For the past twelve years, every time you've scowled at me, it's felt like a knife being shoved right through the center of my chest."

"I don't scowl…"

"We've been over this, Laney. Your scowl is fucking terrifying." I roll my eyes, but there's a hint of a smile on my lips. "But the thing is, I'm pretty sure I know what happened that night, but I feel like I'm missing something too."

"Fletcher…"

"Please, Laney."

This is it. This is the opportunity for me to let Fletcher know how he made me feel all those years ago.

But what happens after?

Does it change what's happening between us?

*Laney, the lines between you two are so blurry, not even a magnifying glass could clear it up.*

Sighing, I say, "Okay."

A breath of relief leaves his lips. "Thank you."

"Don't be thanking me just yet, Fletcher Adams. You're about to find out why I've been calling you Lucifer all this time."

# Chapter 20

**Laney**

*Age Eighteen*

**The Night that Changed Everything**

"You did the right thing, George." My mother's voice stops me in my tracks as I head toward the kitchen.

"I know, but I still feel shitty about it. What if he tries to sue us?"

I peek around the corner and see my mom framing my father's face with her hands. "He doesn't have a leg to stand on. You had just cause for firing him."

"Everything okay?" I ask, interrupting their moment even though I probably shouldn't.

My mom smiles at me as she releases my father and moves back to the stove. "Everything is fine, Laney."

"Dad?"

"Just work stuff, kiddo." He walks over to me and kisses me on the top of the head. "How was your day?"

"Ugh. Boring. I can't wait to graduate."

"Only a few more months," my mother says. "I can't believe we're going to be empty nesters soon, George."

"I know, honey. You remind me about it every day." He looks over at me and winks.

"At least Laney will be with Rhonan at Florida State. That makes me feel better," Mom says while stirring the contents of the pot in front of her. She reaches up and rubs her temples a few times.

"Still have that headache?" my father asks.

"Yeah. I don't want to take any more medicine, but I think I should."

My father goes to the medicine cabinet to retrieve some pills, handing them to my mom along with a glass of water. "If you're in pain, you need to take something."

Rolling her eyes, she obliges my father's request. "There. Happy?"

"I'd be happier if you didn't push yourself so hard."

My mom eyes my father over her shoulder. "Well, that's the pot calling the kettle black."

"You both work too hard," I interject. "But with me and Rhonan down in Florida, perhaps you guys will be forced to take a few days off and come visit us."

My mom rolls her eyes. "Good luck with that. I've been trying to get your father to take a vacation for years, Laney, and haven't had any luck."

My dad crosses his arms. "Fine. Let's go somewhere this weekend."

My mom freezes. "What?"

Dad shrugs. "You're right. We never go anywhere, and after this week with Daniel, I think I need it."

"You're serious?"

My father walks over to Mom and wraps his arms around her waist. "Yes, Elizabeth. Let's get away for a few days. Laney will be fine by herself. Besides, Rhonan said he's coming home this weekend to visit and grab a few things from his room, so she won't be completely alone."

My mom turns to me. "Are you okay with this?"

I nod enthusiastically, not only because I think my parents deserve some time away, but because I know that Fletcher is coming back with Rhonan, which means there's an opportunity for us to be alone and there will be two less people to worry about finding out.

"You two deserve it. Maybe go to the coast. I hear Carrington Cove is beautiful this time of year." My father smiles. "That's what I was thinking. And while we're there, we can sit down and plan that trip to Aruba you've always wanted to go on."

My mother's eyes widen with excitement. "Who are you and what have you done with my husband?"

Dad laughs. "I'm just a man who loves his wife and was reminded this week that running this winery has robbed me of time I'll never get back. I'm trying to live in the moment, honey. Let me, will you?"

My mom presses up on her toes and kisses my dad, which is a sight that should make me gag. But honestly, watching my parents just helps me keep faith that two people can find each other in this crazy thing called life. I want what they have more than anything, and my heart wants it with Fletcher.

And this weekend will be the perfect time to finally go after it.

"Fine. Tell me when to be ready and I'll have my stuff packed." My dad smacks her on the ass as she walks away. "Hey!"

"Ugh, Dad. That's gross."

He turns to me and shrugs. "You can leave the room if it bothers you, but I won't apologize for appreciating your mother's body."

Mom giggles and turns red at the stove. "Dinner still has about fifteen minutes, Laney, if you have some homework to finish up."

"I do, actually. Just call me when it's ready."

"Sure thing, sweetie."

I race back to my room and grab my cell phone, lying down on my bed with my phone poised above me, opening up the text message thread with my brother.

**Me:** *Breaking news: Mom and Dad are going away for the weekend.*

He texts me back immediately.

**Rhonan:** *WTF? Has hell frozen over?*

**Me:** *I know. But you know what would be fun while they're gone? A party.*

**Rhonan:** *You wanna have a party? Yup. Hell has definitely frozen over.*

**Me:** *Come on. I'm eighteen now and I'm about to be in college. I need the practice.*

**Rhonan:** *18 is not 21, Laney.*

**Me:** *Newsflash: You aren't 21 either.*

**Rhonan:** *But I'm closer than you.*

**Me:** *Come on, it'll be fun! I can invite people from school, you can invite your friends you never see anymore...*

**Rhonan:** *Fine, but only because Fletcher just saw my phone and agrees it would be fun.*

Knowing that Fletcher approves of the idea makes me even more giddy.

**Me:** *Yay! Let me know what I need to do.*

**Rhonan:** *We'll talk later. I have to finish studying for my midterm tomorrow.*

**Me:** *Okay. Love you!*

**Rhonan:** *Love you too, sis.*

"Oh my God!" I whisper-shout to myself, tossing my phone to the side and staring up at the ceiling as I process everything that's transpired in the last ten minutes.

But then my phone chimes with another text.

**Fletcher:** *You want to have a party? Who are you and what have you done with Laney?*

My heart starts racing as I contemplate my reply. But suddenly, this wave of confidence rushes through me.

**Me:** *Actually, there is something I want to talk to you about. Perhaps we could sneak away to discuss some stuff at the party.*

**Fletcher:** *Uh oh. Am I in trouble?*

**Me:** *LOL No. I just... really want to talk to you.*

**Fletcher:** *Sounds good, angel. See you in a few days*

When I read his last text, I toss my phone to the side and kick my feet in the air.

This is the perfect time to tell Fletcher how I feel. We'll have the chance to be alone, I'll be at his school in less than six months where we could actually be together, and then all of these feelings for him I've been holding inside can finally come out.

It's perfect. It's fate.

I just hope that my gut is right and that he feels the same way.

***

"Who are all these people?" Rhonan asks as we stand in the kitchen, surveying our house full of people.

"Honestly, I'm not sure."

"Jesus, Laney. Did you invite the whole school?"

"No, but people must have told other people, and you know what happens when word gets out about a party, especially in Blossom Peak."

Rhonan takes a sip from his beer. He and Fletcher brought so much alcohol and now that I'm looking at how many people are here, I'm glad. However, I know neither of them are twenty-one, so I'm not sure how they got their hands on it. I don't want to know though, so I don't ask.

"Not many parties these days, huh?" he asks.

"My class isn't as adventurous as your class was."

"Not everyone can be as cool as us," Fletcher says as he walks up to us, reaching out to poke my nose. I swat his hand away. "Great party though, Laney. Watching all these high school kids drink just reminds me of how much better I am at holding my liquor than I was at that age."

"How drunk are you?" I ask, because my plan to talk to him tonight might have to be put on hold if he's not coherent enough to remember the conversation. Although, if he gets drunk and turns me down, it might be easier to pretend like the conversation never happened. I wipe my sweaty palms on my dress for the hundredth time.

He holds up his red cup. "This is my first drink."

Rhonan scoffs. "Dude, I'm on my third. Catch up, will you?" Someone calls out to him from the living room. "I'll catch you two later," he says before walking off, leaving me and Fletcher alone.

Fletcher moves in closer to me. "It sure is good to see you, angel."

Staring up at him, I study the lines of his face. He looks different and yet the same. Only seeing each other sporadically over the past two years means each time we're face-to-face, I spend several minutes cataloging his features for my daydreams and fantasies. "You too, Fletcher."

"So, what is it that you wanted to talk to me about?" He leans against the counter behind us, crossing his arms over his chest while still holding his red cup.

"Oh. Well, we don't have to talk about that now."

"Nonsense. There's no time like the present." He grabs me by the hand before I can argue and pulls me down the hallway to my bedroom. He stops at the door, rattling the knob.

"You locked your room?"

"Um, yeah. I didn't want people fucking in my bed."

"Good thinking. You're the only one that should be doing that."

My cheeks turn red because not only does the mention of sex make me blush, but he has no idea I haven't experienced that yet. "We can talk out here."

I lean up against the wall as Fletcher rests his forearm above me, his other hand still holding his drink. "All right. We're alone. Now spill."

I drop my eyes to the center of his chest as I begin to fiddle with my hands in front of me. "Well, I uh...I sort of have feelings for someone and I'm not sure how to tell him."

When I look up at him, I see his eyebrows rise. "You have a crush? Is it someone at school?"

I shake my head. "No."

"Do I know him?"

I nod. "You do."

The corner of his mouth lifts. "Then tell me. Maybe I can talk to him, tell him to run in the other direction."

My mouth drops open in shock. "You wouldn't dare!"

He laughs. "Nah, I wouldn't. In fact, any guy who's got your attention is one lucky son of a bitch."

My eyes bounce back and forth between his. "God, you're so blind."

His boyish smile almost makes my knees buckle. "That's not true. I can see very well. Now tell me...who is this boy you have your sights on?"

"He's a man, not a boy. High school boys aren't worth my time."

"You're damn right about that." He reaches forward and pinches my ribs, making me squeal. "Spill, Laney."

With a shaky hand, I reach up and brush his hair from his face, lowering my voice. "I can't believe it's not obvious to you."

His eyes bounce between mine. "Use your words, Laney."

Swallowing down the lump in my throat, thankful for the liquid courage I consumed earlier, I whisper, "After all these years...you honestly haven't noticed how I look at you?"

His smile falters and, for a moment, I regret it all—I must have misread this.

Licking my lips, I prepare to bolt, but when his hand cups the side of my face, I freeze. A pinch in his brow forms, and then something shifts in his gaze. Determination? Permission?

Whatever it is, his spine straightens from his newfound confidence, and then he whispers, "Fuck, Laney. I—"

"Fletcher!" A guy I don't recognize calls out from the other side of the house. "Come on! We need you for beer pong!"

He glances over his shoulder and takes a step back from me. "I'll, uh, be right there!" he calls back.

Disappointment races through me as he creates even more distance between us, brushing his hand through his hair and blowing out a breath. "Christ," he mutters before meeting my eyes again, so many thoughts swirling in his.

But I cut him off before he can make this more awkward. "It's fine. Go."

His brows draw together again. "Laney..."

Smiling, I shrug. "Don't worry about it. It's nothing..."

"Fletcher!" The guy calls again.

And before Fletcher can say another word, I walk away, willing my heart to calm down as my pulse hammers relentlessly.

"Laney!" he calls after me, but I don't turn around. I need space, I need time to deal with his reaction because it wasn't exactly what I was hoping for, but it wasn't a rejection either.

When I enter the kitchen again, I find Dilynne pouring herself another drink. "Hey, where have you been?" she asks me as I bump my hip with hers.

I get as close to her as I can before whispering, "I was talking to Fletcher."

Her eyes widen. "And? Did you do it? Did you tell him—"

"Shhh!" I hiss, cutting her off. "And sort of?" I say, even though it comes out more as a question.

"How do you *not* know if you told him how you feel about him?"

Sighing, I bury my head in my hands. "I told him that I can't believe he hasn't seen how I look at him, and then his face fell."

Dilynne winces. "Yikes."

"Yeah, and then before he could actually respond, someone called for him to play beer pong, so I left and told him not to worry about what I said."

She shoves my shoulder when I lift my head. "I can't believe you did that!"

"What?"

"This was your opportunity, Laney. All these years you've wanted this guy, and you just walked away from him?"

"Well, he let me."

"Yeah, probably because he was a little shocked."

My brow furrows. "I'm confused. You're the one who thought I was crazy for liking him."

"Yeah, but that doesn't mean I don't want you to get what you want." Her face softens. "You're my best friend and you have been pining after him for so long, I wanted to see you get your happy ending." She shrugs. "Maybe it's the secret romantic in me."

I blink. "You? A romantic? Has the alcohol changed you already?"

She rolls her eyes. "Ha. Ha. Don't tell anyone, okay? I need to protect my image."

I mimic zipping my lips. "Your secret is safe with me."

She winks at me before finishing making her drink. When she's done, she spins around to face me again. "Okay, so you need to go find him."

"I don't know..."

"I *do* know. Don't let tonight end without making your intentions clear, okay? Find him at a point when he's alone and be crystal clear this time." She pushes me in the chest.

"What was that for?"

"Puff out your chest. Stand up straight. Be the badass Laney Hart that I know."

I square my shoulders and nod. "Okay. You're right."

"I'm always right." She takes a sip of her drink. "Now, if you'll excuse me, I need to find a guy to talk about cars with because none of these girls are ever on my level about that."

"Hey. I'm not on that level either..."

"No, but you're grandfathered in. We've been friends for so long that you knowing anything about cars is irrelevant now."

I nod. "Okay. Good to know I'm safe."

Dilynne walks off, leaving me alone in the kitchen as people mill around me. The music coming out of the surround sound is making the walls rattle, couples are making out all over the couch or dancing in the living room, and more noise is coming from outside, so I decide to check out that scene.

As I enter the backyard, I see Fletcher high-fiving his teammate in his game of beer pong. I decide to stand off to the side and observe, but he catches me watching and narrows his eyes at me. Not sure what that means, but once he realizes where I am, his eyes drift to me between every play of the game.

I wish I knew what he was thinking. I wish I had any inclination of what his reaction was to what I shared with him. But then part of me doesn't want to know at all because what if that glare means he's mad at me for putting him in this position in the first place?

I turn around and go back into the house to find Dilynne again, standing next to her in silence as she talks about transmissions with some guy around Rhonan's age that I've seen around town a time or two. After about twenty minutes, I see Fletcher walk inside, making eye contact with me as he does. He watches me for a few seconds before turning down the hallway that leads to my parents' room, which I know for a fact is also locked. There are other rooms back there too, though, so maybe he's looking for a place to get away from everyone.

Or... Maybe he wants me to follow him?

Not sure what to think, I decide the risk is worth taking and head in the same direction he went. I shake out my nerves as I wander down the hall and notice one of the bathrooms has a light on and I don't see Fletcher anywhere, so I assume he's inside. I knock gently but don't hear anything over the music, so I check the knob and find it unlocked.

Bracing myself for the conversation we're about to have, I reach for the handle to the door and turn, pushing the door open. But nothing could have prepared me for what I see.

Fletcher is leaning against the wall furthest from the door, his hands braced behind him for support, and a girl is kneeling in front of him, her hands on his thighs.

*Oh my God. Is she...*

It doesn't take me long to figure out what I just walked in on, and when it does, my heart slices in two.

Before they notice me, I slam the door shut and run down the hallway, as far away from that scene as I can get. But running won't erase it from my mind. I don't think anything ever will.

Sobs wrack my body as I push my way through the house to my room, pulling my key from my pocket and unlocking my door, and locking it behind me before falling onto my bed and crying myself to sleep.

Looks like I know where I stand with Fletcher Adams now, and it's nowhere near where I wanted to be.

***

Pounding wakes me from a deep sleep. I lift my head and notice it's just after four in the morning. The inside of the house sounds quiet, so I'm guessing the party died down.

Pushing myself out of bed, I glance at my reflection in my mirror. Mascara streaks paint my face from all my crying, my hair looks like a rat tried to make a nest in it, and I still have on the same clothes since I never bothered to change before I passed out.

The pounding continues, and I make my way to my bedroom door. When I open it, I find my brother on the other side, eyes bloodshot and tears streaming down his face.

"Rhonan? What's wrong?"

He stumbles into my room, pulling me into his chest. "Laney..."

"You're scaring me. What's going on?"

It takes him a few moments to gather himself before he lifts his head and meets my eyes. "It's Mom. Dad just called me, and..."

Dread fills my body. "What? What happened?"

"She—she's gone, Laney. Mom died."

***

"Thank you for coming," I say for the hundredth time as another person from our town comes up to me and Rhonan, offering their condolences—like those words are going to take away the pain from living the rest of our lives without our mom.

It's been one week, and I already feel like the pain in my chest is permanent.

"How long do we have to let these people hang out in the house?" Rhonan mutters beside me, his voice low.

"I don't know. I've never held a wake before." My eyes scour the room, looking for our dad, but I don't see him anywhere. I wonder if he's gone to hide, which is exactly what I feel like doing right now.

Rhonan closes his eyes and shakes his head. "I feel like I'm living in a nightmare."

"You and me both. But this is as real as it gets. Mom isn't coming back..." I choke back the emotion threatening to spill over, but Rhonan pulls me into his chest before I fall to the ground.

"I know, Laney. Fuck. I know." He rests his chin on top of my head.

We hold each other for a few minutes before Elliot walks up to us. "You guys doing okay?" he asks as Rhonan releases me and I wipe under my eyes.

"I don't even know how to answer that right now," my brother replies.

"I'm so fucking sorry, you guys. I know I keep saying it, but…"

Rhonan places his hand on Elliot's shoulder. "I know. Thanks, man."

"Have you decided what to do about school yet?" Elliot asks my brother.

Rhonan's eyes drift to me for a second then back to his friend. "Yeah. I'm not going back."

"What?" I practically shout and then lower my voice once I realize I've drawn people's attention. "When did you plan on telling me this?"

Rhonan clenches his teeth. "We can talk about this later."

"No, we can talk about this now. You can't quit school."

He steps closer to me. "Yes, I can, and I am."

I open my mouth to argue with him, but Fletcher walks up to the three of us, and my words get caught in my throat.

"Hey, man," he says to Rhonan. "You hanging in there?"

"The best I can, man."

Fletcher's eyes move over to me. "How are you doing?"

But before I can reply, Brittany comes up behind him, placing her hand on his shoulder. "There you are. I was wondering where you ran off to."

He doesn't look back at her, his eyes still trained on me. But seeing them together, hearing the ownership in her voice makes the crack in my heart completely split in two.

I divert my gaze from his. "Fine." I think that's only the fifth word I've said to Fletcher since *that* night, but right now, it's all I can muster without the threat of getting sick on the floor in front of everyone.

When Fletcher woke up and found me and Rhonan crying on the couch, holding each other, he instantly knew something was wrong, and after crying all night over *him*, I was surprised that my body still had any tears to spare. But losing my mom was a pain I was not ready to face at the age of eighteen, especially on top of the heartbreak that the man standing in front of me was responsible for.

Rhonan and I left for Carrington Cove later that day, and when we were reunited with our dad, the three of us broke apart together. What was supposed to be a trip away ended with our mom dying from a brain aneurysm—something that no one could have predicted.

After losing her, though, the thing with Fletcher doesn't matter now. Nothing does, as far as I'm concerned. Without my mom here, life has lost meaning. Without my mom here to help me heal from heartbreak, it's easier to focus on anger.

But seeing the pain in Fletcher's eyes is almost too much to bear, especially because I know how much he loves our parents and appreciated our mother.

"Fuck. I just wish these people would leave," Rhonan mumbles to the boys.

Elliot and Fletcher share a look. "Say the word and we'll clear them out," Elliot declares.

"Seriously?"

Fletcher nods. "Yeah. If you two aren't feeling up to this, you don't have to smile and act like you want to talk. If I were you, I would want to be alone too."

Rhonan looks at me for approval, which I give him with one nod. "I just want to be alone, Rhonan. I don't know where Dad is, but he'd probably feel the same."

He turns to his friends. "We'll be in the office," he tells Elliot and Fletcher before grabbing my hand and pulling me down the hallway. When we enter, we find our father crying at his desk. And so we lock ourselves in my parents' office and break apart in solitude, where I cry myself to sleep with my head in my brother's lap and pray that I wake up from this nightmare, even though I know that won't happen.

# Chapter 21

**Laney**

*Present Day*

*The Truth and Taking It*

There it is. Everything I've kept buried for twelve years, just sitting between us. Fletcher stands across from me in my kitchen, his hands clenched at his sides. But the look on his face is the same one he had right before he kissed me in my office.

"So, this is why you cut me out of your life?"

Suddenly feeling self-conscious, I wrap my arms around my waist. "Yes, Fletcher. You—you broke my heart on the worst night of my life, and—"

He closes the distance between us, pinning me up against the cabinets much like he did the first night he came to my house. "You listen to me, Laney Hart, and you listen good."

I nod, frozen by the intensity of his stare. "When you told me how you felt that night, I was shocked, but not because I didn't feel the same way. I was shocked and confused because, for the first time in four years, I *knew* that you felt the same way I did and suddenly, I had the opportunity to do something about it."

"Then why–"

"I just didn't know how to act on it. There were so many things to consider, and the only thing I wanted to do was lock us in your room and worship you for hours, but I couldn't. Your brother..."

I sigh in defeat, closing my eyes. "Are you telling me that Rhonan is the reason you ended up in the bathroom with Brittany?"

"Nothing happened with Brittany," he declares, which makes my eyes pop open again.

"I know what I saw, Fletcher."

"What you saw was her backing me up against the wall, dropping to her knees, and offering to suck me off after she followed me into the bathroom. But what you didn't see was me telling her no and her slapping me across the face before storming out of the bathroom."

My bottom lip trembles. "What?"

"Did you really think that I would want her when I could have you?"

My heart is pounding as I blink several times. "But why...why didn't you find me and explain?"

"I didn't know you saw us!"

"But after that night... You never talked to me about what happened between us. We never finished that conversation, and then she came up to you at the wake..."

"I tried to find you, Laney. I looked for you for almost an hour, but even Dilynne didn't know where you went. I figured, you went to sleep or something so I'd just talk to you the next day."

"What?"

"And then the next morning? Your mom had just died, Laney! The last thing I wanted to do was make your life more complicated at that time. And Brittany? She didn't take no for an answer, obviously. The girl was desperate for my attention, but we were never together."

Silence rests between us. Fletcher retreats from me, pushing his hat from his head and tossing it on the kitchen counter as he paces through the dining room.

I'm speechless. Dilynne was right.

What I saw was...not what I thought it was.

*God, I think I'm going to be sick.*

Fletcher glances over at me, taking in my stance as I feel myself start to crumble. I close my eyes, trying to quell the building tears, but he rushes over, gripping my waist with one hand. "Hey. Look at me," he says, tipping my chin up and waiting for my eyes to open again. When they do, the regret and sadness I see in his gaze has to be mirrored in my own.

On the one hand, my chest feels like a weight has been lifted. But on the other, I feel like so much time has passed that we'll never get back—all because of bad timing and stubbornness on both our parts.

"This isn't your fault. It's mine," he says.

"No, Fletcher," I croak. "I've been so hell-bent on standing my ground, on hating you because you hurt me. And it was easier to hate you than to admit I still felt something for you... To admit that my chest still ached because I couldn't let you go."

"You had every right to hate me based on what you saw and how I acted, the things that I didn't say..." He drops his forehead to mine. "I'm so fucking sorry, Laney. God, I don't think I'll ever be able to say that enough."

"Me too." I swallow hard, but my next words make me even more nervous than dredging up the past. "Where... Where do we go from here, Fletcher? Everything is happening so fast that I feel like my head is spinning."

"That's up to you, Laney," he says as he toys with my bottom lip. "But I know what I fucking want."

My eyes drop down to his lips. "And what's that?"

"You." Simple. Direct. And everything I needed to hear from him, just twelve years later than I wanted.

"Then take me."

Our eyes lock.

And then, we collide.

Fletcher crashes his lips to mine, pinning me against the cabinets again and then pulling me into his body.

My curves melt against him.

"Fucking hell, Laney," he mutters between kisses. I encourage him to keep going by trying to pull him even closer. I wrap my leg around his hip, and he lifts me onto the counter, pressing his cock into the juncture between my thighs. I moan as I feel him thrust his erection against me, rubbing me right where I need him. "What are you fucking doing to me?"

"I need you to fuck me, Fletcher," I say breathlessly.

A pained groan crawls up his throat as he rests his forehead on mine. "Jesus. You have no idea how much I want to own this body, but..."

I reach down and palm him through his shorts. "I'm giving you permission. Take me. Own me."

He tucks my hair behind my ear as he says, "You've owned my thoughts for so fucking long, Laney. You've been the star of my fucking fantasies. Do you honestly think one time will be enough to satisfy that? There will never be enough time." He nips my bottom lip as I contemplate his words.

"No," I admit on a whisper. "But that just means we'll have to do it again." *And again, and again. Apparently Fletcher opened the flood gates when he gave me that first orgasm, and I don't think there's a limit to how many I'll want.*

"If we cross this line, Laney, there's no going back for me. We're going to figure our shit out, but we're not going to get back to the way we were—we're going to move forward. That's what I fucking want." He doesn't allow me to reply, but it's probably a good thing because I'm not sure what to say right now. His eyes dip down to my lips again as he runs his thumb over them. "Are you on birth control?"

I nod. "I have an IUD."

"Good, because I don't want anything between us when I claim this pussy," he says, reaching between my legs and rubbing his knuckles over my slit through my shorts before kissing me deeply again.

"Please..." I moan, closing my eyes as he continues to torture me.

"So fucking pretty when you beg," he murmurs before leaning down to kiss me again, pulling my bottom lip between his teeth. "I want to be gentle, angel, but I can't promise that I won't lose a little bit of control."

"I can take it."

Our eyes bounce between one another's before he takes a step back, forcing me to drop my hands from his face. With our gazes still locked, he reaches behind his neck to pull his T-shirt up over his head. "Strip, Laney."

"But Ellis," I say, bringing myself back to the moment and remembering that my niece could wake up at any moment, and us naked together is the last thing she should see. "She tends to be a heavy sleeper, but..."

"Shit." He lifts me from the counter and carries me back to my bedroom, closing and locking the door behind us. "You're gonna have to be quiet."

"I can try." With shaky hands, I lift my tank top over my head and throw it to the floor before reaching for the button on my shorts and popping it open, shimmying them down my legs and kicking them to the side.

Fletcher drags his hand down as he studies my body, standing before him in my plain white bra and thong. "God, you're perfect."

But then reality hits me. I reach down and cover my insulin pump attached to my lower stomach, but he rushes to me and covers my hand with his own. "Sorry. I know this isn't sexy—"

He presses his fingers to my lips, silencing me. "Don't you dare fucking apologize. If you honestly think I give a shit about that, then you don't know me."

"I know, it's just—"

"This thing keeps you alive, Laney," he says before dropping to his knees and lifting my hand from my body. He presses a kiss right below the pump. "It's a part of you, and that means it's perfect."

"I'm not perfect, Fletcher."

He stares up at me. "To me, you are."

The last thing I want is to get emotional while this is happening, but when he says things like that, I can't help but tear up while being reminded of the boy I handed my heart over to so long ago. Luckily, he presses his nose to my pussy and reminds my body of the main event I'm craving so badly.

"Touch me, Fletcher." He hooks his thumbs in the strings of my thong and pulls it down my legs. "Thanks for not tearing these apart, by the way."

"I thought about it," he teases before pushing my legs further apart. "But the last thing I want to do is piss you off again."

Chuckling, I watch him lean forward and drag his tongue through my slit, making me moan. "God yes..."

"Take your bra off, baby. Let me see all of you." As he continues to torture me with his touch, I fumble behind me to unhook my bra, letting it fall to the floor. As soon as he sees my bare breasts, he stands up and cups them in his hands. "Jesus Christ." His thumbs find my nipples, rubbing over them softly. "So fucking perfect."

"Kiss me," I say as he toys with my nipples at a torturous pace. But he listens, cupping one side of my face and reaching between my legs with his other hand as our lips meet.

He slowly parts me and slides two fingers inside me easily since my body is more than ready for this. As our lips and tongue collide, his fingers work me over, teasing me deliciously as I widen my legs to give him better access. "I can feel your pussy quivering around my fingers, Laney. And next, it's going to quiver around my cock."

My body starts to tremble as I feel my orgasm begin to bloom, but Fletcher pulls his hand away, making me whimper. "Why'd you stop?"

He takes me by the hand and leads me over to my bed. I watch him take his shorts and underwear off, and that's when I see his cock for the first time.

*Holy shit.*

He reaches down and strokes himself while cupping my face. "Don't worry. You can take it." Nodding slowly, I watch as he sits on the bed, leaning against the headboard and spreading his legs as his hard cock rests on his stomach. Then, he motions me to him.

"I'm ready for you, Laney. Come sit on my cock, baby."

# Chapter 22

**Fletcher**

### *Caveman Tendencies*

"I'm ready for you, Laney. Come sit on my cock, baby."

I can already feel myself on the brink of coming just watching her walk toward me—the sway of her hips, the bounce of her breasts, and the look in her eyes of hunger mixed with nerves.

I know I'll have to face Rhonan soon, especially after what he told me the other day. And the guys too. But none of that matters right now.

What matters is that Laney and I cleared up the misunderstanding that ended us, and we are finally on the same page—at least physically.

*All this fucking time she thought I didn't want her...*

Laney straddles me, holding my gaze, but looking more nervous by the second. I reach between her legs again to make sure she's wet enough to take me. "Hover over me, angel." She does as I say as I position my cock right at her entrance, teasing her as I slide the head through her slit and up and around her clit. She lets out a little moan when I hit that magical button. "You like that?"

"Yes."

So I do it again, swirling the tip of my cock around her clit, over and over until her legs are shaking.

"Fletcher…"

"Take me in."

She looks down at where I'm holding my cock in place for her.

"No. Look at me, Laney. I want to watch your face as you take in every inch of me for the first time."

She swallows hard as her eyes lock on mine, and bracing herself on my shoulders, she begins to move down my length, so tortuously slow that I might come in mere seconds. Fighting like hell to control myself, I stare at her magnificent green eyes and watch her lips part as she works herself down my length, inch by torturous inch until I'm completely sheathed by her hot, tight pussy. "Jesus Christ, Laney," I grate out.

"Oh my God, Fletcher…" She lifts herself up and then slowly moves down again, her mouth open, moaning softly with each slide. My cock grows impossibly harder.

I kiss her roughly as she starts to find a rhythm, moving her hips up and down, swiveling them back and forth, making her grow wetter—so wet that I can feel her arousal dripping down my balls. "That's right, baby. Ride that cock."

Her moans vibrate against my skin as I watch her—eyes closed, head thrown back, her nails digging into my shoulders as she keeps riding me, her sounds turning into my new favorite soundtrack.

Fuck, I'm not going to last much longer. This first time might be faster than I wanted, but it certainly won't be the last time. No chance in hell.

I lean forward and latch onto her nipple with my mouth, teasing the bud as she shivers from the contact. Her hips move faster and her pussy tightens around me. "Are you gonna come, Laney?" She nods. Keeping my mouth on her breast, I reach between us and rub her clit with my thumb, helping her get there as I look up to watch her face. "That's it, baby. Break for me," I mumble around her nipple.

"Fuck...oh, shit!" she whispers as her body shakes and trembles through her release. I keep rubbing her clit, drawing every tremor of pleasure from her body, loving the way she shivers in my arms until she's sated and collapses against my shoulder.

Before she recovers fully, I turn her over on her back and lay her down on the bed, sliding back inside her, moving her left leg up over my shoulder so I can get as deep as possible. She arches her back and claws at my shoulders again. "Goddamn it, Laney. Do you feel how fucking hard I am for you?"

"Yes..."

"We have so much time to make up for..."

She frames my face with her hands. "Keep fucking me, Fletcher."

I bury my head in her neck, kissing and nibbling on her sensitive skin. "God, you feel so fucking good, Laney. Your pussy fits me like a fucking glove, perfectly made for my cock." I lick up the column of her throat.

"You wanted this, didn't you?" I murmur into her ear.

"Yes..." She squeezes her pussy around me, making my entire body shiver. "So much," she moans.

"Fuck, you're gonna make me come." I speed up, thrusting harder and faster as that tingle at the base of my spine builds. She nods, urging me on. "Jesus Christ, I'm coming..." White, hot pleasure races through my body as I empty myself into her, sliding in over and over until the last drop leaves my body.

She kisses me deeply as I recover, and when we part, I stare down at her, feeling like my entire life just changed with that orgasm.

But it wasn't just the sex that blew my mind—it was the fact that I just had sex with Laney Hart.

"Holy hell, angel," I breathe out before pressing a quick kiss to her lips.

She continues to lie there with her eyes closed, catching her breath. When I lean down again to kiss her neck, she lets out a little moan. "Fletcher…"

"Fuck. The sound of my name coming from your lips after you came all over me is perfect." A few minutes pass before we've both recovered enough to stand. As much as I don't want to, I pull out of her and then help her up from the bed. "Let's clean you up."

Laney cautiously walks to her bathroom, turning on the lights when we step inside. Our naked bodies are reflected back at us in the mirror. I step up behind her, brush her hair to the side, and kiss her neck.

"So fucking beautiful."

She spins to face me, and I lift her onto the counter, watching my cum drip down the inside of her thighs as I push them apart. "This is fucking beautiful too," I say, drawing my finger through my release and rubbing it into her skin.

"Are you a closet caveman, Fletcher Adams?" she teases with a quirk in her lips.

I keep spreading my cum across her thigh. "I didn't think I was until I saw this. Fuck…" I drag my hand down my face. "You have no idea what you do to me, Laney."

She pulls me toward her, wrapping her arms around my neck. "I think I'm beginning to understand."

A trip back home to celebrate one of my best friends getting married has developed into finding out why the first woman I've ever had feelings for despised me, and realizing that those feelings are still there. Guilt that's been hibernating in my chest has finally started to subside. Passion I've been keeping dormant has finally been unleashed.

But worry still hangs in the air—because there's no way I'll be able to leave at the end of next week without having to sacrifice something. I'm not sure where I stand on all counts yet, and until I do, I just want to focus on what's right in front of me—the girl I've always compared all others to—naked and giving herself over to me.

I reach for a washcloth from a shelf in the corner and begin cleaning us both up before we get dressed and head back out to the living room. I take her by the hand and pull her into me when we reach her front door.

I press my lips to hers again, and the moan that leaves her mouth travels all the way down my body. "I need to go before I strip you naked and feast on every part of you until you're screaming."

"Probably a good idea."

For a moment, I debate pressing her further, trying to find out where her head is at. But I know this woman—slow and steady is going to win this race.

Even though nothing's official yet, I know the line we crossed tonight isn't one we can come back from. Laney wanted this as much as I did, and for now, that's enough.

Once the wedding's over, I'll face whatever hurdles stand in our way—her brother, my friends, my career...

But now, I press one more kiss to her lips. "Good night, angel."

"Good night, Fletcher."

I walk backwards down the driveway, her eyes on me the whole way.

And as I drive back to my cabin, I know one thing for certain.Laney Hart was always meant to be mine, and I'll stop at nothing until she is.

# Chapter 23

**Fletcher**

### *What Happens in Vegas*

"Perfect. I think lining those up on that side of the bar will be great."

The crew I hired to deliver and unload all the stuff for the party walks through the room and sets up the slot machines along the left side of the bar, lining up the bar stools underneath.

I've already been here for a few hours, but the party room in the back of Hart Winery is slowly being transformed into a Vegas casino. Green felt tables are scattered throughout the space, each set up for a different game. Gold and black streamers line the walls, hiding the usual winery décor to make the room feel like a different place. I've also hired a few cocktail waitresses to serve everyone, and a buffet table is being set up on the right side of the room.

"Well, look who it is," Dilynne says as she enters the room, carrying large cardboard cutouts that I can't see the front of.

Gesturing to the contents of her arms, I say, "I'm afraid to ask, but are those for the games?"

Her smile is mischievous. "Why yes, they are."

"And what game are they for?"

She pulls the cutouts away from me as I try to peek at what's on the other side. "You'll just have to wait and see like everyone else."

"Fine." I fan my arms out, drawing her attention to the rest of the room. "Well, what do you think?"

She surveys the progress so far. "It looks like a lot of debauchery is about to go down."

"Let's just hope that Elliot and Tori have a good time."

"Or we could hope that Tori just doesn't show up."

"Why can't you just be happy for Elliot?" I ask, crossing my arms over my chest.

"I would if I felt like Tori was the right person for him, but she's not."

"And what are you basing that on? How she treated you in high school?"

Dilynne shakes her head, her eyes narrowed. "No, it's a gut feeling."

"A *feeling*?"

"Yes, it's called women's intuition, and since you have a penis, you wouldn't understand how powerful it is."

"You're right. I don't get it, but I do get that one of my best friends is really happy, and I think we should all just put our opinions aside to celebrate that."

"I have been, haven't I?" Dilynne counters.

"For the most part, yeah."

"Then leave me be." Her eyes dip down my body and then back up. "Speaking of intuition, you seem like you have a lot on your mind."

I reach up and adjust the hat on my head. "I do. This party, the wedding…"

"Nope, it's something else." Tilting her head at me, she continues, "It wouldn't have to do with my best friend, would it?"

"What are you trying to ask me, Dilynne?"

She takes a step closer to me, lowering her voice. "You sure are going to a lot of trouble here. Is it all for Elliot and Tori?"

"I'm just taking my duty as the best man seriously."

"And what about booking appointments at the salon, or showing up to yoga at the winery, or buying Ellis a new bike and delivering it to her at Laney's house, or hacking Laney's app for her glucose?"

"I'm still waiting for you to get to the point."

She pops her hip out to the side, squinting again. "This better not be a fucking game to you, Fletcher."

"I thought games were the whole point of tonight."

She arches a brow. "You know damn well what I mean. Laney—"

I drop my arms and step closer to her, lowering my voice. "Laney and I are figuring shit out, all right?"

Her eyes bore right into mine. "That isn't exactly reassuring."

*Jesus, what does she want from me?*

Does she want me to admit that for the past twenty-four hours, all I've been thinking about is how this is supposed to work between me and Laney after this wedding is over? That now that I've kissed her, tasted her, fucked her—I can't imagine going back to a life where I don't get to do that every fucking day? That after she told me what my dad said, I stayed up all night wondering if I truly have what it takes to be the man he never could be? I'm so fucking afraid to fail in that regard, especially to fail Laney.

All this time, she's hated me—the old me, at least. But is the new me ready to be the man she deserves? Or am I just doomed to repeat history and make the same mistakes with her that I already have?

"What do you want to hear from me?" I ask Dilynne.

"What's your end goal, Fletcher? Because Laney's life is here, and yours is in Charlotte."

"I fucking know that, Dilynne."

"So is this just some vacation fling? Because if it is, I need to be prepared to pick my best friend off the floor again when you leave, just like last time." She lowers her voice. "You have no idea how much that night hurt her. How fucked up she was over it."

The thought of Laney being devastated at the end of next week makes me want to fucking punch something. But as much as I want to give her everything, I still don't have enough answers to erase all of Dilynne's doubts.

"I understand that now."

"Do you? Because my best friend let her guard down—for *you*. She hasn't done that with anyone since you rejected her and her mom died. Not even with Spencer and they were engaged."

"This isn't a game to me, Dilynne. Laney could never be that inconsequential to me," I grate out. "But unfortunately, I don't have any more information for you right now."

I hold her stare so she knows I'm being honest. There's only so much I can say right now that can quell her doubts, but even if I had more to say, Laney would be the one to get those words first.

With a nod, she says, "Okay. But just know that if you hurt her, I have plenty of tools I can use to torture you, and I know of several scrap yards where I can hide your body."

"I wouldn't expect anything less."

She drops her arms and smiles as if she wasn't just threatening my life. "Now, if you'll excuse me, I'm going to go hide these until the big reveal."

"Does Laney know you are surprising us with this?"

"Of course. But even she doesn't know the full extent of what's about to go down." With a wink, she saunters off with her cutouts down the hall toward a storage closet.

"Jesus Christ," I mutter to myself and then get back to work, making sure this room looks perfect for when everyone arrives.

***

"I just want to thank everyone for coming out tonight," Elliot says, raising his beer. "And a special thanks to Laney and Fletcher for making this night happen."

My eyes meet Laney's across the room. She arches a brow and then rolls her eyes, playing her part so perfectly. Little does everyone here know that I know this woman's body intimately now, including how that eye roll looks when she comes.

"To Elliot and Tori!" I shout, lifting my glass. Echoes of agreement ring out and then the entire room of people takes a drink to toast the bride and groom to be.

Elliot walks up to me. "This party is fucking incredible, man. How did you and Laney pull this off?"

"Let's just say I made a few calls and threw some money around."

He slaps me on the back. "Well, it's very much appreciated." His eyes lift to the top of my head. "Nice haircut, by the way."

Reaching up, I make sure it's styled in place. "I was way overdue. Laney hooked me up."

"Glad to see she didn't kill you while you were planning all this." Elliot fans a hand around the room.

*Nope. She was too busy enjoying orgasms and riding my cock to kill me,* I think to myself.

"It was a close call there for a second, but we were able to compromise."

"Good call on the food too. Everyone loves the menu at Blossom Brews, especially the onion rings."

"That was all Laney."

He takes a sip of his beer. "Well, I'll make sure to extend my gratitude to her as well."

Henley and Rhonan stride up to us, holding their own drinks. I jut my chin toward Rhonan. "I brought some Pappy Van Winkle, if you're interested?"

His brows lift. "No shit?"

"Yeah, I figured it was a worthy occasion."

He drains the rest of his beer. "Does that mean you're going to have some with us?"

My instinct is to deflect, but maybe it's time to tell the guys the truth. "I actually don't drink anymore."

All their mouths drop open slightly.

"Seriously?" Rhonan asks. "Since when?"

I rub the back of my neck but then straighten my spine. "Since I was drafted."

Henley nearly falls forward. "Holy shit. Any particular reason?"

*Because my father is an alcoholic and I never want to end up like him.*

My subconscious doesn't let me admit that, though. "I just really hate the way it makes me feel, and I wanted to be able to play my best. I make a lot of fucking money playing a game that I love. I don't take that for granted."

"I get that, but not drinking at all?" Elliot lifts his beer to his lips. "It just seems extreme."

Defensiveness builds inside of me. "What's weird to me is that my choice to *not* drink is considered odd. Why should I be judged because I don't want to put poison in my body?"

Henley clears his throat. "No judgment, Fletch. At least from me. Do what's best for you."

"So, is that why you've taken up yoga?" Rhonan smirks as Elliot and Henley groan simultaneously.

"Dude, you have no idea what kind of torture that was," Elliot says.

Rhonan bursts out laughing. "And I don't plan on ever finding out."

Henley clears his throat. "I was actually thinking of going again next week."

All of us spin our heads toward him. "Really?"

"Look, all I know is that I was more sore after yoga than I am when I lift weights some days. There's nothing wrong with working on flexibility. In fact, research has shown that flexibility is a key factor in the quality and longevity of life."

Elliot looks at him like he's grown two heads. "You were doing research about yoga?"

Henley shakes his head, taking a sip from his beer before answering. "No. Yoga videos just started popping up on my phone after we went and I kind of got sucked in." Turning to me, he says, "Did you know that goat yoga was a thing?"

"I did not."

"Well, maybe you should tell Laney about it."

"Tell me what?" As if we summoned her, the woman I can't stop thinking about comes up behind us, pushing her way into our circle.

"Yoga with baby goats. I think it could be fun. Baby goats are really fucking cute."

Laney fights back her laugh. "You want to do yoga again after last time?"

"Apparently it helps with longevity *and* flexibility," Elliot quips.

Laney nods, glancing between the four of us. "It does. Well, I'll tell you what. I will commission goat yoga if you can get Rhonan to participate in a class."

Rhonan snorts. "Ha, not gonna happen."

Henley looks over at Laney. "Give me some time."

Elliot laughs. "Well, this was not the conversation I was expecting to have at my bachelor party." He slaps me on the back. "Save me a game of blackjack, will ya? I need to go mingle for a bit."

"Of course, man. Enjoy yourself."

Elliot heads toward a group of people I sort of recognize from around town, smiling from ear to ear.

Laney clears her throat. "I'm gonna go see if the bartenders need anything." She gives me a brief look and then saunters off.

"I need a refill," Henley announces before walking away as well, leaving me and Rhonan alone.

"Where's that bourbon?" Rhonan asks, shaking his empty bottle around.

"The bartender has it. Just tell him your name, and he knows what to do."

"Thanks man." I watch Rhonan head in that direction. The second he gets far enough away, I let out the breath I didn't realize I was holding.

I hate feeling like I'm betraying him, but Laney and I have too much shit to figure out before I potentially jeopardize our friendship.

Henley comes up beside me, leaning in close and lowering his voice. "By the smile on his face, I'm guessing you weren't just telling Rhonan that you have feelings for his sister."

My head spins toward him so fast that I nearly fall over. "What are you talking about?"

"Dude, if you're going to eye-fuck Laney, you need to be more subtle about it."

Glancing around, I realize that we probably shouldn't be having this conversation where other people can eavesdrop. Motioning for him to follow me, I lead him down the back hallway.

When we're alone, I ask, "Was it really that fucking obvious?"

Henley lifts his beer to his lips as he shrugs. "I don't know if other people noticed, but I sure as hell did."

"Fuck." I rake a hand through my hair. "I guess now's the time to admit that I wasn't in the bathroom when I disappeared on you at The Charming Bull."

His brows knit together. "What do you mean?"

Rubbing the back of my neck, I stare down at the ground. "Let's just say Laney and I have a history."

He blinks a few times and then closes his eyes. "You fucking didn't, man."

"Not back then," I cut him off quickly. "But as of last night..."

Henley covers his face with his hand. "Jesus Christ. Did you forget the pact?"

"No, but it wasn't just some heat-of-the-moment thing. It was mutual," I whisper, moving in closer to him. "It meant something, okay?"

"You slept with Rhonan's sister," he says, like I haven't already been haunted by that fact for the past twenty-four hours.

My back straightens as I reply, "I did and I'd do it again because it was always meant to happen."

If there's one thing I know now, it's that my feelings for Laney aren't wrong, no matter how it may make Rhonan or the other guys feel. No, my feelings for Laney are the only thing that's felt right in the past twelve years, and it took my coming home for Elliot's wedding to admit that.

Henley's phone rings in his pocket. He takes it out, declines the call, and shoves it back in. "Freaking Meghan again."

"She's still calling you, huh?"

"Yup."

"Well, maybe you should finally talk to her and see what she wants?"

"She'll get the hint eventually." Shaking off his irritation, he goes back to our previous topic. "So what does this mean? Are you moving back here? How is that going to work with football?"

I let out a heavy sigh. "I don't have all the fucking answers right now, Henley. All I know is that for the first time in years, I feel like a part of me just snapped back into place." I tap the center of my chest. "I can't explain it, but Laney and I... It's real, man."

Henley crosses his arms over his chest while widening his stance. "Then let me warn you—you need to figure out some answers to those questions fast because Rhonan deserves to know, and Laney doesn't deserve to be strung along."

"I'm not stringing her along."

"So, she's in this then?" he asks, waving his hand back and forth between us.

"It's...complicated." The last thing I want to do right now is explain to Henley what's transpired over the last few weeks.

He blows out a breath. "I just don't see this ending well."

"It has to," I say, even though in the pit of my stomach I know the risks I'm taking here—not just for me, but for Laney too. The moment we slept together, everything shifted. Nothing will ever be the same between us. "But fuck, man...she's..."

My words trail off as Dilynne and Laney round the corner and begin walking right toward us.

*Mine*, my mind finishes for me as I watch Laney saunter toward me, her hips swaying in her dark red dress, her lips painted the same hue, and her long hair down, straight and silky.

"What are you two doing out here?" Dilynne asks. "The party is that way." She points behind her.

"We were just having a private conversation," Henley responds.

"You two have conversations about your privates?" Dilynne wrinkles her nose. "Eww, gross. You should be talking to your doctor about those sorts of issues."

Henley flashes his sister a deadpan look. "Hilarious."

She shrugs. "I thought so. Now, if you'll excuse me, you're standing in my way." Pointing to the storage closet behind me, she says, "I need to get my cutouts for my game."

Laney looks at me, shrugging. "I'm just here to help with supplies, apparently."

"You left my sister in charge of games?" Henley asks. "Jesus, I thought you were smarter than that, Laney."

"I needed help, and she saved the day for me, all right?"

"Exactly. Coming up with adult-themed bachelorette party games is my superpower, apparently."

"I'm so happy to know my sister has many talents." Henley heads back toward the main room. "I'll see you guys back in there."

Dilynne walks into the storage closet, retrieving the cutouts, handing two of them to Laney. "Come on, Laney. Let's get this game set up so I can see everyone's reactions."

Dilynne heads back toward the party, but as Laney moves to follow her, I reach out and grab her hand, pulling her back to my chest.

"Fletcher..."

"You look so fucking sexy, Laney." I drag my nose up the side of her neck, pausing to nibble her earlobe. "Fuck, I want to find out what's underneath this dress."

She turns her head to meet my eyes, a mischievous grin on her lips. "Nothing."

"What?"

"I don't have anything on underneath this dress, Fletcher," she says, making me grow even harder than I already was. "That's what you wanted from me, wasn't it? No underwear for easier access next time we saw each other?" She rubs her nose against mine.

"Fuck, angel," I growl out, kissing her neck. "Meet me in this closet in fifteen minutes."

Her mischievous smile disappears. "But Fletcher... We can't." Her eyes bounce around the hallway. "We shouldn't..."

"I honestly don't give a fuck right now. I need to taste you, feel you," I say, desperation lacing my words. "I need to know that this is real."

She closes her eyes and sighs as my lips move down to her collarbone. "It *is* real."

Popping my head up, our eyes meet again. "Then prove it. Meet me here in fifteen minutes."

"Fine," she says before I release her hand and she walks away from me, glancing over her shoulder before returning to the party.

And as I reach down to adjust my cock that might just be permanently hard at this point, I accept that I'll probably burn in hell for wanting my best friend's little sister. But at this point, I don't even fucking care.

＊＊＊

"Oh. My. God," Laney says as Dilynne stands proudly in front of the cardboard cutouts of me and my three best friends.

"It's amazing, isn't it?"

Laney shakes her head back and forth slowly. "I'm... I'm literally speechless. You've finally done something that I have no words for."

Chuckling to myself, I cross my arms over my chest and admire Dilynne's creativity, but only because the picture she chose for my cutout is one of my favorites. It's from the Carolina Thunder calendar that Glenn had me sign last week, and I was Mr. April.

I wonder if Laney knows why I chose that month.

All the guests have gathered around the left side of the room where Dilynne has set up her game.

"Now, I'm sure most of you have played the classic game of Pin the Tail on the Donkey," she starts. "Well, may I present to you, pin the object on the men of the Blackjack Brotherhood."

Rhonan turns to me. "Who the fuck calls us that?"

Elliot wraps his arm around both of our shoulders, wedging himself between us. "I don't know, but I fucking like it. It has pizzaz. Sounds badass, but also smart. Like we could kill you with our bare hands or know the odds of winning a hand in a card game so we don't have to get our hands dirty at all."

Henley rolls his eyes. "I'm so glad that y'all find this amusing."

Elliot laughs. "The alcohol is helping."

"Now, for the objects," Dilynne continues, Vanna White style. "For Fletcher, you'll be pinning the football on his junk."

My smile falls. "What the…"

"For Rhonan, a pair of handcuffs," she says cheekily, holding up the laminated pieces she made for each of our cutouts. "For Elliot, a gavel." Elliot beams with pride next to me. "And for my brother, a snowboard."

"Fuck, she nailed each one of us on the head," Rhonan mutters beside me.

The women of the party eagerly line up to be the first ones blindfolded, but one woman in particular hangs back.

*Good girl.*

Tori comes up next to us, her cheeks flushed, presumably from the alcohol she's consumed. She wraps her arms around Elliot's waist, and looks up at him with pouty lips. "I don't like the idea of women pinning your junk."

He dips his mouth to hers, coaxing her lips open with his tongue, like we're not all standing right here. The rest of us look away until he resurfaces. "Don't worry, baby. You're the only one that gets the real thing."

Tori giggles. "Good." The sound of ringing pulls her from their moment. When she retrieves her phone from her pocket, she groans.

Elliot's jovial mood instantly sours. "Seriously? He can't leave you alone for one night?"

"Let me just see what he wants." Tori answers the phone and disappears down the hall.

Elliot drains the rest of his beer as I clear my throat. "Who was that?"

"Her fucking boss, man. I swear, he can't fucking blink without her help. I can't wait until she quits working for him."

I pat him on the back. "Soon, man."

"Yeah, I know." Shaking off his irritation, he rubs his hands together, plastering his goofy smile back on his lips. "All right. Which one of you am I going to try to 'pin' first?"

Henley holds his hand out toward the games. "You're going to participate in this?"

"Contrary to how I feel about your sister and her asinine ideas most days, I think this is one of her best."

"Don't let her hear you say that, or you'll never live it down," Henley says.

Elliot teeters his head back and forth. "Good point. Maybe I shouldn't play." Then he turns to me. "Are you gonna take a stab at this?"

"Fuck no."

"Dear God, there's more," Henley mutters as Carolina comes waltzing into the room, pushing a rather large cake on a rolling cart before I can escape.

Stepping up to her, I peer at the cake. "Carolina, what the fuck is that?"

Smirking, she stops at the buffet table, lifting the cardboard slab from the cart and sliding it onto the table. "Ask Dilynne to explain. I'm just the delivery person."

My head spins to find Dilynne tiptoeing over to the table. "Ah! It's here!"

Laney steps up to the table, examining the cake as well. "Dilynne Marie Clark. You didn't! You were just supposed to come up with a game."

"Well, I got another idea and couldn't resist." Dilynne loses all composure as she grips her stomach, laughing above the noise of the room full of people. "Oh my God! Carolina, you just made all my dreams come true."

Carolina takes a dramatic bow. "Glad to be of service. Y'all enjoy. And remember, there's cream filling." With a wink, she pushes her cart back out the way she came.

Rhonan shakes his head. "Cream filling. How appropriate."

Elliot walks over to check out the cake for himself, but when he sees the penis-shaped cake with his and Tori's pictures on the testicles, his smile from before evaporates.

"What the actual fuck?"

"Hey. This is for the ladies. At a bachelorette party, there would normally be a phallic-shaped cake. I just decided to make it special and put your faces on it."

Elliot glares at Dilynne. "You're deranged."

"Well, if you didn't want my input, you shouldn't have invited me." Peering around the room, she yells, "Who wants to cut the penis?"

"I'm going to the bathroom," I say, turning to the other guys. "Can someone watch Elliot and Dilynne, please? Especially when the knife comes out?"

"I'm on it," Henley says.

As I head toward the hallway, I glance back to make sure Laney sees me. We make eye contact for the briefest moment and then I walk straight to the storage closet, stepping inside to wait for my girl.

*Fuck, what is this woman doing to me?*

Relationships have never been on my radar. Sure, there have been women to scratch an itch when necessary, but not one of those women ever made me feel or want the things that Laney does.

*None of them have ever been her.*

Despite what I may want to admit, I think I've always measured women against her, and that's why none of them ever stuck—because they never were, and never could be Laney Hart.

I'm so fucking screwed.

A few moments later, a soft knock sounds on the door. "Fletcher?" Laney whispers. "It's me."

I fling the door open and pull her inside, shutting the door just as quickly. My mouth crashes to hers, hungry and unapologetic.

"You wore this dress to torture me tonight, didn't you?" I mutter between nipping her lips.

She drags her nails down the back of my head. "Maybe."

"Well, now you're about to get fucked in this dress."

She leans back. "Fletcher, we can't."

"Oh yes, we fucking can," I say as I unbutton my slacks and shove them down along with my briefs. "Prop your leg on the shelf behind you." Laney glances behind her and then moves back, lifting her heel-covered foot to the nearest shelf. "Now lift your dress and let me see that pussy."

She licks her lips and holds my stare as she hikes the hem of her dress up slowly, baring herself to me. And fuck, her obedience brings out my inner caveman even more than the sight of her glistening and ready for my cock. This woman is normally ready for a fight. But when she lets me take control, it's such a fucking turn on.

I pump my cock in my hand. "This is gonna be fast and hard because we don't have a lot of time, but if I don't get inside you again, I'm going to fucking lose my mind."

"Fletcher," she moans as she reaches up and grips the shelving behind her.

"Every time you say my fucking name, Laney...it makes me want to brand you as mine." I step up to her and drag the head of my cock through her slit. She's already fucking soaked, so ready for me. When the head meets her clit, I swirl it around that little nub a few times.

"God, Fletcher. Please…"

"Already begging?"

"Yes. I need you."

I cup the side of her face, line my cock up to her entrance, and push inside as I lock eyes with her and say, "I fucking need you too, Laney. You have no fucking idea how much." When I meet her end in one smooth stroke, we groan simultaneously, but I reach up quickly and press my finger to her lips. "You've got to be quiet, baby." She nods against my finger as I withdraw from her and thrust forward again. "Fucking hell, Laney. This pussy will be the death of me."

She lets her head fall back as I pick up the pace. "Oh…" *Thrust.* "My…" *Thrust.* "God…" *Thrust.* Her moans and words just spur me on.

I wrap my hands around her wrists, pinning them to the shelves before finding her lips with my own, thrusting long and hard, shaking the shelving behind us, even though the last thing I should be doing is making more fucking noise.

"This party is insane," Henley's voice outside of the closet makes us both freeze.

"I know. Laney and Fletcher really outdid themselves," Rhonan says next, which makes my heart beat even faster.

My cock is buried in his sister, and he's out there singing my praises.

*Fuck. I really am going to burn in hell.*

"I wanted the four of us to play a game of blackjack, but I can't find him," Rhonan continues.

I lock eyes with Laney while I start thrusting in and out of her again, not even her brother's voice stopping me from making this woman come on my cock.

Her breathing grows more shallow and small moans escape her lips as I pick up my pace, so I reach up and gently cover her mouth to stifle the noise.

"You're getting close, aren't you?" I whisper. She nods, eyes wild. "You're going to come all over my cock, aren't you, baby?" Her eyes widen as she sucks in her breath even faster. "Don't fucking come." My hand tightens slightly over her mouth. "Don't you dare fucking come until I say you can."

She whimpers, but all that does is make me want to fuck her harder.

God, this woman makes me crazy

All these years, she hated me because she thought I wanted that inconsequential girl instead of her. If only she knew how hard it was to walk away from her that night. I will spend the rest of my life apologizing for making her feel that way. I can't take my past actions back, but I can prove my feelings for her through my actions now, including fucking her as much as I can to make up for lost time.

My lips rest against her ear. "Do you fucking feel what you do to me, Laney? Do you feel how fucking hard you make me? Do you feel how slick your pussy is as I stuff you full of my cock? Do you feel every ounce of desire I've held for you pouring out of me as I fuck you?"

"I'm pretty sure he's in the bathroom," Henley says from beyond the door. "Come on, let's get back to the party. I think Elliot is gonna try to pin the cuffs on your junk next."

"Fucking Dilynne," Rhonan groans and then the sound of their feet gets softer until I can't hear them anymore.

Laney's eyes are still locked on mine as I reach down and rub her clit with my thumb. "Come for me, angel."

With my hand still over her mouth, she falls apart as her eyes roll into the back of her head. I lift my hand and replace it with my mouth, swallowing her cries as I fuck her through it.

As soon as I know she's done, I thrust a few more times and then spill myself inside her, my forehead resting on hers as my body twitches. "Jesus...fuck."

"Fletcher..." Her forehead rests on my shoulder.

"You make me insane, Laney."

She moves to shove me away once her post-orgasm haze dissipates, but I don't budge. "My brother could have heard us."

"But he didn't." Cupping her face, I pull out of her and then check her wrists as she puts her foot down. "I didn't hurt you, did I?"

"No." She brushes her hair from her face, her eyes still dilated. "I'm pretty sure that was the most intense orgasm I've ever had, though."

"Me too, baby." Breathing out a sigh of relief, I slowly kiss her until my heart rate returns to normal. We get cleaned up as best we can and then I reach for the doorknob. "I'll go out first."

"Okay."

"But Laney?"

"Yeah?"

"Don't make any plans tomorrow night."

One of her brows lifts. "And what's happening tomorrow night?"

"You're staying over at my place."

She pops her hip to the side. "I am, am I?"

"Yeah, baby. You are. Because the next time we fuck, it's going to be somewhere that you can scream as loud as you want."

"Fletcher—" she starts, but I cut her off, cupping her face in my hands again.

"Don't overthink this. Just feel it." Placing my hand on the center of her chest, I plead with her the best way I know how.

I know she can't deny what's happening to us, but it doesn't mean we have to label it right away either.

*You're kind of running out of time though, Fletcher.*

I press one more kiss to her lips and then release her from my grasp. "I'll see you back out there."

Her voice comes out as a whisper. "Okay."

Turning for the door, I flash her a wink before leaving her in the storage closet, even though that's the last fucking thing that I want to do.

But when I close the door behind me, I run smack dab into Rhonan.

"There you are," he says, his brows drawn together.

Clearing my throat, I struggle not to freak out. "Uh, yup. Here I am."

"What were you doing in the storage closet?"

*Quick, Fletcher. Think.*

"Uh, Laney asked me to look for something, but it wasn't in there."

"Well, what did she need?"

I scratch the back of my head, trying to buy time. "You know what? I don't even remember."

Rhonan eyes me curiously. "You forgot what you were supposed to be looking for?"

"Yeah, I think my lack of sleep has finally caught up to me." I force out a yawn.

"Okay then." Rhonan pushes his shirt sleeves farther up his forearms. "Well, the boys want to play blackjack. You in?"

"Naturally."

"Then let's do it." Rhonan motions me to follow him back to the party as I release the breath I was holding in. But as I do, I glance over my shoulder to the closet where I know Laney is still hiding.

Running into Rhonan just made the consequences of my actions more real.

I have to figure out how to make this work.

I need to figure out how to convince him that our pact was juvenile and doesn't make sense anymore.

But more importantly, I need Laney to see what can be possible between us, because if she doesn't want the same things as me, the rest doesn't matter.

# Chapter 24

**Fletcher**

***Spaghetti and Hot Tub Admissions***

I fluff the pillows on the couch for the third time as I walk past them again. Fuck, I'm nervous. I don't know why, but maybe it's because tonight I'm going to lay everything on the line with Laney, and I only hope that she's open to a future for us.

When I texted her this morning to let her know where I was staying and when to be here, she insisted that we at least use this time tonight to work on a few wedding things so we don't have to scrape anything together at the last minute like the bachelor and bachelorette party—even though everyone had a great fucking time last night, Elliot and Tori especially.

I had planned on ordering dinner for us since I'm not that great of a cook and didn't want to risk food poisoning, but Laney insisted she cook for us instead. And as I stand in my rental cabin, waiting for her to arrive, that gesture makes me feel even more inadequate.

What I have to offer her isn't much. In fact, besides the size of my bank account, I have a grueling career, a lack of relationship experience, an alcoholic father who puts me in a bad mood any time we speak, and a group of friends that all agreed we would never date each other's sisters—a detail I'm choosing to ignore as I ask Laney for a chance for us to be together.

A knock on the door pulls me from my thoughts. I race to answer it, and when I see her on the other side dressed in a simple navy cotton dress with her hair pulled back from her face and a nervous smile on her lips, my chest instantly relaxes.

"Hey, angel."

"Hi." She holds out a grocery bag to me. "Can you take this, please? I need to get the wedding stuff out of my car."

"I can get it," I say, preparing to drop the groceries on the ground and retrieve the rest of the stuff for her.

"No, it's fine. There's some cheese and stuff in that bag that needs to go in the fridge anyway. Start unpacking it and I'll be right back." She moves to walk away, but I reach for her hand before she gets too far, spinning her back into my chest. "Fletcher..."

I swallow her words with my mouth, not wanting one more second to pass without feeling her lips against mine. Her mouth opens for me as I coax her tongue with mine, teasing her and drowning in the way this woman makes me fucking feel—like she was always meant to be mine.

"Sorry. I just needed that real quick."

She rolls her eyes. "You act like you didn't just see me last night."

"Yeah, but it's been almost twenty-four hours."

"You're ridiculous," she says, a quirk of amusement on her lips as she heads back out to her car. I watch her the entire time, and when she returns and realizes I'm still standing there holding the bag of groceries, she scoffs. "I told you to unload those."

"I wanted to make sure you got back inside okay," I reply, shutting the door and locking it behind her.

"It's not like someone was going to kidnap me in your driveway."

"You never know."

"This is Blossom Peak, Fletcher. Our crime rate is like nonexistent."

I step up to her and pull her into me by her waist. "But if anything were to happen to you, I'd lose my fucking mind."

Her eyes bounce back and forth between mine. "Your caveman is showing, Fletcher Adams."

"Well, you bring him out of me, Laney Hart."

I release her as she starts taking items from the bag and placing them on the counter. "You know, I've survived twelve years without you just fine."

"Only because you thought you hated me."

"Who says I still don't?" she fires back, a playful quirk in her lips.

"Well, the way you were screaming under my hand last night in the storage closet sure didn't sound like you hated me. In fact, it sounded like you were having the best orgasm of your life."

She rolls her eyes again. "Eh, I've had better."

"Then you were lying to me yesterday?"

She squeals as I lift her up and place her on the counter.

"Hey!"

Holding her chin between my fingers, I lower my voice. "Just admit that no other man who has had the honor of being with you has fucked you the way I do, Laney."

"You already know that." She runs her hands up my arms to my neck, wrapping her arms around me.

"Damn right. And you know why?"

She sighs dramatically. "Why, Fletcher?"

"Because none of them were me. None of them had our history." I nip at her bottom lip. "None of them has wanted you since they were seventeen…"

*And refuses to let you go again.*

Softly, I press our lips together, fighting to keep myself from spilling my guts to her this early in the evening. But when I pull back, that's when I actually take a moment to assess the items she's brought with her.

"Are you…making spaghetti?"

"Yeah. My mom's recipe," she answers so easily, as if she didn't just make me fall in love with her even more.

"You have no idea how much I want to cry right now."

Her giggle makes my heart beat even faster. "It's just spaghetti, Fletcher."

"That spaghetti was one of the only things I looked forward to for years, Laney. Being invited to have dinner with your family gave me an escape from the hell of living with my dad. It gave me stability, calm, and hope—that is until I ended up in your room that first night, and then it was your smile, your eyes, and your heart that kept me going."

"Fletcher…" Her eyes are shining from unshed tears, but she doesn't say anything. Instead, she pulls my mouth to her this time. When we part, she hops down from the counter, but I press one more kiss to her lips before I let her go completely. "Do you want to help me?"

"I don't want to fuck it up," I say, referring to more than just spaghetti.

"You won't," she assures me. "Besides, you should learn the recipe. My mom would want you to have it."

I can only hope that Mrs. Hart would have approved of me for her daughter.

***

"I watched the draft," Laney admits from her spot next to me in the hot tub. We ate dinner, cleaned up the mess, finalized the place cards and seating chart for the wedding, and now we're enjoying drinks—wine for her, water for me—in the hot tub on the back patio.

"You did?"

"I did. And your first game. I cried when you made your first catch."

"Jesus, Laney. There's no crying in football."

She laughs, pushing back my hair with her hand. "I was so proud of you, even though I hated you."

"I think we've established that you hated me, babe."

"I hate that I hated you for so long."

"Let it go, Laney. Please," I say, pulling her lips to mine. "I have—because being like this with you is so much better."

"I actually have your jersey too," she adds.

I lean back, narrowing my eyes at her. "You do not..."

"No one knows, not even Dilynne. It needs to stay that way too, got it?" she threatens, twisting my nipple in between her fingers.

I yelp. "Jesus! Why can't anyone know?"

"Can you imagine if Glenn found out? Dear God, I'd never live it down."

"Oh, Glenn. He seems harmless."

"He really is, but he's also the one who's contributed to the Lucifer jar more than any other person in the salon."

"Speaking of which, can I stop being Lucifer now?"

She purses her lips playfully. "I don't know…"

"When did that start, by the way?"

Sighing, she moves her hands through the water in front of her, avoiding my gaze. "After your first season with the Thunder. People around town were talking about you like crazy. Everywhere I went, I heard your name. You weren't even here, and I couldn't escape you. So, I made it a rule that no one was allowed to say your name in my salon, that way I had one place where I could block you from my mind."

"Did it work?"

"No," she admits. "You were always there."

"You've always been on mine too, angel. Especially when I came back to town and you wouldn't come around."

She brushes my hair back again. "I was trying to move on, Fletcher."

Testing the waters metaphorically, I say, "Did you ever wonder why my picture was in the month of April for the calendar?"

"Because that's when my birthday is," she replies.

"Bingo. I tried to move on too, Laney. There were times I had to force myself to block you out just so I could focus on my job. But I've kept tabs on you—following the salon on social media and through your brother, seeing pictures of you at car shows with Dilynne, staring at pictures of you and Ellis that your brother has posted over the years."

"I haven't googled you in two years," she admits. "I was pretty proud of that one, considering that I used to do it every night."

"Damn. Why are you so obsessed with me?" I tease her, tickling her ribs.

"Um, I think you're talking about yourself, mister break-into-my-phone-to-access-my glucose-monitor."

I pull her mouth to mine. "And I'd do it again. I like knowing that you're okay."

"I'm not used to people worrying about me," she admits on a whisper against my lips.

"Well, you'd better start getting used to it, because that's something I want to be my responsibility now."

She leans back, assessing me, her brows drawing together. "What do you mean?"

"Fuck, I was gonna wait until later to say this, but..." Lifting her hair from her neck, I bury my head there, pressing my lips to her skin until I make my way up to her ear. And then I pull her onto my lap and whisper, "I want this, Laney."

"Want what?"

I lean back and look right into her eyes. "You. Me. Us. I—I want to make this work."

Her whole face transforms—pure shock written all over it. "Oh my God, Fletcher—"

Pressing a finger to her lips, I silence her. "Don't say anything right now, but just know that I've never been more certain of anything in my life. Last night, it all became so clear to me—because not being able to hold you and let everyone know that you're mine was killing me. This possessiveness that you bring out in me had nowhere to go. I know we have so much to talk about and things to figure out. I'm sure you have questions, and I sure as fuck know that I don't have many answers right now. But what I do know is that I've wanted you since I was seventeen. And now that we've finally uncovered the truth of what happened between us in the past, I want to try to make this work."

Her eyes are full of tears. "I—I can't..."

"Like I said, you don't have to say anything right now." Pulling her hand from under the water and placing it over the center of my chest, I hold it there. "Just know that this is how I feel and what I want. The final decision is up to you."

The lump in my throat feels like the size of a softball, but at least now she knows how I feel, what I want, and that I'm willing to do whatever it takes to make it work.

"Kiss me, Fletcher," she says, pulling me back to the moment.

So I do what I'm told, taking her request as a sign that at least she's not saying no.

# Chapter 25

**Laney**

### *Face Down, Ass Up*

I have to be dreaming. There's no way that I'm straddling Fletcher Adams in a hot tub and he's telling me that he wants a future with me.

But is that what I want?

"You have no idea what you do to me, Laney Hart. No fucking clue."

Before I can get another word out, Fletcher crushes his mouth to mine, pulling our bodies together so tightly that no space exists between us.

When our lips touch, I swear I can see fireworks and heat blooms all over my skin. My hands are shaking as I bury them in his hair and drag my nails down his neck, extracting a groan from him that ignites even more heat between my legs.

He grips my hip possessively with one hand as he buries the other in my hair, holding me to him, guiding me to tip my head to the side as his tongue passes over my lips, beckoning me to open up to him. When our tongues touch, we moan simultaneously and then I gasp for air on a shaky breath.

Fletcher spins us around, pushing me against the side of the hot tub, pinning me there with his hips and his cock—his long, hard length that I've felt before, but not like this. Not full of this need and intent, not this laced with passion and consumption that makes me want to freeze this moment in time and never leave this house.

Because beyond this bubble is the real world with real problems I'm not ready to face.

Fletcher Adams is kissing me, claiming me, owning me—and it's better than I ever imagined.

"Fucking hell, Laney," he mumbles against my lips, lifting me by my hips and setting me on the ledge.

"Don't stop kissing me."

"You're fucking crazy if you think I'm going to." We claw and pull at each other, trying to get closer. Our kisses become deeper and sloppier before Fletcher starts to slow things down. He trails his fingers up and down my arms, pressing soft kisses to my lips now—teasing and torturing me before finally leaning back and staring down at me as I open my eyes. "Laney Hart..." he whispers, stroking his thumb along my jaw.

My heart is bursting with so many emotions that it's hard to pinpoint if what I feel is excitement or fear. Nonetheless, Fletcher asked me for a chance and if I don't let us figure out what's between us, then that will be a regret I'll have to live with for the rest of my life.

"We need to get inside—now," he says, command in his voice. "I need you naked."

He helps me stand and then climbs out after me, adjusting himself in his swim trunks before leading me back inside the cabin and to his room. We step into the bathroom where he turns on the shower to let it heat up, and then he's back on me, pulling on the strings of my bathing suit top before tossing it to the floor. When his mouth closes over my nipple, I let out an embarrassingly loud moan.

"You're so fucking perfect," he says as his tongue laps at my nipple.

I bury my hands in his hair as he moves to my other breast. "Your mouth..."

"What about my mouth?"

"Your tongue, your words..." I moan again as he drags my nipple through his teeth.

When he lifts his head, the look in his eyes tells me I was powerless to fight my feelings for this man. I thought I was in control, I thought I could protect my heart. But Fletcher's blue eyes have always unnerved me, and right now, I know that I don't ever want another day to pass where I don't get to look at them from the moment I wake up to the moment I go to sleep. We owe it to ourselves to try to figure this out.

"Get naked." His voice is low, commanding. And I don't hesitate. I hold his stare as I push down my swim bottoms and he unties his board shorts, revealing his cock to me.

I lick my lips as my mouth starts to water. God, I want to taste him.

He leads me by the hand into the shower, pulling me under the water with him as the spray rains down on us. "I've got to get us clean before I dirty you up again."

I crack a smile. "Oh really?"

"Yeah, I like you a little dirty, though." He pushes my hair from my face. "There's so many ways I want to fuck you, Laney Hart."

I push him against the wall behind us so the water hits my back. ""Well, I think it's my turn to live out a fantasy."

He watches as I fall to my knees. "Jesus, angel."

Reaching for his cock, I lick him from the base all the way to the head, swirling my tongue around his tip.

I look up at him. "Put your hands behind you on the wall."

He smirks, tipping my chin up with his fingers. "You can't tell me what to do," he says, throwing my own words back at me.

"Really?" I fire back. "What if I said that I bet I can make you come in less than three minutes?"

Fletcher groans as he tips his head back. "Fuck, I can't wait to find out if that's true." I swirl my tongue around his head again before drawing him into my mouth, taking him as far back as I can before I gag. "Gag on my cock like that again and I'm definitely going to come fast."

He reaches to cup my chin, but I pull him out of my mouth. "Hands behind you, Fletcher."

"Yes, ma'am."

I get back to work, taking him in long, slow drags, passing my tongue down his entire length, gagging every time he hits the back of my throat. And when I see him fight to take in air, I reach down and cup his balls in my hand, rolling them gently.

"Fuck!"

This man—this professional athlete with strength that rivals most men—is about to come apart at the seams and I've never felt more powerful.

*Me. Laney Hart.*

*I think I might come from this experience too.*

I release his balls and move my hand to my clit as I continue to pull him in and out of my mouth.

"Goddamn. Yes, baby. Touch that clit. Make yourself come as I come down your throat."

With a few more passes of my mouth and hand, Fletcher and I break at the same time. I moan around his cock as my orgasm slams into me and his cum hits my tongue. His hand fists in my hair, holding me still as he empties himself in my mouth, and when the last drop leaves his cock, I swallow as he pulls me up from the floor and crushes his mouth to mine.

"You just fucking ruined me," he mumbles against my lips, spinning me around and pressing me against the wall, reaching between my legs to find me dripping. "Fuck, you enjoyed that, didn't you?"

"Yes," I breathe out. "But I want more."

"Oh, I'm going to give it to you." Fletcher quickly washes us both and then dries me off. "Get on the bed on your hands and knees. Ass up, head down."

His commands make my entire body heat up and sparks of electricity travel down to the tips of my toes. I do exactly as he says, waiting in my position in the middle of the bed, growing needier for him with each passing second.

I feel him enter the room before I see him.

"Fuck, I wish you could see yourself right now—ass in the air, pussy wet and glistening, begging for my cock."

"Fletcher..." I gasp. "Fuck me, please."

His knees hit the bed. A beat later, I feel the hot swipe of his tongue along my slit before he flicks it lower, teasing my asshole. My breath catches as heat flares between my legs.

"God, I want to ruin you," he practically growls.

"Then give me your cock, Fletcher. Please..."

He rubs my ass before smacking it gently. "Fuck, hearing you beg...it's making me even harder."

"Show me," I plead. "Own me, Fletcher."

He crawls onto the bed fully now, leaning over my back so his lips can meet my neck. "You already own me, Laney."

He teases my opening with his cock, pushing just an inch inside. "God, yes..." But then he pulls right back out. "No..."

"Patience, baby." He smacks my ass again. "You'll get my cock when I'm ready to give it to you."

"I'm ready now," I whine, growing wetter the longer he leaves me here in this position, knowing he's right behind me, so close and yet denying us both what we want. He leans down and bites my shoulder blade, making me gasp. Growing more frustrated by the second, I reach down between my legs and start playing with my clit. I only get a few strokes in before he grabs both of my wrists and pins my hands behind me.

"I didn't say you could touch yourself."

"God, Fletcher. Please. I'm trembling."

With one hand holding my wrists behind my back and the other gripping my hips, he says, "Good. Then you're ready."

And then he slams into me.

"Fuck!" I scream as he pounds into me hard and fast, smacking my ass with his free hand. "God, yes. More."

"I will never get enough of this, angel. Fuck, you should see the way this pussy takes me. So fucking wet, so greedy, so tight."

I scream each time he bottoms out and then he wraps both of his hands around my wrists and pulls me up from the bed so my back hits his chest. His legs widen beneath me as he continues to pound into me. Reaching around my waist now with one hand, he finds my clit and rubs it softly. "Come all over my cock, Laney. Fucking soak the sheets."

"Fletcher!" I scream before my orgasm rips through my body. A few seconds later he finds his release, spilling every drop of his cum inside me.

He releases my wrists and wraps his arms around me, avoiding my insulin pump.

"Goddamn," he breathes out.

"That was…"

He pulls out of me, flips me onto my back, and hovers over my face, propping himself up on the bed. I feel his fingers part me as he moves his cum around my pussy. "I don't think I'll ever get my fill of you. I still can't believe we're here like this…together." His voice comes out low and shaky.

"Me either." My heart is pounding, but not just from the physical exertion.

Fletcher has told me everything I've wanted to hear from him for so long—I just don't know what I'm supposed to do about it. And until I do, I'd rather say nothing at all.

***

"Is that a hickey?" Dilynne asks when she gets in my car.

I reach up to cover the spot where my shoulder meets my neck. "No…"

"It is! Jesus. Is Fletcher insane? Anyone with eyes and half a brain would know what that is."

"I told him not to." Fighting my grin, I turn to my best friend and shrug.

"You'd just better hope that your brother doesn't see it, or better yet, that it fades before the wedding."

"I think I'll be okay, but just to be on the safe side, I should probably try to find a dress that covers my collarbone."

It's Tuesday morning, and Dilynne and I are on our way into Charlotte to find my bridesmaid's dress. There are more shops and options in the city, and the two-hour drive gives us plenty of time to catch up after this weekend. Plus, it's good practice for me to see just how grueling this drive will be if I start making it regularly to see Fletcher.

"Well, given the state of your skin and the smile that hasn't left your face, I take it your weekend went well?"

I sigh as I turn onto the highway. "It did, but I'm also confused."

"Talk to me then. We have two hours to kill, and I need to make sure you're not just thinking with your clit here."

"What?" I ask through a laugh.

"Guys think with their dicks, girls think with our clits. It's an equivalent metaphor."

"Well, my clit is more than satisfied, but Fletcher brought up something this weekend that my clit, unfortunately, can't decide for me."

"Elaborate."

For the next twenty minutes, I recount the admission from Fletcher, his declaration of how he feels, and his request to make a relationship work between us after this wedding.

"Well, where's your head at, Laney?" Dilynne asks when I finish.

"I—I honestly don't know. What he said? It was everything I've ever wanted to hear from him, but things are much more complicated now than they were back then. He lives in Charlotte, I live in Blossom Peak. His career is there, and my business is at home."

"Charlotte is only a two-hour drive. I mean, we're making it right now for a freaking dress." Dilynne smacks her gum as she reaches forward and skips the song on my playlist.

"True, but it's not just the distance. Being with Fletcher means being under a microscope. The entire world will know who I am. And then there's Rhonan to consider."

"What about Rhonan?"

I blow out a breath. "I'm not sure how he would feel about me dating one of his friends. We never really talked about that growing up, but I think it's because he never thought I'd want to date Fletcher, Henley, or Elliot."

Dilynne scoffs. "First of all, neither of us is desperate enough to date Elliot."

I laugh. "By the way, the cake?"

Dilynne smiles proudly. "Seeing Tori's reaction to her face on a freaking testicle was worth every penny."

"I think you're enjoying getting them both riled up a little too much."

"Elliot is a given, but now that I can mess with his fiancée too? Well, that's just icing on the cake, pun intended."

"Anyway," I say, rolling my eyes. "There's so much to consider when it comes to what a life would be like with Fletcher. And I can't help but wonder what my mom would think."

I miss being able to talk to her about things like this, the difficult moments in life that feel like huge ones, the kind of decisions that will change the course of my life moving forward.

"She loved Fletcher."

"Yeah, but when he was just Rhonan's friend. Not sure how she'd feel knowing he had feelings for her only daughter."

"Back then? She probably wouldn't have been thrilled and would have definitely put a stop to him sneaking into your room at night if she knew." Nervous laughter pours out of me. "But now, I can just hear your mom saying that she'd be thrilled as long as you were happy.

Remember when she used to tell us that the most important thing to look for in a man was how he made us feel about ourselves?" I nod, growing emotional from Dilynne's own memories of my mother. "That it wasn't about his looks, his job, the money he made, or how many friends he had… It was all about how he made us *feel*—like we could be ourselves and he wouldn't try to change us, that he would encourage us to chase our dreams, even as they changed, that no matter how hard things got, he always treated us with respect."

"God, I miss her," I croak out as tears fall from my eyes.

Dilynne squeezes my hand. "I miss her too, Laney. She was like my mom too, you know?"

"I do." Dilynne and Henley's upbringing was more than chaotic, but my parents always kept a safe space for her and her brother in our home.

My best friend swipes under her eyes now. "Fuck, okay. New topic, please. I did not plan on crying today, so I didn't wear my waterproof mascara."

"You plan for tears?"

"I have to. Can't risk a streak ruining my image."

***

Dilynne motions for me to spin around. "Yup. That's the winner. Your ass looks amazing."

I stare at my reflection in the mirror, twisting so I can see the same view of my rear as Dilynne. "You don't think it's too sexy?"

The dress I'm currently wearing and contemplating for Elliot's wedding does not, in fact, cover up the hickey that Fletcher gave me.

But with the way this dress fits my body, I know for certain that when he sees me, he'll be itching to get me out of it. Blush satin clings to my curves with a halter style neckline, highlighting my shoulders and the dip in my waist, and Dilynne's right—my ass looks amazing. The dress is simple, yet sexy and classic.

It's exactly what I would pick for the bridesmaids in my wedding.

My eyes drift over to the racks of bridal gowns on the far side of the shop, taunting me with their sparkles and lace. Dilynne walks over to where I'm standing on the pedestal and grips my shoulders.

"You know, while we're here...there's no harm in trying a few of those on."

I bite my bottom lip. "I'm not even getting married."

"But you will someday."

"I had my chance, remember?"

Dilynne spins me to face her. "That's the thing about chances—sometimes you get more than one. And I know for a fact, that they don't come along again for no reason." Her brow lifts before she continues. "You're my best friend, Laney, and for as long as I can remember, you've had feelings for that man. Now, you know he wants you too. Stop overthinking it. Stop second-guessing, I'm begging you. Jump in headfirst for once in your life."

"But what if I drown?"

"Then I'll rescue you. I'm an awesome swimmer, remember?" She winks at me. "But if you don't at least try, you're always going to wonder what if."

"This was just supposed to be about orgasms."

Dilynne rolls her eyes. "You and I both know that was bull-shit. There has never been anything casual between you and Fletcher Adams."

This is what love is supposed to feel like, isn't it? Fear mixed with euphoria, comfort, and longing—like no amount of time with them would ever be enough, but you're deathly afraid that your time will be cut short anyway?

My mom's death has made me afraid to truly put myself out there and open my heart because losing her was the worst pain I've ever felt, and I never wanted to feel that way ever again.

But now I'm realizing that I haven't truly been *living*. I've been staying still, playing it safe, and picking men that don't have the potential to hurt me, like Spencer.

"I guess I just can't believe all of this is happening," I whisper. "I'm so afraid something is going to ruin it again."

"What do you mean?"

"Well, the last time I got the nerve to tell Fletcher how I felt, my mom died, Dilynne." My throat grows tight. "What if Fletcher and I are cursed? What if something happens when we tell Rhonan, or what if we're just not meant to be together and we're tempting fate by trying? I mean, he plays for the NFL, for crying out loud. Being with him means my life will change forever. How in the hell is this supposed to work?"

"Breathe, Laney," Dilynne says, reaching for my hands and holding them to her chest as reality finally hits me. Something about those wedding gowns triggered me, and now I'm having trouble breathing. "Take some deep breaths." With my eyes locked on hers, I focus on inhaling and exhaling until I feel like the panic attack that was brewing is starting to subside.

"First of all, you're not cursed. Your mom's death was a terrible tragedy, something that no one could have seen coming, which means there's no way it could have been connected. And second, you're getting a little ahead of yourself. I know it's hard for you not to think about the future, but I was just joking about the wedding dresses. Your anxiety is in full force right now, so I need you to try to take a page out of my don't-give-a-fuck attitude and live in the moment."

"I'm trying. It's just hard."

"I know it is. That night changed you in more ways than one, honey. And I've watched you cut yourself off from things that bring you joy, be afraid to live because that might mean that you're making your life count even though your mom's life ended early, and avoid relationships because you were convinced that other men would reject you like Fletcher did."

"Did you earn a degree in psychology that I never knew about?" I ask, only half joking.

"Hell no. But I've been through enough shit and watched enough reality television to recognize avoidance issues in other people."

"This isn't some TV show though, Dilynne. This is my life."

"It is, but is he worth sacrificing what you've always known?"

I don't even have to think about it. "Yes," I say.

"Then you've got this. Get through Elliot's wedding and then get ready to become Mrs. Laney Adams one day like you've always wanted."

"He's the only man I've ever envisioned walking down an aisle toward," I admit. "I couldn't even picture myself marrying Spencer."

"Well, luckily he made the decision to call that whole thing off very easy for you. But if the way Fletcher looks at you is any indication, I don't think you'll have that problem with him. I've seen a man obsessed, and Fletcher is a prime example."

"My life will never be the same when the world finds out I'm with Fletcher Adams, the star wide receiver for the Carolina Thunder."

Dilynne shrugs. "No, it won't. But you will still be Laney Hart, my best friend and badass businesswoman. And honestly? That's all that matters."

***

"So, the aisle will be right here, chairs on either side," Anabell says as she walks through the courtyard of the winery, showing Elliot and Tori how the ceremony will be set up. "Usually, we would have you facing the other way, but we're making the adjustments that you requested."

Tori smiles proudly. "I don't want our wedding to look like everyone else's. Besides, this direction will have my good side displayed to our guests."

Elliot rolls his eyes playfully. "Whatever makes you happy, baby."

"Let's go look at the room where the reception will be just to make sure you approve of the plans for the room." Anabell leads Elliot and Tori into the building on the property where the large ballrooms are located for events.

I move to follow them, but Fletcher reaches out and grabs my wrist before I get too far. "Where are you going?"

"To fulfill my maid of honor duties?"

Shaking his head, he pulls me flush against him, letting me feel how hard he is at my lower back. "We don't need to know shit about table centerpieces, angel. In fact, there's something else I want to show you while we're alone."

I spin in his arms. "Okay..."

My dad comes out of the main wine tasting room, heading right for us.

"All ready for us?" Fletcher asks my father.

"Yup. Rhonan is on his way too."

My eyes bounce back and forth between Fletcher and my dad. "What is going on?"

Chuckling, my father says, "Fletcher has a gift for us."

"Us?"

My father grabs my hand and leads me to the tasting room. "I know you've been bothering me to replace the popcorn cart that we use for movie nights," he starts, "But you and I both know why I haven't wanted to." He opens the door and holds it so Fletcher and I can walk through. "Getting rid of the old one felt like throwing away a piece of your mother." My eyes start to sting with tears. "But Fletcher came to me with an idea, and it made me feel more at peace about upgrading the equipment."

I glance over at Fletcher where he's standing away from us with his hands shoved in his pockets, but a look of appreciation in his eyes.

When I look back toward my dad, he's standing in front of a brand-new popcorn cart—shiny, top of the line, and much bigger than the old one. Whirling back to Fletcher, I say, "You bought us a new popcorn cart?"

"I did."

"But the old one is still here too." My dad points to the far corner by the windows, where the original cart stands, only there's a plaque mounted to it now.

My feet carry me over there, and when I read the plaque, my eyes fill with tears.

*In loving memory of*
*Elizabeth Hart*
*Wife, Mother, and Visionary*
*Hart Winery—her dream, her legacy.*

"I can't believe you did this," I say as I turn around and meet Fletcher's eyes through my tear-filled vision.

"Did what?" Rhonan's voice cuts through the moment as he pulls the front door open and steps inside, still in his sheriff's uniform.

My dad shows Rhonan the new cart and the memorial for the old one as I make my way across the room to the man I can't deny my feelings for any longer.

"Thank you," I whisper, wanting to reach up and pull his mouth to mine, but knowing this is not the time, nor the place.

"Just so you know, I've lost count of how many thank you's you've given me now."

Laughing through my tears, I swipe under my eyes in an attempt to dry my face. "This is... You made..."

Cupping the side of my face, he says, "Your mom was part of my life too, angel. And I understand how hard it is to let go of someone."

*God, this man.*

How could I ever have doubted what exists between us?

How can I possibly walk away from him again, even though I know going forward is not going to be without its own challenges?

"Fletcher." Rhonan crosses the room just as Fletcher drops his hand from my face. My brother throws his arms around his friend. "This really means a lot, man."

"I'm happy you guys love it." Fletcher's phone rings, cutting through the heaviness in the room. "Shit, I need to take this," he says, answering the call and stepping outside.

"Well, now that you guys have seen our new gadget, I'm gonna put it away." My father pushes the new popcorn cart down the hall that leads to the offices. Rhonan and I watch him before I turn and find my brother arching a brow at me.

"What?"

"Is something going on between you and Fletcher?"

My stomach drops. *Oh my God. Did he see Fletcher touching me? Does he know that we've been sneaking around?*

"No," I blurt, instantly hating myself for lying as the word leaves my lips.

"You sure?"

"Why do you ask?"

Rhonan looks over his shoulder at the door that Fletcher just walked out of, and then back at me. "I don't want you to get hurt, Laney. Fletcher is..."

"Fletcher is what?" The topic of our conversation steps back into the room, studying both of us.

"Never mind," Rhonan says, pushing a hand through his hair. "Thank you again for the gift, man. I know it meant a lot to our dad."

"Your mom was an incredible woman. She deserves to be honored."

Rhonan nods. "I agree." Sighing, he hoists his pants up on his waist. "All right, I'm headed home to Joanne and Ellis. Not sure when I'll see you guys before the wedding, so if not, see you then."

I watch my brother leave and then release the breath I was holding. "Oh my God..."

"What?"

"Rhonan asked me if something was going on between the two of us!" I whisper, even though I know Rhonan can't hear us now.

"Shit, really?"

"Yeah. I told him no, but I kind of got the feeling he wasn't happy about the possibility."

Fletcher reaches up to adjust his hat on his head. "I was gonna talk to him about us, Laney. But..."

"But what? Is there something you're not telling me?"

He blows out a breath. "Your brother, me, Henley, and Elliot made a pact when we were younger."

"What kind of pact?"

He looks down at me under his dark lashes. "That we'd never date each other's sisters."

Anger swells in my chest. "What? Why?"

"It seemed so trivial back then, but we were young and naïve. All we cared about was being friends forever. So I need you to understand that telling your brother about us isn't just a simple thing. I'm hoping given how foolish we were back then that he'll be a little bit more understanding now, but I'm just not sure how he's going to react to this and if that detail is one he'll hold onto."

Nerves race through my chest. "Is that part of the reason you didn't act on your feelings back then too?"

"Yes," he admits. "But now I know I was a fool to believe you and I could ever just be friends. You're mine now, and nothing is going to change that—not even your brother."

My hands begin to tremble. "You're willing to risk your friendship with him...for me?"

His confidence is unwavering as he reaches for my hands. "I am. I honestly hope I'm making it out to be a bigger deal in my head than it turns out to be, but just know that no matter what Rhonan says, it won't change how I feel. Okay?"

I nod, unable to speak any more words.

If Rhonan doesn't approve of us together, it's not going to change things for Fletcher.

But that's also my brother. He's a huge part of my life, one that I can't and won't leave behind.

"Wait until after the wedding," I say, needing more time for us to figure everything out. Fletcher's words, feelings, and actions are clear, but I still don't know enough on my end to cause a fight with my brother just yet.

"Are you sure?"

"Yes. We need time."

Time. One thing we don't have a lot of.

*God, why can't love ever just be simple?*

# Chapter 26

**Fletcher**

***Hiding the Truth***

"You're getting married in two days. You have the rest of your life to spend Thursday nights at home with Tori, so turn that frown of yours upside down and deal some fucking cards."

Henley smacks the table gently in front of Elliot, whose mouth quirks up into the closest thing to a smile he's had since we kidnapped him earlier and took him to Henley's house for one last boy's night before the big day.

"You're right. I'm just spent. I can't wait to be on a beach next week with my wife."

Fuck. Elliot's words strike a chord with me because I'd love nothing more than to do the same thing with Laney, not that I can tell my friends that.

Her in a pink bikini, her long brown hair cascading down her back, her tan skin shining in the sun. Me on a lounger watching her walk toward me, growing harder by the second. The two of us alone with no one else to worry about...

Fuck. I hate keeping yet another thing from them, but I have to until this wedding is over and I know that Laney and I are on the same page.

"Fletcher? You in there?" Elliot knocks on my forehead.

I swat him away. "Jesus. What?"

"Rhonan just asked if you want to hit or stay."

I stare down at the cards in front of me, realizing that my friends have all been playing the game while I've been daydreaming about Laney. I feel like someone who's only ever seen in black and white finally seeing the world light up with color. My chest feels lighter, my body alive, my mind finally fucking clear.

And it's all because of the woman I'm head over heels in love with.

*I fucking love her. Pretty sure I always have.*

Flipping my cards over, I smile when I see the ten and the ace I've been dealt, tossing them on the green felt. "No need to hit me, my friends. I think luck is on my side this evening."

Henley snorts beside me. "Beginner's luck." He turns to Rhonan and says, "Hit me." When Rhonan flips over Henley's card, he busts. "Shit."

"*You're* playing like a beginner, not Fletcher." Elliot laughs from across the table.

"Well, *my* luck in blackjack seems about as good as my luck in work lately," Henley says as Rhonan tosses a few chips to me and Elliot since we beat his hand as the dealer. Elliot takes the cards for his turn to deal now as we all toss a chip in the center of the table.

Even though my time with my friends is coming to an end, I'm grateful that I feel like I'm part of their lives again. These past few weeks have revived our friendship in ways I think we all needed.

Hopefully, that's yet another thing that will change after this wedding is over.

"What's going on?" I ask.

Henley lifts his beer to his lips. "I've got to hire a few new people at the resort. Business isn't slowing down, especially as we head into winter, and one of my ski instructors isn't coming back this year."

"Have you put out an ad yet?" Rhonan lifts his cards from the table to see what he was dealt.

Henley blows out a frustrated breath. "Not yet. I was going to wait until the wedding is over and I can give it all my focus. Besides—" His voice is cut off by the sound of his phone ringing. "Jesus, this girl just can't take a hint."

"Is that the same woman who's been calling you?" I ask.

Elliot slides his eyes between me and Henley. "What woman?"

"One of my hookups from last year," Henley says as he silences the call and puts his phone away. "She won't stop blowing up my phone. I think I might block her."

"I told him to just answer it and see what she wants."

"I know what she wants," Henley replies. "My dick, and I'm not about repetition, remember?"

Elliot chuckles before taking a sip of his beer. "Don't deny repetition, motherfucker. I used to feel the same way and now? The idea of one woman is all I want."

An awkward silence rests between us.

Rhonan had a wife and lost her. Elliot found someone he wants for the rest of his life.

And I have seen the other side too now.

Henley arches a brow at me as if he can tell what I'm thinking about.

Finally, he breaks his stare and sighs as he calls for another card. "Hit me." Elliot turns over a five, making Henley bust again. "Fuck!"

"Come on. You know better than to hit on eighteen. What the hell were you thinking?" Rhonan asks.

"I'm not. My mind is a mess right now."

"All of you seem a little tense," I observe.

Elliot eyes me from the side. "You're right, but you don't." He snaps his fingers. "You got laid, didn't you?"

"What?" I say through a laugh, even though when I dart my eyes to Henley, he arches a brow at me again. "No, I didn't."

"Now he's denying it," Elliot continues, shaking his head. "Which means it's true."

"I can't just be in a good mood?"

"You can, but your mood is beyond good. You're calm," Rhonan explains, growing more suspicious. And after his question to Laney the other night, my nerves grow stronger. "That kind of calm comes from good sex."

Not good sex. Incredible sex. The kind that makes you wonder if your dick knows the meaning of life now.

Henley chokes on his beer, glaring at me before I reply, "I didn't get laid, all right?"

"Fuck, if I got laid, I'd admit it," Rhonan adds. "I'm going through a bit of a dry spell, if I'm being honest."

"Well, you're a single parent and work insane hours. That's to be expected."

"Was she a fan? Did she offer to suck you off in a storage closet at Blossom Brews or something?" Elliot prods even further.

Henley coughs violently now. He confronted me about what happened between me and Laney in the storage closet at the winery. Turns out, we weren't that quiet. "Shit."

"Did you forget how to drink tonight?" Rhonan asks as Henley stands up and moves to the corner of the room to gather himself, glaring at me from over his shoulder.

"Anyway," Elliot says. "Am I right?"

"No. You're not because nothing happened. And contrary to what you might think, most fans aren't offering to suck my dick the second they meet me."

Elliot snickers. "Such a shame. What the hell is the point of being famous then?"

Rhonan laughs at our slightly candid friend just as Henley makes his way back to his seat. "You okay?" he asks Henley once he's seated.

"Yeah. Beer just went down the wrong pipe."

"Okay. Now that everyone is done talking shit, can we get back to the game?" Rhonan asks, darting his eyes around to the three of us.

"I don't know that I'll ever be done talking shit," Elliot says as he slides the deck to me for my turn to deal.

"We know," the three of us say in unison before sharing a laugh and falling back into the game.

After a few more rounds, I get up to use the bathroom, but Henley follows me. "Fletcher..."

"What's up?"

"Do you know what you're going to do yet?" he whispers, glancing over his shoulder to make sure that Rhonan and Elliot aren't in earshot.

"About..."

He shoves my shoulder. "Don't play fucking stupid. You were sitting in that room just now. You have to tell Rhonan what's going on with Laney before he finds out from someone else."

I lower my voice. "I will. After the wedding."

"Fuck. I have a bad feeling about this."

"Why?"

"I don't know. Something in my gut, man. I can't shake it, and usually when I get this feeling, I'm right."

"What do you want me to do, Henley? You can at least agree with me that this isn't the time, right? Not with everything going on..."

Henley nods. "Okay, but when you do it, just make sure I'm there in case I have to pull him off of you."

I huff out a laugh. "Thanks for the support."

"You sure this is what you want? Laney, I mean?"

I look him dead in the eyes. "I've never been more sure of anything in my life."

***

"Fletcher? What are you doing here?" Laney opens the front door to Blossom Beauty Friday afternoon, shocked to see me. The salon is closed for the day so the girls can get pampered before the wedding tomorrow.

I hold up the bags in my arms. "I wanted to make sure that you ladies had everything that you needed for today."

Ellis peeks her head out around Laney's long legs. "Uncle Fletcher?"

"Hey, princess. I brought cupcakes."

Her eyes light up. "I love cupcakes!"

"I know you do. Now tell Auntie Laney to let me inside." I lift my eyes back to Laney's, only to find her licking her lips.

"This was awfully sweet of you," she says, holding the door open wider so I can walk through.

I catch the sight of her in her pink silk robe and instantly want to pull it open with my teeth. Instead, I set the bags on the receptionist counter and turn to face her. "I can be a sweet guy sometimes." Leaning down, I line my lips up to her ear. "But you like it when I'm a dirty guy more."

Her skin pebbles right before my eyes. "I do."

"Aw, what did Lucifer bring for us?" Yvonne asks as she walks up to the counter, Glenn trailing behind her.

"Food and booze."

Yvonne turns to Laney. "Can he be our boss instead of you? He seems way more fun."

"I'd definitely let him boss me around," Glenn adds. His eyes drop down my body and back up.

Laney glares at them. "I can be fun."

Yvonne snorts. "Yeah, okay. When's the last time you did anything like this for us?" Yvonne asks Laney as she lifts the bottle from the bag. "And do you also bring us champagne?"

"No..."

"Then I've made my point." She glances over at Glenn. "Let's go get some glasses from the break room so we can pop this cork."

Glenn snaps his fingers. "Now you're speaking my language."

"Fletcher?" Tori walks up to us now, her robe sliding open far enough to almost reveal her breasts. I keep my eyes firmly on hers.

"What are you doing here?" she asks.

I start pulling items from the bags. "I brought you girls some snacks and drinks for your spa day. You can't have a girls' day without good food."

"I ordered food from Blossom Brews for later," Laney interjects.

"I know. I stopped by there first and canceled it."

Her mouth drops open. "Why?"

Taking out the containers of the meal I had delivered from a Michelin star restaurant a buddy of mine owns in Charlotte, I open them one by one to reveal the mouthwatering dishes. "Because you ladies deserved something special today."

I grab one of the boxes and pop it open to reveal an assortment of sushi. "This one is for you," I say to Tori, handing her the box. "Elliot said it's your favorite."

"Oh, Fletcher. If you're not careful, I might just make you the groom." With a wink, she takes the container and walks off, but I catch the glare Laney is giving her.

Jealousy sure does look good on her.

Ellis comes up to me now and pulls on my shorts. "Where are the cupcakes?"

I grab that container and bend down to open it in front of her, revealing two dozen miniature cupcakes in a variety of flavors. Her eyes nearly pop out of her head. "You have to try every flavor and tell me which one is your favorite, okay?"Ellis nods, transfixed by the display of sweets. "I'm gonna eat all the cavities!"

Laney grabs the box from my hands. "Why don't we start with a few and see how your tummy handles it first, okay?"

"My tummy loves cupcakes," Ellis declares confidently while rubbing her tiny stomach.

Laney takes four of the small cupcakes and places them on a plate, handing it to Ellis. "Here you go."

The little girl carries the plate over to a chair and instantly shoves one of the cupcakes in her mouth, kicking her feet.

Laney glares at me. "You know, we're the ones who are going to have to deal with her when she's cracked out on sugar."

"When that happens, you call me and I'll take care of her."

"Why did you do this, Fletcher?" she asks, her voice low.

"Because I can," I answer. "And because I didn't want to go a day without seeing you."

Ever since last weekend, Laney and I have spent every night together, either at her place or my cabin. But since Elliot insisted on tradition, Tori is staying at Laney's house tonight, which means no sleepover for us. I do have some important plans to keep me busy this afternoon, though. But besides that, I'm not sure what to do with myself.

Every part of me craves every part of her. She makes me feel less broken, like the scars on the inside have started to fade. Even after cards with the boys last night, I knew she'd be waiting for me at her house afterward, and that's what I want for the rest of our lives.

I'm so fucking in love with this woman. There's no denying it.

And I can't wait until the whole world knows.

I take her by the hand and lead her outside so we can speak candidly.

"How did last night go?" she asks once the door shuts behind us. We didn't exactly do much talking when I got to her house last night, and Laney kicked me out early this morning before anyone could see me leaving.

"It was fine. Elliot is convinced that my good mood is because I got laid, though."

Laney snorts, crossing her arms over her chest, although it does nothing to conceal her pebbled nipples beneath the silk. "Well, he's not wrong. You definitely have a pep in your step that wasn't there when you arrived."

"That's because your pussy is magical."

"Dear lord. Please don't ever say that again."

I reach up and tuck her hair behind her ear. "It's true though." My eyes scour her face, memorizing every line, freckle, and curve as if I'm seeing them for the first time, when the reality is I've looked at this woman's face for countless hours over my lifetime and yet, I don't think it will ever be long enough. "God, you're beautiful."

"I look like a troll," she argues as I press my finger to her lips, silencing her.

"You look gorgeous. No makeup, hair a little messy, glowing skin."

Her smile is soft. "Thank you."

"I love seeing you like this, almost as much as I love seeing you freshly fucked."

Rolling her eyes, she plants her hands on her hips. "You had to go there, huh?"

"Come on. You can admit my dick's a little magical too. It's okay. I won't tell anyone."

Laughing, she shoves at my chest playfully, but I hold her hand there before she can steal it away. "Fletcher."

"I can't wait to see you tomorrow. I'm going to miss you tonight."

"Me too."

"After tomorrow, there will be no more hiding, okay? I promise."

"Okay."

My eyes dip down to her lips. "Fuck, I wish I could kiss you right now."

She takes her hand back. "Soon."

"Enjoy the rest of your day," I tell her, shoving my hands in my pockets so I'm not tempted to reach out and smash my lips to hers.

"I will. Thank you again, Fletcher. You sure know how to make a girl feel special."

"You *are* special, Laney," I say as I reach for the door to hold it open for her. "You have no fucking clue."

She blows me a kiss as I let the door close behind her.

"Fuck," I mutter to myself, adjusting my hat on my head before turning to head back to my truck. I don't get very far before I hear a voice that stops me in my tracks.

"You're an idiot."

Turning to face him, I prepare myself for the impending argument I know is coming, widening my stance while crossing my arms over my chest. "Nice to see you too, Dad."

"I saw the way you looked at the Hart girl. Do you think she actually wants you?"

"Her name is Laney, and that's none of your concern." My pulse picks up as I take him in. He must be recovering from a bender. Anyone else would look at him and think he's fine, but I know the signs—bags under his eyes, an unshaven jaw, and wrinkled clothes. These are all things that he's good at covering up when he hasn't been drinking for almost twenty-four hours straight.

"All women see when they look at us are dollar signs, Fletcher. That's all your mom saw, and then she trapped me by getting pregnant."

"First of all, Laney isn't Mom. And second of all, what dollar signs are you referring to? Because the last time I checked, you're broke and asking your son for money."

"It's the least you can do given everything I've done for you." I laugh humorlessly as his eyes narrow. "And she may not seem like your mom now, but once she gets a taste of that life, she'll hang around just long enough to get what she feels she's owed." He scoffs. "Your mom had nothing to do with my success. I did that all on my own."

"You developed your drinking problem all on your own too, huh?"

He doesn't even acknowledge what I just said, continuing his rant instead. "They say they can handle the demands of the game, but they will never understand what it's like to dedicate your life, your body, every waking and breathing moment, to football. No one will ever fucking understand unless they've lived it."

"You lost the game twenty-two years ago. When are you just going to accept it?"

He takes a step closer to me as alcohol wafts from his breath. Yep, whiskey. That's his truth serum. "You can stand here and judge me all you want, but one day, you'll realize that I was right."

"One day when you've drank yourself to death, I won't have to hear this shit from you anymore." I see the flash of anger in his eyes, the one that used to appear seconds before he'd swing on me. "You want to hit me now, don't you?" He doesn't respond. "Too bad we're out in broad daylight and not behind closed doors."

"So ungrateful," he mutters before clenching his fists at his sides.

I scoff and turn my back to him. "Have a good fucking day...*Dad*." Walking away, I can hear my pulse pounding. My shoulders are up by my ears, and my chest is wound so fucking tight that it takes me a good ten minutes to cool down and relax as I sit in my truck.

My only concern now is that my Dad suspects something is going on between me and Laney, and if he says something to someone else in one of his drunken rants, it could get back to Rhonan before I get a chance to tell him myself.

"Fuck." I slam my palm into the steering wheel of my truck, leaning my head back against the seat as adrenaline races through me.

It's only when I open my eyes and see the time on the dash that I snap out of the sour fucking mood my father always puts me in and crank the engine, headed to an appointment that will help seal my future—because that's what I need to focus on, no matter how much my past keeps trying to drag me back under.

# Chapter 27

**Laney**

***Here Comes the...***

Tori is pacing across the bridal suite, casting glances at herself in the mirror, and I'm watching her from the corner, wondering what the hell is going on.

It's the afternoon of the wedding and we are less than an hour from the ceremony. Tori was glued to her phone all morning, but as soon as she put on her dress, her face lit up. The mermaid-style gown with a sweetheart neckline fits her like a glove, and she decided on a cathedral veil, which makes her entire ensemble look regal.

Even though the woman pacing before me isn't my favorite person in the world, I still love the magic of weddings—the dress, the flowers, the promises of forever.

But is it possible I might get a second chance at my own forever? With Fletcher?

Her phone rings again, snapping me out of my thoughts.

I take a step closer to her, placing my hand on her shoulder. "Are you sure I can't get you anything, Tori? It's my job as your maid of honor, you know…"

"No, I'm okay. It's just nerves, and when I'm feeling anxious, it's better that I keep moving." Her smile looks forced.

"Okay, if you're sure…"

Her phone rings in her hand for the fifth time since we've been in this room.

"It is your parents?" She said they were running late earlier, so I'm wondering if she's just nervous about that, but doesn't want to admit it.

"No." Her eyes widen as she looks at the screen in the palm of her hand. "Oh my God."

I take a step closer to her. "What?"

She suddenly pulls her phone to her chest. "It's… I uh… I'm going to go outside and get some fresh air."

Without a backwards glance, she leaves the bridal suite.

Dilynne pokes her head in a few seconds later. "Where is the Wicked Bride of the West going?" Sliding through the crack in the door entirely now, she walks toward me in her black satin dress that highlights her amazing body that she usually covers up.

"I don't know, but she's acting really strange. She's been glued to her phone all morning, but something popped up on her screen and then suddenly, she said she needed to go outside."

"Do you think she's getting cold feet?" Dilynne asks. "Because if that bitch walks out on Elliot, I'll make it my personal mission to ensure she never sees daylight again."

My brows instantly draw together. "That was a bit…"

"Murdery?" Dilynne finishes for me. "Well, that's how she makes me feel. And even though this is Elliot we're talking about, no one deserves to be left at the altar."

"I'm sure she'll be fine."

Dilynne steps up to the window on the far wall, peering outside into a small alcove behind the building we are in on the back of the property. "Motherfucker."

"What?"

Waving me over, she points in the direction she's looking. "If she's fine, then why is she outside kissing some random guy?"

My mouth falls open as I watch the scene unfold in front of me, like a car crash you can't turn away from. "Oh my God. Who *is* that?"

Dilynne lifts her phone and snaps a picture of the two of them—Tori pressed up against the building, lip-locked with some mystery guy. "I don't fucking care, but now we have evidence. We have to tell Elliot."

"We can't—" I start, but my best friend cuts me off.

"We can't let him marry her if she's cheating on him!" Dilynne practically shouts. But when we turn back to the window, Tori and the man are gone. "Where the fuck did she go?"

We run outside to look, but there's no sign of them. You'd think it wouldn't be hard to spot a woman in a white dress and veil, but she's vanished.

Trying to keep my anxiety in check, my eyes scour the winery, watching employees drift from room to room as Dilynne and I walk through the property. The courtyard is ready for the ceremony. White chairs are set up in rows facing an arch covered in pink roses, a white silk runner is staked into the grass to serve as the aisle, and guests have already begun to arrive.

I just wish I knew if the bride plans to reappear.

"What are you two doing out here?" Henley comes up next to me, adjusting his coat.

Dilynne and I share a look before I lower my voice. "Well, we have a little problem."

"What kind of problem?" he asks. I motion for him to follow us back to the bridal suite. Once the door is shut, I release a breath.

Dilynne's jaw is clenched as she says, "Tori fucking left with some guy."

Henley's eyes widen. "What? Are you sure?"

"I mean—" I start, prepared to give Tori the benefit of the doubt, but Dilynne stops me from looking like an optimistic idiot.

"Yes. We saw her outside kissing some guy, and then the two of them took off," Dilynne confidently overrides my attempt at playing devil's advocate.

"Did you try texting her?" Henley asks me.

"Yes. The last message I sent to her wasn't even read."

"Motherfucker." He rubs the back of his neck. "We have to tell Elliot."

At that moment, my phone dings with a text.

**Fletcher:** *Elliot is so happy, I think he might cry.*

"Oh God."

"What?" Dilynne glances down at my phone. "Shit."

Henley reads the text as well. "Let Fletcher know while we try to figure out something."

"Figure out what?" Dilynne asks her brother. "The bride is fucking gone. There's nothing to figure out. There's no wedding without a groom *and* a bride."

**Me:** *Well... Tori left.*

**Fletcher:** *What? Why?*

**Me:** *I don't know, but she was with some guy outside, and then they disappeared. You need to stay with him and keep him distracted until we figure out what's happening.*

There's a knock on the door, and Rhonan steps in. "Hey. What's going on? Anabell wanted me to check on everyone to make sure we can start on time."

Dilynne pounds her fist into her other palm. "Tori fucking walked out on the wedding. I swear, if I ever see her again, she's gonna wish a house had fallen on her instead of my fist falling on her face."

I place my hand on her shoulder. "What if we're missing something?"

She turns to me, exasperated. "What could we possibly be missing? She was kissing that guy, Laney. That doesn't exactly bode well for the whole marriage thing."

Rhonan places his hands on his hips. "Jesus Christ. Has anyone told Elliot?"

My heart sinks even further in my chest. "I don't want to go there yet. I feel like we're missing something." I turn to my brother. "Did you ever run that background check?"

"No."

"How long would it take?"

"Not very long. Why?"

"Maybe there's something in there that will help us figure out where she'd go? Or at least, who this guy is?"

Dilynne shrugs. "It's not going to change anything. She's the scum of the earth as far as I'm concerned." Growling, she says, "God, I knew I was right about her."

"Okay." Rhonan fixes his cufflinks. "I'll see what I can find."

"Thank you. And Henley? Please go check their house."

Henley shakes his head. "I don't think she's there."

Dilynne snaps her fingers in front of his face. "We don't care what you think. Just go!"

Henley snaps his fingers in front of his sister's face. "No need for the fucking attitude."

"You started it!"

"Did not!"

"Did too!"

I shove them away from each other. "For the love of God, can you two not fight just this one day, please? I can't deal with your childish behavior on top of everything else."

Dilynne snaps her fingers at Henley again. "You heard the woman. Now go."

"Jesus Christ," Henley mutters as he walks out of the room. Dilynne and I follow him into the hall.

Dilynne turns to me. "Elliot doesn't deserve this."

"I agree. But it's gonna be okay, right?"

"How can you say that?"

Shrugging, I reply, "It's just the right thing to say in a time like this."

Ellis runs up to us, her tiny dress shoes clicking on the tile beneath her. Her white princess dress bounces with each step. "Auntie Laney! Is it time for me to throw the flowers yet?"

I carefully kneel down so I'm on her level, careful not to split the seam of my dress as I do. "Not yet, sweetie."

"When is it going to be time?"

"Soon."

"Ugh. Weddings are boring," she whines.

"You won't feel that way when you're older and you understand what an open bar is," Dilynne interjects. When she notices my glare, she reaches for Ellis's hand. "Hey. Let's go outside and practice throwing the flowers, okay? That way you're ready when it's time."

"Yes!" Ellis shouts. "I can be like Elsa, but with flowers."

Even though my niece is completely oblivious to what's going on around her, I'm grateful for her small ray of sunshine to break through what is potentially going to be a thunderstorm of a day if we don't find the bride.

And truthfully? Practicing might be the only flower-throwing Ellis gets to do today.

Trying to remain positive, I head toward the event space to keep up appearances, making sure that the place cards are in the proper place, centerpieces are, well, centered, and greeting guests as they arrive, putting on the best smile I can muster. I tell the photographers that the bride is running behind due to a wardrobe malfunction, trying to buy us some time.

Thirty minutes before the wedding is supposed to start, Henley returns to the winery. "Laney..."

I pull him into the bridal suite so we can speak candidly. "Anything?"

"No. Nothing."

I bury my face in my hands. "Oh my God. She's really gone, isn't she?"

Henley's phone starts ringing. "Hello? Yeah, we're in the bridal suite." He hangs up quickly. "Rhonan just got back."

A few seconds later, Rhonan barges through the door, slamming it behind him. "I *knew* she was hiding something."

I place a hand to my chest, bracing myself for what he's about to say. "What did you find out?"

Dilynne enters the room a few seconds later. "Did the traitorous witch turn up?"

"Jesus Christ," Henley mutters. "No, but Rhonan was just about to tell us what Tori has been hiding."

Fletcher steps inside the room, shutting the door behind him. I want to spiral as a hundred feelings slam into me at once, but seeing Fletcher with his thick hair combed back and his body molded to his black tux actually helps me stay calm.

*God, he looks incredible—and he's mine.*

Our eyes meet and he rushes over to me. "Elliot is asking questions, and I don't have any answers to give him. Bring me up to speed."

"Well, the only thing we know right now is that Tori was kissing some guy and now she's gone. Henley went by their house and said all her stuff is gone."

Fletcher turns to Henley. "Fuck. What the hell?"

"And apparently, she has an address in Nashville that she shares with a man named Barry Eggert," Rhonan chimes in, gaining our attention.

"Who is that?" Dilynne asks.

Rhonan pulls some papers from his pocket displaying Tori and Barry's picture on the paper. The gasp she lets out makes us all jump. "That's the guy she took off with!"

"Let me see." Fletcher says, taking the paper from Rhonan. "Isn't that her boss?" He snaps his fingers and then opens his phone to search for more information. After a few minutes, he brings up the website for the talent agency that Tori works for, which just so happens to be owned by Barry Eggert. "Why the fuck would she have acted so head-over-heels for Elliot and eager to marry him if she's with her fucking boss?"

"I need a better name for her than the Wicked Witch of the West," Dilynne chimes in as we process this detail.

Fletcher turns to me. "I need to tell Elliot."

Tears fill my eyes. "He doesn't deserve this."

"I know, but it's better that he knows now than as he waits at the end of the aisle for a bride who's not coming."

Rhonan clears his throat. "Let me tell him."

"Are you sure?"

"Yes. I think he's going to take it better coming from me, especially when I show him the proof."

Fletcher turns to me for approval. I nod. "You're probably right."

Dilynne steps up to me, her lips pursed in irritation. "Do you want me to go out and send everyone home?"

"Yeah. I think it's best if they're all gone."

Henley straightens his jacket. "I'll tell the caterers to pack up too."

"Thank you. All of you."

Dilynne grabs my hand. "Of course. We're family. We'll get through this."

I look around the room at my brother's best friends, my best friend, and the man I'm in love with, knowing that no matter what happens today, Elliot will survive this because we all have each other.

The weight of what's about to happen is sitting on my chest like a ton of bricks, but I know that our support system here will be the reason we get through this—because what's happened to Elliot with Tori didn't just happen to him—it happened to all of us. A woman infiltrated our lives, lied to our faces, and made us believe she cared about a part of our family.

Fletcher and I find ourselves alone in the room.

He doesn't let me say a word before his lips are on mine. "God, you look beautiful. I know we have other things to worry about, but I just needed to tell you that."

"Thank you. I just can't believe this is happening."

"I know, angel. It's fucking crazy." Fletcher retreats from me as he looks off to the side of the room. "This is going to devastate him."

My bottom lip trembles as I stare at the things Tori left behind in the room. Fletcher notices and rushes over to me. "Hey, it's going to be okay."

"How can you be sure?"

"Because Elliot is one of the toughest people I know. He's been through some shit, and he will survive this too. It's better that he knows now, though, instead of finding out after they were married."

"That's true. I just... I know how much he wanted this, how quickly he fell into the idea of this new life..."

"Maybe that's the problem. It was too quick."

His words sit between us like a truth bomb we're afraid will detonate if we speak.

The entire progression of our relationship has also moved incredibly quick these past few weeks. Does that mean we're doomed to end tragically a second time?

Before I spiral too far, Fletcher leans down and presses his lips to mine. His touch reassures me. For the first time all day, I feel comfort, and as I deepen the kiss, a switch inside of me flips.

Fletcher matches my desperation, pulling me closer to him, fucking my mouth with his tongue. We drown in each other. I claw at his back. He cups my ass with his hands, pressing his erection into my stomach so I know he wants me just as badly as I want him.

The last thing we should be doing right now is letting our lust for one another drive our decisions, but right now, I just want to forget about what's happening.

I move to push his coat from his shoulders, but a voice at the door stops me cold.

"What the fuck is going on here?"

Fletcher and I freeze, turning our heads slowly to find my brother and Elliot staring at us.

Rhonan's eyes bounce between us as Fletcher releases me from his grasp.

"Rhonan..." Fletcher starts as I wrap my arms around my body.

"What the fuck is this?" My brother waves his hand between us. "You and my sister?"

Elliot's eyes are bloodshot, his fists clenched at his sides. "You broke the pact, man."

"Listen, it's not what it looks like..." Fletcher takes a step toward Rhonan.

"Jesus Christ," Henley mutters behind my brother, shutting the door. "I guess we're doing this now, too."

"Then what is it?" my brother asks. "Because to me it looks like you were about to fuck my sister in our winery." His eyes move around the room as anger wafts off him. "God, I fucking knew it. That night with the popcorn cart..." He turns to me. "I asked you if something was going on, and you lied to me."

"I know—" I'm cut off before I can attempt to explain.

"You fucking violated bro code, Fletch." Elliot's voice is low, almost void of any emotion, but the intensity of his body is saying otherwise.

"This isn't just some fling, okay?" Fletcher explains. "I'm in love with her..."

My heart stops. But before I can process his declaration, Henley takes a step forward, holding my brother back.

Rhonan shoves him off. "*Love*? You don't know the first thing about love!"

"You're right. I don't, but—"

Elliot's laugh is maniacal. "Love? Love is a fucking joke!" He points a finger at Fletcher. "You lied to Rhonan! And you knew Tori was gone and didn't fucking tell me!"

"That's my fucking *sister*, asshole!" Rhonan shouts, stepping toward Fletcher. I move to stand in front of him, but I'm too slow. Rhonan cocks his fist back and swings at Fletcher's face, forcing me and Fletcher to both stumble back. The sound of Rhonan's fist connecting with Fletcher's nose is enough to make my stomach turn.

"Rhonan!" I scream, but Elliot rushes him next.

"You motherfucker!" Elliot's fist collides with Fletcher's ribs, causing him to fold in two.

"Easy there, buddy." Henley pulls my brother back before he can get another swing in.

I rush over to Fletcher, checking his face. Blood drips from his nose, staining his white shirt. When our eyes meet, I see the apology in his.

This wasn't how this was supposed to go.

I twist to face my brother. "Rhonan! Are you out of your mind?"

"Yeah, I fucking am!" he yells, his voice echoing in the small space.

"Rhonan..." Fletcher starts, but my brother spins on him and moves to punch him again. Henley steps in front of him this time to stop him.

"Rhonan, that's enough!"

"You'd better go, angel," Fletcher says to me, ushering me toward the door.

"No. I'm not leaving you."

"I'll be fine."

"You both need to fucking leave," Henley barks out as Elliot grabs Tori's makeup bag and throws it at the wall, glass and plastic shattering and spraying everywhere.

"Fucking bitch!"

Henley motions for us to move. "Let him have his moment, and Rhonan needs time to calm down too."

Rhonan glares at us as we leave. "You're supposed to be one of my best friends..." my brother grates out as we move toward the door.

Fletcher pushes me through the door, following closely behind. "Jesus Christ," he mutters as he rests his back against the wood. The sound of Elliot taking his anger out on the bridal suite continues as we stand there, and Rhonan's voice is booming as he yells at Henley for not telling him about us.

"You're bleeding," I say, reaching up toward Fletcher's face. I take the pink silk square from his tux and wipe it under his nose, pressing it to the opening to soak up the blood that's still flowing.

"Your brother has a mean right hook."

"Is it broken?"

Fletcher reaches up and pinches the bridge of his nose. "Doesn't feel like it." Sighing, he looks at me. "I'm sorry."

"What are you apologizing for?"

"This wasn't how this was supposed to go."

"I know." I drag my hand over the curve of his jaw. "But none of today has gone how it was supposed to, not just the part where my brother found out about us."

He lifts my hand and kisses the top of it.

Dilynne races up to us. "Oh my God. What happened?" Guests are starting to gather in the main room, peeking down the hall to get a glimpse of the drama.

"Well, Rhonan and Elliot walked in on us kissing and they both punched Fletcher."

Dilynne nods. "Yeah, I can see that."

A loud crash comes from inside the bridal suite again. "Is Elliot..."

"Taking out his anger on the room?" I finish for her. "Yeah." The emotions of the past hour catch up to me as tears fill my eyes. "I can't believe this. God, that bitch…" The dam holding back my tears breaks as I start to cry.

Fletcher pulls me into his chest. "He's going to be okay."

And then something else dawns on me. "Where's Ellis?"

"Joanne has her," my father announces as he approaches. "What the hell happened to you?" he asks Fletcher.

"Rhonan found out about me and Laney," he explains.

My dad's brows draw together. "You two are together?"

Fletcher sighs as I swipe under my eyes, trying to gather myself. "Not officially, but if she'll have me, she's the only woman I want." He reaches out for my hand. "The truth is I've been in love with your daughter for a very long time. It's just taken me a while to admit it and finally act on it."

My father clears his throat. "I see. Well, I can't say I'm surprised…"

"Well, Rhonan was, apparently." I look over at my father who's taking tissue out of his pocket and handing it to Fletcher. "That's him in there, screaming, and Elliot is the one throwing things."

"Your brother will get over this if you two are happy. He's just…very protective of you, Laney. We both are."

My eyes find Fletcher's, feeling the certainty I've been waiting for. "This is what I want, Dad. Fletcher is who I want."

"But what about the pact?" Fletcher says as the corner of his mouth tips up.

"Fuck the pact," Dilynne interjects. "I think it's ridiculous that y'all even made it." Of course I told my best friend about the ridiculous notion that these boys were going to dictate who we fell in love with.

Rhonan storms out of the bridal suite, and his eyes immediately land on Fletcher. "You're still here? You've got some fucking nerve…"

"Jesus, I can't handle you right now." I push him back, grab Fletcher's hand, and make my way out to the main room as eyes descend on me. Guests that haven't left are waiting around, prying for more information, but I need to get out of here.

"Excuse me," I say, pushing through the throngs of people in desperate need of fresh air. I can feel Dilynne, Dad, and my brother on our heels, but I don't turn back.

Everything is falling apart around me, and I can feel a panic attack coming on.

Fletcher squeezes my hand, leading me to his truck as people stand off to the side, watching our every move.

When we finally make it to his truck, Fletcher's dad is standing there, a pleased grin on his face and a glass of wine in his hand. And I have a feeling this day is about to get worse.

# Chapter 28

**Fletcher**

*Revenge, an Ultimatum, and an Escape*

My body is on high alert as soon as I see my father standing next to my truck, blocking the driver's side door.

"What the fuck do you want?" I pull Laney behind me, keeping her hand in mine but shielding her from him.

The sinister laugh that leaves my father's mouth makes me grip Laney's hand tighter. "Nice bloody nose."

"You *would* approve... You've given me a few yourself."

His smile falters. "Watch your fucking mouth."

"Or what?" I drop Laney's hand and take a step toward the man who abused me most of my life, both physically and mentally, feeling my tolerance for his bullshit evaporate into thin air.

Hell, I've already been in one fight today, might as well make it two.

"Fletcher!" Laney calls out to me, but I put up my hand to silence her.

"Go ahead. Hit me. Show everyone here how you love taking swings at your son."

Henley suddenly appears beside me, holding me back. "Fletcher, people are recording this, man," he says in my ear.

I drift my eyes to the side and notice the crowd of people gathered around us. "Fuck."

"That's right. You wouldn't want to ruin your precious reputation now, would you?" my father grates out, his smirk back in full force. "Although from the looks of it, your little piece of ass there is going to do that for you."

"You motherfucker!"

I slam my father to the ground before landing a punch to his face. Rationality leaves my brain, red clouds my vision, and my fists keep landing on his face as all the rage from my childhood up until now leaves my body.

"Don't you ever talk about her like that!" I roar.

Henley yanks me back before I can get another punch in. "You're not fucking thinking straight, Fletch!"

"I'm done," I snap, tossing my hands in the air, even though every part of me wants to get more hits in—as many as he's delivered to me over the years.

"Get out of here." Henley pushes me toward my truck. "Go! Before it gets worse."

I reach for Laney's hand and help her into my truck before I round the hood and hop inside myself. Gravel kicks up as I peel out of the parking lot.

My heart is racing as I drive away from the chaos. The truck is silent, the only sound the whir of the tires beneath us.

"Fletcher... You shouldn't have done that."

"What was I supposed to do? Stand by and let him talk about you like that?"

"No, but—"

"He fucking deserved it, Laney. Punching him is the least I could do after everything that man has put me through."

"I don't blame you. But the cameras... People were—"

"I know." I slam my palm against the steering wheel. "Fuck!"

"What are we going to do?"

I stare out the front windshield. "Right now? Just be together. Let shit die down. And hope to God I didn't just ruin my friendship with your brother and Elliot, and my career in one fucking day."

***

My phone rings on the nightstand beside me, waking me up shortly after I'd fallen asleep. When I pick it up and look at the time, I see that it's just after two in the morning. Laney and I talked for a while before she finally passed out, but I couldn't shut my mind off.

I kept staring at her, wondering if I was doing the right thing dragging her into the chaos of my life, stroking the side of her face as my heart warred with my mind. The videos of me punching my father went viral at record speed, causing my agent to call me a few hours after we left the winery, chastising me for my behavior. When I told him why I hit my dad, though, his attitude changed rather quickly.

He's the first person that I've told about my past besides Laney, and I have a feeling he won't be the last.

He assured me that he'd spin this in the right way to make sure my career wasn't in jeopardy, including contacting the PR team for the Carolina Thunder. But the other issue I now have to face is that the world knows about Laney. It's clear that we're an item from the multiple videos online, which is yet another piece of information shared with the world, but not in the way I planned.

I see the number on the phone has an Asheville area code, so I'm pressured to answer it, even though I don't know who it might be.

"Hello?"

"Hello. I'm looking for Fletcher Adams."

"This is he," I reply as Laney stirs beside me. When her eyes pop open and she sees me on the phone, she pushes herself up, but I stop her from moving further.

"My name is Dr. Esser," the man continues. "I work in the ER at Asheville Memorial Hospital and your father was brought in about an hour ago."

I sit up, my pulse spiking. "Okay..."

"You might want to come down here. Your father was in an accident, and..."

"Fuck." I bury my head in my free hand. "Did he..."

"He's alive. Damn lucky, if you ask me."

I toss the covers off and head straight for my closet. "I'll be there as soon as I can."

"He's stable, but since you're his next of kin, I'm obligated to contact you."

"Thank you."

When I hang up the call, I find Laney right behind me in the closet, the sheet pulled around her naked body. "Fletcher?"

"My dad got in an accident." I pull a shirt from a hanger and toss it over my head. "He's in the hospital."

"Is he okay?"

"Of course the fucker lived." I twist to face her and find a look of terror in her eyes. "Shit, Laney." I rush toward her, pulling her against my chest. Here I am irritated that my father is still alive, and yet Laney would give anything for her mom to still be here.

She leans back and looks up at me. "I'm going with you."

"You don't have to."

"I know I don't." She inhales slowly. "But I'm in love with you too, Fletcher Adams, and you don't have to face him alone anymore." It takes a few seconds for her words to register, and when they do, my lungs fill with oxygen in a way they never have.

I cup her face in my hands. "I love you so fucking much, Laney." My lips meet hers. "I'm sorry that I said it for the first time in front of your brother, but..."

"It's okay. I know you were just trying to get him to understand that this isn't just a fluke."

"It never was. I think I've loved you since I was seventeen. It just took me a while to admit it."

She rolls her eyes at me, but her smile is blinding. "God, take forever, why don't you?"

"If I recall, there was some avoiding on your part, too."

"Well, I think it's safe to say that we've both made mistakes."

"I'm not perfect, Laney. I mean, fuck. Look at my life. Asking you to be a part of it is a lot. You sure that you want this?"

She drags her nails through my scruff, pulling my lips to hers. "I've never been more certain of anything in my life."

"I don't deserve you," I mutter between nips of her lips.

"Yes, you do. You deserve to be loved unconditionally, and that's exactly what I plan to do for the rest of our lives."

***

Laney squeezes my hand as we follow the nurse down the hallway to my father's room.

"He's on some pretty heavy painkillers right now, so he probably won't know that you're here," the nurse says as she stops outside the door. "Dr. Esser will be by shortly to talk to you more about his recovery. The police have already been by to question him, but I know they wanted to talk to you too."

"Of course. Anything I can do to help."

Laney looks up at me. "You ready?"

"He's not going to like what I have to say to him."

"And you give a shit, why?"

Squeezing her hand, I say, "Thank you for being here."

"I told you, you don't have to deal with this alone anymore."

I push the door open to his room, and even though I know he was in an accident, I'm still not prepared for what I see.

The massive man that raised me and taught me everything about the game we both love is lying in a hospital bed with cuts all over his face and bruises on his arms, and his right leg is in a cast. Honestly, he looks better off than he deserves.

The couple that he drunkenly crashed his car into last night though? They have a long road to recovery. Laney shed tears when we found out that they survived, and I'm grateful they did. I'm beyond relieved that another set of siblings won't have to face the horrifying task of burying one of their parents like the woman next to me and her brother have.

I stand at the side of his bed, gripping Laney's hand still.

"The windows must have shattered," she says. "He has a million cuts."

"Serves him right," I grate out as anger and grief blur my vision. "He deserves much worse."

"I agree."

A groan leaves my father's lips as he blinks himself awake, staring up at me. "Fletcher?"

"You should be dead," I say without pause, my body shaking from the adrenaline racing through me.

"Fletcher," Laney warns me from the side. I know I sound like a selfish bastard wishing my father would have died last night, especially because the woman next to me would give anything for her mom to still be alive. But I can't deny how I feel. I can't deny that part of me wished for that news just so this part of my past could have been buried with him.

"Son..." His lip trembles as his eyes fill with tears.

"No. You don't get to cry. You don't get to be sorry." I point to the hallway outside. "There's a couple out there, fighting for their fucking lives because of you."

"I know." He swallows roughly. "I didn't..."

"You don't get to blame this on anyone else but yourself. You're a fucking alcoholic, Dad. When the hell are you going to admit that?"

"You're right." He reaches out for me, but I back away. "Fletcher..."

Leaning closer to him, I make sure his eyes are locked with mine when I say these next words. "Listen closely because I'm only going to say this once. I'm *done* with you. I am done being your verbal and physical punching bag. I am done covering for you, feeding your fucking habit, and feeling sorry for you because I know that the game was the one thing that made you feel worthy, and you lost it before you were ready. But if there's anything I've learned watching you, it's that football isn't everything."

I glance over at Laney, her eyes brimming with tears as she nods, encouraging me to continue.

"You hit me, took out your anger on me, and Laney was the one who helped me heal. She iced my bruises, she cleaned up my cuts, and she's the reason that I became the man I am today. Not you."

A tear slips down my dad's cheek.

"So here's what's going to happen. You're going to get help, go to rehab, and publicly admit to the abuse and agree that I punched you out of self-defense, or I will never speak to you again."

"Fletcher..." he croaks.

"Your hospital bills are covered, so don't worry about that. But if you decide to call me when you get out of here, it had better be to tell me you agree to my terms, or kindly delete my fucking number and forget that I ever existed."

He closes his eyes and turns his head away from me. When I look over at Laney, she's smiling at me even as tears stream down her face.

I lead her out of the room. She hops up just enough to wrap her arms around my neck. "I'm so proud of you."

I hold onto her like the lifeline that she is. "I'm shaking."

"You're okay. I've got you."

My emotions overwhelm me. "The look on his face..." I mutter as my lips find her temple. Gratitude radiates from my chest as I hold onto her, squeezing her tight enough that I know she's not going to disappear.

"He needed to hear it. If he genuinely loves you, he'll do what he needs to do."

"How can a parent hit their child?" I murmur, asking the question I've never been able to find the answer to. "How could he hit me and say he loved me at the same time?"

She leans back and holds my face between her hands. "I don't know, but *I* love you. You are the man who defined strength and determination for me. You're the man I've measured all others against. And you're the man I want to build a life with. I can't wait to have our own children to love the way you deserved to be loved, Fletcher."

Fuck. This is how I know this woman saved me—because she loved me even when I thought I didn't deserve it.

"That's why you're my angel, Laney."

"And I always will be." Our lips meet and I take as much time as I need to gather myself while holding this woman in my arms.

When I glance down the hall, two police officers are waiting for me, as well as several reporters.

So, with my girl by my side, I tackle this next hurdle in my life, knowing I have her to lean on this time. And soon the entire world will know that this woman owns me—mind, body, and soul.

***

"Are you sure this is a good idea? I thought we were trying to keep a low profile after Saturday."

Lifting Laney's hand, I bring it to my lips and kiss the back of it, continuing to drive as fast as I can away from Blossom Peak. It's Wednesday night, and since all of the wedding stuff is done and my father is still in the hospital for a while, I decided to surprise Laney with a night out, away from the rumors in town and the tension with my friends, but in a place that I know I can still have control over who sees us. Plus, I've waited twelve years to take this woman on a date, and I'm not waiting any longer.

"Angel, I'm about to show you how having money has changed my life."

She rolls her eyes. "Look, I'm not naïve to the fact that you earn an eight-figure salary, Fletcher. But if you think acting like a pompous ass and throwing it around will impress me, then you don't know me as well as you thought."

I glance over at her before focusing my eyes back on the road. "Look, I didn't mean it like that. I'm just trying to reassure you that I can guarantee us some privacy tonight, all right? I have connections and the ability to spoil you, so I'm going to. Tonight means a lot to me, Laney."

"Really? Why?"

"Because it's our first official date and the last first date you'll ever have."

"What makes you think that?"

"Because you and me are endgame, angel. Plain and simple."

I can feel her staring at me from the passenger seat, but she chuckles before directing her eyes back to the windshield. "Then this better be one hell of a first date, Fletcher. Otherwise, I might just have to reassess some things."

I lift her hand and kiss it again. "I promise not to disappoint."

As I continue to drive to Charlotte, prepared to show Laney what our life would be like when she comes to visit me in the city, I think about how I used to fantasize about our first date back when we were teenagers.

"You know, if I were still seventeen, I'd be taking you to a movie tonight, buying us all of the best snacks, and trying to feel you up the whole time."

Her mouth drops open. "What? That's what you had planned for our first date?"

I shrug unapologetically. "I can't deny that my dick came up with that plan. I'd have taken you for ice cream afterward, though."

"Wow. It's a good thing you never got that chance then—because I would have been severely disappointed."

"Yeah, it doesn't sound as amazing now as it did back then."

Laney laughs. "You think?" She clears her throat. "By the way, after my conversation with my dad yesterday, I think we should talk to Rhonan when we get back."

"How's he doing?"

"My dad said he's been a bear, even snapping at Joanne and Ellis, but he made sure to bring him back to reality. The thing is, I think he's more hurt because we weren't honest with him from the start."

I reach up and readjust my hat. "That's my fault. The lack of honesty started the moment I started crawling through your bedroom window instead of his."

"Well, I didn't tell him how I felt about you either, so we both are at fault here."

"Hopefully, once he hears our story, he'll understand."

"My dad seems to think so."

My eyes flick over to her. "You told your dad everything?"

"I sort of had to, but don't worry. He's not mad at you, more at your father and for not picking up on something going on himself, especially when you were at our house so much."

"No one is to blame here, but when we get back, a lot needs to come out in the open."

"Agreed."

I just hope that my friends are willing to listen and understand.

***

"You weren't kidding about being treated differently, were you?" Laney asks as I pull out her chair at the table set for two in the private room I booked for us at Angeline's, one of my favorite restaurants in Charlotte. This is, of course, after we entered through a private entrance and were escorted down a hall that the rest of the restaurant doesn't have access to.

"Like I said, I wanted us to have our privacy. Angelo, the owner, always takes good care of me."

Our waiter waits for me to sit before handing us our menus and mentioning the specials. Once we place our drink order, he saunters off. "This really is romantic, Fletcher. Thank you."

"I told you. I wanted this to be a night you won't forget. Dinner will be top-notch, but I still have another surprise up my sleeve."

She scoots her chair closer to mine, leaning in so our mouths are just inches apart. "Part of me is glad that we didn't get our first date until now."

My eyes dip down to her lips. "Why is that?"

"Because this means so much more after what we've been through to get here." She tilts her head and kisses me softly.

"Fuck, Laney." Sliding my hand up her neck, I pull her closer until I can feel her chest against mine. I kiss her slow and soft, not having to rush, not feeling so desperate because, even though I know I'll never get enough of her, tonight we have time.

*We finally have fucking time.*

We part just as the waiter comes back with her wine and my water. "Are you sure you don't want to have a drink with me?" she asks.

"I'm sure."

Her hand lands on my thigh. "One drink won't turn you into your father, Fletcher."

"I know, but honestly? I don't miss it or feel like I'm missing out on anything. It makes my mind clearer, and I definitely don't miss hangovers."

"Okay. I just want you to know that I won't judge you if you decide differently."

I lean in and press my lips to hers again. "I appreciate that. Thank you."

The waiter comes by to take our order. Laney suggests I order a few of my favorite dishes for us to share. Once I've covered all the bases, she takes a sip from her wine and turns to face me again.

"So, speaking of the season...training camp starts soon, right?"

I finish chewing my bite of the freshly baked rosemary and olive oil bread. "Yes, at the end of July."

"And what does that look like for you?" she asks, dropping her eyes to her lap.

I tip her chin up with my finger, forcing her to look at me. "I think the question you meant to ask is, what does that look like for us?"

Her eyes dart between mine. "That too."

Grinning, I say, "Well, I won't be able to see you at all for two weeks, but after the first week, we can talk on the phone."

"Two weeks?" Disappointment coats her words.

"I know. Usually it doesn't sound like much, but the thought of being away from you for that long already makes my chest ache." I take both of her hands in mine. "This isn't going to be easy, Laney. I've never played football and been in a relationship, but I'll learn to manage it all. You just have to be patient with me."

"This is all new to me too, Fletcher."

I rest my forehead on hers. "Taking you to Charlotte tonight wasn't just about spoiling you with good food and romance, or getting away from the chaos. It was about showing you what our life could be like when you're here."

"I can't move here, Fletcher. My business, my dad and brother and niece, and Dilynne are all in Blossom Peak."

"And I'm not asking you to. We can split our time between here and there. It's only a two-hour drive. Plus, I don't know how many years I have left in the game. I'm thirty-two. I know Brett Favre played into his forties, but I don't want to do that. I don't want to put my body through that. Besides, now that my dad is most likely out of a job, Blossom Peak High School is gonna need a new coach."

Laney inhales sharply. "But if you play this season..."

"I'm not saying this year, but in the future, that's definitely something I could see myself doing, especially if it means a quieter life with you." Her eyes bounce back and forth between mine. "I know I'm asking a lot of you, but Laney? You're the only woman I want in my life, the only one that I need. I'm willing to make the sacrifices to make this work."

She holds my face in her hands. "Me too, Fletcher." She rubs her nose against mine. "I'm all in."

***

After Laney and I sample all of the food we ordered, I escort her back out to my truck and drive her around the city, pointing out my favorite shops, the park where I go running sometimes, and a few museums I said that I'd visit when I moved here, but never got around to doing. She instantly plans out when we can go to each one, and about thirty minutes later, I head for my house, eager to show her my home and the life I've created for myself here in Charlotte.

As we turn into my driveway, I don't miss the gasp that leaves her lips when she sees my house for the first time. "Fletcher, this is gorgeous."

"Thank you."

The white house with pillars that flank the front door is highlighted by the light fixtures on the outside. A column of windows from floor to ceiling covers the entire right side, offering plenty of sunlight when the sun is out, and views of the city lights below at night since my house sits up on a hill. The white brickwork and black roofing is what sold me on the place, as well as the black marble steps that lead up the red front door, giving it the mix of modern and classic that I wanted when I decided to purchase my first home here.

It's not the most extravagant house on the block, but it's the one that stood out to me because it represented everything I did to get to this place—the sweat, the fear, and the bruises from the game and my father that I endured, yet still came out a success.

I just don't understand why my father can't be proud of that too.

When I pull into the garage under the house, I climb out of the truck and help Laney out, leading her inside. I flick on the lights, illuminating the open concept of the first floor.

"This is exactly what I would have envisioned your house to look like," she says as she slowly walks around, taking everything in.

The entire first floor is open, except for my office in the corner of the floor-to-ceiling windows. The kitchen is white with black marble, the hardwood floors are dark walnut, and my black leather couch takes up most of the space in the living room, providing plenty of seating for the massive flat screen hanging up on the wall. The decorations are minimal—just a few brass pieces and frames of moments in my career I wanted to remember.

But as I lean against the wall next to the fridge, I cross my arms over my chest and realize that the presence that was always missing from this place is now standing right in front of me.

"And how was that?" I ask.

She trails her finger down the frame of the picture hanging on the wall of me at the NFL draft, holding up my Carolina Thunder jersey. "Clean. Neutral. Modern, yet a space that suits you."

"We can change whatever you want, make it more of a home. I want you to be comfortable here too, baby."

Tapping her chin, she hums in thought. "I mean, I guess I have a few ideas."

I smile. "Can't wait to hear them." Turning behind me, I press a button on the control panel on the wall, waiting for the surround system to come to life. "Because You Loved Me" by Celine Dion starts playing from the speakers throughout the house. "Now, since I didn't get to dance with you at the wedding, I'd like to have my dance now, if you'd do me the honor." I hold my hand out to her, waiting for her to cross the room to me.

Slowly, she walks toward me until she's close enough that I can pull her into my arms, encasing her against my chest.

"Is this part of my surprise?"

"Yes." I press a kiss to her temple. "Our first dance, but certainly not our last."

With Laney in my arms, I move us around the room, soaking up every second, silently expressing gratitude to the universe for bringing this woman back into my life.

"This was my parents' wedding song," she whispers.

I lean back to see her eyes filled with tears. "Wow, really?" She nods. "I had no idea."

"I know you didn't, that's why I'm crying."

"I just really fucking love Celine Dion."

Laney chuckles. "I just can't help but feel like this was Mom's way of telling us she approves." Our eyes lock as she waves her hand around the room. "You really did this, Fletcher."

The corner of my mouth lifts as I look down at her.

*God, I love this girl.*

She believed in me when I didn't even believe in myself.

She was my safe haven from the shitstorm that was my life.

She was and always will be my *angel*.

"I did, Laney. And I never would have made it here without you."

She runs her nails down my neck. "Yes, you would have."

"No, angel. You don't get it. There were some days in high school when…" I choke down the lump in my throat. "Days when I didn't think I could take anymore."

"What?"

"Yeah… Just a few days before I crawled into your room that first night, I thought about how I might…"

She pushes her fingers to my lips, silencing me. "Don't say it." Tears fill her eyes again. "I can't believe you thought about that."

"I did, until that night when you put ice on my face and gave me someplace safe to hide. And told me that I was a good person who could make it in life when I honestly didn't know if fighting for my dreams was worth it anymore. When I told you that you saved me, Laney, I fucking meant it."

She presses up on her toes and wraps her arms around my neck. "Kiss me."

Our mouths meet in a slow, heated kiss, and I slide my hands beneath her thighs, lifting her into my arms. She gasps softly, her body melting against mine as I carry her up the stairs to my room. I lay her down gently in the center of my bed, her long, dark hair fanning out around her, her eyes reflecting the light drifting in through the windows.

"I want to touch every inch of you tonight." My voice is low, reverent, as I begin working open the buttons of my shirt, one by one.

"I want you to feel me everywhere, for you to know that no part of you isn't mine."

"Yes... Touch me, Fletcher," she whispers.

"Take that dress off."

She rises slowly from the bed and stands at my feet, keeping her eyes locked on mine as we both undress. My shirt on the floor. Her dress and underwear pooled at her feet. My pants and boxer briefs kicked to the side.

When she pinches the clasp on the back of her bra and lets it slide down her arms, revealing her bare, beautiful body to me, I reach out and trace her collarbone with my fingers. She moans as I trail my fingers over her skin and tilts her head to the side as I move my hand lower, rubbing circles around her nipple with my thumb.

"So fucking perfect."

She reaches out and wraps her hand around my cock, stroking me, dragging her nails gently up and down my shaft.

"Yes, baby. Just like that. Stroke me."

She leans in, still working me with her hand, and presses her mouth to mine, soft at first, then deeper, hungrier. The combination of her kiss and her touch nearly undoes me.

She pulls back, her eyes heavy with need. "Make love to me, Fletcher," she whispers.

I cradle her face in my hand, lowering my mouth back to hers before reaching between her legs, testing her wetness.

"Always fucking ready for me."

"I've wanted you for so long that I don't think that will ever change."

I lay her back down on the bed, resting my hips between her legs. "I want you so desperate to come tonight that you can't fucking stand it."

"Please," she moans as she reaches between us, lines my cock up to her entrance, and lifts her hips, guiding me inside her.

I only give her a few inches before I withdraw. "I'm going to tease the fuck out of you so you know what I feel like whenever I'm around you—aching for you, craving you, waiting until I can have you again. I'm going to show you how you turn me inside out."

She whimpers and reaches for my ass, trying to pull me deeper, but I don't move. "Fletcher..." Her eyes close and she turns her head to the side.

I make short, shallow thrusts. "I'm in control tonight, angel. Trust me to give you what you need."

When she looks back at me, eyes pleading, I slide in further, loving how her mouth parts as I fill her completely. Then I pull back again, slowly entering and withdrawing from her so she can feel every fucking inch of me, and vice versa.

"So good," she breathes, arching against me.

"Fucking perfect."

"Your cock, Fletcher." She sighs as I pick up my pace slightly, only to slow down again.

"Tell me, baby. What about my cock?"

"You make me feel so full...so wet."

"You're fucking soaked, dripping all over me and the blanket." I lift her legs, pushing them back until her knees nearly touch the mattress. "Let's see if we can make you messier."

"Oh." *Thrust.* "My." *Thrust.* "God." *Thrust.* "Fletcher!"

The sound of us fucking fills the room as I pick up my pace again, feeling her grow wetter, hotter, and tighter around me. "Fuck, Laney. Are you getting close?" I brace myself higher on my hands, giving me more leverage to thrust deeper. I wanted to make this last, but this angle is making her cunt grip me so tight, there's no way I'm going to hold out for much longer.

"Yes. Don't stop."

My hips start moving like they have a mind of their own, hitting her deep, over and over again until I lean back on my heels, move my thumb to her clit, and fight like hell not to break before she does. "Come for me, Laney. Right fucking now."

She continues to hold her legs open as I watch my cock sliding in and out of her, glistening from her arousal.

"Fuck. I'm coming!" she screams, twisting her head to the side and gasping for air between each tremor. Pumping just a few more times, I find my release seconds later, collapsing on top of her as we both fight to catch our breath.

"Fletcher... I... That was..."

"I know, baby." I lift my head, smoothing her hair away from her face. "And it's only going to get better from here."

# Chapter 29

**Laney**

*Taking Responsibility and a Postcard*

The past few days have been some of the most emotional of my life—not just because of Elliot's wedding that never happened, but because I witnessed Fletcher stand up to his father in a way that I knew he could this entire time. Fifteen-year-old me was so gratified as I listened to him tell his father exactly what he needed and deserved to hear.

And then our trip to Charlotte reminded me that all the bullshit we've both gone through to get here has been worth it. However, now it's time for me to face my brother, and for Fletcher to face his friends.

I've been trying to call Rhonan since Saturday, but he won't pick up the phone. None of the boys are speaking, apparently. Rhonan's pissed that Henley knew about me and Fletcher, and Elliot is pissed at Rhonan for running a background check on Tori, and Fletcher for not telling him that Tori left the winery. Not to mention, Fletcher knows that the cloud hovering over all of them is the stupid pact they made, so there's a ton of issues to work through.

When I talked to my dad to get an update on my brother, he said that he's calmed down finally, so I took that as a sign to stop putting off the inevitable.

Fletcher offered to go with me to see him, trying to give me the same support that I showed him. But this is different.

I need my brother to hear my side of the story before he speaks to Fletcher again because he's not the one who crossed the line—I did. Our entire history came down to the moment that I told Fletcher Adams I had feelings for him. I wouldn't take that decision back for anything, though, knowing that I would end up where I am today.

All of the hurt, the hate, the agony—it was all worth it, especially now that Fletcher and I are moving forward together.

Joanne opens the front door to the house before I make it up the driveway. "Hi, Laney."

"Hey there." I walk past her into the house. "Should I be scared?"

Joanne laughs. "Your brother doesn't scare me, so I'm not sure how to answer that. But, I will say this...I have an older brother, and their innate need to protect us never goes away. Don't be too hard on him, but at the same time, stand up for yourself too."

"Oh, I plan on it."

Chuckling, she says, "I didn't doubt you for a second. But just so you know, every woman on the planet is going to hate you now for tying down Fletcher Adams."

I blow out a breath. "That's going to take some getting used to, but he's worth it."

Joanne squeezes my shoulder. "True love is always worth it."

I make my way inside the house, heading for the living room. Rhonan and Ellis are sitting on the couch together watching a movie. But when my brother sees me, I can tell that his mind is on anything but Elsa finding out what her ice powers can do.

Ellis sees me a second later, jumping from the couch and running over, wrapping her arms around my legs. "Auntie Laney!"

"Hi, sweetie."

"Did you come to help make Daddy smile again?" Her brown eyes are so full of hope, it slices my heart in two. "He's been really grumpy, like a bear."

"I'm gonna try."

Rhonan scoffs. "Yeah, good luck with that."

"Hey, Ellis?" Joanne asks from behind me. "Why don't we go get some ice cream?"

Her smile is radiant. "I love ice cream!"

"Me too. Go get your shoes." She races back to her room while Joanne turns to me. "Text me when you two are done talking, okay?"

"Thank you, Joanne."

"Anything for you, Laney. You're family."

Ellis comes bounding back into the room, and Joanne scoops her into her arms. "What flavor should we get?"

"All of them!"

"That's my girl." Joanne winks at me over her shoulder. "We'll be back in a bit."

The front door closes behind them with a soft click, leaving me and my brother alone.

Slowly, I step into the living room and take a seat on the couch, leaving a bit of space between us.

"Hey."

"Hey." Rhonan stares at the now black television.

"Are you ready to talk like adults?"

His jaw clenches. "I guess I don't have a choice."

"I'd just like to point out that you're the older one here."

Annoyance radiates off him. "Just say what you came to say, Laney."

Taking in a deep breath, I prepare to say the words I've been practicing over the past few days. "First, I want you to know that Fletcher and I never meant to hurt you."

"But you did choose to lie to me. Both of you."

"Can you blame us? I mean, look at your reaction."

He taps a finger to his chest. "Can you blame *me*? I found out one of my best friends is fucking my sister, and another friend was left at the fucking altar. I'm not exactly having the best week of my life here."

I tilt my head at him. "Yes, it's been a hard week for everyone. But are you ready to hear the truth, instead of being angry at Fletcher for something that he wasn't responsible for?"

"What do you mean?"

I tuck my legs up under me and lean my arm on the back of the couch, propping my head up in my hand. "Fletcher and I have a history, Rhonan. A friendship that you know nothing about."

His eyes narrow. "What?"

"It started my sophomore year. Do you remember that game when he made that incredible catch and came over to our house for spaghetti afterward?"

Rhonan thinks for a moment. "There were several games like that, Laney."

"Well, this was the one that started it all. Dad took him home after dinner, but he came back that night and crawled through my window."

Rhonan grows serious. "Did he touch you?"

I roll my eyes. "No. He thought it was your window and ended up in my room by mistake. But he came back because he was running away from his dad."

"Why?"

I look my brother dead in the eyes. "Fletcher's dad used to hit him, Rhonan. And it happened more than once."

He launches himself from the couch. "Are you fucking kidding me?"

I tug on his hand, urging him to sit back down. "You haven't been online over the past few days, have you?"

"No. You know I can't stand that social media crap."

"Well, after you punched Fletcher in the bridal suite, Fletcher got in a fight with his dad in the parking lot of the winery. Luke said some nasty things to him, and Fletcher gave him a taste of his own medicine."

"Jesus Christ. How come he never said anything?"

"Because it's not that simple. Fletcher buried it, like a lot of people do, especially when the person hurting you is supposed to love you."

"But he told you?"

"Not by choice. But after the second time he ended up in my room with an injury, I started to put two and two together. It took a while for him to actually admit what was going on, and then he made me promise not to tell anyone."

Rhonan's still processing, his hands curled into fists.

"And," I add quietly, "most of it happened after Luke had been drinking. I don't know if you ever noticed, but that man's never far from a bottle. The whole reason they moved here was because he got fired from his previous job because he showed up intoxicated."

"Jesus. And you've known all this time?"

I nod. "I have."

"So you two have been sneaking around since then?"

I laugh. "God, no. If you hadn't noticed, over the past twelve years, Fletcher hasn't exactly been my favorite person."

"I mean, I thought he just annoyed you. He can be a cocky motherfucker sometimes."

*Yes, he can, especially in the bedroom.*

"Oh, I'm aware. But I avoided him because the night Mom died, I told him how I felt about him at that party, and he didn't have anything to say in response. In fact, he avoided me the rest of the night. And when I went looking for him, I thought I caught him with another girl."

I shake my head. "Turns out I was wrong. But at the time? It wrecked me."

Rhonan stands from the couch, pacing back and forth. "So, you had feelings for him, but he didn't feel the same way?"

"Actually, he did, but he didn't act on them because he didn't want to betray you." Rhonan freezes. "Yeah, that little pact you four made is another reason it's taken twelve years for us to figure our shit out," I say, arching a brow at my brother.

"Laney. I—"

I hold my hand up. "I don't care anymore. I just want you to know that Fletcher honored your stupid pact rather than act on his feelings toward me because that's how much your friendship means to him."

Rhonan begins pacing again.

"I know this may be hard for you to hear right now, but I love him, Rhonan." Our eyes meet. "I always have. And he loves me too. We just want to be together, and we will, no matter how you feel about it. I'm hoping that you can be supportive, but if you can't, I'm still going to be with him. You're the one that gets to decide what our relationship and your friendship with him will look like moving forward."

My brother drops back down onto the couch, resting his head against the cushions behind him. "This is a lot to take in."

"I know, and trust me, the last thing we wanted was for you to find out the way you did. We had planned to tell you after the wedding, but..."

He turns his head toward me. "I can't believe his dad used to hit him, and I never put it together. All his bruises..." He rubs his forehead. "Fuck, I'm a shitty friend. It's just... When I saw you two together... I thought you were just a casual thing to him, and I didn't want you to get hurt."

"There has never been anything casual between me and Fletcher Adams."

Rhonan goes silent for a while. Finally, he turns to me and asks, "You really love him?"

I cover my heart with my hand. "I do. He's the only man I've ever loved. In fact, when things ended with Spencer, I wasn't nearly as devastated as I was the night I told Fletcher how I felt about him. But he needs his friends right now more than anything." I prepare to tell him the rest of what's transpired. "People recorded the fight between him and his dad. It's all over the internet, like I said, but there's more."

"What?"

"That night after the wedding, Luke got into a car accident. He ended up in the hospital. He's alive, and the couple he hit are too, but in critical condition." Our gazes meet again. "They have two children—two kids that could have lost their parents." A sob crawls up my throat before I can stop it.

Rhonan pulls me into his chest, rubbing my back as I cry. I've been holding it in, trying to be strong for Fletcher, but being able to share in this grief with my brother is exactly what I needed. "Shhh. It's okay."

"I miss her so much, Rho."

"Fuck, I know. I do too, Laney."

"I can't help but wonder what our lives would be like if she didn't die."

He kisses the top of my head. "I think about that every day, especially now." We sit there for a minute, letting everything I just admitted settle between us. "Where is Fletcher?"

"He's in Charlotte. He had a meeting with his agent and PR team on how to tackle this thing with his dad." I sit up tall again, wiping my nose on my sleeve. "When we went to see Luke in the hospital, Fletcher gave him an ultimatum. He either goes to rehab to get help and admits that he hit his son, or Fletcher doesn't want to hear from him ever again."

"What did Luke say?"

"I don't know what he's going to do. We left before Fletcher gave him the opportunity to respond, and then Fletcher took me to Charlotte to let everything die down here until you guys could hash it all out."

"When will Fletcher be back?"

"In a few days. I hope by then you can find a level head so you two can talk."

"He makes you happy?" he asks as I stand. "Treats you well?"

"He makes me so ridiculously happy that I'm terrified. But he loves me for me, Rhonan. That's all Mom and Dad ever wanted for us. And one day, I know you'll find that again too. I hate that you lost Sarah, but I hope you can remain hopeful that you're not destined to live a life without a partner again. I thought that was my fate for the longest time, but Fletcher has shown me that timing is everything. We just have to be open to the opportunity."

***

When I pull into my driveway, I sit in my car for a few minutes before making my way inside. Fletcher has only been gone for two days, but I already hate how empty my little house and my world feel without him.

The space he takes up here isn't nearly as much as what he occupies in my mind and my heart, but in just two short weeks, his presence became a permanent fixture in my life that I never want to live without again.

As I pop a frozen pizza in the oven for dinner, I realize I haven't checked my mail. I head back outside to the mailbox, and when I open it, I gasp when I see what's inside.

A pink tulip lies on top of a postcard with a picture of Cincinnati on the front. I pull them out of the mailbox and flip the card over to find Fletcher's familiar handwriting.

*My dearest Laney,*

*Cincinnati was the first city I traveled to for an away game in the NFL. I was walking through the airport and I saw a display of postcards and instantly thought of you. Since that day, I bought a postcard from every city I've been to, even though I never knew if I'd get the chance to send them to you. But now I finally do get that chance.*

*You—my angel—have given me so much more than I can ever thank you for. Your light, your smile, your body, your love. I am eternally grateful. This is just the first postcard of many that we can share with our grandkids when we're old and gray. And maybe our granddaughter will put them on her mirror in her room to use as a symbol of love to look up to—because our love is eternal, baby. Nothing can ever come between us again.*

*I love you. See you soon.*

*Fletcher AKA Lucifer*

I can barely see the words on the card as I laugh through my tears.

"Are you crying?" Dilynne walks up to me. "I saw you from the window and got scared when you looked like you were staring down at the ground."

"I'm good." I lift my head to look at my best friend, a smile on my lips and tears still streaming down my face.

"You don't look like it. You look like you need to invest in some waterproof mascara." I hand her the postcard and then lift the tulip to my nose, inhaling deeply. "What's this?" Dilynne grows quiet as she reads Fletcher's words, and when she looks back up at me, she has tears in her eyes too. "Damn it, Adams." She swipes under her eyes.

"I know." Sighing, I pull her into my side. "I'm going to be Laney Adams one day," I say, staring off at the mountains in the distance.

"Yes, you are, my friend. Yes, you are."

# Chapter 30

**Fletcher**

*A New Pact*

"Fletcher."

I walk into my father's house to find him sitting in his recliner, his full leg cast propped up on the footrest. He was released from the hospital a few days ago, but I was still in Charlotte dealing with the aftermath of the week before.

Laney let me know that he made it home, and checked on him last night, even though she didn't have to.

*My angel.*

"Hey."

"Thank you for coming."

Taking a seat on the couch across from him, I keep my walls up because there's no telling what my father will say. I've learned over the years never to underestimate him and always be prepared for a fist to swing in my direction.

"I can't stay long. I have plans with Laney."

He smiles, but I can tell that it's painful for him. "She loves you."

"Yeah, she does."

Nodding, he stares down at his hands in his lap. "I could tell when she was with you in the hospital. And when she came by last night, she made sure to give me a piece of her mind." It's so strange to hear him speak completely sober, almost like there's a completely different person sitting in front of me.

I can't fight the proud curl of my lips. "I'm sure she did."

"I've thought about what you said and honestly? The thought of never speaking to you again is something I couldn't live with."

My throat grows tight. "Well, you know what you have to do then."

He nods. "I do. The hospital gave me a list of rehab centers they recommend, and Laney did as well."

"You have a problem, Dad."

He shoves a hand through his hair before turning his eyes on me. "I do. I always told myself that it wasn't that big of a deal, and contrary to what you might think, I've been doing better over the past few years. But then you showed up out of the blue..."

I cut him off, instantly irritated. "Don't try to blame this on me. It's a goddamn miracle that you hadn't gotten in an accident until the other night, let alone that you didn't kill that couple in the other car."

His jaw tightens. "You don't get it, Fletcher. Seeing you live out your dream, seeing the man you've become and the success you've achieved? All it's done is remind me of all the ways I fell short. I'm fucking jealous of you!" he shouts before his lips begin to tremble. "There! Does that make you happy?"

I stand from the couch. "You think hearing my own father tell me that he's jealous of me makes what you did okay?"

"No! It's not okay. I'm a piece of shit, all right! I fucking admit it." He pounds his fist into the arm of his chair. "But I want to do better, be better. I don't want the rest of my life to feel like this—this shame, this regret, this hatred for me that is so clearly written all over your face."

And that's when it dawns on me. Laney may have hated me for the past twelve years for something that I couldn't control, but I've done the same to my own father.

His actions? They weren't about me. They were about him.

If I'm going to move on with my life, I have to let it go. I have to find a way to forgive him—not for his sake, but for mine.

"Then get help."

"I will. I—I promise."

"Good."

"Son?" he says as I turn my back toward him, preparing to leave.

"What?"

"I'm proud of you," he croaks out, making my eyes sting. "You are ten times the player I ever was."

I glance over my shoulder, fighting back my own tears. "And I'll be ten times the father you were too. We'll talk again once you're clean," I say, and then leave him there all alone, wondering if he'll actually follow through on his promises for once.

I want to believe him. The boy in me will always want a relationship with his dad.

But all that matters at this point is Laney, and our future. So that's my focus until I can start to trust my father again.

***

Laney jumps into my arms the second I get out of my truck and crashes her mouth to mine. "God, I missed you."

"This is such a better greeting than the last time I returned to Blossom Peak."

She giggles against my lips before a moan travels up her throat, egging me on to kiss her deeper and harder.

Fuck, I missed her too. More than I'll ever be able to articulate.

"Thank you again for my postcards."

While I was away, I sent her a total of three postcards, and fuck if she didn't have me tearing up when we talked about them on the phone late at night. "You're welcome. I'm glad you loved them."

She leans back in my arms as I carry her up to the main building at Hart Winery. "I can't wait to show you later just how much."

Groaning, I find her lips again as we walk inside, but a throat clearing to my left has me pulling away from Laney's mouth, only to find George Hart standing in the main tasting room, assessing us.

Laney slides down my body, concealing my cock that's straining against the zipper of my shorts. "Uh, yeah. I probably should have said something earlier, but..."

George extends his hand. "Fletcher."

I nod, shaking his hand. "George."

He shoves his hands in his pockets. "I know you're in love with my daughter, but do you mind keeping the PDA to a minimum when you're around me? That's still my little girl."

Laney rolls her eyes at him, but I nod. "I can do that, sir."

George clears his throat. "I want to apologize to you, Fletcher."

"Why?"

"For not seeing what I should have seen when you were a kid."

Laney rubs my arm at my side. Dropping my eyes to the ground, I clear my throat of the lump developing there. "It wasn't your responsibility."

George steps closer to me. "That's where you're wrong. *It was.* Any adult should be watching out for a child, especially when that child is part of the family. I'm sorry, Fletcher."

Meeting his eyes again, I reply, "Thank you."

"And because I think of you as family, I hope you'll understand why I've asked you to be here."

I look over at Laney and she squeezes my hand. "It's okay. I think tonight has been a long time coming."

George leads us through the winery back to his office. When he opens the door, I find my three best friends sitting around a blackjack table, along with three other men I vaguely recognize, chatting light-heartedly. But as soon as they see Laney and me holding hands, the room goes silent.

Laney presses up on her toes, planting a kiss to my cheek. "Don't be nervous."

Rhonan speaks first. "Laney, I know you're all in love with Fletcher, but that doesn't mean I want to see it."

Laney plants her hands on her hips. "Get used to it, Rhonan. I've waited a long time for this," she says, looking back at me and winking over her shoulder. "Now, should I stay out here in the hall in case I need to call the police to break up another fight, or can I leave while you all talk and promise not to kill each other?"

I meet Rhonan's eyes, seeing the same remorse in his that I feel in my own chest before turning back to Laney. "I think we'll be okay, baby."

"You'd better." She presses up on her toes and kisses me once more before turning and leaving the office.

George clears his throat. "Let me introduce you to some friends of mine." I follow him deeper into the room. "This is Anthony Gonzalez, Brian Thomas, and Henry Collins. Gentlemen, I'm sure you remember Fletcher Adams."

Anthony stands up from his seat first to shake my hand. "We've actually met before when you were younger, and I've been following your career. Congrats on the success."

"Thank you." I reach out to shake the hands of the other two men as well, and that's when I realize I've also met them.

"I've asked my friends to be here tonight to hopefully get through to you guys," George says as he takes his seat at the blackjack table. It's at that moment that I glance in Henley's direction as he acknowledges me with a nod, and then when I take in Elliot, my chest fucking hurts.

He looks like shit—dark circles under his eyes, his hair a mess, and a beard growing on his jaw that he clearly hasn't shaved since the wedding.

"What is there to get through to us about?" Elliot grates out. "I think we can all agree that we aren't as good of friends as we thought."

"Elliot," I start, but his glare makes me pause.

"No. Don't try to come up with some excuse, Fletcher. You fucking lied to us all, not only about Laney, but also about Tori. I was acting like a lovesick idiot while you knew she'd left."

Sighing, I fold my hands together and rest them on the table in front of me. "You're right. I did. I kept shit from all of you, but I wouldn't take it back."

He tilts his head at me. "Really? So you're perfectly fine with lying to your best fucking friends?"

George chimes in. "Can I say something really quick?"

Elliot leans back in his chair, his icy glare still apparent. "Fine."

"You know, the four of you remind me so much of Anthony, Brian, Henry, and myself." George chuckles. "Best friends from a young age, but that doesn't mean that our friendship has always been perfect."

Anthony nods. "In fact, I don't think we realized what true friendship was until George lost Elizabeth."

Rhonan looks back at his dad. "What is he talking about?"

George leans forward. "It's easy to think being someone's friend is enough when life is good. But when life gets hard, or in my case, borderline unbearable, that's when friendship is truly tested." He juts his chin toward the other three men. "If it weren't for them, I'm not sure I would have survived losing my wife."

"But you were strong after Mom died," Rhonan says.

"Because of them, son. Anthony came over and dragged me out of the house. He took me to her grave, made me talk about her, and made sure that I was fucking eating."

"And after you left for the Marines, I took your father to a therapist," Brian says. "My wife is the one that suggested it, but I'm the one that picked him up for his appointments and took him home to make sure he actually went."

"You never told me this," Rhonan says.

"Well, you were gone, and I didn't want you to know how badly I was struggling. I regret that now. In fact, I think as men we need to be more honest about how much we struggle with shit life hands us. We're human, too."

Elliot glances at Henry. "Is that why you were at the winery so much during that first year after Elizabeth died?"

Henry nods. "Yup. I was making sure the business was staying intact while George found his new normal."

My friends and I all exchange glances.

"So, the reason I'm bringing this up is because I think all four of you are dealing with shit right now, and I want to remind you that instead of questioning your friendship, this is when you lean on it." George nods toward his friends. "Loyalty, promises, and history mean nothing if there isn't action behind it."

He turns to Elliot. "And as for your 'pact,'" he says, putting air quotes around the word, "there is no reason why any of you should be angry about that. For one, you were fourteen when you made it, and two, there is no way for you to predict how life can change in an instant. I think your new pact should be to work through your shit, trust that your bond is stronger than you realize, and then agree to be there for each other, even when shit gets hard."

George and his friends stand from the table, but Brian speaks next. "I know we're not your fathers, but as men who've been around longer than you, maybe trust that we know a thing or two. And if worse comes to worst, consider therapy, gentlemen. It's life-changing."

The four of them head for the door, leaving me and my best friends alone.

Our eyes move from one person to the next before Rhonan sighs, breaking the silence. "You and my sister then, huh?"

Nodding, I straighten my spine. "This isn't just some fling, Rhonan. I've been in love with her for a long fucking time."

He clears his throat. "I know. Laney told me everything." My pulse picks up. Laney told me that Rhonan knows about the shit with my dad now, but it still makes me nervous to see his reaction in person. "Why the fuck didn't you tell any of us about your dad?" His eyes bore into mine, even though there's confusion and hurt on his face.

"Tell us what?" Elliot asks, his animosity from before far less than it was.

Rhonan turns to our other two friends. "Fletcher's dad used to fucking hit him."

Hearing those words out loud from someone else feels like a knife slicing through my skin, but demons escaping from the cut this time.

It's painful and healing.

It's honest, yet a dark truth that I've been carrying alone up until now.

Henley glares at me. "Are you fucking kidding me?"

Elliot shakes his head. "More fucking lies."

"It's not lying if you never asked. And besides, I knew you guys wouldn't have let it go if I had told you."

"Damn right, we wouldn't have," Rhonan says.

"And it would have jeopardized everything I'd been working toward, Rhonan. Do you get that? There would have been investigations. I could have been placed in foster care, might have even had to move."

"But you told Laney," he counters.

"I did, but only because I'm a shitty liar and she knew better."

"But what about the pact?" Rhonan snaps.

"The whole point of the pact was to establish a level of friendship that was strong, a foundation of loyalty. But you know what really makes us strong? The ability to get through shit like this. To admit when we're fucking struggling, to not hold in stuff because doing so has just made us fucking miserable, and I'm done feeling that way. Laney has helped me see that too."

"She's too good for you," Rhonan says.

"I know."

"She's too good for anyone, really," Elliot adds, shaking his head.

"Don't have to convince me of that."

Rhonan sighs, lifting his eyes to meet mine. "But she loves you."

"Believe me, I'm still trying to wrap my head around it." I direct my eyes back over to Elliot. "Do you remember that conversation that we had in your office three weeks ago?"

He eyes me curiously. "Vaguely. What about it?"

"You told me that one day I'd find a woman that would make me want to be irrational for the first time in my life, and I did—I just found her at seventeen, Elliot, and it took me this long to figure out what I want. Did I go about it the honorable way? Not at all. But was it honest for me and her? Yes, so I don't regret it. I followed my fucking heart for once, and it led me to where I'm supposed to be."

Elliot lowers his gaze, shaking his head. "Then you're fucking lucky, because following my heart ended up with mine fucking split in two."

My chest aches for my friend because I can't imagine how I would feel if Laney left me like that. But I also know that Laney and I want the same things, and it's clear that perhaps Elliot and Tori didn't as much as he thought they did.

Rhonan stares at the green felt on the table before looking back at me. "I've watched my sister avoid relationships for years, watched her pick the wrong guys, give so much of herself to others, and avoid moving on in life because of what happened with our mom. But this past week? It's like I got my sister back," he croaks.

"Fuck, man." I push a hand through my hair and stare up at the ceiling. "You're gonna make me fucking cry again. I've cried more this past week than I have since your mom died."

Henley sniffles. "Pansies."

The door swings open and George pops his head in. "Crying is a good thing, guys. Let it out."

Rhonan huffs out a laugh. "You're fucking listening to us?"

"Damn right, I am. I don't want you four to suffer for the rest of your lives. You have a chance here to move in the right direction, change the course of your futures, and giving each other shit for crying isn't going to help that. If you need to cry, fucking cry." He tosses his thumb over his shoulder. "Anthony has a great shoulder for crying on if you need a spare."

"Jesus Christ, Dad," Rhonan says, chuckling as George shuts the door again. "What the fuck is going on here?"

"I think your dad is trying to tell us that feeling shit isn't a bad thing, and I think all of us have been avoiding feelings for a long fucking time," I say, knowing it's how I'm interpreting this conversation.

Elliot scoffs. "Speak for yourself."

Henley looks over at him. "Look, I'm really fucking sorry that Tori walked out on you, but George is right." Looking at me and Rhonan, he says, "You're going to get through this, and we are here for you with whatever you need, but we're not just saying that this time." He looks around the table. "Saying it and doing it are two different things, and I think it's time our actions back up our words, guys."

Elliot mutters, "Yeah? Well, what I need is a goddamn drink."

"Because alcohol makes everything better," I reply sarcastically. "Need I remind you of my alcoholic father who used booze to cope, Elliot?"

His bloodshot eyes bore into mine. "I'm not your fucking dad, Fletch. But if I want to numb myself right now, let me."

Rhonan covers Elliots hand with his own. "Right now, you do what you need to. But just know, this pain won't last forever." He clears his throat. "Losing Sarah was the worst thing I've ever felt, but maybe my dad is right. I've never truly dealt with it. I was too busy trying to take care of my daughter to really understand how much it fucked me up."

Henley nods. "I can't deny that hearing your dad and his friends talk about shit is making me think."

"I booked an appointment with a therapist yesterday," I say, pulling the attention of all three of my friends.

"You did?"

"Yeah. I'm fucking tired of letting my relationship with my father affect me as much as it has. Part of the reason I never come home is because of him, but Laney deserves better than that. She deserves a man that isn't afraid to face his past."

Henley nods. "Well, that makes a fuck ton more sense now."

Rhonan stands from his chair and walks over to me. I stand to meet him, pulling him in for an embrace. "I'm fucking sorry, man. I'm sorry for not thinking better of you, for not asking questions when I should have."

"Thank you."

"Just promise me that you'll take care of Laney, all right? I can't lose her too," he mutters in my ear. "I promise."

We release each other and wipe our eyes. "God, I'm done fucking crying too," he says through a laugh.

I turn to Elliot. "I'm sorry again about Tori, but she doesn't deserve you, man."

Elliot scoffs. "Maybe this was all a good thing, makes me remember why I decided against relationships for the longest fucking time. I just need my parents to back the fuck off about it now too."

"What did they say?"

Elliot rolls his eyes. "My mom was devastated but has been pressuring me to reach out to her. Like that's going to fucking happen."

"Do you think if you did though, that it might help?" I ask.

Elliot glares at me. "I never want to see that woman again."

Henley slaps him on the shoulder. "Then we will support you with that."

I look around at my friends. "I fucking love you guys, but if there's one thing I've realized over the past few weeks, it's that being older has not made us wiser."

Rhonan huffs out a laugh. "You think?"

"I thought by this age, we would have more shit figured out, but there's still a lot we need to learn—not just about life, but about each other. I'm sorry that I've kept things from you. I'm sorry that I didn't feel like I could confide in you or be honest about how I felt about Laney. But I think I needed to figure out how I felt about those things myself before I could articulate them."

Henley nods. "And do you feel that way now?"

"Yeah, I do, and it feels fucking amazing. I want that for you guys too. It's not about being perfect, because lord knows none of us are. It's about facing shit instead of running, and honoring our truth. Laney has helped me learn that, and I hope all of you can figure that out one day as well."

"Then maybe what we need is a new pact," Henley suggests.

The four of us look around at each other, nodding in agreement.

"Yeah, I think that's exactly what we need."

***

"Are you taking me up this mountain to make out in your truck? You know, living out another teenage fantasy? Or is there where you murder me and leave me for the animals to feast on?"

My brows draw together as I look over at Laney sitting in the passenger seat of my truck. "Have you been watching Unsolved Mysteries with Dilynne again?"

She nods. "Yeah, and I think I need to stop."

"I think you do too."

A month ago, I would have been more concerned, but after learning much more about Dilynne and Laney's friendship and how it's evolved over the years, I'm just glad that my girl has someone to lean on during the breaks that we're going to have apart coming up.

My truck sways side to side as we drive along the dirt road, inching closer to the spot that I've been waiting to show to Laney since I met with the realtor right before Elliot's wedding that never happened.

I only hope that this is everything she envisioned because if not, I still have a few days to back out of escrow.

Turning left, I pull into the vacant lot that sits on a flat part of the mountain, shifting into park before turning to take in her reaction. "We're here."

It's her turn to be confused. "Okay. What are we doing here?"

Once I help her down out of the truck, I take her hand in mine and start walking through the dirt, pointing as I speak. "I'm thinking six bedrooms minimum—three for kids, one for us, and two for our offices." Her eyes widen. "I want a gym in the basement, a playroom for the kids, a movie room, and an indoor pool so we can go swimming while it's snowing outside, and watch it fall all around us through the glass-covered ceiling. It will be like being in a snow globe, and the kids will love it." I take her over to the most important spot. "But this right here? This is where your picturesque window will go, looking out over Blossom Peak, just like you wanted. And right in front of it will be your desk, the desk where you're going to sit and write your first book."

Moisture clouds her eyes, but I keep going, dropping to one knee in front of her. She stifles her gasp with her hand. "But if this isn't the way you dreamed it, we can find another plot of land to build our dream home together. I don't care where it is, as long as it's exactly as you dreamed it, and the two of us are there together."

"Fletcher Jared Adams...are you..."

"Laney, I could have fucking lost you," I say, fighting the crack in my voice. "You could have married someone else, and I never would have had the opportunity to make you my wife." I pull the black box from my back pocket, opening it to reveal a pink diamond ring that matches her mother's necklace. "So yes, I am proposing to you. I know it's fast, Laney, but we've lost so much time, and I don't want to waste another second. I want you to be my wife. I want everyone to know that you're mine. I want you to be Laney Maddison Adams." Swallowing roughly, I prepare to ask her the question I've been waiting to ask her since the first time I realized she was the one, but our phones chime at the same time, interrupting our moment.

Closing my eyes, I groan. "You need to eat something. Your blood sugar is low."

"I swear to God, Fletcher Adams...if you make me eat something before you finish what you're about to say, I'm going to murder you up here on this mountain."

I shake my head at her, my chest bouncing with laughter. "Fine. But after, you're eating."

She pats her pocket. "I have a snack right here. Now, you were saying..." She folds her lips between her teeth.

Taking a deep breath, I finish what I came here to do. "Laney Maddison Hart, will you marry me?"

She jumps up and down in place, screaming, "I'm going to be Mrs. Fletcher Adams!"

I throw my head back laughing before standing to my feet. "Is that a yes?"

"That's a hell yes!" She jumps at me, wrapping her legs around my waist before crashing her mouth to mine. "I can't believe you did this."

"I can't believe I finally got to." My finger traces her face. "All this time you thought you hated me, Laney Hart. But it turns out, we just had to wait for that hate to turn to love."

"I love you so much," she whispers against my lips before I set her down and gently place the ring on her finger, watching her admire it as the sunlight catches it. "Mom would approve."

"I thought so. Your dad certainly did."

"My parents love you, Fletcher."

"I love them too. And I promise to honor them both by loving you the way they loved each other—unconditionally and forever."

# Chapter 31

**Laney**

***One Month Later***

***Looking toward the Future***

***Wait, is that a...***

"Here's to making it to the Super Bowl this year!" Rhonan shouts as our friend group in the back room at Hart Winery raises their drinks up in agreement. It's Fletcher's last weekend in Blossom Peak before pre-season games start, so we decided to have a small party with everyone together before life gets very intense for the two of us. He got back from training camp last week, so the season starts very soon.

God, those two weeks were brutal being apart. But when he finally came home to me and found me wearing nothing but his jersey, we instantly made up for lost time—over and over and over again.

Fletcher nods his head. "We're going to do our best." He kisses me on the cheek. "I have a new good luck charm this year, so hopefully that makes the difference."

"Way to put all the pressure on me," I reply sarcastically.

Dilynne tosses me a look. "He's not wrong. You have a duty now to the Carolina Thunder. You must make sure this man is well-fed, well-rested, and well-fucked."

Hazel walks over to our table, her drink poised at her lips. "Uh, what the hell kind of conversation did I just walk in on?" Her husband, Gage, comes up behind her, wrapping his arm around her waist.

The two of them finally set aside some time to visit Blossom Peak, primarily so she could meet Fletcher before the season officially started. Having her here has meant so much to me, especially because she knows how hard it is to fight for the ones we love.

Rhonan glares at my best friend. "I just want to say thank you for the reminder that one of my best friends is sleeping with my sister."

Dilynne leans closer to him, smirking. "You're welcome. He's about to be your brother-in-law too."

"Next summer," I correct her because even though Fletcher was adamant about proposing quickly, I was insistent on giving us time to plan a wedding and adjust to our new lives together. However, Fletcher decided he is only going to play for two more years, that way we can start a family sooner rather than later.

"God, I can't wait to help plan that bachelorette party. The cutouts are gonna come out again, but elevated."

I close my eyes. "Good God."

Dilynne walks away, making me question her sanity for the thousandth time in our friendship, but rest assured, no matter what she has planned, I'm going to marry this man and give him as many babies as he wants because getting to watch Fletcher become a dad and love his children will be the last thread he'll need to be completely healed from his past.

It's only been a few weeks since Luke entered rehab, but Fletcher and he have agreed to attend counseling sessions once a week once he's done with his program, and Fletcher has been going to therapy on his own.

After the conversation he had with my dad, his friends, and Henley, Elliot, and my brother, he's been even more eager to heal from his childhood, and I couldn't be prouder of him.

Fletcher is still keeping his guard up with his father, but I can tell that he's optimistic that Luke will finally be able to turn a corner in his life. The scars that he left on him though will only fade with time.

Henley, Elliot, and Rhonan have their own issues to process now, too. I know the four of them have grown closer through all of this, but I'm proud of Fletcher being the first to show them what is possible.

Yvonne steps up to me, wrapping her arm around my neck. "So, when do I get my keys?"

"Tomorrow, like we discussed."

"Come on. Just give them to me now." She holds her hand out in front of her, fanning her fingers.

"Why are you so eager for these keys?"

"Keys equal power, Laney. I'm about to be the boss when you're gone, and I feel like I've been training for this my entire life."

I roll my eyes at her dramatic declaration. "I don't know, maybe I should have asked Glenn if he would like to become my new manager."

Yvonne glares at me. "You and I both know that if Glenn were in charge, you'd come back to chaos and glitter everywhere."

I cringe. "God, I hate glitter. It's the herpes of craft supplies."

" Exactly." She fans her grabby hands at me again. "Just let me have the keys, that way you can sleep in tomorrow and don't have to worry about waking up to open the salon."

Fletcher comes up behind me, burying his face in my neck. "She does have a point. I'm sure we could find other things to do tomorrow morning if you don't have to get up and go to work."

Closing my eyes, I focus on the feeling of his lips moving across my skin before handing Yvonne the keys. "You're lucky I'm addicted to this man."

"Lucifer was alluring, and people gravitated to him for a reason. I'm just glad you finally gave into him." Winking, she saunters off.

I let out a heavy sigh.

"You all right?" Fletcher asks me as he takes a seat on the stool next to me.

"Yeah. It's just weird."

He kisses my shoulder. "I know, but Yvonne loves that salon as much as you do. She's going to do a fabulous job of running things during the season for you."

When Fletcher and I discussed our living arrangements for the next five to six months of the season, I knew I would have to give up time at the salon to make this work. It was difficult, but the idea of spending more time away from Fletcher was harder to imagine. So, I asked Yvonne if she would be willing to step up and she agreed eagerly.

As much as Blossom Beauty has been my love for the past six years, my new love is now my focus, and I'm vowing to pour as much energy into my relationship as possible. We break ground on our house next month too, so in between living in two different cities and finally sitting down to write my book, I'm already stressed just thinking about all the changes. But I'm definitely not complaining.

If there's one thing I've learned over the past two months, it's that the "broken" people will always be able to love harder than most. Once you've been in the dark, you learn to appreciate everything that shines.

I wanted this, and I'm going to appreciate every single second of the chaos.

Dilynne walks up to us again, holding her drink. "Uh, have you seen my brother?"

I glance around the room. "I feel like he was just here a second ago."

She looks to the arched entrance to the room just as Henley walks through, holding a baby carrier in one hand and a diaper bag in the other. "Is that a baby?"

When he makes his way over to us, Dilynne prods. "Why do you have a baby? You're aware that a baby is in that thing, right?" She points to the carrier in his hand.

Henley's face looks pale as he sets the carrier on the table. The baby dressed in a pink outfit is sleeping soundly inside, but everyone's eyes are locked on him. "I finally figured out why that girl Meghan has been calling me so much."

"Who's Meghan?" I ask.

"Shit," Fletcher mutters beside me. "Meghan is a woman Henley slept with last year, and she's been calling him for months."

"Okay..." Dilynne drags out the word, not putting two and two together yet.

"Your brother thought she just wanted a repeat with him, but I'm guessing that wasn't the reason she was calling." Fletcher flicks his chin in the direction of the baby.

Dilynne gasps as everything clicks. "You have a daughter?"

"I—I guess I do."

Dilynne assesses her. "How old is she?"

Henley clears his throat. "She's three months old."

"And where's Meghan?" Fletcher asks.

Henley takes a deep breath. "She's gone. She never wanted kids, so she left the baby with me."

Our group of friends look between each other, completely shocked and at a loss for what we should say.

Henley has a kid.

Looks like the man who never wanted any responsibility is about to eat his words.


**THE END**


***


**Want a glimpse into Fletcher and Laney's future? What happens when his team makes it to the Super Bowl?**


**Click HERE for an exclusive Bonus Epilogue!**

*Scan for
Bonus Epi-
logue*

***

**And are you ready to find out how Henley handles his
surprise baby without falling for his new nanny?**

**Pre-Order On Borrowed Time Today!**

# Also By Harlow James

**Blossom Peak Series**

<u>All This Time (Fletcher and Laney)</u>

<u>On Borrowed Time (Henley and Elodie)</u>

<u>Test of Time</u>

<u>It's About Time</u>

***

**<u>Carrington Cove Series</u>**

<u>Somewhere You Belong (Dallas and Willow)</u>

<u>Someone You Deserve (Penn and Astrid)</u>

<u>Sometimes You Fall (Grady and Scottie)</u>

<u>Someday You Learn (Parker and Cashlynn)</u>

Somehow You Knew (Gage and Hazel)

***

**The Ladies Who Brunch (rom-coms with a ton of spice)**
Never Say Never (Charlotte and Damien)
No One Else (Amelia and Ethan)
Now's The Time (Penelope and Maddox)
Not As Planned (Noelle and Grant)
Nice Guys Still Finish (Jeffrey and Ariel)

***

**The Newberry Springs (Gibson Brothers) Series**
Everything to Lose (Wyatt & Kelsea)
Everything He Couldn't (Walker & Evelyn)
Everything But You (Forrest & Shauna)

***

**The California Billionaires Series (rom coms with heart and heat)**
My Unexpected Serenity (Wes and Shayla)
My Unexpected Vow (Hayes and Waverly)
My Unexpected Family (Silas and Chloe)

***

### <u>The Emerson Falls Series (smalltown romance with a found family friend group)</u>
<u>Tangled (Kane & Olivia)</u>
<u>Enticed (Cooper & Clara)</u>
<u>Captivated (Cash and Piper)</u>
<u>Revived (Luke and Rachel)</u>
<u>Devoted (Brooks and Jess)</u>

***

### Lost and Found in Copper Ridge
A holiday romance in which two people book a stay in a cabin for the same amount of time thanks to a serendipitous $5 bill.

### Guilty as Charged
An intense opposites attract standalone that will melt your kindle. He's an ex-con construction worker. She's a lawyer looking for passion.

### McKenzie's Turn to Fall
A holiday romance where a romance author falls for her neighborhood butcher.

# Acknowledgements

It feels AMAZING to finally have this book out in the world, especially after the trouble it caused me.
The first draft of this book was NOT what you just read. LOL But I am beyond thrilled with the final result AND this series. It's fresh, emotional, and steamy. These men are down bad for their girls, and are willing to put in the work to keep them.
With each new series, I pinch myself that I get to write love stories and people read them. It is truly is an honor, and I hope to keep doing this for many years to come.

To my husband: Thank you for believing in me and cheering me on every step of the way. Thank you for traveling with me, investing in my success, and being my person, my best friend, the man that inspires all of my book boyfriends, and my official Book Bitch. I love you.

To my beta readers: Emily, Keely, Carolina, and Kelly: you four are the best voices I have in my corner. Each of you gives me the advice, feedback, and support that I need in your own way. I'm so grateful to have the four of you on my team still after all this time. I love you all and appreciate you more than you'll ever know.

To Kait, my P.A.: Hiring you has been one of the best decisions I've ever made. Your friendship and professional support have helped me so much this year. Thank you for being my newest cheerleader!

To Jess, my social media manager: You have single-handedly made my life better! I have so much more time to focus on writing and other aspects of my business thanks to you. Your time and creativity is appreciated SO much. Thank you from the bottom of my heart for doing what you do for me.

To Kari, my content team leader: I'm SO honored that you agreed to help me with this new aspect of my team! You are such an incredible support and I'm looking forward to how much we can grow this team together.

And to my readers: thank you for supporting me, whether you've been here since the beginning, or you're brand new. I LOVE this hobby turned business of mine. It's an amazing feeling to be able to create art for someone to enjoy and forming a relationship from that. I never take my readers for granted and know that there would be no Harlow James without you.

So thank you for supporting a wife and mom who found a hobby that she loves.
And a future career that I'm working toward with each passing day.

# About the author

Harlow James is a wife and mother who fell in love with romance novels, so she decided to write her own.

Her books are the perfect blend of heartwarming, addictive, and steamy romance. If you love stories with a guaranteed Happily Ever After, then Harlow is your new best friend.

When she's not writing, she can be found working her day job, reading every romance novel she can find time for, laughing with her husband and kids, watching re-runs of FRIENDS, and spending time cooking for her family and friends while drinking margaritas.

# Connect with Harlow James

Follow me on Amazon

Follow me on Instagram

Follow me on Facebook

Join my Facebook Group: https://www.facebook.com/groups/494991441142710/

Follow me on Goodreads

Follow me on Book Bub

Subscribe to my Newsletter for Updates on New Releases and Giveaways

Website

www.ingramcontent.com/pod-product-compliance
Lightning Source LLC
Chambersburg PA
CBHW061045310726
48969CB00004B/1092